OPEN YOUR HEART

"Shelly," he said softly, "don't leave. I've been unfair. I don't know what got into me. Will you stay?" His face turned toward hers, his eyes spoke volumes that his face hid.

"I think it's best if I go," she managed. Another emotional discourse like they just had would be too much. She needed time to think, and right now it proved to be difficult with Justin's face less than six inches from her. His puffs of breath touched her head. She glanced at his lips and reiterated to herself, *I think it's best*.

"Well, I think otherwise. I want you—"

Startled, her eyes flew to his.

A wicked grin stole across his face. ". . . to stay. I think we understand each other. What do you say?"

A yearning in her burned and it only prodded her when Justin was in her thoughts and especially when he stood close enough for her to tiptoe and kiss his lips. A smile wavered at the thought. She licked her lips nervously.

"I'll take that as a yes."

OPEN YOUR HEART

Michelle Monkou

BET Publications, LLC
http://www.bet.com
http://www.arabesquebooks.com

ARABESQUE BOOKS are published by

BET Publications, LLC
c/o BET BOOKS
One BET Plaza
1900 W Place NE
Washington, DC 20018-1211

All Kensington Titles, Imprints, and Distributed Lines are available at special quantity discounts for bulk purchases for sales
promotions, premiums, fund-raising, and educational or insti-
tutional use. Special book excerpts or customized printings can
also be created to fit specific needs. For details, write or phone
the office of the Kensington special sales manager: Kensington
Publishing Corp., 850 Third Avenue, New York, NY 10022,
attn: Special Sales Department, Phone: 1-800-221-2647.

First Printing: November 2002
10 9 8 7 6 5 4 3 2 1

Printed in the United States of America

This book is dedicated to my mother, Doreen Monkou,
for teaching me never to give up, and to my father,
Charles Monkou, for encouraging me to reach
for the stars.

ACKNOWLEDGMENTS

Smooches to my gal pals, Julia Canchola, Cecelia Dowdy, and Celeste O. Norfleet, for encouragement and feedback.

Thanks to my supportive buddies from RWA's Washington (DC) Romance Writers chapter and especially, Cameron Darby, Lisa Kamps, Karen Lee Smith, and Susan Webb.

Much love to my husband Bryan Samuels, my brother and sis-in-law, Malcolm and Donsha Monkou, and my kiddies, Gabriella and Lex.

For making my dream a reality, my gratitude extends to my editors Karen Thomas and Chandra Taylor.

One

Justin Thornton barely discerned the yellow advisory road sign—SHARP TURN AHEAD. Sheets of rain provided a hazy curtain that made it difficult to see into the inky night. He'd driven Crescent Drive enough times to know each curve by heart, and the rain-slicked road didn't deter him.

"Slow down, Justin," his wife pleaded.

He eased his foot off the accelerator. "You lied to me."

Oncoming lights blinded him. Justin squinted in an effort to see past the distorted high beams directed his way. He tried to increase the speed of the wipers. Its furious metronome whipped back and forth across the windshield already at full speed.

"I did what any woman would do to keep the man she loves."

The headlights drew steadily closer.

"Justin, please talk to me."

"There's nothing to say." His hands gripped the wheel and he bit down the rage burning a hole in his gut.

"I'm your wife. I made a mistake. A lousy mistake." The woman's voice broke. "Remember our vows? Remember 'for richer, for poorer, in sickness and in health?'"

"But it wasn't one mistake. A business trip here, a night out on the town with girlfriends there, a weekend getaway to a spa." She must have thought him a perfect, gullible fool. He grinned evilly at her registered shock. "Yes, I know all about your many trysts. It cost me to know, but it was worth signing off on the five-digit check." He wanted to rage, to pound something. "When did it end for us? God, I was so blind." His throat tightened. "What a fool you must have seen in me to make me believe that you were pregnant. That was the ultimate." He banged the steering wheel with his hand. "And it was all a lie." The tears crested and he bit down on raw edges of his grief. "A damned lie," he whispered.

"No one is perfect. You put me on a pedestal that I couldn't live up to, but it never meant that I didn't love you. I just can't be the person you want me to be. I thought I wanted more, something else." She reached out to touch his arm.

"Take your hand off me, Wanda." He turned his view from the road and gave his full attention to glare at his wife. Her high-fashion beauty and thick, luxurious hair no longer made his pulse race. Betrayal warred with cherished memories that he couldn't turn off. He wanted ice to run through his veins and freeze his heart against the sound of her voice, the warmth of her touch; against all the things she'd promised him when he lay in her arms.

"Oh God, look out!"

His gaze shot back to the road. Headlights came toward him.

No. They came *at* him.

In his lane.

Then the driver swerved widely back onto his side of the road.

Justin exhaled. His stomach muscles unclenched. "What the heck was that!"

A split second later the knot in his stomach bunched again. The car, now a few feet away, skidded back into his lane.

Wanda screamed.

Goose bumps prickled on the back of Justin's neck. He yanked the wheel to the right to avoid a head-on collision. Brakes locked. In a flurry of motion, he grappled with the steering wheel trying to pull away from the soft shoulder. Tires hit the graveled edge and kept sliding. With the back of the car now leading, the vehicle broke through the guardrail with a decisive snap.

Justin looked over at Wanda; her lips mouthed his name. As the car shot backward crashing through trees and bouncing off rocks, Justin prayed for a miracle. He imagined that the Old Walker River, probably swollen by the constant rain, churned hungrily for its newest victims.

Waiting for the impending impact, he deliberately reached over and took his wife's hand.

"Forgive me," she whispered.

The car flipped completely over, throwing them violently against the steering wheel and dashboard. The window next to him shattered into a spiderweb pattern. They landed upside down in the river with a massive splash. Within a minute, the car slid in an all-consuming, black, watery grave.

Justin awoke. A strangled scream locked in his throat. He breathed deeply until his bearings settled. The red LCD of his clock read three A.M. Another night of horror had visited. He rubbed the tight knot at the base of his neck. Adrenaline pumped through his body and he waited for the sensation to ease. The familiar exhaustion followed, winding its way through his tight muscles, chasing the jittery edges of nerves. Its aftereffect sagged his shoulders into a slump.

Fully awake now with a dull headache, he didn't want to sit in the unwelcomed darkness any longer. Walking barefoot into the kitchen, he relished the cool tiles beneath his feet. Sweat beaded his brow. His thirst burned a scratchy trail in his throat. Without turning on the light, he found his way to the refrigerator. The pitcher of lemonade called to him and he gripped it with a shaking hand. It was tart and refreshingly cool; he gulped it, disregarding the occasional spill down the sides of his mouth. Finished, he wiped his mouth, set down the pitcher in the sink, and closed his eyes in a meditative moment.

He had lived. Wanda had died.

The kitchen lights flickered on, brightening the area with an unwelcoming glare.

"Those dreams eating at you?"

Justin jumped at the sound of his father's voice. "Why are you up?"

"There's a rerun of my favorite sitcom coming on in five minutes. Join me. I want to talk to you."

"Pop, not now."

"You're not going back to sleep. Even if you go to your room, you'll sit there and brood until the sun rises. Might as well spend a few hours with me."

Justin followed Phillip's slow, uneven gait down the hallway toward the family room where his father eased into his favorite armchair. The decision to sit or beg off his father's invitation for a late-night chat turned over in his mind. He didn't want anyone probing his mind, analyzing his emotions. Remaining silent, he sat in the sofa opposite his father and watched him switch on the television to view the sitcom until the first commercial played, after which his father clicked the MUTE button.

"I'm repeating myself, but those dreams are eating at you again? What keeps torturing you?"

"What do you mean?"

"Just look at yourself. Are you going for the gaunt look? Those dark shadows under your eyes make you look like kin to a raccoon. So, what is it?"

"What do you mean 'what is it?' What is it always?" Justin shrugged, frustrated at not being able to articulate the depth of what he was feeling. "There's nothing you can do. Nothing."

"Damn it. You're my son. My life. It's killing me to see you day after day wither and die inside. Hell, you're only thirty-seven and you behave like the grim reaper."

"It's a little hard playing sunshine boy when your wife is dead and everyone thinks you killed her."

"What does it matter what they think? The police investigated and the matter is closed. And has been for over a year. You're the one holding on to the demons. Let it go."

"How can I when the newspapers continue to publish snide editorials? *Was there really another car? Why didn't that driver come forward? What did Justin Thornton have to gain?* And the worst—*Did he kill his wife in a jealous rage?*"

"Nonsense. Utter nonsense. I'd think by now you'd have developed a thick skin. Otherwise, you'll second-guess your entire life, like you're doing now."

"I hear you, Pop, but it's not that easy. Living with constant accusations and malicious gossip is having an effect. It seems I have enemies who would rather see me squirm. I'm a prisoner serving a sentence that may not have an end."

His father leaned forward and peered at him with an intensity that made him shift uncomfortably. "That's not the only reason for your distress."

Justin leaned his head back on the chair. Pop could always pull his secrets out of him. "Why don't *you* tell me what the other reason is, then?"

"Okay, I'm guessing that if you believed in self-flagellation, your back would be striped from a cat-o'-nine-tails. What are you ashamed of?"

"Maybe you should have become an FBI profiler."

Phillip chuckled. "I got all my skills from watching TV. I also know when someone is trying to evade the question."

Justin didn't know how to answer. It shocked him that he'd been unable to put a name to what he was feeling, always assuming that it was mere guilt. "She—Wanda—asked me for one thing before she died. I didn't give it to her. And I could have, but it wouldn't have been sincere." He rubbed his temples, keeping his eyes closed. He didn't want to witness any changes in his father's face that would reflect his disappointment. "What kind of person does that make me?"

"Justin, stop it. Look at me. How can you think that you're any less of an honorable, loving person? You moved back home to care for a sick, old man. Always you've put your family first and that's because family, honor, and love are values near and dear to your heart. It's understandable that you're going through turmoil, but the key is to go through all that while you still maintain an active part of life."

It all sounded easy. "Thanks, Pop." Justin got up and kissed his father's cheek. "I'm glad I'm home too; maybe we both can help each other."

Shelly Bishop heard the phone ringing as she stepped off the stairs leading to the second floor. Her garden apartment was the first on the left so she didn't have far to sprint. Laden with groceries, she fumbled with keys to unlock the door. Once inside, she dumped the bags in the corner of the living room and grabbed the phone on a side table.

"Hello," she greeted, breathless.

"Shelly, it's me."

"Oh, hi, Mom."

"Don't sound so disappointed."

"Sorry." Shelly laughed.

"Heard from Tanya?"

"Nope. I said that I'd go with her to her classes, at least

to meet her teacher, but she never showed. My main goal is to find out how much work she's missed for the semester."

"That girl's gonna give me gray hairs."

"In your case, she'd have to give you black hairs."

"Ha ha, Miss Smarty-Pants. I'm really worried about that child."

"Me too, Mom. Considering my sudden change of scenery on her behalf and her latest malfunction, I'm not feeling her right now. As soon as I get my hands on her, we're having a little talk."

"Don't be too harsh. The girl's had a hard life. She's just a might stubborn in the face of reason, like you."

"Yeah, well, I had my reasons, didn't I?"

Silence.

Shelly could have kicked herself for going down that path.

"Mom, if I see her, I'll tell her to call home."

"Bye." Her mother's voice echoed a tiredness that Shelly only just noticed.

Bags emptied and all the groceries tucked away in the cupboard and refrigerator, Shelly needed a shower to get her second wind to make dinner. She looked forward to the pounding spray of water to ease away her tension.

Minutes later, she dried off, preoccupied with what she would cook. The doorbell chimed, interrupting plans for baked salmon and pasta primavera. Grabbing an oversize T-shirt and leggings, she hopped and stumbled to the door while pulling up the leggings. Hopefully, it wasn't her persistent neighbor bugging her about a date. His fast-talking, player lingo grated on her nerves.

She put the chain on the door before opening. For a few seconds, she stood openmouthed in amazement. Undoing the chain, she opened the door in welcome. "Well, well, if it isn't the prodigal niece."

"I don't smell dinner." The teenager walked past Shelly bumping her shoulder with lots of attitude.

Shelly counted to ten and closed the door. "Good for you. Your fingers may not be working to dial home, but your nose deserves a medal."

"Can I get something to eat?"

"Ooh, the manners—gas tank must be on empty."

"Look, you're the one who wants to play big sister. Now I'm here, you're giving me grief."

"Grief isn't all I'd like to give you right about now. Don't play me, Tanya. As you may have heard through the family grapevine, my head's not wrapped too tight and I will kick your butt around this apartment if you keep up this tough rebel-without-a-cause attitude."

Shelly studied her niece standing with hands on her hips. Her T-shirt showed off a vulgar innuendo. Anger fairly crackled off her youthful body as she passed on a defiant stare.

"You're sure you didn't get fired from the hospital in the Big Apple," Tanya accused.

"No, instead I got a distress call from my mother begging me to come back to this shoe-box town and tend to my niece who was walking a thin line with the law. Here I am, fully into my nursing career, saying, 'Hmm, family needs me.' I take a leave of absence, sublease my apartment, and head to the good ole town of Hopetown to stop you from sinking in your crap."

"Wah wah wah. Let me tune up the violins. I can take care of me, okay? Grandma was cool when I was younger, but I'm an adult now and it's time for me to be on my own. My father and mother are both gone, making new lives with their families and once in a while they write me a note or send a few dollars and want me to come visit them. *Visit,* not live, with them. But I'm not crying over that 'cause it's made me stronger and I certainly don't need a baby-sitter. I appreciate you thinking—"

"Hold up, one second. No, you don't appreciate jack. Yes, you experienced a lousy childhood and there's nothing you and I can do about the past. But your parents are trying to make amends. Your grandmother, who should be rocking in a chair on a porch enjoying your occasional visits, worries about you, and I don't want to see you make the same mistakes as I did." Shelly looked into Tanya's eyes, willing her to stay.

What the heck was she doing here, pretending as if she knew what to do? The one thing that she did know was that Tanya was like her. They both had suffered their fair share of knocks and scrapes from life that left a fragile shell of resistance camouflaged with a tough-girl image. She took a deep breath. There was no plan, no guide to handling this situation—her niece—but she was going to try her best.

"I'm going to make the first step here, like an adult. Come in, wash up, and have dinner with me. No conditions. No pep talks. No interrogation. We'll eat, watch TV, then sleep."

"Fine. I'll go wash my hands. By the way, what's for dinner?"

"No, baby girl. Go wash your entire body. Please." Shelly held her nose and her niece giggled. "Come on, follow me."

Dr. Calloway's office had buzzed with activity since the doors opened for business. Shelly craved a second cup of strong black coffee and it was only ten o'clock. Her mind screamed from tiredness. She and Tanya did talk, mainly to convince Tanya to stick around at her place for a while. After four hours, Tanya relented. No guarantees could be made, but Shelly hoped that a meal and a safe place to sleep would continue to entice Tanya before she ran off again. Victory couldn't be claimed, as yet, but Shelly enjoyed the small steps toward it.

"Hi, Shelly. How's my favorite nurse?"

"Hello, Mr. Thornton. You're trying to butter me up. Favorite nurse, indeed. All the other nurses fall over themselves for you."

"Exactly! All except you. Guess I'm too old for you."

"Have a seat on the table, please. I have to take your blood pressure." Phillip Thornton was a delight. His lighthearted banter always brought a smile.

"Shelly, are you from around here?"

"Yep."

"Never thought of leaving?"

"Yep."

"Never got around to it?"

"I did."

"What brought you back home?"

She popped the thermometer in his mouth, slowing down his probing questions and allowing herself a few seconds to decide on whether to respond. The smirk he turned her way hinted that he was on to her delay tactics.

"*Home* would be an overstatement, Mr. Thornton."

"Are you staying for the long haul?"

"It's looking that way. I've been back for nine months and my New York job is pressing me for my plans." She sighed and recorded Phillip's vital statistics. "The problem isn't quite under control and it would be premature for me to leave." She wrapped her stethoscope around her neck and gathered his file.

"Once that matter is all wrapped up, I'm out of here," she vowed in a subdued voice.

"Do I detect a hint of remorse? It's okay, my dear, home will always be where you make it. But I will say this, you can call a different place every week home, but your roots, well, your roots remain the same. There's no running from them."

"That would depend on where you came from, wouldn't it? The right side or wrong side of the tracks."

"You know, I like your spunk, Shelly. You don't hold back, do you?"

"No need to or people will take advantage of you."

"Not everyone's the enemy."

"Maybe not, but I don't have time to figure out people. So I react to what I see or feel. But for the most part, I keep to myself."

"Seems lonely holding the world at arm's distance. You're making me think—"

"Uh-oh."

"Seriously, I'd like to help you out while you tend to your business."

Shelly paused from her task of drawing blood. Her smile dissipated. It didn't take long for her senses to go on alert as she waited, tense and wary. "What do you want, Mr. Thornton? Why do you want to help me?"

"I didn't mean to alarm you. It's only that I'm looking for a personal nurse and can pay you much better than this place. It's a win-win situation."

"You don't know anything about me. And for that matter, I don't know anything about you."

"I've had nine months getting to know you. You're conscientious, have a healthy work ethic, and our conversations make me feel better. You don't disrespect my age or worth, for that matter, and I appreciate your special touch."

His compliments embarrassed her. "So, it's all about you."

"I guess you got me there."

Shelly stripped off her gloves and gathered the vials of blood. Despite Phillip's easy manner, she remained cautious out of habit. There was one thing on her mind and that was Tanya. There was no time to get distracted or entertain any other options. "The doctor will be with you in a few minutes."

"What's the answer?"

"I'll take it under consideration. You have a good day, Mr. Thornton."

A couple of hours later, Shelly entered the break room with her bag lunch. Some of the other staff were already huddled at one of the round tables. One table remained vacant, however, much to her delight. As she walked by, the animated conversation at the occupied table dropped to husky whispers. A gossip tidbit must have come their way, Shelly surmised. But the turn of their eager faces toward hers meant only one thing. She was the subject of the whispering.

Now what?

"Well, aren't you the lucky one?" The leader of the group spoke up first.

"Why do you say that?" Shelly sat at the empty table, having no desire to join the group. Her curiosity was piqued, yet she would not feed into the buzz. Quite deliberately she took out her turkey sandwich and laid out the rest of her lunch.

"You got the Thornton man falling under your spell," Theresa, the leader of the gossip pack, remarked.

"He's a sweet, older man," Shelly defended.

"Can't disagree with you there. But he's not the one that gets my heart humming," Patsy, Theresa's sidekick, added, with an exaggerated fanning of her hands. "Have you seen his son?"

"Didn't know he had any family. But, then again, he doesn't say much about anything. Just likes to ask me questions," Shelly answered. "What's the big deal?"

"One day his son came with him," Patsy offered. "Talk

about gorgeous. I was like a fish out of water, my mouth opening and closing."

"She's not lying. I happened to be walking by and almost walked into the files. You know me. I'm not into making a fool of myself over a guy, but this time was an exception," Theresa said.

"Sounds fascinating, ladies, but I'm not interested even if he was dipped in gold."

"So you say," Theresa shot back. "I can lay down a bet—and I'm not a betting person—that one look at Justin and your panties will be in a bunch."

"If my panties are in a bunch, then it's time for a bigger pair." Shelly proceded to eat. Lunch would soon be over and she wanted some fresh air before heading back for the next round of patients. She paused. "Justin, you said?"

"Justin Thornton."

The name mentioned, Shelly's heart reacted. But more than her heart responded. Memories from a happier time brought a warm rush through her. She left the break room with a small smile on her face.

Outside, a gentle breeze rustled the trees. Shelly turned her face upward to the sun rays, soaking them in. *Justin Thornton*. The name was a blast from the past. Most women remembered their first everything. In her case, her first kiss was indelibly marked and placed in her hall of fame of memories. The keeper of those fabulous lips belonged to the light brown, smooth-talking J.T.

Maybe there was more than one Justin Thornton. She shook away the silly memories. They were ancient and from a different time when her niavetë got the best of her.

The latest delivery had arrived. Shelly and Theresa passed the downtime with restocking the supplies.

"Deep thoughts. What's up?" Theresa inquired later that day.

Shelly shook her head. "Something was said earlier that jogged an old memory."

"Something like what?"

"Oh, nothing." Shelly stood on tiptoe to slide a box of bandages on the top shelf. "Well, it's the Thornton name. Sounds familiar."

"Really," Theresa exclaimed. "Which one? Justin?"

"Yep."

"You had something with him?"

Shelly laughed. "No, hardly."

"Did you want to?"

"That's a bit personal." Shelly added silently, *Yes, indeed I did.*

"Sorry."

"It's okay. His name brought back some memories best left forgotten. I'm surprised that I didn't make the connection with his father."

"Phillip is a sweetheart. Lost his wife about five years ago. He's a trouper with his illness and all. He doesn't get out as much as he used to, though. I think his visits to Doc are a highlight for him."

"He seems down-to-earth. I like that in a person."

"Hey, you want to go bowling with me and a couple friends after work?"

Shelly guessed that she must have passed the test with the group. It only took eight months to get an invitation. Maybe her slight admission to past adolescent behavior was the key. Acceptance didn't feel so bad. "Sounds like fun, but I'm busy. Another time, maybe?"

The drive to the next destination offered some thinking time. The rush hour traffic crept at an annoying pace. The trail of cars, bumper to bumper as far Shelly could see, left no alternative but to reflect.

Creeping up on a minor fender-bender later, Shelly thought about her volunteer work at the center. Regardless of how rough her day was, once she entered the building, her tension would ease from her body. She wasn't sure what had prompted her to volunteer. If her few friends could see her they wouldn't believe that Shelly Bishop, the hermit would spend two hours a day, three times a week volunteering. Her work obsessed her with a ten-hour a day grueling schedule as an emergency room nurse. Happy hours, hanging out with the girls, and dating barely occupied her time. Work filled her thoughts. Home provided refuge.

All her life she followed her heart, inevitably getting her in trouble. Her mother accused her of being impulsive, a most annoying habit. Shelly didn't know any other way to function. One day she made up her mind to volunteer and she did.

She turned her car into the parking lot and stepped out with a sense of purpose and anticipation. In keeping with her ritual, she paused to read the sign arched over the doorway—WOMEN'S CRISIS CENTER—before entering. Then she read the day's inspirational message written on the blackboard for attendees: HANG UP YOUR CLOAK OF RAPE VICTIM AND PUT ON YOUR ARMOR OF EMPOWERMENT.

Two

Suicide.

He'd opt for suicide. On second thought, that wouldn't be a voluntary act. It had to be a homicide, then. It would be a first in legal history to convict someone for boring him to death.

Justin's head throbbed. No place to escape.

The banquet room capacity had to be at its max with an excess of politicians, business owners, and socialites, drinking and networking. Justin could pick each type out of a lineup. He couldn't be too harsh, though, since he slipped into each role as the situation required. Tonight, however, he simply wanted to remain in the background. Lately, these shindigs irked him, leaving him restless and looking for the exit at an early hour.

The wall of people entrapped him. Their bodies were tightly packed in conversational groups, with wine sloshing over the sides of glasses. A battle of heady scents from perfume, aftershave lotion, and hairspray waged in the tight confines. His senses cried overload. Fresh air made it to the top of his list of immediate needs.

He pulled at his starched collar, miserable when he spotted a large contingent of reporters and camera crews staked out at various spots. Instinctively he retreated behind his protective shield of a polite, cool, public persona.

Maybe luck would pay him a visit and head off the in-evitable, invading questions.

Since his father's retirement from the public eye, questions and gossip raged about the outcome of the family-owned business. Would he carry on the legacy? *Could* he carry on the legacy? The stodgy banking world wanted proof. A guarantee sounded good right about now. He sighed. It only took one reporter to take the first bite and the frenzy would begin.

"Mr. Thornton! Hello there."

Justin jumped. The shrill voice that had annoyed him for the past ten minutes rang in his eardrum. He didn't think the woman paused once.

"You're not paying attention," Mrs. Greene admonished. "I was saying that Laverne is planning to move back to Maryland." She slapped his arm, ignoring his wince. "Left that good-for-nothing in Atlanta. Wait till I tell her who I saw tonight." She rolled her eyes, clapping her hands excitedly. "A real-life *millionaire* bank owner. Wow!"

He cringed at her wide grin, sharklike and hungry. Time to change the subject. "Ah, and who might this be?" he asked, deliberately turning his undivided attention to the unhappy teenager now pinned in an iron grasp beside Mrs. Greene.

"This is my youngest, Sadie. A bit shy." Mrs. Greene leaned forward and her glasses slid to the tip of her blunt nose. "Too shy if you ask me. Not a bit like Laverne."

He studied the young girl, noting the constant snap of her gum. His nerves snapped right along with it. Her boredom with the subject of Laverne had far outpaced his.

"Laverne is different. Did you know she won Miss Maryland Young Teen? Then she acted in the community theater. Now she's a dancer. Oh, and she models. Maybe you've seen her." She giggled and pushed the offending glasses back into place. "You probably wouldn't have, though." She leaned toward him and the glasses promptly slid to the tip.

Justin bit his cheek to keep a straight face. The glasses didn't impede the torrent of words spewing from her mouth.

"She advertises feminine products. I could go on, but—" She paused.

Here was his chance to run. "Actually, I do have to—"

"Yeah, yeah. But look at her picture." Mrs. Greene beamed as she presented the wallet-sized photo of her daughter.

Justin looked at the picture, making sure to keep his expression neutral. Any sign, whether of interest or disinterest, from him would spell disaster. Judging by Mrs. Greene's presence at every civic or social event he'd attended in recent months, he surmised that she was on a mission.

He'd experienced persistent women, but when mothers took up the challenge, the rules changed because there weren't any. The ultimate goal had only one ending with their beloved daughter and him standing before a minister saying "I do" whether they meant it or not.

A chill slithered to the pit of his stomach at the thought. Since Wanda's death, none of the women he'd dated ever contained their excitement over his net worth. One in particular had an expensive and embarrassingly public birthday party catered on his behalf and then sent the bills to his accountant for payment.

He remained convinced that a woman unfazed by his lifestyle did not exist. If any did, as his father optimistically insisted, they were married or in a convent that turned its back on personal possessions.

Mrs. Greene's wide smile, which he swore started from one ear and looped to the other, had earned her way onto his I-told-you-so list.

Justin nodded, smiled, with the occasional "Ah, yes" as she chattered. He glanced at his watch for the third time. It was now or never. "Ladies, do excuse me. I must head over to make the opening remarks." He shrugged and hoped his rueful smile seemed genuine. Without waiting for a response, he turned and squeezed his way through the crowd.

He blew a sigh of relief as he regained control of his personal space and headed toward the podium, his mind still pounding from the onslaught. Frankly, she'd worn him down and a minute later he might have surrendered and accepted the blind date with Laverne. He shook his head at his bald-faced lie.

If he was lucky enough, he could present the award and get the heck out before being bombarded again. He took the folded paper with his speech from his inner pocket, casting a cursory glance over the tables below him.

He paused.

Man, oh, man.

The evening might be interesting, after all. He stroked his beard, studying a woman sitting a few feet from him. A lazy smile eased across his face. Admiring was acceptable. Safe. He couldn't make out the conversation at the table. From the look of things, the young woman sat with her parents, her resemblance a combination of the two. He guessed the older of the two women was the mother, who laughed and carried on an animated conversation with the entire table.

Everyone appeared to participate, either laughing or responding, except the woman who'd caught his eye. No laughter, not a whisper of a smile from her, only the continuous twisting of her napkin. Her focus fastened on nothing in particular.

The ebony beauty intrigued him. Where had she been hiding? It was his business to know all the politicians. She didn't fit that bill. Maybe a business owner, a shy one, though, but the mystery had its possibilities. The alternative

was a socialite. Her whole look reflected elegance and he
wondered why he hadn't run into her at other gatherings.

Her quiet nature provided a startling contrast to the
clank of silverware hitting china, the rippling melody from
the harpist, and the heady chatter. She sat unaffected, far
removed from the din.

Snap out of it. He had to begin the program. There'd be
time to make her acquaintance.

He picked up the discarded speech cards. He wished she
sat elsewhere, though. "Ladies and gentlemen, welcome to
Hopetown's Community Celebration." He continued with
the program, awarding various citizens for their contribu-
tions, recognizing philanthropists for their donations, and
inserting his witty remarks.

At last he came to the final award to close the program.
"And now it's time to bestow the highest honor from the
community to a deserving citizen. Several nominees, all of
whom have volunteered significantly in their neighborhood, made it a tough decision. We are all proud of you
and hope that you continue to serve as role models for
each of us and especially our younger generation. Although my father could not be here this evening, I'm proud
to stand in his place to present the Volunteer of the Year
award to Shelly Bishop."

Justin looked up, anticipating the recipient's approach
to the podium. The standing ovation concealed the lucky
person. It wasn't until the ebony beauty, as he'd begun to
think of her, came up the small stairs that he attached a
name to the person—Shelly Bishop.

Time slowed as he savored the moment that couldn't
have gone better. From the close-cropped hair framing her
face and neck—what a beautiful neck, a ballerina's neck,
he'd decided—to her bared shoulders and gown that fit her
brown body like a full-length gold glove.

The designer of this knockout piece didn't disappoint

him with a slit to the thigh that allowed peekaboo glimpses of her leg and matching shoes.

She now stood a foot away from him. He couldn't tear his gaze away from her solemn face. Her eyes briefly lit on him before she shifted her attention. Long enough for him to appreciate her most attractive feature: heavily lined eyes, almond shaped with a slight slant upward like an exotic minx's. Something nudged him in the back of his mind about this woman. It must be her eyes. Yes, that was it. Even as he thought that, it felt wrong. He studied her face and his gaze fastened on her lips a bit longer than even he thought appropriate.

Several seconds ticked by before he remembered to shake her hand, present the award, and wipe the silly grin from his face.

Shelly Bishop.

Was she imagining that her name had been called? Leading up to the event she had mixed feelings. She wanted the award, not to satisfy an ego trip or to show off to her family and friends, but because it would provide a chance for her to be courageous, to show her gratitude. The other side to that wish meant someone who truly deserved the honor wouldn't be recognized.

"Go on, honey," her mother urged. "That's my girl," she bragged to the neighboring tables.

Shelly struggled to squelch the fluttering butterflies performing somersaults in her stomach. It was time to follow through with her resolution. The clapping and congratulatory remarks faded into background noise. She looked from her father's proud smile that was a part of his distinguished figure with salt-and-pepper hair to her mother's animated gestures, pumping her fist triumphantly in the air. No censure or judgment marred the loving gazes they showered upon her. Their happiness warmed her, giving her the strength she needed to go through with her plan.

Her mother pulled her close in a tight embrace. "I'm proud of you. Now go on and get that award." She kissed Shelly's cheek. "By the way, now you'll be face-to-face with Dapper Dan since you didn't want to check him out during dinner."

Shelly chuckled. Her mother's knack of being lighthearted and upbeat kept her out of the doldrums more times than she could count. How could she possibly check out anyone now? She hoped that somehow she'd manage to walk up onto the stage without tripping over her feet. Her thoughts spun and she couldn't focus on the cheering crowd, the cameras flashing, or even how she looked. Maybe later she could recall the details to experience some type of belated sense of excitement. Only a few feet away from the podium, the flurry of activity moved into her periphery. The steps to get her award felt like the longest mile. Like a magnet, her eyes fastened on the man—a familiar figure who rattled carefully locked away emotions—holding her award.

It was Justin.

Her Justin.

For one moment, she thought of turning around and running through the exit. But, reality slapped her awake with the realization that he probably didn't even remember her. She continued forward with her mother's admonishment playing her head. Close up, he was worth the discreet glances and whispers the women at her table indulged in during dinner. In her defense, any of those women would have also fallen under the spell.

Justin definitely could stop traffic. It wasn't just good looks he had to his credit. A certain charm surrounded him, drawing and holding her attention like a magnet. The tailored suit could put him on the pages of any magazine featuring heartthrob business execs. His contoured face fashioned a beard expertly shaped along his jawline and mouth. A mouth that broke into an easy broad smile as he gazed intensely at her, dispelling any thought of him being boyishly anything.

"Congratulations, Miss Bishop." He smiled.

She shook his hand, thinking that his teeth didn't have to be so perfect. He probably hadn't had to endure anything like her nine-month sentence of painful braces. Her returning smile got lost in the attack of nerves and she could only gulp. "Th-thank you."

He guided her to the microphone with a gentle touch to her elbow. The contact, although brief, still made her flush like a smitten schoolgirl. She watched him take up his position some distance away.

With a sigh she shook herself out of her adolescent reaction. No need to fool herself, her interest in any man never went past arm's-length admiration. There was too much to risk otherwise. It meant opening up, trusting, sharing. She'd rather reject first than face the inevitable rejection. She pushed Justin Thornton and his good looks to the back of her mind—and that kiss.

There were other matters to take care of, like her thankyou speech. "Ahem. Thank you so much for this award. I honestly feel that I am not worthy of such an honor." She paused, keeping her eyes downcast. Gathering her nerve, she continued, "I say this because people volunteer from their hearts, sharing their talent, zest for life, and the positive parts of their lives with others. When I volunteered to work at the Women's Crisis Center, I had selfish reasons that are not in the spirit of volunteerism."

The room quieted. Shelly licked her lips, desperate for a sip of water. Her hands shook and she gritted her teeth to keep the tremor from taking over her entire body. She clutched the crystal award, allowing its sharp outline to sink into her palms in an effort to keep her grounded. "You see, two years ago someone I mistook for a friend betrayed my trust. That sense of security that I'd taken for granted had been shattered. Since then, I worked as a volunteer at the Women's Crisis Center looking for answers. Some reason that told me why a friend used his strength against me. Why did splitting my lip and pulling my hair make him feel like a man? I heard stories here that made mine pale in comparison and other stories that continue to haunt me. Those are the women, the survivors, who deserve your honor and respect."

Her tears welled and spilled down her cheeks. "It took a fighting spirit and let me tell you, it's a daily battle. It took faith to fight the demons of depression. And it took my family's love to mend me back together. Thank you, Mom and Dad, for not judging me. Thank you for your love and patience. It's still a long road ahead. I know that the new family I've discovered at the Women's Crisis Center will continue to help me on my journey." She held the award in the air. "And this is for you, my sisters." She blew a kiss.

She was given a second ovation with everyone enthusiastically clapping. Several women openly wept, while a few men shifted uncomfortably, fighting back emotion.

"Here," a familiar voice said. A handkerchief was presented and she took it.

"Thank you." She wiped her eyes. "I owe you one." She turned to face Justin Thornton. Looking into his thoughtful, dark eyes filled with sympathy shook her resolve not to be a weeping willow. She tried to smile again and only her lips quivered in response. His dark brown eyes swallowed her with their compassion. She had to get away or crumble into hysterics.

"Excuse me, please." She hurried back to her table. Each dab at her nose with the handkerchief provided a pleasant whiff of crisp-scented cologne.

"You did good, girl," her mother said, beaming, her makeup streaked with dried tears.

"Even if I fell flat on my face, you'd say that, Mom."

"Yes, I would because you would do that well, too."

Her father squeezed her hand. "I'll always be there for you. You're my favorite daughter."

"And you're the *bestest* dad." She was a card-carrying member of the daddy's-girl club, and his broad shoulders had always been a good place to cry. As the only daughter, she never lacked for attention. It spoiled her, but she wasn't complaining.

"Well?" Her mother tapped a red nail on the table. "What did you think?"

"What difference does it make what I think?"

"Don't play games with me." Her mother playfully pulled at Shelly's curls. "He hasn't taken his eyes off you since you returned." She looked over Shelly's shoulder, waved, and nodded. "I think he wants to talk to you."

"Mom!" Shelly couldn't believe her mother's audacity. "Don't call him over here. If he comes, I'm gone."

Her mother stared at her as if she'd grown another head. "What's the big deal? A simple hello, here's my number, here's your number, invitation to family dinner. Nothing heavy at all."

"Like I would be crazy enough to bring him home. He'd never pass your third degree. Besides, I am not dating any-one anytime soon. The few men I've wasted my time dating claim they understand that I want friendship first, but they never really do." She played with a crumb on the table. That fact hurt more than she cared to admit. No man wanted to take the time to build a foundation.

"Fine, but if I was five years younger, I'd give him a run for his money." Her mother pulled out her compact and powdered her nose.

"Why?" her father asked. "So he can call you 'old girl'?

Five years? Please! Better be about fifteen years." He winked at Shelly.

"You know something, Bill, no one asked you anything."

"Then why don't you leave Shelly alone, Clara?"

"You don't know what you're talking about."

Bill pointed in the direction of Justin. "Why would you want to hook her up with the gigolo man? You can tell he's used to women falling all over themselves for him. My daughter is too sensible for that."

"Weren't you the same way? Yet we fell in love and look at us now."

"I rest my case," Bill retorted with another wink toward his daughter.

Why did he have to go there? His comments inflamed the situation, and her high-strung mother was ready to come out swinging. As her parents bickered, Shelly fiddled with her evening bag, hoping that Justin wasn't standing close enough to hear the exchange. Finally her parents rose, readying themselves to leave.

"One moment, please."

Shelly didn't have to turn to recognize the deep timbre of Justin's voice. A tingle of anticipation rippled through her. He towered over her where she sat, and to lessen the difference she stood, only able to meet his shoulder.

"I didn't get a chance to say what an inspiring message you shared."

Gosh, he looked good. He would stand out in any crowd with the natural red-brown hair neatly close cut. Like redheads of any persuasion, she thought the dusting of freckles complemented his beige skin. "Thanks. I hope it was inspiring for at least one person."

His hand covered his heart. "It was for me."

Shelly smiled. He was *still* smooth, she had to give him

that. The twinkle in his eyes let her know that he agreed with her assessment of him.

"I'm Justin Thornton, by the way."

She shook his hand for the second time, noting that it easily swallowed hers. "I'm Shelly." She laughed. "I guess you know that already."

He nodded.

Her father stepped up protectively at her shoulder. "And I'm her father, Bill Bishop." His face set hard with displeasure, glaring eye-to-eye at Justin.

Shelly held her breath at the standoff. Justin didn't back down or blink. He remained stoic. Although her thirtieth birthday was in a few months, she was reliving the traumas of her first high school date.

Justin addressed her parents, a smile tugged at the corners of his mouth. "Glad to meet you. You've got a beautiful daughter."

"I know. What exactly are—"

Clara took her husband by the arm. "We'll be in the lobby. Don't hurry on our account. Your father and I are going to have a talk." She looked back at Shelly and gave a dramatic thumbs-up sign.

"Shelly, we'll be waiting for you," her father shot over his shoulder.

Embarrassed, she remained silent. Nervously her finger smoothed a curl at her neck. She wished he'd say something.

"Nice parents."

"They really are, just a little protective."

"I meant it. It's nice to see such closeness. I'm close with my father. Couldn't imagine it any other way. Well, I won't keep you. I just wanted to come over and congratulate you. Here's my card. If the Hopetown Savings Bank or I can help you in any way—"

She turned the card to read. No point in denying it, she

wanted this to continue. Since the conversation didn't develop, no thanks to her father, the unspoken invitation lay at her feet. Her limited dating experience followed a pattern where the men figured a couple of dinner dates and a night on the town were payment for a few hours in her bed. She wasn't that desperate. Yet she longed to believe that the vibes she read in Justin's considerate attention and thoughtful eyes guaranteed something wholesome.

She studied Justin's retreating form. He walked with a smooth, unhurried gait. Her father was probably right. A man in Justin's position would have women, and lots of them, at his beck and call. His family's money and social position could prove to be a downhill charge into a bad experience. Once was enough for her. She tore the business card in half and laid it on the table.

The ride home didn't prove to be any better on her nerves. She should have driven her car to avoid her mother. Her mom questioned her with the skill of a wartime interrogator. Shelly hid her feelings, grateful to be sitting in the back of the car concealed by the darkness. As her father navigated through the deserted streets of Baltimore's inner city, she identified with the eerie emptiness that hid the city's forgotten souls.

"I agree with you, Mom, that he is everything most women would want, but I'm not interested," she replied, frustrated by her mother's latest comment that goaded her into reacting defensively.

"That's my girl," her father joined in. "No man *should* be good enough for you."

"I don't care for the combination of money and power," Shelly stated.

"Don't rush her, Clara," her father advised.

"I'm not rushing her," her mother snapped. "But she can't live behind a wall of fear either."

"She won't have to because next time I'm gonna kick some butt." Her father nodded to her in the rearview mirror.

Another time, another place, she would have laughed. For Bill Bishop—who'd spent his teenage years in prep school, attended an Ivy League university, and now wore his trifocals full-time—to be kicking anyone's butt would be a sight to be seen.

The fabric of her family life appeared to be unraveling and it made her angry and frustrated. Her father, known as the gentle giant, had his world turned upside down as much as she did. Her mother remained preoccupied about whether her daughter would ever trust another man again and become a wife and mother someday.

Shelly accepted the blame, the weight pressing on her shoulders. She had asked them, begged them to follow her request. By signing some darn papers, she had sold her soul, and her parents had had to swallow their rage.

Half an hour later, her father turned the car into the parking space in front of her apartment building. She craved the solitude, thankful that she hadn't moved back home upon her parents' urgings.

She stepped out of the car. The summer night's humidity draped her in an uncomfortable moist cloak. It took no time for her curls to untwist and hang like a limp cap. She tapped on the passenger window. "Guys, I'll be fine. Tanya is staying with me until I can help her back on her feet. She enrolled with the Hopetown Girls Club and they went on a retreat this weekend. In the meantime, I have enough to do to keep me busy."

"Good, glad to hear about Tanya. I really hope you can make some headway with her. However, you take care of yourself. Don't hide from life. It hands us a bum deal every now and then, but it's got a lot to offer too." Her mother kissed her cheek. "Besides, you don't need to end up like your spinster great-aunt in South Carolina, living alone with a million cats running around your ankles. You're too young to pass up fun things."

"Nothing wrong with cats."

"People need people."

"Good-bye, Dad," Shelly said pointedly. Her father took the hint and started the car.

Stepping into the apartment, she flicked on the lights bringing her living room to life. As her stay had lengthened indefinitely, she had spent some money decorating her entire apartment with the right colors, furniture, and drapes. After a stress-filled day like this one, she welcomed the chance to come home and enjoy the calming effects of her earth tones, featuring sienna browns and reddish clay hues. She kicked off her shoes and padded barefoot into the kitchen.

A cup of chamomile tea beckoned to her. While the water came to a boil, she unzipped her gown and freed herself from its confines. The pleasures of living alone afforded the unabashed opportunity to be au naturel. The stockings had to go too and she promptly rolled them down her legs. A few minutes later, teacup in hand, she ran her bath. A hot soak and tea were a ritual at the end of a stress-filled day. In this case, an emotionally draining day counted as such.

Minutes later, Luther Vandross's deep soulful voice floated out to her as she prepared her bubble bath with a touch of peppermint oil. Submerged in scented suds, she sipped her tea humming to the tune. Luther crooned about loneliness and she drifted along with its melody. His words stoked the sadness that lately she seemed unable to keep buried away from everyone.

Shelly remembered that awful night after a Halloween

party. Her parents had stood horrified after the doctors led them into the emergency care unit. All she could do was sob in her mother's arms, unable to deal with the recent terror. The evidence of what she'd endured lay plain to see with the bruises and swelling, skin covered with black and blue splotches, clothing torn. She had fought with everything in her and managed to escape. All she had wanted at that very moment was to curl up and disappear. The police had treated her with cool detachment. Toby Gillis, the man who had violated her trust, had already contacted them. By the time they visited, her role as a crazed, rejected girlfriend had been established.

The weeks that followed continued her walk through hell. Toby's lawyer had passed on his thinly veiled threats of reprisal if she didn't sign papers demanding her silence. A list of so-called witnesses waited in the wings to testify if necessary. Her parents had complied with her final wishes with great reluctance, and they did whatever it took to make her feel better.

Shelly stepped out of the tub. It had been a while since she had relived the entire experience. The nightmares had decreased to infrequent visits, but she wished they would drip off her body and swirl down the drain like the water in the tub. She dried herself and slipped on pajamas. Running was the last thing she wanted to do. There were so many things she wanted to accomplish and places to visit. Most importantly, she wanted to share those dreams with someone special who cared and loved her. Retreating from life had gotten old.

She slipped under the quilted cover and snuggled into her pillow. One day her prince would brave the brambles and slay the dragon that held her heart hostage. A familiar face with sexy freckles teased her sleepy mind. She yawned. Her life was reduced to fantasizing about fairy tales, but at least the role of the prince was a done deal.

* * *

The telephone's shrill ring jarred Shelly awake. It couldn't possibly be morning. She groaned sleepily and pulled an extra pillow over her head. It only muffled the sound, chasing any further hope of her falling asleep.

She reached for the receiver, knocking over her bedside clock. "Hello," she croaked.

"Good morning, Miss Bishop," a contrasting crisp voice greeted, full of annoying cheer.

"Nancy? Is that you?"

"Yes, Miss Bishop. Just calling to tell you that your vacation is over." She pronounced the word "ovah" with an exuberance that grated on Shelly's nerves.

Shelly knew for a number of years that she was not a morning person. She'd even tried to make that point clear to Nancy, but it was obvious that there was a communication breakdown. Nancy's perky tone and exaggerated pronunciation added to Shelly's crabbiness.

"Shelly, are you still there? Wake up!"

"Shh. I'm here. I'm here."

"I have a job for you. The interview is at ten-thirty this morning. Get a pen and paper for the details."

"That's nice, but I am employed, remember? You got me that job."

"Yes, but Doc Calloway was already contacted and he's willing to give you up. Before you blow a fuse, he didn't have any complaints. It's just that he got a call from an old friend asking for a favor."

"Okay, go ahead. You certainly got my attention." Shelly sat up and got a pen to take down the information. It would help matters if her head didn't feel as if it were filled with pea soup. Two glasses of wine earned the blame.

"The client has had a relapse after a one-year remission phase. He has a full-time nurse but wants a companion and chose you. The address is 12002 Elm Street, upper-crust side of Hopetown. It should take you twenty minutes to half an hour."

The fog in Shelly's head cleared. The Gold Coast! Interesting. The westside of Hopetown had neighborhoods catering to six-figure-and-above incomes. Grand homes covered great expansive properties that were as much a part of the natural landscape as the famous white oak trees that lined the roads like sturdy sentinels. As standard amenities, houses came equipped with tennis courts and swimming pools for the prominent lawyers, doctors, and business executives. With the improbability of being a home owner in the fashionable high-priced district a stark reality, she'd settle for being an employee.

"How long is the assignment?" she asked, biting the tip of her pen.

"It's indefinite, with lots of flexibility."

"I think I may skip this one, Nan." There was no reason to change jobs, especially since her coworkers accepted her and the job was stress-free. Most of all, it wasn't about the job because her focus had to be Tanya.

"Sorry, kiddo. The client asked specifically for you."

"Who is this person?"

"Darn it! One sec. I just knocked the paperwork off my desk." Paper rustled. "Ah, here it is. The name's Thornton."

Shelly didn't realize that she'd held her breath, until she noisily exhaled at the mention of the familiar name.

"Thornton?"

"Phillip Thornton to be exact," Nancy clarified.

"And he asked for me? I guess he wasn't kidding."

"Excuse me?"

"Oh, nothing. What else did he say?"

"He said he was referred by a friend. Said he'd heard only good things about you and that you came highly recommended."

"I guess I should be flattered," Shelly replied, with a big grin. Phillip was certainly persistent. "Thanks, Nan. I'll let you know how it goes." She placed the phone down gently, already speculating.

One major reason existed for playing along with Phillip's elaborate scheming. The money would certainly come in handy since her current pay wasn't up to New York standards.

But that was the sensible reason for taking the job. Being sensible bored her. The more exciting reason allowed her to enter the world of the Thorntons, where Justin was prince of his realm.

Three

An hour later Shelly turned down Elm Street and thought she had driven into an artist's rendering of an idyllic view of suburbia. Sturdy white oak trees, weeping willows, and various evergreens provided a lush, green background. The morning sun peeped through branches, promising to deliver another onslaught of a hazy summer day. In no hurry to reach her final destination, Shelly cruised at the posted speed limit to gaze at the stately homes behind fences and security booths.

The neighborhood didn't appear too busy as she watched a few people jog, the hired help pushing strollers or holding an infant's hand, and a lawn service person unloading his equipment to begin mowing.

A car approached her, the yellow lights on the four-wheel-drive flashing. It slowed as it drew closer and Shelly fastened on to the driver, a uniformed security guard. He stared at her through mirrored glasses as he drove at a crawl past her. She gave a shaky smile and a short wave. No response. Shelly took it as her clue to end the sightseeing and be on her way.

At the end of the street where it ended in a cul-de-sac, she pulled up to massive iron gates marked with the address she sought. She'd heard of people's jaw dropping, but never believed in such a thing. Yet, there she sat with mouth agape.

"Wow!" she exclaimed.

The impressive sight before her could not be mistaken for the traditional, four-bedroom colonial like her parents' home. And there was no comparison to her matchbox apartment.

This estate spoke volumes about her new client. She leaned out of her window and pushed the button on the speaker box. No one answered immediately and she took the opportunity to get a better view. Leaving her car, she walked up to the gates and gingerly touched them, hoping that she hadn't triggered an alarm. Tall columns with ornate scrolled crowns, borrowing the palatial magnificence from Greco-Roman architecture, framed the front of the residence.

"What a life!"

Suddenly a man appeared dressed in a black suit. He stood powerfully built like a human Mack truck, stone-faced, able to scare the heck out of her in a dark alley.

"Can I help you?"

"I'm Shelly Bishop. Here to see Phillip Thornton."

He pulled out a cell phone, dialed, and said her name. Seemingly satisfied, he snapped the phone closed.

Only after she displayed her driver's license and he jotted down her license plate number, did she gain access. She swallowed her teasing remarks about rent-a-cops when she spied the holstered gun at his side. Actually, his cold, assessing eyes equally served as a deterrent.

She rolled onto the property in her Ford Escort, feeling like a mouse entering a lion's den. The gates clanked into place, locking her in its gilded cage. In her rearview mirror, she watched the guard staring after her car, one hand casually resting on his gun.

One thing she knew for certain, Phillip Thornton was an important man.

A cobbled driveway wound its way from the gate to the

house into a crescent shape. She parked in front, suddenly conscious of the car's minor dents and rust appearing as large wounds against the backdrop of grandeur. She shrugged, not much she could do, but it didn't stop her from trying to wipe clean a smudge on the side mirror with ragged tissue from her pocket. Besides, renting a limo to come to work wasn't in her budget.

Shading her eyes from the sun, she scanned the area for signs of anyone. The only activity came from squirrels cavorting from tree to tree. Birds whistled contentedly perched in front of various birdhouses around the expertly manicured gardens. The flower of choice seemed to be the rose, which grew in full abundance intertwined in the iron fence, softening the image of a fortress.

Additional wine-colored roses framed the house walls, a stark contrast against the walls' bright white color. Burgundy shutters on either side of the large, full-length windows completed the impressive picture.

Shelly approached the front door, passing between small evergreens, neatly trimmed, encased in large, round brass pots. Overall the house was a perfect model for a luxury home magazine. She wondered what was on the other side of the door as her finger poised over the doorbell. Taking a deep breath, she pushed the button and almost immediately saw a distorted image of someone approach through the stained glass panel in the door.

The door swung open, and a dour-faced woman stared down her nose at her. She didn't return Shelly's smile, which wavered and then dissipated. "G-Good morning, ma'am. I have an appointment with Mr. Thornton. My, er, name is Shelly . . ." Shelly's voice trailed off into uncomfortable silence.

The woman took in Shelly's uniform, sizing her from the top of her head to her white-stockinged legs and shapeless nurse's shoes.

"I am aware of who you are," she remarked in a precise, clipped manner. Then as if Shelly passed the woman's unspoken test, she stepped back and motioned for her to enter. "Mr. Thornton is not here at the moment. Follow me and I will take you to his office. You may have a seat in there. He is due to arrive shortly."

Shelly nodded. *Yes, Drill Sergeant.*

Obviously this woman ran the household with an iron fist. She didn't wear a uniform, although the brown shapeless dress appeared to be her style. Brown must be her color also because the dress, hose, and shoes matched perfectly—a good shade of mud. From the formal way she referred to Mr. Thornton, her position probably was housekeeper, which likely meant that nothing occurred without her approval or knowledge.

As Shelly followed the woman, she rated the first encounter at the Thornton house as "barely passing." It was clear that this formidable woman didn't like her and didn't feel it necessary to introduce herself. It wasn't Shelly's first time working under such conditions, but she would tolerate it as long as it didn't get hostile and she was able to do her job without undue interference.

The older woman opened the office door and stepped aside for her. The office was neat and carried a faint lemony scent of furniture wax.

"Have a seat, please. Is there anything I can get for you?"

Shelly shook her head. Although the question was asked, her guide's face didn't encourage any requests. Shelly actually looked forward to waiting in the office out of her sight.

Once the door closed, she studied the room to gain some clues about her new employer. That was a half-truth. Really, she wanted to discover whether her intuition was correct, whether Justin called this modern-day castle home.

Walls lined with numerous volumes of books, none of which appeared to be pleasure reading, surrounded her. On closer inspection, the titles displayed banking, marketing, and various other banking-related topics.

"Banking! It's all banking," she muttered. She ran her fingers over the spines. The books felt expensive with leather bindings and gold imprint. This time she didn't fight her mind's rebellious wandering as it flashed various angles of Justin's face like a slide show. A nervous flutter started in her stomach. Her pulse quickened.

She'd have to wait and see if her guess was correct.

Where could Phillip Thornton be? More precisely, were the two Thorntons related? She had the impression that he'd taken a turn for the worse. Requiring a nurse didn't bode well. In a few minutes, all of her questions would be answered. She walked over to one of the windows and looked outside. Her breath caught at the sight of a large expanse of manicured lawn.

Shelly surmised that Mr. Thornton must have liked the outdoors and all its natural beauty. To a large extent, nature and its gifts had been preserved. Folding her arms, she stood at the window and thought about what it would be like to spend a quiet afternoon under one of those trees reading, listening to music, or having a romantic picnic with that special someone.

Problem.

She didn't have a special someone.

A door opened and closed behind her.

She jumped and swung around to face her client, equipped with a ready smile and sincere compliment about the garden on the edge of her tongue.

Her smile froze. The compliment fled her mind.

"Shelly, er, Miss Bishop?" Justin stood in front of her. His expression reflected equal surprise.

"Mr. Thornton?"

Justin motioned for her to go first.

Confused and suddenly nervous, she wet her lips with the

tip of her tongue. "Mr. Thornton, I wasn't expecting you. I mean—I thought that I was meeting Phillip Thornton."

"Oh," he replied distracted, shaking his head in disagreement. "No," he protested. "That couldn't be. Since his illness, he doesn't hold any appointments. That's my job, so to speak." Justin jammed his hands in his pockets. A frown played, appearing and disappearing, as if a great decision weighed on him. He crossed the room and stood behind a massive cherry-wood desk that gleamed with a rich sheen.

"What can I do for you?" he asked, visibly relaxing with the desk between them. "I received a message that I had to come home regarding my father. Then I get here and Mrs. Beacham tells me someone is waiting to see me in the office. I wished she'd told me that it was you. I would have had you come directly to the bank. I would rather have made the donation to your charity there, but I can be accommodating." He flashed her a brilliant smile. "Coming here was probably out of your way." He pulled a ring of keys from his pocket, unlocked the desk drawer, and retrieved a checkbook.

"Mr. Thornton, I appreciate your willingness to give me a donation." Shelly stopped him, mainly for her benefit. "You've already been more than generous. However, I'm not here for that purpose." Shelly didn't understand the personality change that she'd just witnessed. First, excitement, then suspicion, and now a frosty nip penetrated the space between Justin and her. "Why then are you here?"

No time to explore the twinges of disappointment. Did he think that she dressed like this for kicks?

"I'm here on a job," she explained, watching closely for reaction. Her announcement stopped him in the midst of fishing for his pen. His hand stayed in his inside jacket pocket. A chilled gaze studied her with a piercing look full of speculation. All the while her nervousness escalated, hovering at panic level.

"Job?" His tone dropped a notch. With deliberate calm-

ness, he adjusted his jacket and slowly closed the checkbook, placing it back in the desk. Then he sighed and
pinched the bridge of his nose between his eyes. "Not
again," he mumbled under his breath. The frigid stare he
nailed her with had enough power to drop the room's cool
interior another few degrees.

This day was not unfolding the way she had planned or
hoped. Confused, she didn't like feeling as if she'd committed a crime. She had done nothing wrong.

Bracing herself, she met his quelling stare. "Let me start
at the beginning," she began calmly, despite the rapid beat of
her heart. "I am a nurse when I am not volunteering at the
center. My agency called this morning and said to show up
for a job here."

A snort marked the first clue that Justin didn't believe her.
"Cut the bull! Either tell me what it is you think you're
doing, or I'll have security throw you out on your pretty
behind."

"Excuse me?" Enough was enough, how dare he! "Look,
Mr. Thornton, I was sent here. I didn't go for a morning
drive and end up in your house." Was the man crazy? She
didn't think that she was overreacting, but the furious gleam
in his eye spoke volumes. He might not wait for security to
throw her out on her "pretty behind." He'd volunteer.

"It's true." She fumbled in her purse and took out Nancy's
business card. "Here. Call this number." She willed her outstretched hand to remain steady. His scorching words had
blasted a hole in her that left her raw and bruised.

He snatched the card from her and punched the numbers
never once taking his eyes off for any longer than necessary.

"Nancy Boyd, please. Ms. Boyd, Justin Thornton here. I
have a Miss Shelly Bishop here in my father's house, claim-
ing that she is on a job for my father. Mmm. Mmm. Who
was your contact? Thank you." He finished the call by slamming the receiver down in its cradle.

From what Shelly heard on her end, he didn't get the news he expected. His anger, which lay barely beneath the surface, suffused his face, tightening by the second, and if possible, steam would have escaped from his ears. Shelly's eyes locked into the pulsing muscle in his jaw as it worked to an internal beat.

"You!" He pointed at her. "Stay put!"

What was happening? Justin stormed out of the office, slamming the door shut behind him. His mood churned, one second happy to see that Shelly had acted upon his veiled invitation, but perturbed to find her in his father's home. Coincidence? Not a chance.

Yet she was in the office looking demure and sweet in her white pantsuit hired as an employee. It all fit too neatly for his liking and he was determined to get to the bottom of it. The initial rush of—what? He couldn't put his finger on it—when he saw her standing at the window set off alarms in his head.

"Damn!" He wasn't comfortable with being out of control. And he refused to cave in to juvenile reactions toward the sound of her husky voice or the soft-scented fragrance he noticed when he entered the room.

Standing outside his father's door, he tried to regain some semblance of calmness. There had to be a reasonable explanation. At least he hoped there was one. He knocked first, then entered.

His father sat at the window reading a magazine. His slightly rounded shoulders emphasized his overall fragility. It amazed him that his father always had a smile or some motivational tidbit to share with him.

"How are you, Dad?" Standing next to his father, he made a contrasting figure with his youth and vitality.

"Oh, hello, son. Didn't expect you so soon. Is everything all right?"

"Well, not quite." Justin stopped in front of his father

to maintain eye contact. "Dad, are you up to your tricks again?"

"Tricks?"

"Are you playing matchmaker? There's a woman in the office who claims you hired her."

"Justin, have you gone crazy? Ever since the last time you chewed my ear off, I haven't given your lack of female companionship another thought." His father put his wheelchair in reverse and maneuvered it around him. Over his shoulder, he explained, "I did hire a nurse, if that is to whom you are referring. Would you send her in, please?"

His father's nonchalance didn't go over on Justin. Running his hand over his hair, Justin huffed, his exasperation building. Something just didn't ring true with his father's story, but he knew the stubborn man would hold fast to his story if pressed.

"Okay, Dad, have it your way." He raised his hands in surrender. "One day you're going to pick the wrong girl and have a heap of trouble on your hands. I guess when it backfires, then you'll come running for me to clean up the mess. Lecturing to you won't do any good, so I'll send her in and the two of you can plot away. But let me warn you, the minute she gets in my way it's out she goes."

"In case you forgot, dear boy, I hired her. And only *I* can fire her." His father flipped through the magazine in his lap without acknowledging his scowling son. "However, so you don't get even more paranoid, she wasn't hired for your entertainment. I'm bored and lonely. If I'm going to go, I don't need to be climbing the walls from being stuck indoors."

"Stop it, Dad. Your situation is nothing to joke about and you've managed to beat it. Let's not talk about failing. We'll look back on these times as a brief unpleasant moment."

His father motioned for assistance from the wheelchair to the bed. "We've been through this before," he replied. "I've had a wonderful life and continue to enjoy every moment.

We'll all die eventually. It's simply a matter of how we'll go. Agonizing about the way I will leave God's green earth is not how I plan to spend my time. No regrets, though. I thought, at least, I'd passed on that same love for life to you. But day after day you never fail to show me that cynical, jaded soul you possess, and *that* breaks my heart.

"The bank has become your obsession, but when the day has ended, does the bank greet you at the door and ask about your day? Does the bank massage your problems away? Does the bank hold you in its arms until you fall asleep? Life is too short, son."

Justin retreated to the door without answering his father. A debate on his obsession with the bank was not his intent. A relationship had too many unknowns and his father's legacy was a curse sometimes.

A young, black man with attractive financial holdings, living the life of a bachelor, acted as a magnet in the worst way. If there was anything he valued highly, it was his personal space. He didn't care for gate-crashers, nor did he have the patience to invest in finding a soul mate. Why couldn't his father understand?

"I'll send her to you."

Outside, Justin took deep breaths. His insides ached from the wretched state to which his father was reduced. He tried to be strong for him and it was all he could do to keep from breaking down at his father's bedside. But they had been given a second chance and he wanted to bottle each minute—just in case.

On the other hand, his father's obsession with his single state seemed to have grown since the doctor announced his relapse. Settling down as a married man would probably be the first order his father ever gave him that he could not truly fulfill. He wasn't ready to let go of his father or the dismal future. So being thankful for what life offered was not going to be easy. It came with too many strings attached.

It was amazing, though, that cancer didn't stop his father's optimism. He dearly loved his father's ability to swipe obstacles from his path. It was a quality he envied about the old man.

Justin's life was too cluttered, a state he deliberately created and maintained. The bank, the extra business functions and conferences played central roles in his hectic life. Not to mention his social calendar, which remained filled with him acting as host for charitable functions or sponsor of numerous foundations.

How could he find the time to have a relationship where he could trust, love, and honor a woman—his wife? He shook his head. No, he was better off alone. He had his flings, and they would have to suffice.

If it was indeed his father's intent that his new nurse was going to be the next Mrs. Justin Thornton, he would be disappointed. Justin might not be able to cope with his father's condition, but Miss Bishop was a different matter. The familiar tick in his jaw worked. He refused to fall into her man-trap, looking at him with feigned indignation. Never mind that his gaze drew to her pursed lips, full and tempting. His father might have outdone himself with this temptress.

Justin decided to make an exception this once; he'd play along. His father and this conniving woman might have concocted the game, but he was about to change the rules. He hoped she had the stamina to keep up with him.

Shelly heard Justin's footsteps strike the hardwood floor before he appeared at the door. His short absence gave her time to compose her shattered nerves. It was quite obvious that Justin wasn't pleased that she was an employee. The reason for his displeasure, however, was lost on her. Where had that lazy, sexy smile disappeared to or the concerned, assessing eyes that showered her in a warm glow?

Taking a seat, she crossed her legs and pretended to minister to her nails. She would not give the younger Thornton the satisfaction of making her feel on edge. Her spunk was back.

He flung open the door, standing in the doorway like an angry warrior. His eyes, angry and dark, glared at her, his brows like straight dark dashes. She shrank back. Okay, maybe half of her spunk was back.

"It would appear that you have lost the first round." A small smirk played on her face, adding sting to her remark.

Justin turned menacing, dark brown eyes on her. His penetrating stare transmitted his wish to vaporize her on the spot; however, she stood her ground. Three male cousins had trained her for such occasions. Despite his earlier temper tantrum, Shelly decided he was still very handsome and still could cause a strange, new stirring in her.

"Shall I ring for the housekeeper to take me to your father?"

"First, don't get cocky," he snapped. "You may have won the first round, but you won't be around to finish the fight. Second, *I* will take you to my father."

"Mr. Thornton, I am not trying to be impertinent, but I was not the one who requested my presence. I think we should call a truce while I'm in your father's employ." She extended her hand in an act of friendliness.

It was clear he didn't remember her from several years ago. Their first meeting outside a postgraduation party had lasted fifteen minutes. What more could she expect? After a moment's hesitation, Justin crossed the room and took her hand, his expression still highly suspicious.

Standing a few inches away from him, Shelly concentrated on keeping her breaths even so he wouldn't see her distress.

"Okay, let's go, I have to get back to the office." He looked at his watch to drive home his point that she was an inconvenience.

The hallway he led her down was gaily decorated. Shelly had no time to sightsee since she had to match two steps with every one of Justin's. At the end of the hall, they entered a wing built away from the main part of the house. Dark wood doors barred entry.

Justin pushed open the doors. A nurse sat in the reception area. After writing on a patient chart, she looked up at the couple. "Mr. Thornton, back again?"

"Hi, Mildred. Yep, I'm back, but not staying. Dad wanted to meet the new nurse." He pointed to Shelly and made introductions.

"Nice to meet you, Miss Bishop. I'm Mr. Thornton's nurse."

"Please, call me Shelly. I hate formality."

The two women shook hands. Shelly immediately felt comfortable. Mildred's easygoing demeanor and ready smile set her at ease. They would get along. She breathed a sigh of relief. So far, the housekeeper and the son were ready to kick her to the curb.

"Well, ladies," Justin interrupted, "I have to go. Mildred, please take Miss Bishop in." He gave Shelly a mock salute, turned, and left.

When Shelly followed Mildred into Phillip's room, she braced herself for the worst, especially since he'd missed a couple of appointments at Doc Calloway's office. However, the man who lay among the pillows was not the picture of hopelessness. There was a spark of determination that held a strong presence in the familiar twinkle of his eyes. This fighting spirit warmed her. Phillip would be a pleasure to attend.

"Miss Bishop, thank you for accepting my offer." Phillip was clearly exhausted, but he made an effort.

Shelly brought her chair closer to his bedside. She liked his smile. Actually it reminded her of Justin's. When his son managed to show it.

"I must be honest with you, Mr. Thornton, I'm a bit curious as to why you wanted me. From the look of things, you're well taken care of."

"I know, but remember I offered you that job. You said you would consider, but I couldn't wait any longer. All I did was ask the same question in a different way." He grinned like a little boy proud of his creativity.

Shelly nodded, not because she understood. Instead, she was even more confused at the lengths that Phillip went to get her. Looking around the room at the efficiency of his home life, she determined that he lacked spontaneity. She served that purpose, a role that she was willing to tolerate and accept.

"Okay. You are properly staffed, so what exactly did you want me to do?"

"I know I appear extravagant." When she shook her head, he chuckled. "It's okay. I know I am. According to my son, extremely so. But I wanted a companion who would read and talk with me. Someone who wasn't afraid of my condition and could help chase the blues away. Think you can handle that?"

Shelly was relieved. It would be great to be paid to talk and keep someone company. "Yes, Mr. Thornton, I think I can handle that."

"Good. Mildred will fill you in on the details. I need to rest so I'll see you tomorrow."

Outside the room Mildred brought Shelly up to date on her employer's health, his typical day, and how they could complement each other without being in each other's way.

Mildred grew serious. "I have to ask how many terminal patients you've dealt with."

"Five," Shelly answered. "My experience spans a wide range of age groups in the seven years I've been a nurse."

"So you're used to worst-case scenarios?"

"Yes, I am. Makes me appreciate what I have even more."

Mildred nodded grimly. "Just checking your experience because although he's pretty active and has a good attitude, he just learned that he's out of remission. I'm hoping for the best, but frankly, no one knows for sure whether this is long or short term." She looked at Shelly and asked candidly, "Can you handle it when the situation turns?"

Shelly understood the nurse's questions. It would not do for her to have emotional breakdowns in front of the patient. Besides, Mildred might need her medical assistance and she would not be of any help if she could not be emotionally detached.

"Yes, I'll be able to handle it." She loved her profession and cared deeply about each of her patients. It was what helped her through the upheavals in her life. Smiling at Mildred, she reassured her. "Phillip Thornton will be in good hands."

"Good. Now for the rules." Mildred pointed to the other chair in the reception area. "You might as well have a seat. The rules are a bit lengthy, provided by Mrs. Beacham, our taskmistress. If you want to remain employed here, don't cross her and don't forget the rules."

Mildred paced, counting the rules off on her fingers. "First, you are an employee. Second, you are not equal to Mrs. Beacham. Third, do not use the front door. If you forget, then you will be told to use the side entrance in a five-minute lecture by Mrs. Beacham."

Mildred's voice droned on with several more rules all piling on top of each other. Shelly knew that it would be a matter of time before she violated a sacred rule. She would have to deal not only with Justin, but also with the formidable Mrs. Beacham.

"Thanks. I think." They shared a laugh.

Shelly felt confident and excited with her new assignment. It promised to be challenging, but it was exactly what she needed right now.

Justin, however, was a different matter.

That afternoon, pulling out of the Thornton's driveway, Shelly wondered if she'd made the right decision. The Thornton men elicited two distinctly different reactions. Phillip made her feel at ease. Her goal was simple. Make him comfortable and share anecdotes with him. She looked forward to sharing in his vast life experiences. His stories promised to be endless and entertaining. Being his companion would be a pleasure and an honor.

His son, on the other hand, made her uneasy, although the feeling wasn't malevolent. Instead it made her aware of him in a refreshingly new way. Everything about him caught her attention and scrambled her senses. Agreeing to work in the house held a similar danger like playing with matches near a gas pump.

Sooner or later, the odds increased that a spark would ignite.

Four

It was almost time.

He paced in front of the window with an occasional glance at his Rolex. Moments later, he saw the familiar burgundy Ford Escort round the bend. Even though he restrained himself, his pulse skipped a few beats when Shelly parked and stepped from the car. He appreciated his father's decision to get rid of the unflattering white uniform. Her casual attire of blue jeans an oversize shirt and her hair styled in tight curls appealed to him. Very sexy.

Mrs. Beacham, prompt as usual, appeared in the hallway to open the door before Shelly knocked. Justin retrieved his briefcase off the dining table and paused in the doorway for a few seconds just so Shelly would see his casual approach.

Common sense warned him to keep a safe distance between them. The exact time when his attitude toward Shelly had changed, he wasn't sure. Maybe it happened each time Shelly visited his father. Phillip always appeared to be energized and animated after Shelly left for the day. His gratitude toward Shelly ran deep because his father's stubborn decision to hire her proved to be the medicine he needed.

Women before Shelly never got this close, never had him considering possibilities that, frankly, scared the mess out of him. Just like that, his determination graduated to his bold action to make the first move.

"Oh, good morning, didn't expect to see you here," Shelly greeted.

"Late start."

"You're the boss, so I guess it's okay." She laughed.

The sound warmed him and he had the sudden urge to trace the outline of her adorable lips, which showed off a cinnamon-brown gloss. He especially loved the fullness of her bottom lip, lined with a darker shade that highlighted its movement when she talked.

He gulped the remainder of his juice, hoping that something witty and hip popped into play. He set down the empty glass on a side table. "Any plans for the weekend?"

"'Fraid not. I've some work to do at home."

Now what? After asking a moronic question like that, he had to give a reason for his interest. Besides, she hadn't asked about his plans. From the suspicious tilt of her head, he shouldn't hold his breath either.

"Something is nagging at me." Justin frowned. "I've met you before."

"Really?"

"Yes, but I can't remember where."

"I guess that would be your loss."

Undeterred, he forged ahead. "It wasn't high school because I went to an all-boys school. Maybe college?"

Irritation flashed across Shelly's face. "Unless you went to school in New York, I'd say you're wrong." Shelly gave a short wave. "Time for me to get to work. Nice chatting with you."

"Bye," he replied. His mind urged him to stop making a fool of himself and move toward the door for an exit with dignity. However, his traitorous feet remained rooted to the spot as his senses drank in the soft floral scent surrounding her.

Wuss! his conscience berated.

Shelly tucked a stray strand behind her ear, nodded, and

walked past him. Her gaze never stayed on him for more than a second and her every movement held his attention. Heck, everything about her held his attention like her smooth, rich brown skin, free from layers of makeup, revealing her natural beauty.

"Damn!" Justin growled.

Memos and multicolored report folders cluttered the desk in his office. He rubbed his tired eyes and yawned. His mind zigzagged in several directions, thinking about his father, the bank, his life—all demanding too much of him.

And what a life! His jaw twitched from the bitter loneliness always on the horizon of his emotions. It was the familiar growing ache that needled his desire to see one person. He wanted to experience that bright smile and carefree attitude that his father enjoyed when Shelly was around.

These feelings were new and unwelcomed. They opened him up to more than he wanted to deal with because, despite this hectic scene, a woman with sex appeal and intelligence created a different type of havoc in his very soul. Since Shelly Bishop had landed in his life, his common sense seemed to have fled.

In the meantime, his schedule didn't cooperate with his preoccupation. It was his fine luck that the following week he had a meeting with the executive vice president of commercial banking to study the bank's corporate loan portfolio. Despite his best efforts, he couldn't concentrate on the printed words or numbers.

An irritated review of his planner told him that he couldn't afford to put off studying the draft report. Every hour had an appointment written in until eight that evening. His typical day brimmed with appointments, meetings, and corporate schmoozing. Thinking about his workload made the tension in his neck muscles bunch into painful knots.

Then there was his father. His courageous fight against prostate cancer had leaked to the media. The news attracted expected talk about the bank being sold. Debate waged on whether he, the son and sole heir, could continue its success; whether he had the experience; whether he had the raw talent and business savvy. Anything he overlooked, any mistakes he made, could be the end to what his father had built.

Vulnerability nipped at his heels. His shoulders carried their familiar droop. He dropped his head in his hands and rubbed his temples in an effort to erase the pressure and regain control.

"Doris!" he barked into the intercom. "Do you have a minute?" His fingers drummed on the desk blotter as he impatiently waited for his executive assistant. "Doris! Are you there?" Slamming his palm on the desk, he wondered where she'd gone. If she didn't appear in the next few seconds, he would have to go find her.

"Yes, Mr. Thornton." A woman in her fifties answered his bellow, standing in the doorway, the picture of professional efficiency.

"Where is the report from Mr. Shandler? I don't see it anywhere."

She stepped midway into his office and stood her ground, peering over her half glasses at him. He hated when she did that. It made him feel like a truant little boy. Justin rifled through the papers. He muttered another curse when a pile placed close to the edge of the desk fell into a disorganized heap onto the floor.

"Mr. Thornton, I told you yesterday that Mr. Shandler will bring the report by this afternoon." Without raising her voice or showing any outward signs of being flustered, Doris came over and picked up the papers.

"Oh, yes, I remember now." Justin glared at her, his jaw twitching furiously. He didn't miss the edges of Doris's mouth lifting slightly upward. How satisfying to see the new boss lose his mind. Thank goodness she wasn't a gossip or his faux pas would be a banner for the entire bank's amusement.

He had to get out of his office, get some air, clear his mind. Although the executive office came equipped with a wet bar, bathroom, and luxurious leather suite, he felt confined. He still saw it as his father's domain with his decorations, furniture selection, and arrangement. Rearranging or replacing anything seemed like an act of betrayal.

"I'm going down to the cafeteria, and when I return, I don't want to be disturbed. I'm going to finish up with the report, return a few calls, and then I've got to get back to the house." *To see Shelly.* "So, I'll need to change my schedule."

"Yes, sir. I'll make the necessary changes."

There was too much work for him to really go anywhere. His distraction now meant longer days later. Short term, however, a quick walk around the office building would do him good. It allowed his employees to become accustomed to seeing him in the new position. And he had mighty big shoes to fill, trying to match his father's success. He set off on his tour of the four floors that housed the corporate headquarters, while thinking about how to gain the employees' trust.

Despite his best intentions, Justin didn't acknowledge the many greetings or he simply waved without noticing. It wasn't that he distanced himself from his employees, but his thoughts continuously betrayed him.

Shelly. It was always Shelly Bishop.

To talk only about her physical attributes, she was nothing short of being gorgeous. But his fascination filtered past the obvious. Maybe it wasn't deliberate, but he couldn't deny the attraction. Shelly wove a web that had him securely fastened and the more he fought its hold, the tighter it became. The pain she described about the assault had drawn him in and he wanted vengeance against the monster that had obliterated her innocence and enjoyment of a natural relationship.

Yet on the other hand, he couldn't help but feel that it wasn't sheer coincidence that this beautiful young woman showed up at his father's house to play nurse. He didn't believe it because his life hadn't dealt him a lucky hand lately.

"Mr. Thornton, how are you doing today, sir?" An exuberant young man waved in his direction.

Justin sighed. An interruption. He returned the wave and hoped that Joe Pease would keep his attentions to only a greeting. If the man knew the height of his irritability, he would seek safer ground.

No such luck. The assistant vice president from marketing hurried toward him. An eager, self-appreciative smile plastered on his face. Any other time, Justin would have patiently entertained the man's chatter.

"Do you have a quick minute, Mr. Thornton? You know I was thinking about efficiencies and I came up with this great idea that will cut costs. Not putting anyone down or anything, but there are a few things that can be improved here and there. I've made a list of those who are not quite meeting the standards that I know you personally want here at the bank. And, well, sir." He beamed. "I'm your man to make it happen." His steps quickened to match Justin's.

"I'd love to hear about it, Joe. Have you run it by Williams yet? You know how I feel about skipping the chain. It can lead to communication gaps." He paused, meaningfully. "A personal pet peeve of mine."

"Well, no, I—" Joe's bravado withered. "Well, I have to be getting back to work."

The man's thinly veiled ambitions grated on Justin's nerves. There was no place at this bank for the usual competitive, territorial shenanigans that occurred at his competitors'. The family-like atmosphere and team spirit mentality marked Hopetown Savings Bank's unique features that his father had spent a lifetime creating. And he hoped to maintain it in his father's stead.

Justin shook his head at the dejected figure. Pease had potential, but he annoyed him with the millions of ideas that featured him as the solo star. He continued on his way, deciding to take a stroll through the cafeteria. Nothing like an unexpected visit from the boss to give people indigestion as they tried to eat and sound insightful at the same time.

Justin had almost made it into the eating area, but was snagged by another vice president.

"How is Mr. Thornton?"

"He's still hanging in there. Thank you for asking, Peter." The time wasn't right for him to make any official announcements. It would be up to his father. He chatted briefly and then excused himself.

The bank's employees expressed genuine concern about their boss' condition. Many of them had worked with him for years. Besides, he had a successful, hands-on management style that had developed strong loyalties. It was only natural that the employees would also worry about their future should anything happen.

Back in his office, Justin felt at ease. Stretching his legs and getting away for a few minutes had cleared his head. Maybe he could get Doris to shift the appointments for the remainder of the week.

He'd carried a lot on his plate in the past few months. Today for the first time he took notice of the weight. He wanted to rest, to relax and have everything the way it used to be. His father healthy and working.

And his wife. Well, no rehabilitation could have been done with his marriage. Wanda lied with no finesse or fear of discovery. Remembering his comment about pet peeves, he thought a revision of the list was in order. His real irritation was lies. People who underestimated him and tried to take advantage of him with lies earned his wrath. But, ultimately, he hadn't wanted her to die. No one deserved that as punishment.

Opening a file on his desk, he forced himself to concentrate and finish at least one item that day and have it cleared off his desk.

"Sir, your twelve-thirty appointment is here," Doris interrupted over the intercom.

"Blast! Doris, take me off the speaker. Is everyone out there? I thought I told you to reschedule my afternoon appointments." He looked at his planner. Sure enough, it was neatly written in Doris's handwriting. "You're doing this to me deliberately."

She cleared her throat softly, a dead giveaway of her amusement. "Shall I bring them in, sir?"

"Yes," he hissed.

Justin watched the group file in. His knotted brows caused them to ceased their bantering, casting a pregnant silence around the office. Maybe he could push things along. Then he was definitely leaving for the day. His crankiness had returned with a vengeance. When he left, he was not taking the pager and the cell phone would be off. Playing hookey once in a while was a necessity.

"Ladies and gentlemen," he prompted, "let's get started. We need to take a look at how we're managing our risks, including where our weaknesses lie. Colette, why don't you take over and acquaint everyone with our strategy and then we can get into each person's role."

The woman whom Justin addressed laid down a thick package of varied-colored paper. The graphs that Justin could see from where he sat induced an instant headache. It would be a long day. He wished that he could unbutton his starched white shirt, loosen his navy blue tie, and kick his black oxfords to the side.

Colette distributed handouts. "Risk must be identified

in each line of business so that we can contain it and optimize our profits. . . ."

Justin agreed there was risk, pure and simple. He made an effort to keep a handle on Colette's report, but her words had a different meaning for him. It *would* be a risk to ask Shelly out on a date.

There. It was out in the open.

The disclosure made him drop his pen. The slight disruption brought a halt to the presentation. All eyes on him, awaiting his comments.

"Oh, sorry. Go on, please." He opened the bound report and flipped through it so he would at least look as though he were paying attention while his mind pleasantly wandered.

"Next is, how will the risk be measured? . . ." Colette's voice faded.

The risk could only be measured with a harassment suit. How was he going to get around asking a woman under his employment out on a date? He reasoned that technically she was not under his employment, but his father's. There had to be a way around it. He couldn't let it go without an effort. The fact that she didn't fawn over him and maintain some reservation when she was in his company impressed him. She had a brain and wasn't afraid to use it. The hour melted away quickly as he thought of the possibilities.

And then there was always that great body. He smiled.

"Then you agree, sir?" Collette and five other pairs of eyes looked expectantly at him with reciprocating smiles on their faces.

"Uh—um—well," he stuttered, hoping that one of them would give a clue as to what he was about to agree to. "Okay, I think it's a great start, but let me think on that a little more before we go any further. I vote for a break and we reconvene later."

They nodded and Justin, the attentive host, escorted

them to his office door. If he kept this up, there would be no Hopetown Savings Bank.

Once he'd talk himself into surrendering to his feelings, he had to act. He picked up his jacket, swung it over his shoulder, and left his office, whistling.

Driving down the street, he decided to call ahead. He took out his cell phone and dialed.

"Hi, Mildred. How is my father doing?"

"He's doing fine. Actually went out on the balcony with Shelly."

"Good news. Ah, is she there?"

"No, sir. This is her volunteer day. She only comes in for a few hours in the morning. Do you want to speak to your father?"

Justin swallowed the disappointment. His foot shifted to the brake. He flicked on the left signal. "No, Mildred. I'll catch him later. Gotta go." He stabbed the END button. Disappointment left him flat.

At the next traffic signal, he made a U-turn and headed back to the bank. No point in going home.

Activity hummed at the Northern District police station. The early morning didn't slow the handcuffed lawbreakers waiting to be processed. Shelly closed her eyes and counted to ten. When she got her hands around Tanya's neck, she promised to strangle her until her tongue popped out.

It was now seven o'clock. There was no way she would make it on time. She hung on to a small sliver of hope and decided to wait before making the I'm-stuck-in-traffic-call.

Wiping slightly sweaty palms on her slacks, Shelly approached the main desk. Her throat locked up. No sound emerged for her to inquire about Tanya. The yells and curses flying around her head unnerved her. But leaving without talking to Tanya wasn't an option, either.

"Ma'am, is someone helping you?"

"No. I'm looking for a girl who was brought here. Tanya Bishop."

The officer tuned to a computer and typed in the name. "She was brought in an hour ago."

All Shelly could do was stare at the policeman. How could Tanya pull such a stupid stunt like this? "May I see her?"

"Yes, this way. The detective who brought her in has a few questions for you."

Her stomach lurched. She merely nodded and followed the policeman to an office. Shelly stepped into the small office filled with metal file cabinets. *Dismal* came to mind. The walls appeared gray and dingy, as ancient as the nicked furniture in place.

She saw Tanya sitting in one of the chairs at the far wall. The spunky teenager was disheveled and visibly distraught. Her individual plaits partially hid her face and rested on her shoulders. Nervous fingers pulled at the edge of her blouse, each finger flashing a silver ring. Shelly looked down at the black platform shoes and wondered how she hadn't managed to twist her ankles.

Then Shelly noticed another person, a very serious cop, standing behind the desk with his hands in his pockets. The cold stare he passed from Tanya to her made her knees weak.

"Have a seat, Miss . . ."

"I'm Tanya's aunt, Shelly Bishop."

"Detective Tucker." He shook her hand and crushed it. "Let me cut to the chase. I caught Tanya early this A.M. at Del Ray's Bar, using a fake ID to purchase liquor."

He tossed the identification card in Shelly's direction. With a small movement, she dragged it closer with a finger to see the object that would take them all down. The laminated identification was such poor quality that the bartender would have to be blind and just born into the world to accept it. Shelly leaned back in the chair and waited for the rest.

"This bar has served alcohol to underage teenagers, which is why I was on the job. First of all, this town has a curfew for teenagers, so she blew it on that front. Then, she and her friends, who are also being held, passed these IDs. Now that you're here I want to give her a couple of choices. If she tells us who made the IDs, we won't book her. But if she ever tries this stunt again, then she'll wish that she'd never met me." He walked around the desk toward Tanya, who kept her focus at the floor. "So what will it be, Tanya?"

Silence.

He turned his attention toward Shelly and stabbed at her with a long finger. "That's where you come in. Talk some sense into your niece, or else I'm going to book her. Honor student or not, cheerleader captain or not, she's in for a rough ride. I'm going to talk to the other parents." He paused in the doorway.

Shelly watched his eyebrows blend into one long hyphen as he frowned, lips curled in displeasure. "You got ten minutes."

Shelly stared at the door after the cop left, her mind scrambling to get around the situation.

Tires squealed around the Thorntons' driveway. The morning sun already high drove home the point that she was late. Shelly slammed the car door and ran around to the side of the house to see if she could spot Mildred through a window. Out of breath, she placed her forehead against the window. Using her hands to shield the sunlight around her face, she tried to see if Mildred sat at her desk. It took a few seconds for her eyes to adjust.

She blinked and refocused. Great! Mildred stood in the waiting area. The nurse moved forward. But when the face emerged from the shadows, it wasn't Mildred's.

The door near the window opened with a stern Mrs. Beacham pinning her with a disgusted look.

"Thanks." Shelly inched past her. Her feet moved with heavy reluctance.

Why did this woman make her feel like a juvenile delinquent? Maybe it was the way her lips disappeared with open distaste; the cold, dark eyes that bored through her; or the depressing, shapeless dresses that made Shelly think of a warden.

"My car. It wouldn't start." Even to her ears, the excuse sounded shallow. She would have to resign herself that she would never measure up to the housekeeper's standards.

"Mr. Thornton asked for you." Mrs. Beacham turned to leave. Over her shoulder, she added, "Your pay will be adjusted for your tardiness."

Shelly stuck her tongue out at the stiff figure retreating down the hall. A hearty chuckle from behind startled her. She spun around and saw Mildred emerge from one of the many rooms, looking thoroughly amused.

"I tried to wait for you," said Mildred, still chuckling. "Then, the old bag made her rounds, which by the way, she does each morning and late afternoon. So, there is no sleeping in late, nor is there any slipping out early."

"I don't know what happened. Last night I couldn't sleep. Then early this morning, an unexpected errand came up. Believe me, this is not how I do business."

Mildred waved her hand. "Please, girl, you don't have to explain to me. As we agreed, it's not as if you're giving him the medication. That's what I'm here for. But now he's all yours. He's been asking for you."

Shelly walked into the room to see Phillip sitting at the edge of the bed reading an inspirational book designed for daily use. The picture he presented in a brightly colored Hawaiian shirt and khaki slacks with bedroom slippers lightened her mood. It was ironic how, no matter what mind-set she was in, Phillip could manage to bring a smile to her face. She remained out of sight until he finished.

Observing him, she noted that they had a common thread. They both relied on inspirational and spiritual sources for self-help through life's difficulties.

"How are you this fine morning, Shelly?" He stood slowly, wavering slightly until he could gain his balance.

She came forward, but didn't offer assistance. It was important that she show confidence in his abilities.

"It looks like you're better than I am."

He waved aside her compliment. "I was determined to get up off that confounded bed and move around to get the old juices flowing. You think, later, we can go outside for a walk?"

"I don't see why not. The weather has been absolutely superb and I haven't heard of any rain in the forecast for another day or two."

"Good, good." He offered the crook of his arm and she took the invitation.

"I'll warm up by giving you a tour of my suite."

She nodded. "I'd love that." She'd learn about not only Phillip, but his elusive son.

He led her slowly to one end of the room. Various framed photographs, some black and white, were centered on the wall between each window. On closer inspection, there were many notable persons in each of them. The list of celebrities included the mayor of Baltimore, governor of Maryland, owner of the Washington Wizards, and the two Maryland senators.

"Wow!" exclaimed Shelly. She gazed at the photograph of Phillip Thornton shaking the president's hand.

"I know how you feel. Even after many years of hobnobbing and rubbing elbows with the upper crust, I can't believe it."

"You're just amusing me. Aren't you the upper crust?"

Before answering, he led her over to an armoire. From the top drawer, he retrieved a worn black-and-white photo. She leaned closer to make out faces in the fuzzy images of a man and woman with a small child standing between them. The threesome posed in front of a brownstone in their Sunday best. Shelly guessed it was taken in the forties.

Phillip pointed to the man in the photo. "That's my pop. He worked for a brick-making company, and then in the evenings and on weekends he worked for a furniture store. Didn't see him much, but his long hours paid for me to go to college. My mother, holding my hand in the photo, worked as a maid. I was the youngest of three boys. By the time it was my turn to leave the nest, they could each help me. Without them, I wouldn't be where I am today."

"It's nice to know how important family is to you. Sometimes I feel like an only child. There's a ten-year gap between my brother and me. I often wonder what a large, close-knit family would be like."

His fatigue showed and they walked back to the bed. Mildred was already getting his medication in order.

"As long as you have strong ties, it doesn't matter if the family's large or small," he replied, shifting himself into bed. "That familial bond can never be broken. And believe me, there's always something or someone threatening to destroy it."

"I agree." She wondered if he had the answers for what to do if the person who destroyed the bond happened to be her. Taking the cowardly way out had damaged the family ties.

Shelly left the room so Mildred could be free to administer the medicine and attend to Phillip's needs. She returned an hour later to find him in a fitful slumber. The pride he felt for his family and their role in getting him where he needed to be shone through. Making sure not to awaken him, Shelly exited quietly.

The gardens beckoned to her and the promise of the warm sun rays made the invitation more appealing. She didn't want to read anything. Just enjoying nature was enough. Hesitating, she decided to use the forbidden door, reasoning to herself that the flower beds she'd admired sat closer to this side of the house. She sucked her teeth, like a rude child, at the image of Mrs. Beacham's disapproving face, but she couldn't help looking over her shoulder, just in case.

A door slammed with a loud bang. Voices argued. She stopped at the sudden commotion, not wanting to intrude. The conversation, if the shouting and angry words could be deemed as such, leaked out of the closed room.

The verbal battle grew more vicious, increasing in volume. She hurried back into the house to get back to her area of the house. Uneasy, she stepped farther down the hall, curious yet frantic at the notion of being caught in a compromising position. Her heart hammered away in her chest. The male voices, of that she was sure, literally traded insults. Alarms clamored in her head warning her of danger.

She stepped into a room next to the one where all the commotion was taking place. The speakers and their voices became more distinguishable. An uncontrollable trembling erupted, leaving her legs in a rubbery state. She gripped the back of the nearest chair for support.

Icy slivers of dread crept through her body like a slow, thick liquid. A wave of vertigo hit. She swayed. Her breakfast threatened to reverse its route as nausea overcame her.

That voice.

She *knew* that voice.

Toby Gillis.

Here in this house. A few feet from her. There was no mistaking the arrogant twang of a South Carolina upbringing. His characteristic laugh had more animal qualities than human.

The man who had attacked her and made her life hell stood in the house in the next room. She hadn't seen him after the attack and the numerous visits from his attorneys. Only a wall stood between them. Her thoughts were seized in the terrifying moment. Never in all her dreams of revenge did she imagine this time or setting.

Terror continued to hold firm to her body. She remained frozen, sucking in her breath, as footsteps stomped toward the door opposite her. No place to run to, except the library, which had a connecting door to the office. Tiptoeing over, she prayed that she could remain hidden there until it was safe for her to head back to neutral ground.

The office door slammed against the wall. The reverberation shook the walls. A small gasp escaped and Shelly clamped her hand over her mouth. She wanted to hide, to tuck herself into a ball and shut the voice out of her life, out of her memory.

Shelly ran lightly over to a high-backed chair, which offered a small hiding place in the corner of the room. There she crouched with her eyes tightly shut. Only her ears witnessed the continued angry exchange.

". . . But as the saying goes, a chain is as strong as its weakest link. And, brotha man, you need to wake up."

"You're no better than a snake," Justin snarled. "You and your father won't get any part of Hopetown."

"We'll see," Toby quipped.

"No! We won't."

Shelly listened to the footsteps heading toward the front door. It opened.

"This will be the last time you enter this property. Not that we have anything else to discuss, but it will be done away from here."

"Whatever, Justin. It's no use trying to keep it from the

old man. Hell, it may be what he needs to hear before he makes that final journey, considering all he's got is you as the pathetic heir apparent. This is a golden opportunity. Don't screw this up for him like you're doing with the bank. I'm pretty certain that you'll be given a couple of resignations. And in a few months, more rats will abandon your ship."

The door slammed. No returning footsteps came her way and she tried to guess where Justin was. It wouldn't do for him to see her crouched in a corner.

"Miss Bishop!"

Shelly jumped with a startled yelp.

Mrs. Beacham!

Five

Shelly looked up into Mrs. Beacham's face glowering down at her. The housekeeper moved the chair aside, fully uncovering Shelly in all her shame. Feeling naked, she wished that she could remain curled up and hidden; instead she straightened slowly to face her gray-haired tormentor. In a few seconds, the situation graduated from a small spark to a furious blaze when Justin popped his head in through the connecting door to his office to see what Mrs. Beacham had unearthed.

The disgust plain on his face made her go cold. His eyes flashed with fury, assessing the situation, and Shelly braced for the harsh words and one-way ticket to the door. If the relationship between them hadn't recently warmed up with semifriendly greetings and snippets of pleasantries, this setback wouldn't have hurt as much.

"What's going on in here?" he demanded.

"Sir, she was eavesdropping."

The accusation hurt, stabbing at her self-esteem. It burned its way through her conscience as she hit a wall of frustration because she couldn't defend herself. Once again, she'd have to face Justin's anger and snap judgmental attitude full of accusation.

"I . . . I," she began weakly. Her mind raced for a reasonable explanation. "I was going for a walk and then I heard . . ." Her voice trailed. She plucked at the wisps of curled hair at the base of her neck. This was what quick-sand felt like, she thought, and she was sinking fast.

"Mrs. Beacham, thank you. I will tend to this matter."

Justin folded his arms and stood with legs apart, rocking on his toes. Shelly couldn't see over his shoulder to the safe haven of the doorway. She was sure that he had had his full limit of her, but he obviously wasn't going to rush the process.

The housekeeper shot her a contemptuous look and left. Flashbacks of her grandmother came to her. There was no getting over Grandma Ada and there was no getting over Mrs. Beacham. In all fairness, the woman did her job, protecting her employer's interest. It wasn't any shock to Shelly, given the frigid treatment that Mrs. Beacham showed her at their first meeting, that the housekeeper wouldn't have given her a chance to explain privately. Shelly reasoned that, if the tables were turned, she would have reacted in the same way. Yet she'd hoped for some clemency, since nothing in her behavior had posed a threat.

"Miss Bishop," he snapped, "follow me." Justin strode toward his office.

Shelly kept a safe distance behind Justin, wondering how much longer he planned to make her squirm in misery. Embarrassment still heated her face and tears of self-pity sprang up, which she roughly wiped away rather than have Justin turn a scornful gaze on her. Besides, it had been one hell of a day. She followed his march to the next room, his heavy footsteps thudding against the wooden floor.

But once the door closed, she was sure he'd give vent to his fury. Her steps slowed at the doorway. It wasn't Justin's anger that made her hesitate or filled her with panic. Instead the thought of Toby standing in this room a few minutes ago made her stomach clench in knots.

She had to bite down on her lip and feed on the pain to

keep from running. Running to escape her nightmares that, in one swift luckless afternoon, had turned into a reality.

That voice, a sickening drawl, had cursed her and called her vulgar names now a permanent part of her memories.

Justin disliked her, that she was certain, and he probably wanted her several miles away from him. However, he didn't evoke the sense of evil that Toby could lay claim to as his own. Toby had managed to screw up her life once again, as she faced her first experience of being fired.

"Come in here, Miss Bishop." Justin resumed his kingly stance. His jaws clenched and unclenched. "I don't know what your motives are. Why you're here and so on. But this latest performance doesn't leave me with any confidence. I don't care what my father has promised you or what you have weaseled out of him, but you've just spent your last minute here."

Well, there it was finally. *Fired*. With the sentence came the humiliating task of listening to her character being ripped apart. She stared into his eyes, dark and stormy, returning her stare with an intensity that didn't bother to hide his disdain. The mouth that she had once admired as strong and attractive, now was inflexibly turned down.

She didn't know how to defend herself, but she couldn't just let it be. Pride stirred beneath the weight of the accusation. It inspired her to accept her punishment, but not before having her say. "Mr. Thornton, may I explain?" She rubbed her hands together, gathering her thoughts.

"Why?" His voice thundered. "What possible explanation could you give me that justifies your betrayal in my father's house? Do you think me a fool? Do you think me gullible— like my father? I have to protect what he's built. A legacy that you couldn't possibly imagine, and at the same time I have to deal with people like you and Toby Gillis."

She shook her head from side to side. "Please, don't include me in the same league with Toby Gillis," she whispered between trembling lips. "I heard what he said to you. And I would never—"

"And I'm supposed to trust you? Who are you, Shelly Bishop, that I should trust you? Hell, for all I know, you'd run your happy little behind out of this house and tell the same newspapers who crucify me on a weekly basis about what happened here today." He pinched the bridge of his nose with a tortured expression.

Shelly didn't expect Justin to be her number-one ally. After all, he didn't know her or know anything about her, save what she'd said at the awards banquet. But his vicious attack and searing judgment against her was too much. If ever there was a time to scream, now seemed to be perfect. "You have the freedom to play prosecutor, jury, and final judge, but not before you listen to what I say."

He snorted. "Go ahead. Explain. But let me warn you not to tempt your fate by lying to me. I have little patience for any bull."

Shelly remained tongue-tied, knowing that the only way to extricate herself was to lie. Her hesitation proved to be her downfall as he shook his head and turned to head back to the door.

"I'll advise Mrs. Beacham of your immediate departure and I will see that you receive a check for services rendered." He flung the words over his shoulder.

Breathing was difficult. His ferocity pressed against her chest and she felt herself begin to buckle beneath its weight. She desperately wanted his understanding, instead of his treatment of her as if she were something gross stuck to his shoe. "What about your father, shouldn't he have a say?"

"My father will have to understand. Despite his best intentions, he can't control the natural order of things."

He was almost out the door, not bothering to address her directly any longer.

"Justin?"

The name hung in the air. Her slight questioning tone stopped him. As if against his will, he turned slowly. The two faced each other, no further words spoken, while the undercurrent of tension sizzled. Shelly's impulse was to brush away the deep frown wrinkling his forehead and succumb to the urge to fully disclose her most private feelings. It mattered what he thought of her. She wanted the same look of respect and even attraction that she saw when she had confessed her inner feelings at the awards banquet. There was a connection that she was sure wasn't her imagination. She wanted it again. She wanted him to look at her and be affected in the same manner as he had been that evening.

"Why do you dislike me? Why can't you trust me?" she asked, almost to herself.

Justin hesitated, clearly considering her question.

"Because you're perfect. Or appear to be. From my experience that's a warning signal of trouble ahead. You've heard the saying 'nothing is what it seems.' That's my new motto because the more gloss and glitter, the worse the imperfection. And while you may have been awarded Miss Volunteer of the Year and possess beauty that makes a man say halleluia, I don't plan to buy into your Pollyanna disguise." He took two steps toward her and leaned forward. "Before you get me, I'm getting you."

Considering she was the one who didn't trust men, now that the tables were turned on her she didn't like it one bit. "You shouldn't judge," she countered. "I may not be good enough for your high and mighty ideals, but I'm a woman of principles. Your insecurities are your business. I meant no harm to you, your father, or the precious family bank. I was embarrassed at overhearing your *discussion* and preferred hiding to placing you in an embarrassing situation. But you're unfair. And I cannot stay here any longer because I will not allow you to strip my dignity from me with sarcasm and disdain." She brushed past him. Her face burned at her boldness and the itsy-bitsy diversion from the real reason. "Good-bye, Mr. Thornton." She didn't expect him to retract his words, but she'd managed to defend herself, whether he believed her or not.

"Let me advise you to keep what you heard to yourself. If I find out that you—"

"Don't threaten me," she said, swift and indignant, between gritted teeth. "I am a nurse. I do know something about discretion, thank you very much. You don't have to stomp on my intelligence and bully me in the process."

Good. He had the decency to look embarrassed.

"I didn't stomp. I just—"

"I know." She held up her hand. "You're protecting the precious legacy that I know nothing about but had the nerve to blindly enter the elite world of the Thornton dynasty. Silly me." She rolled her eyes. "You know what, Justin? Get over yourself. You're sounding like an eighties nighttime drama." This time she walked past him. Her teenage pageant experience came into play as the cool, unhurried walk and erect carriage helped her exit on a high note.

Justin followed.

Seconds ticked. Justin rubbed his jaw studiously. "Ms. Bishop—Shelly." He sighed. "My nerves are a little wracked with everything, however, it's no excuse for my rudeness. I wish we could have met under different circumstances."

She slapped on a saccharin smile and faced him. "We did, once. Although it's clear that it meant nothing to you, I, however, lay awake many nights after you first kissed me." She laughed at how wide his eyes opened. "Let me take you back to the postgraduation party at Stevens Hall. Midnight. I'd just been dumped by Warren, who'd made up with his ex-girlfriend, Shirlene, on the dance floor. You'd followed me outside while I bawled my eyes out."

"I remember." His face reflected wonder. "You know what it is?" Justin pointed at her. "Your hair was past your shoulders and you wore the most god-awful baggy clothes. I had come out to smoke when I thought smoking was cool. You were sitting on the steps looking abandoned. I talked to you for a few minutes to make sure you were okay and then I kissed you good-bye."

"For me it was a kiss that said 'hello.' You were my first."

"I kissed you on the cheek."

"It still was my first." She sounded defensive even to herself.

"If it was so special, why didn't you call me the next day?" He frowned. "As a matter of fact, I went to your friend's house asking for you. She said that you weren't interested in me and had already left for New York."

The ancient history stirred to life. "I should have known Freda was up to her tricks." Her eyes widened with sudden realization. "Oh my gosh, did she snap you up after that?" Shelly covered her mouth, but not before a giggle escaped.

"It's not funny. You broke my heart."

"Oh, please, spare me."

"No, I'm serious. I tried to find you, even went to your ex-boyfriend for information." He shook his head with a rueful smile. "Not to mention that I spent the remainder of the summer trying to detach myself from your psycho friend."

Shelly wasn't buying it. She agreed he might have been a bit curious about her, but he was a player then, and probably a player now, only older. "I knew we weren't from the same circles, friends or moneywise. I wasn't going to set myself up for another rejection." She gave a harsh laugh. "From the looks of things, one way or the other, rejection is sure to follow me."

"I'm truly sorry." He approached her with an outstretched hand.

His apology touched her, but she ignored his hand. "Apology accepted. You're right, under different circumstances maybe we could have been friends. I'll go get my things."

Shelly saw the renewed interest now that she'd jogged his memory. He stood in the doorway, studying her with a slight smile. She walked toward him aware that he had not stepped aside. Holding her breath, she sidled past, her chest brushing his arm. Its muscled hardness against her soft curves sent a tingle and she could feel her breasts react with a tightness.

"Shelly," he said softly, "don't leave. I've been unfair. I don't know what got into me. Will you stay?" His face turned toward hers, his eyes spoke volumes that his face hid.

"I think it's best if I go," she managed. Another emotional discourse like they just had would be too much. With Toby Gillis sniffing around this close, it would be a matter of time before he discovered her. She needed time to think, and right now it proved to be difficult with Justin's face less than six inches from her. His puffs of breath touched her head. She glanced at his lips and reiterated to herself, *I think it's best*.

"Well, I think otherwise. I want you—"

Startled, her eyes flew to his.

A wicked grin stole across his face. ". . . to stay. I think we understand each other. What do you say?"

Yes. Her answer was *yes*. But they played a dangerous game. A yearning in her burned and it only prodded her when Justin was in her thoughts and especially when he stood close enough for her to tiptoe and kiss his lips. A smile wavered at the thought. She licked her lips nervously.

"I'll take that as a yes."

She didn't object, although her mind in usual logical fashion called her an array of names for giving in.

"Are you available tonight?" Her smile turned to shock. He continued quickly, "Please, don't misunderstand. I have a dinner meeting at eight o'clock at the Columbia Lakeside Inn. And I thought that I could finish apologizing and if you were free, well, if you could join me at seven." Before she answered, he added, "Don't feel that I'm pressuring you, or that you have to accept." He raised his hands in defense.

Her thoughts raced, keeping time with her erratic pulse. The first reaction was a decided no.

But that changed to a decided yes. "Okay, I'll meet you. This isn't a date or anything, right?"

He nodded.

"You'll just apologize and admit what a jerk you were?"

He grinned. "*Touché.*"

Legs shaking, victory within reach, she excused herself. "I must be getting back to your father."

Activity in the hotel lobby seemed brisk for the lateness of the hour. Then Shelly remembered that was to be expected because of the airport's proximity ten minutes away. A glance around the area didn't reveal Justin. After asking for directions she made her way to the lounge area. She blew out a shaky breath as each step closer made her panic increase. To avoid being teased, she hadn't told her mother about this latest development.

Her emotions warred. Now wasn't the time to reawaken a crush on the boss's son, especially when he obviously didn't care for her in that manner. A few steps past the elevators Shelly stopped to reconsider. Businessmen and women passed her in blurry motion, but her mind was preoccupied with what-ifs. What if she didn't show up? What if she was making a fool of herself? What if she got back in her car?

Put one foot in front of the other and keep walking. The signs to the lounge led her deeper into the hotel where the heavy flow of traffic lessened and softer lights set the mood. On cue, she followed the music filtering out from the lounge. Her legs shook slightly, but she took a deep breath and entered. The decor harbored more soft mood lights, mirrored walls, and small tables with two or three barrel-shaped chairs surrounding a bared portion of the floor.

An attractive woman crooned a familiar song. Shelly recognized an R&B hit. The singer swayed to the lazy beat as her powerful voice filled the room. Shelly joined the applause at the end, appreciating the talent before her.

She surveyed the small crowd and self-consciously adjusted her black blazer, feeling dowdy and plain in black jeans and a casual beige knit blouse. She had dressed simply, intent on playing down any hint that this was a date. The semidarkness and the couples smiling at each other over drinks cast the romantic air.

She spotted Justin immaculately dressed in a dark suit, cuff links glittering under the lights. Before Shelly could call to him, the singer strolled over to Justin's table. Shelly had not given her much attention, other than admiring her vocal power, but that was before she performed sultry moves and sashayed over to Justin's direction. Annoyance stole over Shelly, prickling her self-control.

The tender scene unfolding slapped a bit of practicality into her head. A man who had the devastating good looks, charm, and financial strength that Justin possessed had to have a pretty, young thing in tow. If the woman shared any qualities with her, it would be to fall for those wonderful freckles.

The lady sat sideways on Justin's lap, and he wrapped his arms around her slim waist interlocking his fingers. She sang to him as if he was the only one for her. In return, he granted her a huge smile. Shelly's heart constricted. She continued to watch as the singer's hands played with his hairline, tracing it above his ears, and then her bloodred fingernails traced the outline of his profile before she gave him a quick peck on his lips. She moved off back to the platform, finishing the song.

Shelly wanted to leave. There was no reason why watching him with another woman should have affected her. But she couldn't trust herself to remain rational and not pluck every fake red nail.

Flushed, Shelly came to a standstill a couple of tables behind Justin's. It bothered her to see the woman and him share a tenderness that she could only hope to experience someday. The first night that she saw him at the awards dinner didn't reveal this carefree attitude. Then he had seemed too controlled. As if he was master of a game where only he knew the rules, she remembered how his eyes had admired her, thoroughly examining her with an appreciative glimmer. With this woman, he smiled with abandonment. Its openness transformed him from the pensive, difficult man to a fun-loving, charismatic hunk.

"Shelly, over here."

Shelly pretended she had just seen him and waved.

Justin rose. The easy smile was replaced with a shaky grin. "Have a seat."

She sat across from him, gaze averted. "Um, I hope I'm not intruding." She tilted her head toward the stage. "You did say seven o'clock." She paused. Her heart hammered against her chest. His closeness always set off her pulse.

"Oh, Melinda?" He smiled and waved at the woman. "You're not intruding. Business with Melinda was over a long time ago."

So she was his ex-girlfriend. Great! The news didn't make her feel better. Well, it served her right, entertaining outlandish thoughts.

The waitress came over and Justin ordered a refill on his drink. Shelly wanted something strong to numb the jealous pangs, but alcohol on this occasion was not a good idea. So she ordered a cola, hoping the caffeine could have a safer intoxicating effect.

"Melinda and I had a very physical relationship," Justin continued, seemingly unaware of her discomfort. "The final straw was when she punched me in my nose in fourth grade." He chuckled, shaking his head at the memories.

Shelly joined him, first giggling and then breaking out in laughter. Her clenched hands relaxed in her lap. But what if Melinda wanted to make amends? Her laughter stopped abruptly. She turned to study Melinda. She had come a long way since fourth grade. A few things had developed since then—her breasts and her hips and those darn legs. Shelly wanted to button up her blazer. She slouched, accepting defeat. "With such memories, I guess she's special to you?" she inquired without looking at Justin.

"Yes, she is."

Shelly closed her eyes briefly. She wished she could block out the sincerity in his statement.

The waitress returned with the drinks and she took a big gulp of her cola. It was cool and delicious, but did nothing to mute the jealous jabs in her head.

"Would you care for something? They don't serve meals here, but we can get a light appetizer. How about a shrimp cocktail?"

She nodded. Although shrimp was her favorite, it probably wouldn't make it past the lump in her throat. It didn't help that Justin wore a soft smile whenever he looked in Melinda's direction. Out of the corner of her eye, she saw a couple approaching. It was Melinda accompanied by a giant.

"Hi, Justin, just wanted to say thanks for coming." The singer turned to Shelly, extending her hand. "Hi, I'm Melinda Sharpe and this is my husband, Theo." Shelly gasped, and gave Melinda her brightest smile. Melinda continued, "Well, I won't interrupt, but I know I can always count on you, Justin, to come see my performance whenever I'm in town."

"Please join us." Shelly was in high spirits now that her fear had been extinguished.

The shrimp arrived. Shelly dived into the appetizer

while Melinda, Justin, and Theo caught up on the latest news about his father. Life was grand. They could have been discussing nuclear physics for all she cared. She dipped a plump shrimp into the cocktail sauce, glancing intermittently at Justin chatting.

Shelly watched the power he had to draw people out and make them comfortable. She knew at that moment that she was no exception because she could fall under his spell. The admission almost caused a chunk of shrimp to slide down her throat.

Friendship.

She refused to think beyond that and for her, friendship was a big step past the employee relationship. Later she could blame it on her euphoria or the seductive songs Melinda had crooned.

A few minutes later, Melinda and her husband left.

"Sorry about that." Justin touched Shelly's hand lightly. "I know you must have been bored as we caught up, but I don't get to see her often. So we're both revved when the opportunity arises." He glanced at his watch, shaking his head ruefully. "Darn, it's after eight. I wanted this to be a breakthrough in our relationship."

Shelly shook her head. "It's okay. Another time?"

"Sure." He frowned, resting his chin on his cupped hand. "But what do you do when you're not at my father's?"

"I spend most of my time at the volunteer center. Eventually I want to become a counselor." A counselor for women who had the misfortune to experience terror like she'd known.

"That's commendable. I can understand why you must have a strong sense of responsibility. I admire that. May I call you at home?"

"Thank you," she murmured and hastily took a sip of her drink. She wrote her number on a piece of paper, hands shaking slightly. She was such a basket case around him.

To her surprise, he took her hand and held it within his warm one. His thumb rubbed the back of her hand. "Shelly, despite not having much time to really talk tonight, I did enjoy your company." His words melted her heart and she hung her head, bashful at his compliment. "And, I will call you. We have unfinished business." He turned her hand over, palm up. His head lowered, as if to kiss her wrist at the point where her pulse leaped irregularly.

Thankfully she was seated because her knees weakened as she imagined his lips softly touching her skin. A blaze of heat raced through her, causing all kinds of sensations. She pulled away from his hold afraid that she'd make an even bigger fool of herself. "I must be going." She hastily excused herself and left.

In her car, she sat for a minute while it idled, waiting for her nerves to settle. "Whew," she exhaled.

Breathing calmer, nerves in check, she drove out of the underground parking lot and headed for home. Tonight would be a sleepless night. This time it wasn't because of Toby. Instead it was because of feelings that she had never known existed and desires she had never thought she would have with a man who had ignited her sensual fantasies.

A week passed and there was no call from Justin. A few days she came in early or stayed late to catch a glimpse of him. She wondered if he stayed there at all. What a fool he must have thought her. Her schoolgirl crush must have been great amusement for him. He would have to be obtuse to miss the impact he had on her. He probably was occupied with a more experienced willing prospect that made him think of her as child's play. Bitterly she examined her behavior. *Well, it won't happen again.*

* * *

"Hi, Shelly." The Tuesday morning group spoke to her as they arrived.

One of her duties was to sign in each person before the session began. Women of different ages, sizes, and ethnic backgrounds signed the registration pad and entered the room. Shelly greeted each woman who walked past her. This group was in the middle of the entire counseling program. Shelly was always amazed at how much these sessions helped those who experienced the most difficult situations. Each woman had been raped, had been in a situation that almost led to rape, or currently gave support to a suffering relative or friend.

"Shelly, will you be joining in the discussion today?" Leesa, the counselor, waited for Shelly's response.

Shelly attended all the sessions, but remained in an assistant role to Leesa. A few times she contributed to the discussion, but she always held back. She wasn't ready to unleash her anger and hurt and guilt that haunted her. It scared her that she might not be able to stand herself once she bared her soul. Leesa always tried to ease her into the discussions. Today was no exception.

Today, however, she felt a change. Unexplainable, she didn't try to fight it. Surrendering to it, she wanted to share a part of her. Shelly followed Leesa in and took her place among the other women. Before long it was her turn.

"First, I feel out of place because I wasn't actually—" She kept her head bowed, chin tucked in.

"You can say it. Raped! You weren't raped," spouted one of the women, matter-of-factly.

Shelly nodded. "But, I still have those feelings that you all discuss. At times, I wondered if I overreacted and it really wasn't going to end in . . . rape."

"Don't be a fool. In your heart, you knew what was up."

One of the members came to Shelly's defense, "Don't call her a fool, Kim. I know what she means."

Kim frowned. Her body tensed ready to launch into a tirade.

Leesa intervened. "Ladies, remember. We must respect each other, especially when we disagree. Please continue, Shelly."

Her squirming revealed how nervous she felt. "Kim's right. I am a fool. I never pressed charges. I allowed them to frighten me into keeping silent."

The eldest woman of the group prompted, "It's not too late, you know."

"No, it's not," Kim echoed in her special way. "Actually, girlfriend, leave the cops out. They don't care nothin' 'bout you. Relying on them will only end up with the rapist getting a slap on the wrist with some light sissified sentence." She patted her chest proudly. "I know some guys who'll take care of him. Just say the word."

"Kim!" Leesa snapped. "None of that in here."

Kim pouted, arms folded belligerently. It was her trademark sign that she would participate no further.

While Leesa lectured the class on the last outburst, Shelly thought about Kim's message. Toby had to feel the fear and panic that he was responsible for. She wanted him to bleed and hurt with his chest burning to catch his breath. Kim was the mouthpiece to Shelly's emotions. Frankly, it scared her. Never had she felt so full of rage that went hand in hand with a desire for revenge. But common sense prevailed, albeit weakly. She knew she had to get on with her life. At least that's what everyone preached at her.

Like a mirage playing with her mind, Justin's face— strong, determined, and endearing—reminded her of what joys in life awaited her, if she would only release.

After class ended, Leesa and Shelly cleaned up the room, arranging the chairs for the next group.

"I want you to put Kim's invitation out of your mind."

Shelly laughed. "I'm not that crazy."

"Well, many have tried desperate things and I can sense you're on the edge of where to go from here." Leesa stopped and stared at her.

"Psychic now, are we?" Shelly remarked in wonder. Leesa's precision rattled her.

"Nope. The fact that you saw him recently will put new fears in your head."

Shelly didn't answer. New fears and nightmares paid their nightly visit.

"I want you to continue coming to these discussions and not just to volunteer, okay?" She gave Shelly's arm a squeeze, and the two hugged. "I'm also here if you just want to talk."

"Thanks."

Despite her best intentions, Shelly raced home each night to check her answering machine for the one call she wanted. Most times it was her mother or a friend inquiring about her well-being.

Approaching her apartment, she heard the faint ringing of her phone. She ran up to the door, fumbling to get the house key. It proved to be an elusive task. She muttered a string of curses after dropping the keys in a heap at her feet. Meanwhile, the ringing continued.

Successful at last, she dropped her purse and jumped over the additional three steps leading into her home and sprinted down the hall to the phone mounted on the kitchen wall. Shelly's hand paused over the receiver. She was out of breath and didn't want to appear as if she was anxiously awaiting the call—if it was Justin.

Breathing in check, she picked up the phone. She could hear the click of the caller hanging up before she uttered a breathy hello.

"Geez!" She slammed down the phone and stomped to her room. It could have been him and she missed it. Sitting at the foot of her bed, she looked at her reflection in the full-length cheval mirror.

Girlfriend, you need a life! With that statement, she threw herself back and stared at the ceiling.

The phone rang again. With a split-second roll across the bed, she answered.

"Shelly?" It was Justin.

She kicked off her shoes and made herself comfortable, smiling with sudden elation. "Yes."

"I was busy with the bank examiners last week. Sorry I didn't call."

"Please, it's okay. I'm fine," she lied. "I've been having such a busy week that I would've missed your call anyway."

"Oh." Shelly caught a trace of disappointment and her smile widened.

"Is it too late to share a cup of coffee?"

"Not at all. Where should I meet you?"

The doorbell rang, interrupting her call.

Reluctantly, she put him on hold and went down to see who it was. Her mom had casino night, which she attended on Wednesdays, so it couldn't be her. Unless Tanya had escaped her grandparents' watchful eyes, she was under tight curfew. And her father always called before coming to see her. There were her friends, but right now, she was between friends. Many she had alienated after the traumatic event.

She tiptoed and looked through the peephole.

Face enlarged because of the magnifying glass in peepholes, Shelly knew those features from memory. She pressed her face to the door, her hand on her heaving chest. Opening the door would be like turning the page in her life. Her hand rested on the doorknob.

Six

Justin stood in the doorway, cell phone in hand. A thickening shadow of new growth along his jaw added to natural ruggedness. His smile melted away any reservation Shelly had about her surprise visitor. The hard-nosed businessman softened his image with stonewashed blue jeans and a casual white shirt unbuttoned at the neck, revealing a gold-linked chain.

Her pulse tap-danced at a hyper beat. "Come in," she invited, gesturing toward the living room. "Were we supposed to meet tonight?" she asked, nervously tugging on a lock of hair.

He waited until she sat before he took his seat. "Nope. I guess I'm acting a little impulsively . . ." He paused. "Not really knowing whether you were up to company."

She admired his long legs casually outstretched. "It is a surprise." A bit shy from his scrutiny, she never let her gaze linger to catch his. "But a pleasant one. How did you know where I lived?"

"I confess," Justin began to explain, looking a little uncomfortable. "I kinda took a peek at your personnel information." He affected the demeanor of a little boy caught in the act. A cute little boy—or rather, a cute hunk of a man—caught in the act. Freckled face and eyes full of mischief, he grinned.

His determination to see her impressed Shelly. An un-

expected opportunity landed in her lap on her turf. Possibilities wove their way through her imagination. As they
exchanged small talk, she went to the kitchen to prepare
coffee. As the coffeemaker bubbled and hissed a new
batch, Shelly fought the urge to call someone—her
mother, Leesa, anyone—to tell them that Justin Thornton,
the most handsome man she had ever met, was sitting in
her living room. Being laughed at for her adolescent crush
served as a good inhibitor. The machine beeped after completing its cycle and the rich smell of freshly brewed coffee
wafted through the kitchen. She followed his instructions
on how he preferred his coffee.

"I do have coffee cake from a bakery I went to this morning," she offered, balancing a tray of two matching mugs.

"Thanks, but no, thanks. I've done too much damage at
dinner." He sipped his coffee.

Shelly watched him covertly over the rim of her mug
every time she took a sip. Image wasn't everything, but it
didn't hurt either. His creamy brown skin, smooth and un-
marred, could leave women in envy. Thick arched
eyebrows framed dark brown experienced eyes that reflected a touch of cynicism. Yep, here was a man who
knew the kind of reaction he got from the sistas and didn't
care about how many hearts he broke in the process.

Without warning, his eyes met hers in a similar, studious
gaze over the rim of his mug. Being caught red-handed, she
gulped the hot coffee. "Ouch." She flinched as it burned her
tongue and throat. She moved the mug away for safety since
her senses whirled from his frank assessment.

Thankfully realizing her discomfort, he deliberately
looked around as if admiring the African prints on the
wall. "Love your taste. Those are unusual."

His gaze stopped at a pair of pencil-drawn pictures of an
African boy and girl in traditional dress. Each portrait mat-

ted in black frames matched the earthy, clay tones of several ornaments decorating the room.

"I bought those at an art show at the Art Institute in Washington, DC. I can get prints or originals of up-and-coming artists. It also affords me the luxury of having unique pieces without breaking my bank account. I have quite a few signature pieces at my home in New York."

"You seem quite at home here."

She took a deep breath and nodded. "This will always be my first home. There's no denying."

Justin opened his mouth to talk, but reconsidered. He took another sip of coffee. "I've also begun collecting a few pieces of a particular guy I met in New York. Actually, he's going to have an exhibition in Baltimore in two weeks."

"Really?" She could kick herself for sounding so eager.

"Would you like to attend? I do have an invitation and you could accompany me as my guest."

"I would love to go but I'm not sure whether it would be appropriate, well, you know." She played with her bracelet, hoping he would understand her hesitation.

"I think I understand. And I won't push you. I'll leave that invite open." He raised his hand at her protest. "Hear me out. As I've said, we'll leave that open, and meanwhile, would you have a simple lunch with me?" He opened his arms to add an unthreatening gesture to his second proposal.

Shelly didn't respond immediately. It was still a "date" with the boss, although not as official as the exhibition.

"Look, before you turn me down, how about lunch tomorrow at that cheesecake place?" As if reading her mind, he added, "The place is always packed and fast paced. It wouldn't be my ideal choice to take a date."

She blushed at his bluntness. It wasn't the location that made her hesitate. A simple situation had so much potential to turn into a disaster. The last mess she'd landed in still carried repercussions. Yet being in Justin's presence sent her emotions spiking with a new energy that she fought to restrain.

"What do I need to do to convince you?" He stood in front of her, hands tucked into his pockets. A deep frowned marred his forehead, eyes boring into hers, seeking an answer.

She shrugged. "It's not so easy."

"It's a simple yes or no, but let me add that if your answer is no, I'm not leaving."

Her short chuckle clearly surprised him. He probably expected her to argue. If he only knew that his ultimatum was not as unattractive as he tried to make it seem. He could stay forever for all she cared—that is, if the practical side of her wasn't such a nag. "Okay, you win. When and where?"

"Tomorrow at noon." Now it was his turn to laugh at her shocked expression. Without waiting for a response, he took her hand. In comical fashion, he laid it against his chest where she could feel his strong heartbeat. "I do appreciate your granting me the honor of your presence. And now that I've accomplished my mission, m'lady, I bid you adieu."

She giggled, but underneath, his deep voice, rich with sensuality, softly flicked aside any lingering doubts. Completely under his spell, she followed him to the door, remaining there until his sleek sporty convertible glided out of the parking lot. Her fingertips still tingled from the closeness of his skin. She'd felt the hard thickness of his muscular chest and couldn't help but wonder how it would feel to run her hand over his entire body. She slammed the door shut to destroy the scintillating thoughts.

"My, oh, my, dear Aunt Shelly. I'm so jealous."

"Oh, my gosh!" Shelly whirled around and fell into the closest chair. "Geez, Tanya, how the heck did you get in here?"

Her niece sauntered out of the den and dangled a silver key. "Grandma. She hadn't heard from you all day and I told her that you were very busy with your new job." Tanya flipped the key into the air and caught it with a flourish. "Now I know what or rather who is making you keep long hours. Hmm, looks like I need to call Grandma."

"Touch that phone and die! How did you get here?"

Tanya raised another key.

"And how did you manage to come alone?"

"Gastons has a mega sale at the mall and Grandma is following her second mission on this earth."

Shelly put her hand to her chest in an effort to calm her breathing. "Exactly what is her first mission?"

"It's a tie—for me to stay out of trouble and for you to find a man."

"Humph," Shelly muttered. It would appear that either case was a distinct failure. "Didn't you have to pick her up?"

"No. Grandpa said he'd do it after his golf game."

"Don't just stand there, come help do something. Take these mugs to the kitchen. And now that you're here, it's time for you to give me your decision."

"What decision?"

"Don't play games. I'm not in the mood."

"I can't help that. Maybe you need Mr. Hot-to-Trot to come cool your heels. Probably been a while since your engine got anywhere close to warm."

Shelly stared at her niece for a full second, swallowing the urge to throttle her disrespectful body. She walked over to the telephone in the kitchen and pulled a business card off the refrigerator that was held by a magnet. Blank faced, she dialed. "Detective Tucker, please. Tell him this is Shelly Bishop letting him know that it's no deal. I'll hold, thank you."

Tanya ran over with a finishing slide into Shelly. She pressed down on the button, disconnecting the call. "Auntie Shelly, no," Tanya wailed. "What's going to happen to me?"

"I'm no law expert. But I expect that you'll be standing

before a judge. Maybe you'll get probation, and then, you might not."

"How can you be so coldhearted? I'm seventeen."

"Yes, you're seventeen and old enough to know right from wrong. Old enough to remember what your family has taught you. Obviously, your friends are more important. Well, now your friends can help you get out of this mess." Shelly grabbed her niece's arm. "By the way, how many friends called to see how you made out?"

Tanya pulled her arm away and moved to the safety of the couch. She sank into the cushions. Her bottom lip shook as she fought the emotions that resulted in tears streaming down her cheeks. "You want me to say the person's name?"

Day after day, her niece plucked a nerve. This time she wasn't backing off the teenager. Shelly walked over to the sink to keep from getting worked up.

"It's easy for me to say yes because I know that it would mean a second chance for your sake. But I want you, of your own free will, to say yes because you're ready to turn the page in your life. Drinking. Bad company. What's next, Tanya? You're playing too close to the flame."

Tanya blew an exaggerated sigh. "Can't you just let it go?"

"Let it go! Did hell freeze over? What possessed you to think that half-ass ID card would get you some liquor? And don't think I'm not going to get on you for drinking. But first things, first."

"Maybe you should just exorcise my demons. All of a sudden, you're acting like a Goody Two-shoes."

"I'm going to have to accept the fact that you will choose to use immaturity to deal with your problems. What you fail to understand is that age and responsibility are not on your side. You can't get away with the cute, naive high school delinquent attitude."

The bedroom door slamming shut marked Tanya's response.

Shelly kicked at the air, frustrated that she always managed to get sucked in by Tanya's negativity, leaving her ready to fight back.

Shelly opened the door. "I've tried to get you to see the error of your ways. And I don't know what to do. Right about now, I think that you should seek professional help. I can call—"

"Professional help! You mean like a psychiatrist? Do I look crazy to you?" Tanya paced the room, her unease matching the constant movement.

"Yes, a psychiatrist. A therapist. Even the psychic Jamaican woman on TV is an option right now. I can't help you, Tanya." The weight of her frustration brought tears. "I don't know how to help you."

Tanya stopped her constant march and sank down onto the bed. "Please don't give up on me. I don't know what's wrong with me. But you're all I have on my side. I'm angry about a lot of things. I guess stuff gets into my head and then I act before thinking."

"Oh, hon." Shelly walked over and hugged Tanya. "I'm angry about a lot of things too. I also know that you can't keep running." Shelly closed her eyes tightly to fight back the floodgate of tears. Her frustration at Tanya was more about herself. "Think it over tonight, Tanya. Follow that inner voice and trust it."

Tanya wiped away her tears. "But Detective Tucker may be issuing a warrant right now."

"No, he won't. I didn't call him, I called the weather line." She lifted Tanya's chin. "But tomorrow morning is my deadline. I mean it this time."

"I guess I should say thanks for not telling Grandma and Grandpa everything."

Shelly gripped her niece by her shoulders and gave a slight shake. "Tomorrow, Tanya."

Justin's car purred down the road without disturbing the solitude of the night. Traffic was minimal as he cruised at an easy speed. Soft sounds of the latest slow jams escaped from his car joining the whizzing sounds of the few cars he passed.

He mused, how funny things turned out to be. Although he didn't believe in coincidences, it couldn't be pure luck that had brought Shelly Bishop front and center to his life. His life was one thing, but now she dominated his thoughts.

When all else failed, he turned to his father. It had been a while since they had a father-son chat. Justin needed to hear his advice to confirm whether he was losing his mind or his heart. His watch showed nine o'clock; there might still be a chance he was awake. Turning into the garage, he noticed the light through the partly open curtains of his father's room. Without bothering to go to his own room first, he went straight to him. The thought of baring his soul agitated him, but he needed his counsel. He badly wanted someone to tell him to stop wasting his time; not to follow his whims; to realize that any woman, Shelly, in particular, would eventually do him no good.

His father was up, eating a bowl of ice cream while watching TV. He waved Justin over, motioning to the chair at his side. Justin relaxed, pleased to see his upbeat attitude. He glanced over to the TV to see what caused the old man's intermittent bursts of laughter.

Sitting back, observing his dad, it occurred to Justin that he was not spending enough time with him. In his trying to prove his competency with the bank, work had also become the obstacle. But his father did not appear to need his sympathy, as a zestful gleam radiated off him.

Justin waited for a commercial because he didn't know how or where to begin.

"What brings you here, son? Looks like you've got lots on your mind."

Justin shrugged. His father didn't know how close he was to guessing the truth. "I just wanted to see how you're doing."

"Okay. Now what?"

"And to talk."

Phillip grabbed the remote and turned off the TV. "Is it the bank?"

"Oh, no. No. Actually, it's about a, ah, woman." Even to his own ears, Justin sounded like a nervous boy. He couldn't stop his fingers from picking imaginary lint off his pants.

"Anyone I know?"

"Yeah."

"Stop spoon-feeding me. I can't take it."

Justin paced, eyes focused downward. Why on earth was he feeling so inexperienced? "It's Shelly."

Complete silence.

Justin looked up to see an enigmatic smile, small at first, graduating to a huge grin, pinned onto his father's face.

"What?" Justin always hated that look that revealed nothing, but he sensed something big underneath it all.

"Nothing, nothing at all." His father shook his head. "It's just that wonders never cease. This, by the way, is the same woman you accused me of bringing here to trap you."

A slow burning crept up Justin's neck as embarrassment covered his face. Dad wasn't going to make this easy.

"Okay, I won't tease you. What's the matter? There's something wrong?"

Justin sighed and pulled up his chair closer to his dad's bed. "We'd met years ago after high school. That's not all. Did you know she won the Volunteer of the Year award? Boy, did she look good! All class. Then she landed on your doorstep and, at first, I thought she had other motives." He squinted at his father. "And I still do, by the way. But I figured that I would stay a couple steps in front of her. I'd beat her at her game. Figured she was like the others. But she's different, down-to-earth. And, she doesn't seem to be impressed by my position at the bank. Frankly she's never asked me about the bank." He buried his head in his hands and sighed. "I'd wanted a fling, nothing serious. Have some fun, no feelings hurt and go our merry way."

"Until you eventually get tired of her."

Justin didn't contradict. Any attachment spelled disaster. It had many times before, and he wasn't a green young man baring his heart for the first woman to stomp on it. Most times he sabotaged any resemblance to a relationship before the net was cast over him.

"Instead, it's not quite happening that way. I have the feeling that she's interested, but she's so reserved that sometimes I doubt my instincts. Then I put on this air of bravado, but I never know if I'm pushing too hard. I want to invite her to the reception that the Bankers Association is sponsoring. She's so beautiful and intelligent, a perfect companion—for the evening only, of course. Plus, a part of me wants everyone to see her on my arm, but she is against dating me—her employer."

"Son, what would you like me to say or do?"

"Fire her!"

His father chuckled. "What would that do?"

"Then I wouldn't have to feel guilty about dating her. I wouldn't have to follow any rules or code."

"Now what are your intentions? I hear you talking and it's obvious that you find her physically attractive." Phillip raised his hand at his son's quick defense. "No, you're being honest. But, if there is nothing more than the old one-two skudoo, then leave her be."

His father's words shocked him. To Justin's ears, his own

admission did sound shallow. With an effort, he reached deep within himself where he kept his yearnings and emotions in check. The process was like a visit to the dentist. Ultimately, it would do him good, but from start to finish it was torture. "I can't let her go because what I feel I've never felt before with anyone."

"I think that's a good thing. So, you really like her? And you're sure it's not just physical?"

Justin frowned.

"I've seen the way you've looked at her the few times you hang around late in the morning until she arrives."

"I don't hang around, as you incorrectly think. *And,*" he emphasized, "I am not a leering pervert."

"Those are your words, not mine."

Justin slapped his knees. "She is more than a pretty face. There is a certain style in the way she carries herself that touches me. I feel like I have a rare gift where the entire package is perfect. That's what I'm uncomfortable with; that's what's restraining me. What do you do when someone has all the qualities you only expect in books and movies? I feel like a teenager with a crush. All I want to do is be with her all day long." Justin felt as if he had just run a marathon with that confession. But it was out in the open. He waited for his father's comments.

"That's how I felt when I first met your mother. It was a feeling that was new and beautiful. She made me come alive." His eyes watered at the memory. "You're not alone. Build her trust. Let her feel comfortable and a friendship will naturally develop. She won't disappoint you."

"Dad, you're forever the wise one and the optimist. How do you know she won't disappoint me? If I started counting now, several have done just that."

"But she's different. I know and I can feel it."

"Thanks, omnipotent one," Justin replied, bowing in

mocking fashion. He kissed his father on the cheek, just like old times.

"G'night, son."

Justin shook his head again at his father's impish smile. "I swear every time you smile like that you're up to something. Sooner or later, I'll find out what's bringing that devilish sparkle to your eye."

Shelly prepared for bed. Tanya had settled in for the night on the couch. Snuggled between the pillows, Shelly watched the shadowed patterns on the wall. A yawn escaped and she dreamily thought about her niece, hoping that she'd experience some self-actualization process overnight. A bigger yawn followed and she snuggled deep beneath the covers.

The sun beat warmly on Shelly's shoulders. She stood with Justin in a vivid green field dotted with little wildflowers that bathed the surroundings in pink, purple, and white. In his arms she nestled, enjoying his physical strength and security. Justin kissed her face, lightly touching his lips against her skin. Each kiss taunted the threshold of her passion. Her hands went up around his shoulders, fingers pressing into his muscles. She hung on afraid that she would faint dead away as he nuzzled her neck. When his tongue traced a line to her earlobe, her head fell back with dizzying effect. Her neck arched even more for easier access. Her world spun slowly and she gave in to headiness, sinking deeper into the moment. No words uttered. None needed. He sensed her needs and deepest desires.

Her eyes closed.

When she reopened them, the idyllic scene had vanished.

The dark, stormy clouds rolled in as if by an unseen force. The grass and flowers no longer fluttered under the soft breeze. Instead, they drooped in defeat. Each stem, each stalk bowed. Shelly floundered under the great weight pressing her down, threatening to suffocate her. Fear gripped her. She gasped for air, clawing to escape. She pushed against Justin's body, crying into his shoulders. She had to keep fighting. No matter what, there was no giving up. A leg brutally forced her legs open. Justin raised up.

The face staring back at her wasn't Justin's. Instead Toby leered at her and then tossed his head back, laughing at her.

Shelly awoke suddenly, her nightdress drenched with her sweat clinging to her body. Breathing ragged, she lay on the bed until her eyes adjusted to the darkness. The nightmare sapped her strength, leaving her fatigued and shaky. The sheet had wound around her legs and arms, restricting her.

A few seconds later, she felt strong enough to get out of bed. Her throat was parched and a glass of cool water seemed like a good idea. She hoped that she hadn't made a fool of herself and screamed. Not that anything could wake Tanya.

She made her way to the kitchen for a glass of water. The lasting effects of her nightmare were evident because the glass she held shook so badly that water sloshed over its sides.

Wide awake, she walked into the living room to see if any magazines lay around. Not wishing to wake Tanya, she tiptoed behind the couch and glanced down to look at her niece. Her shock registered upon seeing the blanket thrown back and a handwritten note placed on the pillow. Shelly picked it up, dreading the contents of the message.

Dear Aunt Shelly,

Please don't be mad. I've taken everything you said into consideration and I've made my decision. I hope you will be proud of me. I'm going to get some evidence to back up what I'll tell Detective Tucker. I'll be in touch by tomorrow. Thanks for everything.

Love, Tanya

Seven

"Bill, honey, come and sit. Shelly has something important to tell you."

Shelly's father walked into the family room, wearing a puzzled frown, looking from his daughter's face to his wife's. He sat in his chair near the fireplace, cleaned his glasses with the edge of his shirt, and after settling them back on his face, waited.

"Tanya was arrested a few days ago."

"What?"

Shelly cringed at her father's roar. "She had been taken into custody for using a fake ID to buy drinks at a bar."

"Clara, did you know about this?" Bill turned accusatory eyes toward his wife.

"No. I'm as shocked as you."

As the second part of the relay team, her mother then shot her a look full of blame.

"The cops want Tanya to give up the person who made the ID. We talked about it. I thought she would do it this morning, but when I woke up, she was gone." Shelly pulled out the note, now crumpled, from her pocket. "This is what I found, instead of her."

Her mom took the note, the piece of paper wavering in her hand. Shelly remained standing, her back against the wall ready to face the firing squad. Her parents anxiously pored over the note, looking for answers from the few cryptic lines.

Although she dreaded every second of her revelation, Shelly could no longer hide Tanya's deeds from them.

"What does this mean?" her father asked. "Do we call the police and have them find her? It sounds like she's going after the guy. By herself."

"I called Detective Tucker and he's going to push for a name from the other kids who'd been picked up with Tanya." Shelly kept her worst fears to herself. The longer it took for her to find Tanya, the worse her situation. Plus the reality of where Tanya's case fell in the priority of a busy city precinct left little doubt that she and her family could not rely on the police for significant assistance.

"So we're just supposed to wait?" Her father continued to bark his questions.

"They'll make you wait twenty-four hours unless we can prove she's in grave danger." Shelly pointed to the note. "Technically, there is no evidence of a threat."

"It's time to call her parents," her mother declared.

"Good idea. We're doing all we can do and it's time for them to know about their child's well-being. No sense keeping anyone in the dark," her father finished, with a stern glare tossed her way.

A large knot twisted in Shelly's stomach. She didn't want to call her brother or his ex-wife. She didn't want to admit that she couldn't help Tanya. She couldn't deal with failing her niece who had turned to her for help and guidance. All in all, her purpose for moving back home seemed empty and a monumental failure.

"I'll go call Patrick now," her mother said.

Shelly watched her hurry off, while her father left the room. The situation had been taken out of her hands. A deepening frustration enveloped her. She wanted to scream at the top of her lungs that she was sorry. What good would it do? Besides, her family had heard that word from her too many times as she dealt with her own problems.

Standing in the family room wasn't going to get her niece. An idea formed. She pondered the possibilities and decided that she didn't have a choice. As she headed toward the front door, she heard her mother.

"Faye, we have a problem. It concerns Tanya. We need you."

Shelly walked out the door as her mother's voice faded. *We need you.* The same words that her mother had used when she had asked her to leave New York and return home. In some mixed-up fashion, she'd heeded the call with a hidden purpose to purge her demons so that she could move on with her life. Now failure settled on her shoulders, again.

Shelly closed the door behind her and took a deep breath, squinting from the morning sun. This time, she had to make things right. She had to bolster her own self-confidence because there were others who depended on her. Right now it wasn't about her, but finding Tanya. Everything else had to move to the back burner.

"Okay, I can't hold it in any longer. What are you up to?" Mildred's face was only a few inches away from Shelly's. Not missing a thing, she kept her hands on her hips waiting for an answer.

"What are you talking about? I'm not up to anything." Shelly groaned within, her stomach queasy. All morning she had sensed Mildred's keen eye on her. Every move she made, watched. Though she had wondered what could have given her away, she'd hoped that she'd been mistaken about the intense scrutiny.

A jittery mess as the day went by, she bemoaned her agreement to lunch with Justin, especially during work and given everything else that happened earlier. It was no wonder that she had managed to break a glass, misplaced Phillip's newspapers, and been caught twice daydreaming.

These misgivings stirred up guilt and embarrassment, while Mildred taunted her with snide remarks.

"I should be the one asking what you're up to. You're leaving early. What's up with that?"

"I have a date, Miss Missy," Mildred replied with a smug smile. "But unlike you, who would rather die than admit she had a date, I don't have a problem telling the world my plans. Plus, I don't know who you think you're fooling." Mildred walked around the room, imitating Shelly's actions. "Miss Missy, you've been walking around, humming and looking all dreamylike one second. Then a few minutes later, you look like the saddest pup in the world. And then Phillip's been talking to you. Heck, he'd be better off talking to the television screen with the amount of times he repeats himself." She paused, eyes narrowed to slits, mouth set sternly.

Shelly knew these signs. Mildred was only getting started.

"To make matters worse, every time Justin visits his father, which I might add has become quite frequent of late, you get all fidgety, and you can't say a complete sentence without stuttering."

Shelly rolled her eyes to throw her off the mark. "Mildred, you and your overactive imagination. I suppose looking at all those soap operas during the day is finally having an effect." She pointed at the nurse. "You're mistaken. I may have been a bit absentminded, but your reasoning is way off base. You, my friend, are totally clueless."

Mildred sucked her teeth and waved aside her denial. Clearly she couldn't claim victory over duping Mildred, especially with such a weak-sounding defense.

"Here, help me change the sheets before Phillip comes back from the doctor," Mildred ordered.

The two ladies stripped the soiled linens and efficiently replaced the sheets with a crisp, patterned set.

"I'm not done with you, Miss Missy. You know, if I

didn't know better I would think that you and Justin have a little somethin' somethin' going on."

"You need to stop sniffing that nail polish you're always using. I don't have anything going on with anyone here or anywhere." Shelly gulped in reaction to Mildred's brazen remarks, but to an even greater extent, from the accuracy of her words.

Alarm bells and whistles went off frantically in her mind. Technically nothing had really occurred between Justin and her. But her firm resolve was only a facade. She threw the pillow in frustration at Mildred, happy to see it hit dead center in her face.

"Why the spiffy hairdo and makeup? Dinner date?" Mildred took one of the figurines off Phillip's night table, held it up dramatically to address it. "My friend, lend me your ear," she whispered. "On one side, we have the wealthy son—a fine redheaded specimen of the male variety—that any woman would love to grab hold of. On the other side, we have the curvaceous employee—she's got that naive girlish quality under a healthy helping of bod-e-liousness. Hollywood couldn't pen a better script for an affair between the sheets. Need I say more?" She placed the figurine back on the shelf.

"Shut up, Mildred. Gosh, you make me sick. You know what you can do with your innuendoes. For your information, I'm here as a favor to Phillip. Remember him, the terminally ill patient? There's no room for *stuff* with anyone, including his son. And, another thing, I don't care about his money or who wants him or his redhead or his freckles . . ." Shelly stopped, frantically searching for a way to repair the slip.

Mildred clapped. "Ladies and gentlemen, winner of the bull blankety blank award—Miss Shelly Bishop. Woo woo, Miss Bishop, can I get your autograph? You look somethin' pretty with your hair all finger-waved. Yeah, I caught that slip of the tongue."

Shelly turned her back on Mildred. With a quick glance in the mirror, she gave herself a pat on the back for selecting the plum lipstick because it perfectly matched the purple shade of her blouse.

Stepping up next to her, Mildred addressed Shelly's mirror image. This time her countenance didn't reflect any teasing merriment. "I don't go for the boss-employee thing, but you're gonna do what you want to do. Be on your guard and don't let your heart make any decisions you'll regret later. I've been where you've been and despite all the promises and niceties, you're the one who will end up on the short end of things." She put her arm around Shelly's shoulders. "Don't mind my teasing, girl. I like you and that's why I put in my three cents."

Shelly nodded. The words poked her conscience, but her friend's sincerity softened her stark advice. It never entered her thoughts to change her mind and cancel.

Lunchtime arrived sooner than she was prepared. Mildred said nothing further for the remainder of the morning, even when she left on the excuse of having to run personal errands. But, the knowing look on Mildred's face told everything.

A definite bustle surrounded the front of the restaurant. It sat in the busy downtown area, nestled among office buildings. Justin glanced at his watch, figuring that the small crowd waiting for available tables was on their lunch break.

He smoothed down his jacket and pulled at his sleeves. Of all the conferences and meetings he had to attend, this lunch with Shelly wracked his nerves. He surveyed the waiting area for her familiar face.

Most of the patrons wore business attire. It was the hot

spot for corporate lunches and other business-related power
sessions. Justin selected it because it did not cast a romantic
air with the steady traffic of servers and the boisterous
stream of customers. He wanted Shelly to feel comfortable
in an open environment, while he made his case. No pressure. But this was his all-or-nothing attempt to break through
some of her defenses to get her to give him a chance.

He glanced at his watch—ten minutes late. He didn't
know her style, so he wouldn't panic. But maybe she had
changed her mind and left a message at the office. He'd wait
a little while longer, although he agonized over the urge to
check his messages. He didn't want to face disappointment
so quickly.

After glancing at his watch for the sixth time, he saw her
immediately as she walked through the door. Despite the
number of people standing in the entrance, his gaze fastened
on her familiar face. An appreciative smile appeared as he
admired her hairstyle. His chest swelled with pride—"heav-
enly" was an apt description—and he wanted her.

Looking the picture of relaxed elegance, he remained
seated twisting his glass. Nothing could be further from the
truth because his heart galloped and at any moment, he expected to keel over from a heart attack. So focused, he
missed the seductive looks women tossed his way as they
walked by openly admiring him.

The hostess escorted Shelly over to the table. With a winning smile, he stood, taking her hand. Her small hand was
completely covered in his. Its coldness struck a mental note
that she might be just as nervous as he. Or, maybe she
dreaded the meeting. The thought jabbed him in his gut.

"You look stunning," he complimented.

"Thanks," she replied. "You look great too."

"I guess then we can sit here for an hour and just dazzle
everyone with how good we look."

She laughed at his remark. The aroma of different dishes wafted past, causing Shelly's stomach to rumble in protest.

"Don't worry," he reassured, recognizing her embarrassment. "Mine has been rumbling ever since I sat down. I'm glad to see we're on the same wavelength. Here comes the waiter, do you see anything you like?"

"Everything appeals to me, especially the thought of the cheesecake." Desserts were her weakness.

"The cheesecake is awesome. That's the restaurant's trademark."

After placing their order, Justin inquired about his father.

"He's doing well. Today he went to the doctor's for a routine checkup, and he was a bit worn down from the outing. But overall, his whole demeanor is upbeat."

"I credit his improvement to you." Justin smiled showing his perfect white teeth. "No." He raised his hand in protest. "Listen to me. It's true. Before you came, it was as if he was just waiting to die. There was nothing for him to look forward to. Every day was the same routine. Then, you arrived. Ever since, he seems more excited about his life. I actually saw him writing down an itinerary, which means he's planning, looking ahead. And that makes me feel good." Taking her hand in his, he continued, "I'm truly grateful to you for that accomplishment. It means a lot to me."

It took a moment before Shelly responded. Justin hoped he'd not offended her. Maybe she didn't take him seriously.

"I think you give me too much credit, but thank you," she said softly, pulling her hand away from his.

His holding her hand must have displeased her because he watched her rub the area where he'd touched her.

Their food arrived promptly. She had a chicken sandwich smothered with mushrooms and Swiss cheese and he had a grilled chicken salad with house dressing. They dived in with gusto and laughed at each other because of the comic picture they presented with bulging cheeks. Conversation remained neutral as they exchanged opinions on the food and the restaurant, both favorable. Hungry for the most part, and with the high quality of their meals, it didn't take long to consume the fare.

Appetite satiated. Justin fought with himself on how to guide the conversation to a personal subject—them. Nothing seemed appropriate as a segue.

"So, where do we take this from here?"

What a question, how was she to answer? He kicked himself at her startled look and immediate withdrawal. What an idiot, he reprimanded himself. The fact that she didn't smile, that her eyes didn't light up, that she didn't answer immediately told him loud and clear.

She was not interested.

He counted on his ego being bruised because he had considered this reaction. Twisting his glass furiously, he stared at the ice clinking against it. In a swift gulp, he drained it, and imagined the cold liquid blending with a strange emptiness in his gut.

"It wasn't suppose to be a brain buster. I'll just take your response, or lack thereof, as answer enough." His words tumbled over each other, adjusting to his mood to hurry up and get the heck out of this noisy box.

"Give me a second. I'm not going to pretend that I don't know what you mean," she answered, hesitantly. "But I can't answer the way you want me to."

"You're a remarkable woman."

"Ah, now it's flattery." A sad smile barely emerged on Shelly's face. "I have what many would call too much baggage. There's no room for anyone else."

"So do I."

"Yeah, right. Granted your father's health must be a major concern. But there's the money, power, and people who want to be around the 'light.'"

"Are you afraid of the light?" Justin studied her, trying to understand the turmoil behind her stormy brown eyes.

"Yes," she answered, sincerely. "Ever seen what those lighted bug zappers do to an insect? I think I could stand to learn a lesson or two from that."

"If I'm the light, I must be a thirty-five-watt version. If you hadn't noticed, the newspaper takes great pleasure nipping at me. My so-called friends compete for the honor of gossiping and telling lies about me." A bitterness crept into his tone.

"Why? Is it the bank?"

"The bank. My leadership. My father's legacy in the community. Take your pick." He suddenly wished he had ordered a vodka tonic. It might help to keep the hostile edginess out of his voice. "Then there's my wife."

Shelly's glass slammed down onto the table. Her eyes as wide as saucers, stared back at him.

"Wife?"

"I'm a widower."

"Sorry." Indecision to sympathy flashed across her face in a heartbeat.

"How long ago did she die?"

"It's going on two years."

"How do you go on?"

Now, she was in awe of him, all for the wrong reasons.

"Can't afford not to," he answered.

"You said the newspaper attacked you?"

Justin signaled to the waiter for refills on their sodas. He'd opened the door to his private world. Even his own action surprised him, but he followed the gut feeling that he could bare his soul to her without her taking advantage.

"A smear campaign if I ever saw one."

"Why?"

"They think I killed my wife, Wanda."

Again, Shelly's eyes grew round. This time she coughed and only recovered after taking a sip of her soda.

"I would say that I agree with you, then," Shelly stated, nodding her head.

"About what?"

"Man, do you have baggage! How did you do it? And why?"

"I hope you're not enjoying my disposition?"

Shelly shook her head. "You're knocking me over with stuff, that's all."

"I didn't kill her." He swirled his glass, watching the ice cubes churn a spiral into his drink. A downward spiral that matched his life ever since he had met Wanda. "But at that moment before the car accident, I wanted to break her neck."

"All righty, then." Shelly squirmed. "Too much information."

"Yes, I guess this is getting too deep. Let's just say that my wife died. I'm sorry that she died, but I'm not going to pretend to be the grieving husband."

Justin looked over at Shelly, willing her to look back at him. He wanted her to look squarely at him, not at his neck, his hands, or the table. It didn't seem that he'd have to worry about her taking advantage; instead, he might have to worry that he'd scared her or, worse, repulsed her by his honesty.

"What about you?" he asked, trying his best to pull her back from wherever she retreated.

"I'm dealing with some things, as a matter of fact. Some I'd rather not talk about."

"Oh, yes, I understand." He left unsaid his recollection of her speech and the devastating circumstances that had befallen her. The thought of someone daring to hurt her made his blood boil. He wished that he'd known her then.

Her attacker would probably have been drinking his meals through a straw for the rest of his life.

"Some things will always be a part of my life. Right now, I have a problem with my niece."

He listened as she explained the bare facts of her situation. She spoke as if repeating a laundry list with a background sketch leading up to the sting operation and then the almost sure possibility of her brother and his ex-wife coming into town. He keyed in on what she didn't reveal, sensing her desire to right the wrong for which she took responsibility.

"Do you have a photo of her? I think I may be able to help you, Shelly." It was too soon to know for certain, but he couldn't fight the urge to make her dependent on him. She handed him the photo. He would move mountains to live up to his boast. "No promises. I'll make a few calls and see if I can locate your niece."

A sudden smile radiated her, unrestrained.

"Promises aren't necessary. They tend to be difficult at times to live up to."

"True." But nothing she said dampened his triumph. He took responsibility for changing her mood and looked forward to doing that more often. He could grow addicted. "Feeling better?"

"Yes, I am," she answered firmly and laughed.

"Good. I prefer seeing you smiling."

"Oh, geez, look at the time. I've got to be getting back."

Justin agreed and settled the tab. They strolled out of the restaurant toward the parking lot.

"Thank you for everything," Shelly said, her face partially turned away from Justin's.

He looked at his watch to give himself something to do. He was his own boss and she worked for his father. Time didn't matter. But, he'd behave. "Yeah, I guess we had better be on our way. Where are you parked?"

She pointed toward the next row of cars. He recognized her burgundy Escort and followed her to it. He didn't want to let her go. When they reached the car, his mind raced through several reasons why they should see each other again.

Looking down on her face and into her eyes, he knew that he was lost. She gazed at him and then dropped her glance to his mouth. He took the plunge.

Shelly wanted him to kiss her. Throughout lunch, she'd fought a schoolgirl's giddiness because every facet about him evoked a strong physical response. His cologne had Shelly taking deep breaths, almost causing hyperventilation. His voice, rich and smooth, stroked her into a hypnotic state, as she hung on to the rhythm of his words. She couldn't forget those lips, prominent and wide, with a ready smile.

She leaned forward, ever so slightly, flirting, hinting that she wanted his full lips to touch her. He seemed hesitant and she prayed that he would not back away. It was too late for either one to back out and she wanted his kiss. Tentatively he pulled her toward him and she could feel his breath against her lips. There was no mistaking the answering smolder in his eyes.

She blinked and the small act cued him.

The instant she felt his lips against hers, she groaned. The sound escaped on its own.

Just before she closed her eyes, he closed his. A man after her own heart. Shelly parted her lips and welcomed his stroking tongue, enjoying the warmth of his embrace. Suddenly, he pulled away from her, but still kept her locked in his glorious arms.

"I've wanted to kiss you from the first time I met you," he declared huskily. "Do you want me to continue?"

She answered him by pulling his head down to hers. She didn't want to talk. Already her lips felt cold and craved his attention. This time she curved her body against his entire frame, a solid sheet of muscle. Then he massaged her back, sliding his hand up to her neck. She whimpered as her body reacted with delight to his touch.

A car horn blared. "Come up for air, will ya?" an exuberant teenage driver yelled.

With the snap of a finger, the mood disappeared. A slow flush crept up her neck. For heaven's sake, her mother would be appalled. Well, not really. Anyway, she was appalled at her own wanton display in the public parking lot.

She straightened her clothes, in an effort to give her nervous hands something to do. He traced the outline of a wave in her hair and she melted when his hand trailed along her cheek.

It would be best if she got on her way before she made a bigger fool of herself. So much for putting things on the back burner. In one single swoop, she'd forgotten about her niece and everything else for that matter. Back to reality.

Opening her door, he waited for her to do a once-over in the rearview mirror. "I'll call you tonight."

Face upturned, she nodded. Then quite suddenly, Shelly burst into laughter. "I'm sorry," she finally said. "Here." She handed him a compact with a mirror.

He looked at his reflection. Then, it was his turn to be amused. He broke into a grin that grew into hearty laughter. His mouth resembled a made-up clown with smeared purple lipstick. He took his handkerchief and wiped any evidence of his lunch pastime.

"Okay, rule number one—laughing at my expense is not allowed."

"Then don't give me any reason to break that rule."

When the car pulled out of the parking lot, he took a deep breath. He felt as if he had taken his first step onto a tightrope. Despite his lack of promises, he was deeply committed. A relationship didn't seem like such a horrible venture.

His heart had already made a choice and he was only too willing to follow.

Eight

Shelly parked her car in the same spot that she'd selected since the first day that she worked at the Thorntons' residence. Her car sat on a blacktop area next to the side of the four-car garage, out of the way of the residence's only driver—Justin. The spot for his BMW gaped.

Actually since the infamous kiss, she'd worked two days without running into Justin. She bumped the car door closed with her hip and swung her pocket book over her shoulder. As usual the grounds were neatly manicured with the sprinkler system in full swing, spraying the lawn with wide arcs of water. The heady scent of the roses lining the house perked her up a little. She took a deep breath and entered through the side door.

The hallway leading to Phillip's suite always brought on claustrophobia. Walls painted a midnight blue with white trimmings hemmed her in with their austere confines. She passed a side table with a huge silk flower arrangement of tiger lilies and stopped briefly to survey herself in the gold-rimmed mirror mounted on the wall. She glanced at her image, noting the puffiness under her eyes, her hair that had seen better days, her lips crying out for lip balm. What a mess! Continuing down the hall to the double doors, she made the personal adjustments.

"Hey there, Mildred."

"Hey, yourself."

Shelly gathered up the newspapers and pulled out the newest selection of books that she'd brought for Phillip's reading pleasure. Their conversations were never planned and she looked forward to discerning his mood to determine what direction they should take. Often he'd select an area of interest for her to investigate and research.

Meditation was last week's pick. At first she had to admit to being skeptical about taking the time to gather information. But their conversations ranged from understanding its origins, to using specific techniques, to inducing the proper environment for meditating. They'd agreed to try what they'd learned and then discuss it. She had nothing to report. The past week may have needed a meditative spirit, but her volatile emotions Ping-Ponged too much for her to settle down long enough to "breathe in with the good and out with the bad."

A muffled ringing of a telephone reached her. Realizing that it was her cell, she pulled the small device out her pocketbook. The number displayed belonged to her mother. It must be about Tanya.

"Yes?" She turned her back to Mildred and wandered away to a corner.

"Where are you, Shelly?" her mother's voice shrilled.

"I'm at work," Shelly whispered, looking over her shoulder to see if Mildred listened.

"Work! At a time like this you're working? Aren't you worried about Tanya? You know, you should be. After all, you were dealing with the child."

The familiar bubbling anger percolated. Her mother had an expert touch to push her buttons, firing her up like a rocket ready to go charging. "Mom, I have to work. I only work a few days a week. We went over this before. Now is not the time."

"Fine. Patrick arrived. I figured you would have liked to be here to tell him firsthand what happened."

Shelly pinched the bridge of her nose, squeezing her eyes shut in an effort to think. "I'll be there as soon as I can, okay? Good-bye." She punched the END button without waiting for her mother's response.

"Everything okay, hon?" Mildred hadn't moved, hovering before Phillip's door with a tray of pills and a glass of water.

"Yeah," Shelly lied. At that very instant, her life was skipping happily into the abyss.

Mildred nodded, an eyebrow raised over an unbelieving glare. "If you ever need to talk, I'm here."

Shelly sighed and followed her into Phillip's room.

An hour later Shelly and Phillip sat in the garden off the back of the house, Shelly on the wrought-iron chair, Phillip opposite in his wheelchair sipping a glass of milk. The early morning sun on its rise to the midday peak provided a comfortable backdrop to a cloudless day. Phillip had surprised her with requesting that they take a morning stroll into the garden. His color looked good and she was pleased to share the moment with him.

"You seem to be a thousand miles away."

Shelly sighed deeply and shrugged. "Sorry, Phillip. I guess I've been a bit preoccupied."

"You can say that again. I've had to repeat my questions. Is there a problem?"

"No," she replied quickly. "I was just thinking about my birthday." She laughed, a quick burst, to cover her lie. The annoying event had rolled around another year.

"When is it?"

"Saturday. The agency did tell you that I wouldn't be available from Friday to Monday?" Well, at least, that part was true, although it wasn't the subject of her thoughts, lately.

"Yes, I remember. Planning to do something fun? I do hope so. You deserve it, too young to be so serious."

"Not much I can do about that," she murmured, looking off into the distance.

"I know what I'd like to discuss this time."

"I'm listening." Enjoying the change of subject, she turned to him and saw in that moment what Justin would look like in twenty to thirty years. Justin's sharper-contoured face would give way to softened edges that still maintained a mature distinction.

A transformation that would, by no means, be unattractive.

Despite all the side effects of chemo, Phillip could brag about his lightly lined face that didn't droop or sag in the usual places. Even her mother would make a big deal of his good looks.

"Birthdays," he remarked, grinning like a schoolboy. "That's what we'll discuss. I suggest that since yours is coming around the corner, you'll be the subject."

She eyed him warily. "And exactly what will we be talking about? I'm really not doing anything special. In the past, my parents rented a boat and we went sailing along the Eastern Shore—great seafood restaurants."

"That's it? No parties? No girls' night out? It's a celebration of a year's worth of living. Think about all the wonderful things that have happened in the year and celebrate. Maybe there's a special someone," he teased with a chuckle, his eyes dancing with mischief.

She considered Phillip's remarks. "I've only been here a few months, remember? Thanks for your confidence, but it might be a tad misplaced. I'll have to pass on any 'special someones.' And that's not a bad thing." She pulled out a deck of cards that she'd brought along in case they were inclined to play a game of gin rummy. She shuffled and dealt. "Believe me, celebrating is the furthest thing from my mind."

"Nonsense. I bet you can name one great thing that happened this year worth celebrating," he scolded. "One thing, Shelly? Come on!"

Pressured, she didn't have to think long or hard.

Justin.

Six feet something of milk-chocolate proportions. Plus their kiss had moved up notches since her college days. She blushed unrepentant from the memory. Yes, he was worth a celebration—albeit, privately. She nodded at Phillip.

"Good. I knew, if you tried, you could find something to be grateful for."

"Oh, Phillip, you always take the time to make me feel good. I feel like you're not getting your money's worth out of me. Look at me, I'm doing nothing but yapping about myself." She squeezed his hand and impulsively hugged him. "I'm sorry. I shouldn't have done that." She folded her arms tightly against her chest to prevent any further embarrassing displays.

"That's okay. A winner always likes to be hugged. Gin!"

Shelly laughed. "I don't know how you do this to me. Every game."

"Let's walk." He eyed her reaction. "Okay, I'll walk, you push the wheelchair, and when I feel faint I'll be sure to tell you."

"Okay." Shelly helped him get up from the wheelchair and allowed him to take hold of one of the handles. "You truly amaze me, Phillip, considering your circumstances."

"You want to know if I'm grateful, right? Well, I want to show you something."

They made their way slowly down a stone path that ran along the back of the house toward a screened gazebo. The path formed the outer perimeter of the in-ground pool, rectangular-shaped with smaller Jacuzzi spas on either end. Natural white stone framed the calm turquoise water twinkling under the sunlight, teasing and beckoning her. The hazy climate, marking the summer month, underlined the need to take a running leap and sink into the cool, refreshing water.

"Isn't that a waste?" Phillip remarked, nodding toward the pool. "Justin used to swim when he was in college. He'd have pool parties and the place would be lively. Now, he goes to the gym to swim. Doesn't make sense."

The image of Justin standing on the diving board with little more than a Speedo popped up as a freeze frame in her mind. A small smile played on her lips.

The smile snapped out of sight when she spied Mrs. Beacham's dour face in a kitchen window. Shelly traditional brown dress stood out against the white trimming of the window. Shelly sighed. The housekeeper hadn't warmed up and apparently had no intention of doing so. Shelly's imagination wandered at length, probing the message behind the stern surveillance. A look that immediately stirred up her defenses about her cushy job.

Phillip finally stopped at a bronze plaque embedded in the ground. A small fence, at midshin level, framed the spot. Shelly stooped to read the inscription.

"There's a time capsule buried here?" she asked, incredulous.

"Yes, and as you can see from the date, it has been here for forty years."

"Do you have any dinosaur bones in there?"

Phillip huffed and stepped away from the wheelchair. He brushed her hand away. "After that remark, I'm gonna show you who you're messing with." He swayed slightly as if under control by a slight breeze. Despite his protests, Shelly remained within reach—just in case.

"Forty years ago when we were brand-new to the house,

my wife, Estelle, and I moved out here." His eyes grew dreamy as he shared fond memories. "We were the first black family to move into the neighborhood. Nothing major happened like you hear about with cross burnings or vandalism. Instead, we were ostracized." His tone sharpened with an edge of bitterness. "No one talked to us. When there was any event that involved the community, we never knew about it. It was a different form of hell." He turned sharp eyes on her, face tight from the hurt. Taking a deep breath, he pushed his shoulders back proudly. "We didn't move, as you can see, nor did we hide. Estelle was a strong woman. And when she determined that she would do something—well, damn it, we didn't have a choice." A chuckle rumbled from him.

It was nice to see the strength of marriage and its sanctity upheld. Her parents also shared a similar healthy and loving relationship in their marriage. Personally, she couldn't buy into matrimonial hoopla. She wouldn't blame her decision on her experience with Toby, but it certainly didn't help it. It was more a question of independence and what she'd have to give up.

"Presumptuous as we wanted to be, we invited ourselves to the events. We visited our neighbors taking cookies, cakes, or whatever we had; and even visited them at their places of worship. We went the extra mile, and it paid off. We won their respect and we helped in getting rid of any preconceived ideas they may have had about me or my people.

"Getting back to what I was saying, though, we came out here to this spot and made a vow. We vowed that we would create this time capsule for our children, grandchildren, and so on to provide a permanent mark in our family history. As they grow up with the easy life, the contents of the capsule buried on this property will be a reminder of where their family came from and what they should be thankful for.

While they shouldn't forget where they came from, neither should they apologize for where they're at today."

Shelly looked at the plaque again. What a legacy! She heard the pride in Phillip's voice and it touched her, causing goose bumps. A small part of her envied the dedication and care that he had for his upbringing, his accomplishments, and his son's future. She wondered if Justin truly understood the depth of his father's gift.

"Ah, I see Pop nabbed another willing victim for his famous history lesson," Justin quipped on approach.

"Actually, Mr. Thornton," Shelly replied, turning away from Justin to Phillip, "I thoroughly enjoyed your story." She glared at Justin, who brandished an impish grin.

"Well, I did too—that is, the first couple of times I heard it," Justin piped in. He winked at Shelly, who quickly glanced over to Phillip to see if he'd noticed. Thankfully, he was still staring at the plaque. It gave her time to get over the strange flutter in her stomach.

Phillip walked toward the house. "Okay, Justin, what brings you home so early? I know it wasn't me with those flippant remarks you just made," he shot over his shoulder. "Shelly and I are now going to the family room to watch our game show and then, the news. More than likely we'll be chatting, so don't bother to accompany us if you're going to be a pain."

Justin quickened his step beside his father's chair, he on one side and Shelly on the other. "I promise to behave if you'll let me into your club." He puckered his lips into a kiss and blew it over his father's head.

Shelly gasped, an automatic response to Justin's ridiculous and dangerous behavior. He acted like an adolescent with raging hormones. This wasn't the contemplative man she'd left at the restaurant and who had playfully teased her.

To worsen matters, he fell behind his father a few paces

and pulled her bodily against him. "You're smelling lovely," he whispered.

Shelly pushed him off and concentrated on not screaming, especially when Justin leaned forward and kissed her lightly on her lips. The flutter in her stomach was joined by an answering chorus of jitters. It didn't help that her signals to stop were met with his great amusement. Why was he risking her job with Phillip?

Anger stabbed.

She chided herself for not realizing that Justin might be deliberately trying to make Phillip send her packing. Regardless of how well Phillip treated her, she was the hired help. She had no intention of taking advantage of his good nature by having a fling with his son. She could thank him for the kiss, even credit him for stoking the fire under long-dormant emotions, but that was as far as she was willing to take it. She'd just have to apologize later that any indication of a continuing relationship was an accident.

Now studying him, she could not see any signs of a calculated motive. But could she trust her ability to be a judge of good character?

"Shelly, dear, I'm going to get into my chariot and I'd like to head into the house. I hate to admit it, but I'm a little tuckered."

Shelly immediately focused on Phillip and assisted him into the wheelchair.

"How are you doing, Dad? You do look a bit washed out."

"I'll be fine." His father waved off Justin's close attention.

The house's cool interior welcomed them. Shelly aimed the wheelchair toward the family room, as was their habit after coming from outdoors. Justin followed, much to her annoyance. The trio passed Phillip's bedroom suite and Mildred seated at a desk outside the room.

"See all of this, Shelly?" Phillip remarked, his head slightly turned in her direction. "It goes to my son, the one and only. No secret, right?" He waited until she nodded. "Wouldn't you agree that it's a bit much for a freewheeling bachelor? Look at me, I'm drowning in the darn house."

Shelly couldn't see Justin permanently settling onto the massive property. Although he took up temporary residence, the sedate mood of the place lay in direct contrast to the workaholic, intense person standing before her.

"It needs life, a woman's touch, some bratty kids—my grandkids preferably." Phillip hit the arm of the wheelchair for each point he made.

"My father thinks I'm so multifaceted that I can run the business and take on the responsibility of being a husband and father. Sorry to disappoint," Justin replied.

Too late, she was disappointed. She shook it off, blaming it on the fact that, although he might not be a good choice of husband for her, she did feel that he shouldn't shut the door on something his father so desperately wanted on his behalf.

"Got something to say?" Justin goaded.

She shrugged, watching him with annoyance, and he dropped another wink.

Justin tried to behave, but flirting with Shelly proved to be too much fun. Her obvious discomfort tickled him and he wondered why she had suddenly turned prudish. Maybe she regretted sharing a deep kiss with a sampling of full-bodied passion just beneath the surface.

So far he managed to witness her quiet side when she sat at his father's side listening to his stories; the nervous side when Mrs. Beacham discovered her in the library; and the determined side when she spoke at the award ceremony. It underscored his perception that she was not only a complex person, but not cold and unmoving, someone who could be his equal.

Mrs. Beacham entered the room. Grateful for the interruption, Justin asked her to bring refreshments. His thoughts had gathered a momentum that he could ill afford. His father's advice haunted him, but he'd rather handle things on his own terms.

"Boy, stop standing there looking all foolish, staring at Shelly."

Justin's face instantly heated. His beloved father with all the cunning of a fox was on to him. "For your information, I was not staring at Shelly." He noticed the panic in her eyes and the way her body stiffened.

"Maybe I misread the situation." His father gesticulated with sweeping motions. "I only thought that if you were a mite attracted, maybe you'd go to a restaurant and get to know each other."

"Now, now, Phillip, not in a million years," Shelly explained.

She'd beat him in answering, but he didn't care for the adamant refusal.

"Ah, here's Mrs. Beacham. My favorite—lemonade." Justin took two glasses off the tray before she could set it down on the table. "Shelly?" He kept the smile hidden when she took the glass without looking at him. Anger fairly crackled off her with her shoulders so rigidly set. "Take a deep sip, my dear," he whispered conspiratorially. "It might douse that temper of yours."

She grinned back at him. Or at least, he took it as a grin, although there was a marked resemblance to the odd occasion when his dog from childhood days had bared her teeth.

He turned and handed the second glass to his father. "Your favorite. See, Mrs. Beacham always looks out for you."

"Always duly noted."

A rare smile peeked through on Mrs. Beacham's face. It amused Justin to notice that only his father could melt the housekeeper's demeanor. A small glimpse of human emotion softened her. He'd never considered that she, too, might be lonely. Until now.

Justin helped his father to his favorite chair and settled the cushions around him. Out of the corner of his eye, he saw Shelly walk over to the couch and hesitate before sitting. He wouldn't let her get off that easy.

"This seat taken?" he asked and plopped down beside her. She scooted over, leaning her body into the armrest. "I don't bite." He flashed a winning smile and was rewarded with her mouth tightening.

The game show theme played in the background. Justin was only dimly aware of the host's introduction and his vivacious letter-turner. He didn't much care for the overly enthusiastic players, nor the so-called challenge of guessing the correct letters to a word. Sitting beside Shelly caused its own distractions.

"You never said why you're here so early," Phillip said.

"Don't worry, I won't interrupt your time with Shelly. I came to get some files and head back to the office. I have a dinner meeting with the head of Valcon Construction. It'll be a real coup if they leave National's and come on board with us."

"Good to hear, son. Work, work, work. When will you relax a bit to focus on you? Shelly, what do you think?"

"Oh, no, I don't want to be in this family discussion." She squirmed uncomfortably and reached for her lemonade, holding the glass tightly.

Phillip snorted. "Help me out here, Shelly. Hypothetically speaking, could you see yourself dating a man like Justin?"

A few seconds ticked by, the silence more damning than if she'd blurted out a sarcastic quip. Justin couldn't believe his father's blatant attempt to force a situation.

Reality jackhammered a sign that read *stupid* on his brain. Like a fool, he'd played right into his father's plan. He fell back into the couch as the sordid affair sunk in.

Shelly and her father had bested him. He'd suspected it, but he couldn't stop himself from wanting to be around her.

This new twist had just the right punch to set the record straight.

"Normally, I'd say yes, I would date someone like him." She looked over her shoulder, sizing him up with cold matter-of-factness. "But, hypothetical and all, the problem would be that he lacks challenge. Don't get me wrong, a girl could have a good time, but there has to be more to him—something deeper, more meaningful. Who has time to deal with a playboy?"

Phillip clapped his hands and chuckled. "You're darn right!"

"Hey, both of you, did you ever stop to think that there might not be any women worth my time? Or maybe I should just rush right out and attach myself to a leech who will suck me dry and everything I've built up over the years—hypothetically speaking." Justin's temper rolled on picking up momentum. "Do we have any nominees? How about you?" He stared back at her, aware that his words had hit their mark.

Phillip tossed a cushion that hit Justin in the face. "That scenario suits me. Shelly, if you're up to it, you can fill the spot. Son, she's got a good head on her shoulders and would be a welcomed addition to the family. Then after she killed you off, she can take over as queen of Hopetown Savings Bank."

"No, thank you. I have my sights set much higher. I heard the mayor may be looking for a wife, though." Shelly spoke through clenched teeth. It started out as teasing, but he'd said a few things that rubbed her the wrong way.

Phillip turned the volume up on the television. "Hold it. Listen."

Previews of the upcoming half-hour local news flashed across the screen. Justin only caught the tail end of one of the highlights. The anchorwoman announced that a rumor from a reliable source reported Hopetown Savings Bank was being courted by an interested buyer. News to follow after the commercial break.

Justin stood, then walked closer to the television. He blocked out his father, Shelly, and the soft scent of peaches surrounding her. His heart pounded as each annoying commercial jingle played. Finally, the news resumed.

A reporter standing in front of his bank's headquarters gave the scoop. An undisclosed interested buyer was looking into purchasing the community bank. The reporter interviewed some of the employees emerging from the building and each showed shock at the news and its implications. The piece ended with the reporter stating that the owner of Hopetown Savings Bank could not be reached for comment to confirm a looming merger or buyout.

Justin swore under his breath. He had to get to the bank. The phone rang, jarring his concentration. Mrs. Beacham stepped into the room to announce the call.

No doubt that since word was out, he would be receiving several calls. "Mrs. Beacham, please take a message. We won't be taking any calls unless it's family or friends."

Justin ran his hand through his hair. "I bet I know who's behind this."

"I think I'll be going now."

Phillip waved Shelly back to her seat. "No, please stay. You will be a target for the media since you work here with me. Believe me, there is nothing to the rumor, not one kernel of truth. I'm not selling anything. I know you wouldn't either, Justin. Someone is trying to tear us apart, but it won't happen." He slammed his fist on the armrest. "It won't happen."

"It smacks of Toby Gillis's handiwork. Before, he was merely a nuisance, but now he has taken things too far, too personal. I'll take care of it. I'm going to call Braxton and find out what we can do legally. Then, I'm going to call Connors to have him dig up what's really going on." Protect. His primary objective was to protect his father. He pinned Shelly with a quelling stare. He had no time for games and wouldn't be fooled by the beautiful exterior. "In the meantime, no one, and I mean no one, is to talk to any member of the press."

Shelly didn't answer. Good, because he wasn't expecting one. It was a command.

"I need to go back to bed." Phillip sat forward, shoulders slumped. He looked as if something had sucked out the vitality he had recently shown in the garden. "I'm not feeling well." He shook his hand at their obvious concern. "Not to worry. It's been a long day and it's ending on a low note." He wheeled himself toward the doorway. "By the way, Justin, you will need to do damage control with the employees in the morning. I would suggest that you give all the department heads a call and get them comfortable."

His father also suffered under the surprise news report. This simply fed the rage burning a path throughout his body. "Don't you worry. I'll have everything under control. You just go and rest. I'll keep you informed every step of the way."

He watched Shelly gently help his father out of the room. She glanced over his father's head once to look at him. It surprised him, the sadness in her face. Other than being concerned over his father's health, he didn't expect her to be devastated over the news about the bank. Yet, he didn't mistake the drawn tension around her eyes and mouth.

Frightened.

She appeared to be afraid. But of what?

Time to face her family.

Half an hour later, after leaving Phillip, Shelly sat in the breakfast nook of her parents' house. It was one of her favorite rooms, next to her old bedroom. The oversize bay windows invited in large amounts of natural light. Soaking it up while inhaling enticing scents of seasonings, marinades, and various meats made it a perfect nook to relax in. However, today it was the room for her debriefing.

"What brought you back here?" Patrick inquired.

Her brother, the ex-college football player, leaned against the marble-top island in the kitchen. His face hadn't changed much since she last saw him. The wide shoulders and beefy build from his days as a defensive end hadn't left him. People always remarked on how much they resembled each other. It was probably the small nose, the lips, and the shape of their faces.

"I only came back for Tanya's sake."

"Which brings me to my next question."

"Before we go there, I want to know where you're working." Her mother, always the plain-talk type, had finally pinned her.

"I'm working for a private home in Hopetown."

"Why? Do you need money? The few hours at the doctor's office wasn't enough? I told you that we'd pick up any bills you have."

"I'm fine. I'm not working all the time."

"Doesn't appear so because I've visited twice and you weren't home. You don't come over for dinner anymore, which is why I was asking about this new job."

"Fill me in on Tanya. I'm not interested about where you're working, Shell," Patrick said. It was like the old days when they'd protect each other from their mother's intensive interrogations.

Shelly gladly reported on her niece's adventures, fighting the urge to be less defensive about her role.

"What puzzles me is why Mom and Dad called you to come and take care of Tanya, instead of calling me. I *am* her father."

Her mother, who had casually leaned against the row

of cabinets, shifted her stance. Shelly took perverse pleasure in witnessing her discomfort. Frankly, she was also
curious.

"I don't appreciate your tone, Patrick. I agreed to be
Tanya's guardian because neither you nor Faye wanted to
uproot her from the familiar. And, well, we called Shelly
because we hoped that by her coming home, she'd reconsider and stay. She just gets all swallowed up in New York.
Look at her!"

It'd been a long day. Everyone had a motive and had her
dancing on their string: Phillip, her mother, and newly
added to the list—Justin. "Maybe if you'd spent less time
focusing on me and more on Tanya, we wouldn't be having this meeting about her whereabouts."

"Oh, really? I'd say that you, young lady, need as much
help as Tanya to get out of the rut you're in. Think I haven't
noticed how you mope and don't bother going to visit your
old friends? Heck, when was the last time you came to
church with me? One good thing, though, is that at least
you're going to the center."

"Hey, remember me?" Patrick waved his hands. "What
are you talking about? Did something happen to you,
Shell?" He grinned. "I bet it's some man problem. There's
lots more where he came from so don't get frazzled."

"Patrick, be quiet. You're not helping," their mother
snapped.

Shelly prayed for numbness. Then this disastrous day
could continue its hellish path and she wouldn't notice. Instead her face was flushed and she was mortified that
Patrick was only moments away from discovering what
had happened to her, thanks to her mother.

"I have to get Faye from the airport." Her mother
reached for her car keys lying on the counter.

"You don't have to, I'll get her. We'll have to face each
other sooner or later. This will give her some private min-

utes to bat me around with that waspish tongue of hers."
He grinned at the prospect. "Besides, I think both of you
need a few minutes to declare a truce." He took the keys
from his mother's fingers. "Where's Dad when you need
him?" He winked at Shelly and left the house whistling the
theme from *Rocky*.

Neither woman spoke right away while the refrigerator
filled the air with its soft humming.

"That wasn't fair," Shelly admonished.

"I know," her mother replied. She kept her head down
and her hands busy picking lint from her pants.

"Why?" The soft asked question hung in the air.

"These past few days have me edgy. I'm sorry."

"That's not good enough. Why did you manipulate me?
I subleased, I had to make arrangements about my job. I
had to put my life on hold. Now, to find out that it's part of
your game really irritates me."

"I was worried about you. You have no friends, male or
female. You have no hobbies. And your house in Brooklyn
has no furniture—what kind of home is that? You're a shell
of who you used to be. I—we, your father and I—can't
stand to see you like this. And then there's Tanya. You're
the one person that she doesn't have any issues with and
looks up to, another reason why I called on you." Her
mother came over to the table and stood behind her. She
rubbed her daughter's shoulders. "Are you ever going to
tell Patrick?"

"One day, but not today," she emphasized for her
mother's benefit. She needed her apartment at this very
minute. Solitude she craved.

"Don't shut us out, Shelly. All of us need each other to
heal and move on. You, most of all," she added. "I'm sure
we'll find Tanya soon. I have faith. But now I want you to
seriously consider making this town your home, again."

Justin had circled the wagons to protect his family, effectively shutting her out. Now her mother was ready to do the same for her. All she had to do was enter and enjoy the homecoming. Her family could provide the warmth and comfort that she needed.

Toby Gillis.

The dark cloud over the ideal fantasy of a quiet life. The longer she stayed, the more likely that their paths would cross, especially given her employment with Phillip. She closed her eyes to her mother's soft touch, stroking her head. She sighed.

"I won't push you. Please realize that the door is always open. I love you, daughter."

Nine

Justin sat behind his desk, hands steepled, looking out the window. The bank's headquarters had prime land next to one of the county's regional parks. Acres of trees surrounded a cleared area with picnic benches and playground equipment. Joggers ran in and out of view along the trail specially carved along the landscape.

He'd taken a quick break to clear his thoughts and refocus. Back to the business at hand, there was a lot of work to be done. Stockholders, employees, and the media demanded his attention. They wanted his reaction. They wanted promises and commitment. Sooner rather than later, he'd have to deal with them.

He popped another two caplets down with lukewarm coffee to take the edge off a mounting tension headache. Eyes closed, he pressed his hand to his temples, willing the pain to subside.

The private line on the phone rang. The shrill chirp jarred his head and he snatched up the receiver. "Justin Thornton."

"It's Connors, sir."

"Any news?" Justin didn't have time for pleasantries.

"Not good, I'm afraid. There are a small number of the boardmembers that have been approached by a buyer. It happened about three weeks ago."

Justin pounded his forehead with his fist and clenched

his teeth. The headache throbbed, radiating from the back of head. "Who is the buyer?"

"No one is talking. Rumor is that it's Gillis, but nothing is pointing that—"

"Of course not," Justin interrupted. "That rat is too smart for that. But he'll make his move soon." The situation called for fast thinking and he was having the hardest time doing just that. "Find out what you can. Do you at least know which boardmembers?"

"Yes, it's the same group that had tried a similar maneuver with your father a few years back. When they had secretly tried to combine their stock. It's not all bad, though. There is another small group that has no ties to anyone and is genuinely interested in seeing the bank an even bigger success on its terms."

It was the opening he needed. His breathing responded to the bit of good news and even his headache had stopped the march over his entire head and receded to being a minor inconvenience. If he could reach out to this group, he could nip everything at this stage. Survival of the fastest became the new motto.

"Good work, Connors." He hung up, already in deep thought about the upcoming employee meeting. In fifteen minutes, he was on. What and how he said things would have an impact beyond today or tomorrow.

Justin walked into the room nervous as hell. The minute he stood in the doorway, the roar of chatter ended. Every seat was occupied, with a few stragglers standing against the wall. The packed conference room housed almost full representation from his employees. He'd come prepared to present the bank's case simulating a theatrical play, where he was the star performer, director, and producer. No sudden moves, no nervous habits, he'd practiced the gist of his comments, noting when to give and hold their eye contact and when to make sweeping motions with his arms in an all-inclusive embrace.

And now the show began.

Justin greeted them and came straight to the point, the reason for an impromptu all-staff briefing. Then Phillip entered the room, the special touch of a cameo appearance. He suggested with no room for negotiation that neither Mildred nor Shelly should attend the meeting with him. Maybe one of them could wait in the limo and that was acceptable. It was important to show the physical strength because it's what people perceived to be the standard for overall prowess in handling anything. There hadn't been time to get a suit tailored to fit his thin frame, but the indispensable Mrs. Beacham had sent a suit to be altered.

His father, with his hair shaved off, walked slowly over to his side. He greeted him in an easy affable manner, relaxing some of the tensed faces. After he took his seat, he flicked the switch to turn on the microphone embedded in the table in front of him. He took a few minutes to address employees who had served under his leadership, reminding them how they had overcome struggles then to become pillars in the community.

Justin relaxed as his father spoke from the heart. He knew then that he could never let Toby Gillis destroy a legacy. With everything he had and more, Justin planned to keep what was rightfully his.

When it was Justin's turn, he crumpled the carefully written script. The queasy taste of doubt evaporated. Confident and inspired, he took the mantle of leadership that his father gave him and underscored a few minutes ago. Hopetown Savings Bank would remain a bank for the community, small businesses, and minority entrepreneurs.

As part of his finale, he acknowledged specific departments and people who had gone above and beyond in helping the bank earn its place in the community and city as a leader.

At the end, the employees gave a standing ovation, clapping enthusiastically. The message of solidarity had been delivered and accepted.

Justin followed up the meeting with a separate, more intimate one among the executives. Unveiling his strategic plan to counterattack any possible damage. The next major move was to determine what damage had been done to the customers' confidences, even if he had to visit each commercial account himself.

Fatigue weighed on Phillip's face. Justin led him to the elevator and rode it down to the car.

"Looks like we did it, Dad."

"Sure did. It felt good to be in the middle of things. But I'm an old man and don't have the stamina."

"Go home and rest. I'll be late, but I'll stop in to let you know how things went."

The elevator doors chimed before opening. Shelly immediately came to his father's side. She didn't greet him or acknowledge his presence. Attentive and gentle, she propped his father against her side and led him to the waiting limo. Justin followed behind, hoping and waiting for a glance, a shy smile.

"Bye, Dad." He felt like the third wheel. His father waved, already chatting it up with Shelly.

He headed back toward the elevator and pushed the button to go up to his office. The floors lit up as the elevator descended and he silently said each number to force himself from turning toward the limo. The doors slid open and he stepped toward the elevator cab. A peek. One last look to see if she'd look at him.

Shelly had closed the door on his father's side and walked around to the other side. She faced him. He waited. She got into the car and pulled the door closed without looking at him. He rode up the ten floors, wondering why he was so disappointed that she didn't notice him. She'd dismissed him and he didn't like it.

Shelly arrived at the center, a bit surprised that she looked forward to the day's activity. With all the turmoil whirring within her, she needed the hour to become grounded. An hour to build herself up after Justin's bruising remarks. He'd thought so little of her that he could be hurtful, even in front of his father.

It killed her to see him this morning in an expensive suit, looking and playing the part of an executive. She steeled herself from looking into those soft brown eyes that made her knees weak. She rehashed his offhand comments about the type of woman he thought she was. It fortified her. It made her see red. The anger kept her from acting like a ninny and she'd left without giving him the satisfaction of seeing her true emotional state.

"Welcome, everyone. It's another week, another new page in our lives. We have a new participant. Everyone, this is Josh Benton, he'll be joining our group." Leesa opened the meeting.

Josh sat on the small metal chair with legs open and slouched over his legs. He wore a baseball cap pulled low onto his forehead and tilted on an angle. Angry gray eyes glinted from under the brim, giving each member a hostile once-over.

"What brings you here? A big burly guy like you couldn't have been raped," Kim asked, noted for her aggressive nature.

He turned his head to her and rolled his eyes before leaning back and closing them.

Kim didn't flinch or back down from the challenge. The young woman reminded Shelly of a fox, with sharp, small features. Shelly noticed the excitement light up her small shifty eyes; she'd sniffed something worth pursuing. "You are here on one of those court order deals."

"And what if I was?"

Shelly felt as if she were at a tennis game, looking back and forth between the two. His latest remark caught her off guard.

"Don't get your feathers ruffled. I'm here because my lawyer plea-bargained. I didn't admit to anything. I just have to show up here for three months."

"Do you realize that most of these women were raped or were close to someone who was raped?"

"What does that have to do with me?"

"It means that sensitivity is necessary from everyone. And we come here to understand, console, and discuss how we feel about the aggressors." Gloria, one of the oldest in the groups spoke up.

"Like you," added Kim.

He looked around the room for the first time. "Since I'm the only male, I guess I'll be sitting in on male bashing sessions. This is bogus."

"No one is getting bashed here, Josh. But for your purposes, you will come to develop an understanding of what the victim feels and the effects of your actions," Leesa informed him.

"Like I said," he reiterated through gritted teeth, "I didn't rape anyone."

"Doesn't matter now, the judge evidently felt it necessary that you join us—so, welcome," Gloria offered. Her maternal touch always managed to dilute any harsh words or overtures.

The remainder of the session went through the regular process as each person shared her feelings and how she was coping. Shelly didn't want to share the latest about

Justin. Any friendship or relationship that could have blossomed died an ugly death. She'd deal with it privately.

Shelly remained behind to help Leesa clean the room after the hour was over. It didn't entail too much effort, basically stacking the chairs against the wall, disposing of any paper cups, and emptying the coffee urns.

Leesa turned out the lights and they walked down the hallway. The counselor slipped her hand into the crook of Shelly's arm. "What's on your mind? Keep frowning like that and those worry lines will become permanently etched in your forehead."

Deep down she did want to tell Leesa about her constant thoughts, but suddenly she felt shy, embarrassed. She shrugged, hoping to throw her off the trail.

She didn't.

"Talk to me, Shelly."

They now stood outside where a slow, steady drizzle showered on them. The air was muggy, thick like pea soup. Even prepared as she was with an umbrella, the dampness clung to her feet and ankles. This was the type of weather that made her want to be indoors curled up with a book and caramel popcorn at her bedside.

"Leesa, I don't know how or where to begin." Shelly focused on the counselor's red and white umbrella. "It's complicated."

Leesa gave an understanding nod and came straight to the point. "It's Toby?"

At first, Shelly shook her head. "I guess in a way it *is* indirectly related to Toby." She sighed wearily. "Nowadays, everything about me is connected to that monster. It's preventing me from living."

"Look at me, Shelly."

Shelly focused on her friend and mentor. When she looked at Leesa, she saw a free spirit. Today her friend wore a two-piece Nigerian-styled dress and pants. It's caramel color contrasted with her cocoa-colored complexion. She added a few inches to her petite frame with a matching head wrap that was bound around her naturally locked hair.

"Let's get in my car and go for a ride—nowhere in particular. We can stop at the donut shop at the corner and get a hot chocolate. I want to talk this out with you and I'm tired of getting wet."

With their hot chocolate, Leesa headed toward the public park that ran alongside the main road in the area. She parked across from a basketball court where young boys played, despite the rain, high-fivin' and talking trash after each successful basket. Shelly envied their carefree lives and easy camaraderie they enjoyed on the courts. Most likely by now, some of their innocence disappeared that would shape their outlook.

"What's troubling you? Work? Home? Family?"

"Out of all this mess, there's someone. Someone I wanted to be close to." Shelly's hands twisted and turned in her lap.

"That's a good thing, right?"

Shelly nodded. "At least I think so. It's not too soon, is it? To want to be with someone?"

Leesa laughed. "Oh, good heavens, no. That's the hard part. I guess there's lots of doubts eating at you at this very minute?"

Shelly sighed. "You got that right. I'm not completely comfortable. One of the problems is that I'm not sure if it's the fear or my intuition. I think he might be using me."

"Whoa, that's deep. Let's see if we can sift through this. Do you have any evidence to back up your feelings?"

Shelly thought about it. "When I first met him, I thought he was pretty cool. Then by chance, I started to work for his father and, boy, did he change! He accused me of coming after him for his money." Shelly's lip curled with disgust. "Anyway, a truce was declared and then things heated up between us. And later, he threw it back in my face that I could be after him for his money."

"Just like that." Leesa squinted thoughtfully.

"Well, some other things happened in between that got him upset."

"Maybe you got caught in those other things and he lashed out at you."

Shelly didn't answer. Seemed logical, but it hurt nevertheless. Plus the money issue would always be divisive.

"Is talking to him an option?"

"No way. It wouldn't matter, anyway. We're from two worlds, distinctly different with values and priorities that are more than an arm's length distance from each other. For a brief time, I lost myself to a fantasy. But I'll bounce right back. It's in my genes."

"Baloney! The only thing in your jeans is your big ole butt. You're letting fear stand in your way. I may not have known you before everything that happened. What I've learned so far makes me proud to know you." Leesa took Shelly's hand and squeezed it. "You're loyal, thoughtful, and determined. Qualities that will bridge any gap."

Shelly took a deep breath, and a small smile shakily appeared. "You're so kind."

"Kind has nothing to do with it. Listen up, Shelly. Your life has been altered by what happened, but don't allow who you were to wither. That inner turmoil that's tearing you to pieces is the 'old you,' carefree, trusting, loving, warring with the 'new you,' hurt, scared, distrustful. You need to be more aware, but it doesn't mean that you have to bury your natural feelings."

Tears slid down Shelly's face as her body released the tension from the past days. "You've helped me more than I could have helped myself. I never thought that I would want a relationship. I didn't want to be in that vulnerable position. And, I certainly didn't go after this situation. Somehow, it is as if we were drawn together and I suppose we both have to battle our inner demons." Shelly hiccuped and laughed at the same time. "I'm still afraid to take the first step. But I'm even more afraid of not doing anything."

Leesa joined her with a few tears. Shelly hugged her best friend, thinking how lucky she was to have such a support system in place. Leesa always referred to the lotus flower and how it blossomed in muddy swamps. She'd need that symbol to keep steadfast in her quest for complete recovery.

Shelly waited for the doorman to announce her arrival. She'd been summoned by Justin's secretary to be there at eight o'clock sharp. The efficient executive assistant ignored her automatic refusal and continued on with her missive that it concerned her niece.

At seven fifty-five, she stood in the lobby of a luxury apartment building, Justin's home. Conflicted with her decision, she was nervous. In a few minutes, she'd be face-to-face with Justin, although he had not personally called her. Yet she could have demanded that she be told the news about her niece, rather than giving in so easily and agreeing to see him.

The doorman got the okay and escorted her to the elevator. He slid a key above the numbered panels, punched in a number, and then stepped out. Whether the doorman accompanied her or not didn't matter. Security cameras in each corner of the elevator had her in their sights.

Shelly studied her reflection in the elevator doors. Everything seemed in order. She'd pulled her hair into a ponytail, made no effort to wear makeup, not even lipstick. It wasn't a social visit. She wore stretch pants and a long cotton shirt with sleeves rolled up at the elbows.

The elevator stopped with barely a bump and the doors

opened. To her surprise, she stepped directly into Justin's living room. He rose from a chair and covered the speaker part of the receiver pinched between his shoulder and head. "I'll be off the phone in a sec," he mouthed.

She nodded. Her heart hammered against her chest. Her system was on overload: Justin in casual crisp white pants and an equally white shirt opened at the chest. His feet, well, they were bare. He looked comfortable in his home. His turf.

She walked in slowly, her head almost revolving in a complete circle.

Nice place.

The living room had a sunken floor. The furniture set had been arranged in a semicircle to face an ornate fireplace. Shelly smiled to see her favorite colas sitting on ice. She grabbed one and walked over to the balcony.

The view of downtown Baltimore took her breath away with the thousands of lights winking along the skyline. The Harbor, Camden Yards Stadium, and even the new Ravens Stadium sat less than two miles away. Several docked boats hosted onboard parties. Shelly leaned onto the rail sipping her cola, enjoying the night air. Up here she felt as if she sat on the top of the world away from the noise and confusion below. She hadn't known what the big deal was about living in a penthouse until this moment.

She heard him approach, but waited for him to address her.

"Hope you didn't mind coming up here?"

She turned around to face him. "Not at first, no. Besides, I was curious to see where and how you lived."

He waved his hand casually. "This is my place, has been for about three years. This is where I hide when I've had enough. But since Dad's illness, I moved back to the house. And I'll be there until the end." His face showed his pain.

She wanted to comfort him and share in his grief. But that was over. "Tanya?"

"Oh, yes, I have some news. I know where she is."

Shelly yelled out a "whoop." She clapped her hands, feeling giddy from the good news. "How?"

"Never mind the details. Actually, I just got the address a few minutes ago. That was the call." He pulled out a scrap of paper from his pocket. "I guess we can call the police now."

"Is she with the guy? The one who makes the IDs?"

"No. She's hiding out in a motel." He looked at the address. "Not in the best part of town, either."

"Call the police for the guy. I want to go for my niece."

"Yes and no."

"Excuse me?"

"The police have been called for the creep. My driver will get your niece. She'll be brought here. Then you and she can talk before going to the family. He'll call to let me know that he's got her."

His words infuriated her. "With a snap of your fingers, you've made it all better. I want to get my niece. I got her into this mess and I have to get her out. Who are you to stick your nose into my family's business? You didn't want me sticking mine in yours." She seethed, ready to explode and rip something apart.

"Thank you, Justin. You're so kind, Justin. I really appreciate it, Justin," he stated, with mocking sarcasm. His mouth tightened, and he glared back at her. "I didn't just snap my fingers, nor am I trying to upstage you. It's really not about you. But you're so busy feeling sorry for yourself that you can't see three feet ahead of you. The girl shouldn't be in that neighborhood. You shouldn't be in that neighborhood, and I sure as hell don't want to be in that neighborhood. Lucky me, I can send my driver into the war zone to get your niece out."

Shelly held the glass against her head. His words made

her ashamed of her behavior. She'd really stepped into this one. Maybe she could throw herself over the balcony.

"I can't help you reach your niece when she gets here. That's up to you. I did what I could to help you." His voice softened. "I did what I did to say I'm sorry."

Shelly gulped. He was turning the screws tighter. The guilty knot tightened in her throat.

He took the glass away from her head and set it down on the table. As each tear fell from the corner of her eyes, he stroked them away gently with his thumb. His eyes held no malice, ulterior motive, or anger. And then he pulled her against his chest and held her. "What would you like for dinner?"

She pulled away, laughing and wiping away the tears. "I'm not hungry."

"I bet you haven't eaten since lunchtime."

He took her silence as an affirmative. "How about an omelet? Come into the kitchen and keep me company while I cook."

The kitchen was not exceptionally big, but everything sat neatly in its place. Shelly perched on a bar stool, positioned herself to see him prepare the meal. With great flourish, he created a three-cheese omelet accompanied by toasted bagels. It was too bad the amount of time consuming the tasty fare didn't compensate for all his time and effort.

"Well, now that we've eaten, let's go relax in the living room. If you don't mind, I would rather not watch television."

The phone rang and Justin picked up immediately. He gave Shelly a thumbs-up sign after setting the receiver down. "She'll be here in twenty minutes."

"Thank God."

She followed him and took a seat on the floor, their backs against his beige leather couch. From his seat next to her, he used the remote to turn on a jazz CD selection. Soft music flowed from speakers placed strategically around the room. Shelly settled back with a satisfying sigh.

"Would you like some wine?"

"No, thanks. I would take another cola." No need to muck up her brain, especially when Tanya was on her way and she didn't have a clue what to expect from her.

Justin replenished her drink and flopped down next to her. His casual attitude set her at ease. She didn't want to question it. She wanted to enjoy the moment and hope that he didn't hold her recent behavior against her.

"Isn't it a beautiful night?" he remarked as they looked out through the open balcony doors. "It's so clear that you can actually see the stars. When I was staying here, I would sit in the dark with the doors open and stargaze." He gave an embarrassed laugh. "Those were the nights I just wanted to be alone. Do you ever feel that way?"

"Yes, I do. It's a great way to end the day after dealing with traffic, bosses, just life's ups and downs. Instead of stargazing, though, I listen to music while I soak in the tub."

He rolled over onto his stomach, grinning wickedly, "That sounds tempting."

"Well, my tub is built for one."

"And mine's built for two, or more, any way you like it."

She grunted at his indecent proposal. Her face flushed with traitorous thoughts. She took a gulp of her cola to cool the burgeoning flames of her passion.

"Shelly," he called softly to her, "I've changed my mind."

She held her breath, waiting for him to continue.

"A while back, I had said, foolishly, that I couldn't promise anything."

She nodded. Her heart pounded and she was sure the vein at the base of her throat visibly pulsated with every beat.

"Blame it on male pride. I couldn't allow anyone, especially you, to force me into a relationship. I ran away from the kind of interpersonal involvement that you read about in the perfect stories or movies, where the man can't exist without the woman."

"Your wife?" She chose not to look at him then. She'd listen to his words, the nuances of his voice, to hear the truth of his relationship with his wife.

"I loved Wanda. And probably somewhere in my heart, there is a part of me that still loves her. But there's a part of me that can't let go of the pain she put me through."

"You don't have to." Shelly heard the mixture of anger and pain in his voice and it affected her. Without knowing Wanda, she disliked the woman. She didn't want him to relive any bad memories.

"In a strange way, it's therapeutic to share this with you." He looked up into her face. "Unless you'd rather not listen."

"No, please go ahead." She touched his cheek to reassure him that she could handle whatever he told her.

"I fell for Wanda with all her faults and wild ways. I believed that I could give her respectability and she would change. That I could love her enough for both of us. That one day, she would learn to love me, just a little. Sounds tragic?" He laughed bitterly. "Instead, I earned her disgust and soon after, her many flings became known to me. She showed no effort in hiding it, almost taking perverse pleasure in having me catch her. I may be a fool, but I was ready to cut her loose. When I dropped the divorce papers on her lap, she announced that she was pregnant." His lips curled with disgust. "Of course, doubt entered my mind that the baby was mine. But I had no anger against the child and decided that until the paternity test was taken, everything would be put on hold. Wanda wasn't in any hurry to get the test. She pretended to be the perfect wife, accompanying me to public events, entertaining my father with gourmet meals. I began to doubt my earlier decision." Justin closed his eyes and pounded his head with curled fists. "Then she had her cycle and I realized that she'd played me for a fool. I gave her two choices, the airport or the bus terminal. I packed her bags and dragged her to the car. I was on my way to the airport when we had the car accident."

"Where was she going?"

"To her sister's in Arizona."

"How do you feel now?"

"I feel sad that her family can't have her be with them. But for me, I feel nothing. She'd killed that a long time ago. I wish that I could forgive her. I haven't been able to and that haunts me because it's the last thing she asked of me, before she died." He took her hand and leaned his head into her palm. "What kind of man does that make me?"

Her heart ached for his pain. "You are a man who makes his father proud. You are a man that makes a woman's heart melt."

"My mother was a beautiful woman. I don't mean in a fashion sense, although she was that. She had the most generous heart and it always had room for one more. When she died, I thought my father would be devastated. Don't get me wrong, he was sad, upset, withdrawn. But they had shared a full life making each moment count. They had arguments and disagreements, but they managed not to have permanent divisive issues between them. I envied that. I want that." He clutched her hand a little tighter.

The phone rang. Justin spoke briefly into it and hung up. "Tanya is on her way up."

Shelly jumped up from the floor, not wishing to seem too casual in Justin's apartment in front of her niece. No need to give the young girl the wrong impression. The ice had melted between them, but she couldn't think for how long.

"Would you button up your shirt? And wipe that silly grin off your face," she scolded, straightening her own clothes. Gosh, she was a mess. Her palms had gotten clammy and she wished that she'd rehearsed what she wanted to say, rather than swooning under Justin's gaze.

"I'll do even more than that, ma'am. I will get my shoes and head out for an hour or so."

The elevator swooshed open. Shelly bit back her retort and waited for Tanya to emerge.

"Hi, Aunty."

"Tanya." Shelly walked slowly forward, reading her niece's face for any signs of hostility or distaste. She pulled her into a warm embrace, blinking back tears of relief. "I'm glad you're safe."

"Can we sit?" Tanya laughed shakily. "My legs feel a bit wobbly."

Shelly led her to the couch. Justin stepped out of his bedroom and walked past the couple. "I'll show myself out. Tanya, I'll make the introductions when I return."

Tanya's face registered surprise. She looked back and forth from Shelly to Justin. "You're living here now?" Her eyes wide with shock and the old teasing sparks.

"No."

"Hmm. Do you want to?"

"I see you haven't changed," Shelly remarked dryly.

Tanya looked down and plucked at the miniskirt that offered little more coverage than a Band-Aid. "I guess it's about time that I do change, huh?"

Shelly remained silent, desperately wracking her brain to come up with the right words.

"I wasn't running away. I mean, I guess I was. But I also needed time to think. My life, my head, it's all screwed up. I don't know whether I'm coming or going." She sighed and leaned back against the couch. "Oh, I better not, everything is so clean and white." She sat up, stroking her hand along the couch. "Obviously, he's never had kids."

Shelly reached for Tanya's hand and clasped it between hers. She noted the nails bitten down to the raw flesh with chipped nail polish. Her heart ached for the teenager locked in a body on the verge of adulthood. "I've listened to your apologies. I've even apologized on your behalf. I've accepted your words of repentance and supported any effort you made to mend your ways. But it's time to face facts that you cannot do this alone. And you shouldn't."

"Please, don't mention the psychiatrist thing again," Tanya cried out in panic.

"No, no," Shelly soothed. "I have a proposal for you, which I haven't even discussed with the other persons involved. As far as I'm concerned, the matter isn't up for negotiation."

"What is it?"

"I want you to move in with one of your parents." Shelly held her breath, but also held on to Tanya's hand to show her support.

"When you hit, you hit hard."

"I learned a thing or two from you."

"Which one?"

"First, I have to tell you that they are both in town. Actually your mom arrived a couple of hours ago. Your father is at the house. I'm not sure where you mother will stay. It'll be a smart move to talk to both of them before making any decisions. It's time for all of you to make a decision as a unit."

"I don't think I could stand to have them see me as a failure. You don't judge me, but they will."

"Don't underestimate them, Tanya. No matter what happens, we're family." She shucked her niece's chin. "Remember that the next time you have an urge to run away."

An important message from the ARABESQUE Editor

Dear Arabesque Reader,

Because you've chosen to read one of our Arabesque romance novels, we'd like to say "thank you"! And, as a special way to thank you, we've selected four more of the books you love so well to send you for FREE!

Please enjoy them with our compliments, and thank you for continuing to enjoy Arabesque...the soul of romance.

Karen Thomas
Senior Editor,
Arabesque Romance Novels

Check out our website at
www.arabesquebooks.com

SPECIAL OFFER!
4 FREE BOOKS

ARABESQUE ®

A PRODUCT OF

BET BOOKS™

3 QUICK STEPS
TO RECEIVE YOUR "THANK YOU" GIFT
FROM THE EDITOR

Send this card back and you'll receive 4 FREE Arabesque novels! The introductory shipment of 4 Arabesque novels – a $23.96 value – is yours absolutely FREE!

There's no catch. You're under no obligation to buy anything. You'll receive your introductory shipment of 4 Arabesque novels absolutely FREE (plus $1.99 to offset the costs of shipping & handling). And you don't have to make any minimum number of purchases—not even one!

We hope that after receiving your books you'll want to remain an Arabesque subscriber. But the choice is yours to continue or cancel, anytime at all! So why not take us up on our invitation to receive 4 Arabesque Romance Novels, with no risk of any kind. You'll be glad you did!

Call us
TOLL-FREE
at 1-800-770-1963

THE EDITOR'S "THANK YOU" GIFT INCLUDES:

- 4 books absolutely FREE (plus $1.99 for shipping and handling)
- A FREE newsletter, *Arabesque Romance News*, filled with author interviews, book previews, special offers, and more!
- No risks or obligations. You're free to cancel whenever you wish... with no questions asked.

Accepting the four introductory books for FREE (plus $1.99 to offset the cost of shipping & handling) places you under no obligation to buy anything. You may keep the books and return the shipping statement marked "cancelled". If you do not cancel, about a month later we will send 4 additional Arabesque novels, and you will be billed the preferred subscriber's price of just $4.00 per title. That's $16.00 for all 4 books for a savings of 33% off the cover price (Plus $1.99 for shipping and handling). You may cancel at any time, but if you choose to continue, every month we'll send you 4 more books, which you may either purchase at the preferred discount price. . . or return to us and cancel your subscription.

PLACE
STAMP
HERE

ARABESQUE ROMANCE BOOK CLUB
P.O. Box 5214
Clifton NJ 07015-5214

Ten

Most of the homes in her parents' neighborhood stood dark and silent. Midnight was only two minutes away as Shelly drove Tanya home. She'd briefly considered having her niece spend the night with her and meet with her parents in the morning. A flashback of Tanya's quick disappearance changed her mind. She'd have to kick herself over being duped twice and her family would be too outdone with her latest decision.

She steered the car along the quiet side streets, occasionally passing another car. Her mind sped ahead, preparing her for the various reactions to her proposal.

"Scared?" Tanya asked.

"I should be asking you that," Shelly replied, grateful for the chance to stop the second-guessing.

"Just a tad. You'll be there with me?"

Shelly turned and smiled. "Yes. I'll be at your side. We'll fight the dragons together."

"Don't let Grandma hear you call her that."

They giggled, more from the case of jitters than anything else. Shelly pulled into the driveway and turned off the engine. She took a few minutes to gather her wits. "Let's go."

She entered the house and disabled the alarm. All the lights were turned off, except for the one on the cooking range. Her mother preferred not having the house in complete darkness.

Patrick must be in the basement in the extra guest room. She was surprised that he wasn't lying on the couch watching TV in the family room. No sound came from upstairs, either. Everyone had gone down for the night, but she expected her mother to be up still and watching the late night talk shows. She motioned to Tanya to go into the family room, while she headed up the stairs to her parents' room.

She'd barely knocked on the door when her mother prompted her to enter. Once she'd told her mother the news, Shelly delegated the job to her to wake the rest of the household. Fifteen minutes later, her father came down half asleep to the family room, while her brother came up because of the footsteps he heard. Neither saw Tanya immediately, who had taken the chair farthest away in the room.

"Oh, my God. Tanya?" Patrick questioned. He blinked rapidly, ridding his eyes of sleepiness. In a grand gesture, he closed the distance between his daughter and himself, grabbed her up in a bear hug, lifting her off her feet. "I'm so glad to see you. Are you okay?"

Tanya hugged her father, resting her head in his thick neck. "I'm okay, Daddy."

He put her down and held her away from him, studying her from head to foot. "You're sure you're okay?"

"Yes. Yes." Tanya's face lit up at seeing her father. Her smile transformed the once sulky child into a vibrant young lady.

"Well, what about me? I want a hug too," Shelly's father prompted.

Tanya walked over and hugged her grandfather. "I really missed you, Grandpa."

"Me too, hon. Did you get to eat?"

"Just tea."

"What the heck is tea! Nothing but colored water from some chopped-up leaves. You need a helping of meat loaf and mashed potatoes. Your grandmother's been cooking up a storm since her baby boy came home," Shelly's father teased.

"Clara, don't stand over there and make the girl have to go to you. Come and hug your granddaughter."

"Humph." Shelly's mother stood her ground with her arms folded around her robe.

Shelly sent a silent wish Tanya's way, hoping that she wouldn't choose this moment to assert her independence. She owed lots of apologies and her mother would not be so easily manipulated like the men.

"Grandma, I'm sorry to have caused you so much grief and disappointment. As much as I wanted to stay here, I really wanted to be with my parents, but I didn't know how to get anyone to listen to me."

"I would have listened."

"I mean no disrespect, but you were so busy trying to win me over with toys, clothes, and giving me anything I asked for that I started to resent the very people that helped me. Then I did stuff for attention, but soon it became a habit. The harder I tried to make it better, the deeper I got in trouble."

"So how long are you at home this time around?"

"That's what I came to tell everyone."

Shelly kept an eye on her mother, just in case she unknowingly made it more difficult than it needed to be.

"I want to go live with my mother."

"What!" Patrick shouted.

"Suits me," a familiar voice sounded.

Everyone shifted attention toward the doorway where Faye stood with a fashionable, full-length robe. A former ballerina, with her tall, slender frame, she stood rigid and erect. For someone who was asleep a few minutes ago, her hair lay neatly in gentle waves past her shoulder. Her Creole heritage added to her exotic beauty, a trait that Tanya shared.

"Hello, Faye," Shelly greeted, wary of the cool assessment that her former sister-in-law gave her.

Faye merely nodded in her direction.

Clara stepped forward, putting aside her reservations. "Everyone, have a seat. Looks like we'll be up for a few hours."

"I don't think so," Faye sniffed. "I need a full eight hours of sleep. Tanya, come here and give me a hug."

Tanya crossed the room and hugged her mother. "I want to be clear, Mother, that I've decided to live with you, not because you have shown me the slightest evidence that you could do a better job in raising me than Grandma or even Dad."

"Really?"

"Yes, really. But I am at a point in my life where I need my mother, now more than ever. I want you to give me attention and don't treat me as if I just came into the family." Tanya walked over to Patrick and put her hand through the crook of his arm and faced her mother again. "I want to be able to come visit you, Dad, as often as I like."

"Demanding, aren't you?" Faye stated, clearly taken aback by her daughter who stood eye-to-eye with her.

"Yes, and only because at first you didn't ask my opinion. You treated me as less than a child because even a child has feelings and can understand things that you take for granted. You left me here without a second thought because it was convenient for both of you."

Shelly was the first to take a seat. Her niece's self-confidence pleased her and she realized that after tonight, Tanya would be okay. She curled up on the couch and watched the family drama draw out, knowing that at the end Tanya would leave with Faye. Patrick would see his daughter more often than before and her parents could once again enjoy retirement, while her mother could now focus all her attentions on controlling certain aspects of her life. It was as happy an ending as could be expected in real life.

* * *

After such a full week, Shelly looked forward to the weekend. Even her birthday couldn't bring her down. Helping Tanya pack her clothes and other personal possessions the night before had put her in a good mood. Patrick had left earlier in the morning, promising Tanya that he would be there for her. Faye and Tanya planned to leave tomorrow morning, with the arrangement that she'd spend the summer with her grandparents.

With her mood on the upswing, it only soared to new heights when Justin offered to take her out to dinner for a small birthday celebration. This time she accepted with no lingering doubts. She'd helped put her family back together, she'd spend her birthday with someone who seemed mildly attracted to her. What more could she ask for?

Prompt and every bit a gentleman, Justin arrived at her door with a single red rose. As they sped down the highway in his BMW, Shelly sank into the leather seat that molded to her rear end and back with plush padding. A gentle breeze whipped through her hair, but she was too happy to care about being mussed. How many times had she enjoyed a twilight drive in an expensive, sporty car, with a devilishly handsome man—friend?

She'd leave the question unanswered, for now.

"Why are you smiling and sighing?"

"You made my day, that's all. The flower. Taking me to dinner." She touched his arm. "It was really sweet."

He patted her knee. "Sweet for the sweet." He gave a sideways glance. "Besides, you're one year closer to forty."

"Hmm. I suppose in a few years, you'll share your first-hand experience."

"Touché, birthday lady."

Shelly admired the scenery, a contented smile on her face. Noticing a few familiar landmarks, she focused on the green sign mounted on an overpass as they approached. A half mile later, Justin exited on the ramp to Annapolis. Puzzled, she wondered if he was taking her to a restaurant on the waterfront. No need to worry, he could have taken her to a shack and she'd be wearing the same silly smile.

Later she'd have him take her to her parents'. The idea popped into her head and she didn't shove it to the back. It would be an official visit to her parents', something that not many men in her life had experienced. Even her mother could be too shocked to do anything embarrassing. She couldn't deny, however, the nervousness from the idea.

"Stop sitting there and staring at me."

"Can't help it. I like the view," Shelly replied, honestly. She enjoyed watching him handle the powerful car. His easy manner exuded confidence. Suits gave him an air of an executive businessman, but the casual white polo shirt and khaki shorts softened the buppie image and made him into one of the regular folk.

"At least tell me what you're thinking? That secretive smirk is getting to me."

"If you really want to know," she teased. "I wondered what my parents would think of you if you met them. They live around here, you know."

"I'm sure I could win over your mother," he bragged.

"No argument there. You'd be a shoe-in with her."

"Your father, on the other hand—"

"That would be fun."

"You'd better not leave me alone with him."

"What's it worth to you?" she inquired, playing itsy-bitsy spider up his arm.

"What's it worth to you? If you don't help me, I'll have to mention how you left your toothbrush on my sink."

She gasped. "You wouldn't?"

"Try me."

"You play dirty."

"All the time."

After a few minutes, she noticed they had driven through several residential areas. No restaurants were in this area, maybe a few fast-food restaurants, but nothing special. "Where are we going?" Her curiosity got the better of her.

"You'll see," he answered.

She knew the neighborhoods and various streets. "Are you taking me to my parents' for dinner?"

Justin turned and answered her with his brilliant smile. "Wouldn't you like to know?"

A few minutes later he parked in front of the house. Its historic architecture was still impressive as it approached its hundredth anniversary. The four-bedroom, redbrick colonial sat back on the property. A snakelike driveway lined with white tulips cut through manicured landscapes from the roadway to the door.

Her parents' cars weren't there. But Justin must have known that because he had obviously gotten directions from them. Worst case, she had her key.

Justin came around and opened her door, offering his hand for assistance. He continued to hold her hand as they made their way up the path. Knocking before she retrieved her key, she waited for an answer.

Deciding that no one was home, she unlocked the door and entered. Justin remained on the porch. Shelly walked into the foyer, looking into the living room on her left and the study on her right. There wasn't any sign of anyone. She kept walking toward the kitchen area, peeking into the family room.

She passed the downstairs powder room and caught a blur of motion out of the corner of her eye.

She froze and let out a short scream.

When her mind reconnected with her body, she turned only to realize that Justin wasn't behind her. The adrenaline shot through her system. She vented an earsplitting scream and ran back toward the door.

"Justin, run!" She barreled into him, pushing him toward the door. The idiot, she thought. What was he grinning at when there was an intruder in the house?

"Surprise!"

Several voices yelled in discordant fashion. She jumped and cringed against Justin's chest. People emerged from different places in the house: behind the massive mahogany bookcases in the living room, the cherry-wood china closet in the dining room, the island in the kitchen, and even from within the pantry closet in the hallway, next to the kitchen. At least ten college friends, a handful of coworkers from Dr. Calloway's office, and even Leesa stepped out, wishing happy birthday.

Justin disappeared and returned from the living room with a huge bouquet of red and white long-stemmed roses and a gift-wrapped box, small enough to fit in his palm, which he presented to her.

She beamed, a bit embarrassed, but pleased at the attention.

Her mother came over and hugged her tightly. "You go, girl."

Shelly responded with a tight hug.

Her father kissed her cheek. "It's not over yet."

All eyes turned toward the family room. Phillip in his wheelchair emerged with Mildred at his side.

Impulsively, Shelly ran over and hugged him, immensely thrilled to see him. They made a complete picture with Justin and both sets of parents, together with her, sharing her birthday.

"I want you to know, honey, this was all Mr. Thornton's idea," her mother confessed, refilling the punch bowl.

"Phillip? How did he get in touch with you?"

"No, not that Mr. Thornton. Justin. He called me and said

he wanted to surprise you." Clara leaned back and looked toward the living room where everyone had gathered. "So you kept your employer a secret from me. No wonder you were putting in so much overtime." She patted Shelly's hand when she opened her mouth to protest. "That's okay, you're forgiven. You know, Shelly, you've landed a fine catch, thanks to me." Clara stepped into the hallway and openly admired Justin, who chatted with Leesa. "He looks good, sounds good, and even smells good." Shelly rolled her eyes at her mother and the two women laughed. "It's good to see that sparkle back in your eye, daughter."

Shelly didn't know how to react to Justin with so many people present. She busied herself in the kitchen, filling the ice trays with water. "We'll see how long that sparkle lasts."

"Stop being pessimistic. It's time for your life to turn around. Don't you think so?"

Shelly didn't want to analyze it. If she did, she could fine a million reasons why she should end it before anyone got hurt. Right now, she'd pretend that her mother's words were absolute.

"You're right." To change the subject, she asked, "Where's the music?"

As if someone heard her, the music blared from the basement. Shelly laughed. It was an ole school jam by Parliament Funkadelics. The seventies' synthesized sounds vibrated throughout the house and she was already swinging her hips and moving toward the source. A group of not so shy guests led the way toward the basement to dance. Shelly kissed her mom's cheek and followed the dance line.

"Oh, my," Shelly exclaimed. Streamers, balloons, and birthday decorations dressed the basement into a festive colorful party room. Someone had even attached a disco ball in the center of the ceiling. A lone strobe light caused the familiar reflective spots of light to dance on the walls in the semidarkened room.

Shelly bobbed to the beat. She felt lucky and couldn't believe that so many people came. For her. For her birthday. Feeling the heavy beat of the music, Shelly started to dance with no one in particular.

Someone grabbed her arm and pulled her around. "You can't dance without me," Justin shouted over the music. He performed a comical routine of poppin', sending Shelly into peals of laughter.

"Are you going to break-dance next?" She wished she had a camera.

He winked at her. "If you insist." With that, Justin began his break dance routine and then dropped to the floor to spin on his back. His body retaliated and he emitted a groan, ending in a tangled heap.

Biting her lower lip to suppress an erupting chuckle, Shelly helped him up.

"Oh, just go ahead and laugh. It's better than seeing your eyes water like that." His irritation just added to the merriment and she obliged.

After an hour of dancing, Shelly begged for a rest. Upstairs she refreshed with a glass of punch over lots of ice. She wiped the perspiration from her forehead and fanned her heated face with a napkin. It provided minimal reprieve. The basement had heated up a few degrees with the serious dancing taking place.

Her mother stepped away from her conversation with Phillip. "Looks like you been working up a sweat down there."

"Yep. I can't remember the last time I danced like that. Gosh, those songs took me way back—college, even high school. I guess that means I'm getting old."

"Let's go out on the patio. It's a little cooler out there." She hooked her arm into her daughter's. "We haven't had a chance to talk lately. How are you doing?"

"I'm fine. Work is great. The sessions at the center are getting easier for me. Overall, I'm feeling better."

Her mother sized her up, smoothing back damp stray wisps of hair around her daughter's face. "You do look better."

Justin walked past the doorway and her mother immediately looked in his direction. She tilted her head toward him. "Shelly, I know that I rib on you a lot about finding someone, especially about him. Mainly it's to get you to move on with your life and not let this ugly experience consume you. But on the other hand, you don't need a man to be complete or whole." She lifted her daughter's chin. "Remember that, okay?"

Shelly nodded. "I know, Mom. I can honestly say that's not what's happening with me and Justin."

"The transformation that I'm seeing before me can mean only one thing." She gave Shelly a look, first questioning and then knowing.

Shelly turned her head away from her mother's sharp eyes. Even as a child, she could keep nothing away from her mother. It was what reinforced the bond between them. "Yes, Mom," Shelly corroborated her mother's intuition. "I'm in love." She said it, pure and simple. And she liked saying those words. Inside, her heart rejoiced. It won the battle.

"Enough chitchat," her father broke in. "It's time to open presents and then cut the cake."

"No one does that anymore, Dad." Shelly laughed at her father.

"What do you mean? Everyone is waiting." Her guests all echoed his sentiment. She raised her hand in defeat.

As she sat in the middle of the living room, her presents were brought to her one at a time with an announcement of who provided the gift. Mounds of wrapping paper grew at her feet, as Shelly uncovered silk scarves, books, jewelry, and even two concert tickets to see one of her favorite singers.

The last gift was handed to her. From Justin. Immediately the room quieted. Shelly blushed under the intense scrutiny. She couldn't think of what it could be and unwrapped it carefully. Her mind raced to think of the possibilities.

After the wrapping paper was gone, the simple white box sat in the palm of her hand. Fingers trembling slightly, she opened the top. Soft tissue, which she picked through carefully covered the surprise.

Her stomach tightened at the exquisite item. A gold charm bracelet sat on cotton padding. Extended from its links was a key and heart charm.

Everyone "oohed" and "ahhed" appreciatively. Shelly gave in to the demands and passed the gift around for all to see. She looked over to where Justin stood. He leaned casually against the wall.

"Thank you," she mouthed, not trusting her voice.

He nodded, a lazy, sexy smile playing on his lips.

"Ooh, look, the heart is inscribed." Mildred held it up between two fingers.

Several heads clustered around eagerly trying to see the inscription. Shelly swallowed the lump in her throat. Her heart beat erratically and her hands turned clammy. She walked over to the huddled group, who parted, creating a path for her. Mildred held the bracelet out and Shelly took it with shaky fingers.

"Go ahead, tell us what it says," her mother prompted.

Shelly licked her lips. It didn't help. Her mouth was dry. Her lips were dry. A kiss from Justin would help. Such scandalous thoughts popped more frequently into her head and they proved to be less shocking each time. But nevertheless, now wasn't the time.

"A promise," she read. She didn't have time to react because everyone clapped and hollered, whooping it up in

raucous fashion. But she didn't mind since it matched the excitement raging inside her.

Still leaning against the door, Justin accepted the teasing from everyone, even her father. A bit shy, but feeling the urge to show her appreciation, Shelly went over and hugged him. Short and sweet.

"Time to cut the cake," her father proclaimed.

"This isn't a wedding, Dad."

"Justin, stand next to my stubborn daughter and cut the cake. I'd like a piece before my birthday."

Side by side, she stood with Justin, feeling as if she were rehearsing for a wedding. Of course, not hers or anything like that. Her mother chattered on with camera in hand, taking turns blinding her and Justin with the annoying flash.

To Shelly, everyone's voices sounded like bees buzzing in her ear. Her attention only had time for the man who stood next to her.

Neither Shelly nor Justin looked at each other, but she was quite aware of him as each movement, however slight, made his forearm touch hers. The soft intake of his breath let her know that he was also affected.

Mildred pushed Phillip forward.

"Oh, Phillip, I haven't had a chance to talk to you."

"That's okay, sweetheart. It makes me feel good to see you enjoying yourself."

She was glad she could contribute to bringing a smile to his face. If only for a few hours, she could take his mind off the bank issues and even himself.

"Blow out those candles and make a wish."

Shelly complied. Eyes closed, she took a moment to think about her wish. A birthday only came once a year and she did not want to waste her wish. Justin had all but declared his intent tonight. So wishing for him was unnecessary. Instead, she decided that she would wish for happiness between them as long as it lasted.

It wasn't a greedy wish. Besides, she was cynical enough to believe that it couldn't last forever. As she watched the wisps of smoke drifting from the candles, she imagined this moment and her time with him to be equally temporary.

"Shelly, stop daydreaming and cut the cake." Impatience ruled the crowd.

"Hostile people. Fine, I've cut the cake. Happy?"

"No," they cried in unison. "Kiss. Kiss. Kiss."

He must have sensed her discomfort because he clasped her hand behind the tablecloth. The small gesture away from prying eyes gave her some courage.

Together they cut into the yellow cake, slicing off a small square for each other. He fed her piece first, which she daintily nibbled from his fingers. Then, it was her turn. She carefully placed a piece in front of his lips. He took it from her, briefly slipping his lips over her fingers. Shelly bit down hard on her lips to suppress a moan.

The two had each locked in the other's gaze. As their heads drew closer, Shelly began to panic. Embarrassment remained a factor, but she was more afraid that she would lose her composure and fawn like a giggly schoolgirl.

Moments before his delicious full lips touched hers, he winked. It broke the tension. His quick peck was welcomed. She squeezed his hands gratefully.

After all the guests had left, Shelly sat with her parents in the family room. Everyone was exhausted.

"Thanks, Mom and Dad. I had a good time. You really surprised me."

"Hey, we can't take all the credit. Justin had a major hand in everything," her father offered.

Her mother perked up. "Did you like your gift?"

"Which one? There were so many."

Her mother threw a pillow at her playfully.

"Yes, it was beautiful, quite unexpected, though."

Justin entered the room. "Mrs. Bishop, the dishwasher is loaded and most of the rooms have been cleared of trash."

"Wow, Justin. You didn't have to do that, but it is greatly appreciated. My feet are killing me." Her mother stood and said over her shoulder, "I bet you must be tired. I'll show you to your room." He followed her out while Shelly sat staring at the two leaving the room.

"Close your mouth, Shelly, that's totally unbecoming."

Shelly stared at the doorway for a few more seconds. "Did I just hear correctly? Justin is spending the night?"

Her father returned her look with seriousness. "Yes, he is. I'm finally going to have someone to play chess with me." Then, he too stretched. "Good night, honey. Catch you in the A.M."

This had to be a dream. First, the whole birthday thing and now Justin was spending the night in her home. That event shocked her, but she couldn't get over her parents acting as if this were the most natural thing in the world.

As if Shelly and Justin were a couple.

Her heart chimed in that they *were* a couple. She loved him with everything within her. She leaned back in the reclining chair. Hugging herself, she closed her eyes and thought about the man she desperately loved.

Eleven

It was the best sleep Shelly had enjoyed in some time. Her room from childhood held many pleasant memories. The white four-poster bed with frilly bed linens, posters of various celebrities, and handbills of activist events from her college days decorated the wall, and her wide array of stuffed animals added to the charm.

The soft pink and white color scheme had a soothing effect. She felt safe on familiar ground. And only two doors away, Justin had spent the night. Too bad she was too tired last night to go on a night prowl. She rolled over on her stomach and yawned.

The enticing smell of a full breakfast meal chased away any lingering drowsiness. She wondered what the day would have in store for her. It had been a while since she looked forward to anything as much as this day.

Light at heart, she showered and dressed in record time. As a special touch, she sprayed on her signature spice scent. She followed a tip she had read in a fashion magazine and placed a dab behind her ears, in the crease in her forearm, and behind her knees.

Now she was ready to face the day—and Justin.

Her father was reading the newspaper when she entered the dining room. The table was already set and the food that she'd so aptly sniffed out was in large serving dishes waiting to be eaten. Her stomach rumbled. No further prompting was necessary.

"Good morning," her dad mumbled without looking at her. His routine had remained the same for most of her life. Today, nothing differed, he focused on the sport pages and all its statistics.

She greeted him, casually looking around for Justin. For the first time she noticed that the table was set for three. Hopefully, he hadn't left without saying good-bye.

Her mother entered with a platter of biscuits. The golden-top fluffy edibles piled high made Shelly's mouth water. She was convinced that her mother cooked in this manner to emphasize what Shelly missed by living on her own.

"Good morning." Her mother placed the mouthwatering fare on the table. "Justin ran out early this morning, but he said to be ready by noon when he gets back." Her mother surveyed the table, refixing the dishes that didn't meet her standards.

Shelly was disappointed that he was gone, but that changed to curiosity. "Ready for what?"

Her mother shrugged. "Didn't say. By the way, your father and I are going golfing in an hour."

Mouth full, Shelly nodded. Well, it seemed as if everyone had something to do, except her. She looked at her watch. It wouldn't be noon for another three hours. With her parents gone, she had to find something to keep her mind off what lay ahead for the day with Justin.

While her mother prepared herself to go golfing, Shelly sat contentedly patting her fully satisfied stomach. Her parents had calmly invited her boyfriend to stay, and after the surprise birthday gift, it was official. She had a boyfriend. No one seemed more amazed than she. But, it had been a while since the sun shone on her side. She leaned back in the chair, hands clasped behind her head, contented.

"So, you really like him, huh?" her father asked out of the

blue. He closed and folded his newspaper, giving her his full attention. His fatherly concern, and a bit of curiosity, showed, but it was understandable.

It was on the tip of her tongue to pretend that she didn't know what he could be referring to. "Yes, I do very much." As an afterthought, she asked, "Do you like him, Dad?" His opinion mattered, and she held her breath, waiting.

"Yes, I must say that I am impressed. You know I'm not fond of these spoiled rich kids that look down their noses." She acknowledged that issue was his pet peeve. Whenever he looked at the news, he spent the next hour discussion the problems of "uppity hooligans." Brow furrowed in deep thought, he continued, "But Justin seems genuine through and through. Besides, I have noticed how googly you get when you're with him." He looked over the top of his reading glasses studying her. "And it's important that my little girl is happy. You deserve a break."

Her father always had the ability to bring her to tears. It wasn't often that they had these heartfelt talks. But his concern and love for her were always clear to her. He was the person that she confided her innermost thoughts to because he didn't judge her. It was true that he wanted her to be happy.

"I'm not only happy, Dad." Shelly spoke candidly. "I'm in love."

He responded with a warm smile, softening his craggy features. They hugged, while Clara stood unseen at the doorway, wiping away tears.

The moment Justin pulled into the Bishops' driveway, Shelly opened the door. Not sure where they were going, she chose a peach short set. The day promised to be hot, but thankfully not humid. The lightweight cotton material would be sufficient.

He beckoned to her. When she got into the car, they both leaned forward for a casual kiss. It seemed so natural.

"You look great," he complimented. "Smelling good, too." He leaned back and demanded, "Are you trying to seduce me, woman?"

"Please, I wouldn't have to try."

"Oh." He laughed. "So, we're all that now."

"And then some." She loved their bantering. He could be so comical and lovable.

"Where are we going?" She could barely contain herself.

Justin shot her a sideways glance. He pretended that driving required his full attention, then threw her another look. At length, he answered, "To the Land of Oz."

Playfully, she jabbed at his shoulder. "Okay, Mr. Smarty-Pants, be that way. But what if I don't like where you're taking me?"

He took her hand and kissed it. "You will."

It wasn't long before Justin parked the car close to the harbor. The area already bustled with tourists and lovers of historic places. The streets lined with several restaurants and quaint shops added to the unique Old World flair characteristic of Annapolis.

"You know I've never come down here before, never had any reason to." Justin admired the nineteenth-century architecture.

Shelly viewed the buildings and surroundings with an equally appreciative interest. "It's funny how you take something for granted when it's always there. But if you go away from it for a while, something happens." She shrugged. "I guess I matured so I have a different perspective."

They strolled hand in hand, Justin leading the way. He squinted out to the area where the boats docked. "There it is."

She didn't know what he referred to, but tried to keep up with his quick long strides toward the target. Boats might not be her strength, but from the pictures she had seen in those luxury home magazines and television shows, this one qualified as a yacht. The sleek craft shone brilliantly under the afternoon sun with stark white and shiny silver trimmings. The name painted on the side read YOUR LOVEBOAT.

She smiled and wondered if Justin had deliberately picked this boat because of the name. He lifted Shelly onto the boat. His hands, strong and huge, encircled her small waist with little effort.

Since she didn't know she would be going for a boat ride, it was convenient that she wore the proper shoes. They were necessary until she got her sea legs because the boat rocked quite a bit as they pulled out into the bay. Shelly had to hold on to the rail for support, while she offered up a quick prayer.

A steady breeze blew across the deck. The sun beamed from directly overhead and the breeze offset the heat, somewhat. Many other boats of various sizes dotted the horizon. As they passed, other seafarers exchanged greetings with them. Shelly was in heaven, enjoying the salty spray as the craft sped on its way.

"You want to try steering?" Justin offered the wheel.

Shelly looked warily at it and decided that she would rather be a passenger. She shook her head.

"Where are we heading?"

"To a restaurant my father recommended on the eastern shore."

"Your father?" she asked, incredulous. "Was all this his idea?" She hoped not. She wanted it to be Justin's idea, not just acting on his father's orders or suggestions.

"No, no. I asked him for suggestions on a good seafood restaurant and that was it. The rest is me—all me. And the drive would be a little lengthy, so I thought of the boat."

Shelly's frown remained.

"Hey." He nudged her. "Don't you think I can be creative, romantic, and resourceful?"

"Creative, definitely. Resourceful, an A plus. But, romantic?" She looked doubtful.

"I bet you've never had a more romantic weekend. No need to think about it. Just go ahead and admit it." He strutted back and forth in front her. "Well?" he demanded impatiently.

Shelly had had a few dates before Toby, but that's all they were—dates. "Okay," she surrendered. "I agree." She pouted at her defeat.

Triumphant, he kissed her. She playfully bit his lip.

The restaurant didn't have the finesse she expected. The long wooden tables were better placed outside. The fish nets decorating the wall for ambience, instead darkened the interior. Because of the open windows, flies battled for the same meal as the patrons.

It took all these ingredients to make the restaurant unique. The food was rated highly and had loyal diners. She feasted on crabs that had the right amount of seasonings.

"I propose a toast."

Shelly raised her glass and waited for him to continue.

"To Shelly Bishop, the woman who has taught me to feel again."

"To Justin Thornton, the man who treats me like a lady."

After a calorie-laden birthday celebration and the huge seafood meal in various cream sauces and butter for dipping that they just consumed, Shelly feared she would have to buy a new wardrobe. With a satisfied sigh, she rested her head against Justin's shoulder.

Justin guided the craft back toward Annapolis. He placed an arm around Shelly's shoulders. "Won't it be wonderful just to keeping sailing, never touching the shores except for food and water and other necessities?"

"Only if it's with you." Shelly snuggled, reveling in their

intimacy. It felt as if they were the only people in the world. Sailing in the great expanse of water with no boats or land nearby, the solitude provided privacy.

He gave her arm a friendly squeeze. "I'm glad that I'm here with you also. We make a perfect romantic picture as we sail into the sunset. I guess we're supposed to live happily ever after."

The sunset was indeed breathtaking. Deep mixtures of burnt orange, vivid yellow, and pink presented a picture good enough for an artist's appreciative eye. Though they were inexperienced in art, they enjoyed the panoramic view nonetheless. Nature's gift to them, it seemed. It felt complete since everyone had congratulated them on being together that now even Mother Nature would do her part for them, blessing them with a radiant sunset and pleasant weather.

Bobbing on the water with only the seagulls for company, Shelly remarked, "I wish this day would never end." She touched his cheek tenderly. "I like being with you."

He looked at her and what she saw in his eyes made her stomach tighten. His raw desire lay open, vulnerable, for her to see. Today it didn't scare her like it first did at his apartment. Instead, she welcomed it.

Her fear she gladly discarded. It weighed on her, making her doubt her abilities. Thank goodness that Justin had remained determined. His success at chipping away the defensive wall she had erected could now be appreciated.

"It doesn't have to end, at least not at this moment." His deep voice with its velvet quality kept her desires stirring. He turned the engine off and sudden quiet descended. There was an air of anticipation.

Justin didn't turn from the steering wheel. He gazed out toward the horizon, only the rise and fall of his chest evident. He dropped his hand from her shoulder.

The next move lay at her feet.

Justin played the perfect gentleman. She had stated the

rules, so only she could break them. In keeping with the sounds of soft lapping water, she whispered what had been uppermost in her mind all day, "Please kiss me."

"Oh, God," Justin said. "I can't kiss you, Shelly. I can't because I can't promise to stop there." He turned to face her, his face tight with restrained emotion.

Shelly took his face and brought it down to hers. It was important that they were on the same accord. She touched her forehead to his. Eyes closed, she allowed her sense of touch to record his expression in her memory. He sucked in his breath as her hands traced his features. With a feathery touch, she outlined his lips with her fingertips.

Following her heart, she kissed him, light and quick. "You don't have to stop. I want you more than I can say." She opened her eyes to see if he understood what she had left unsaid. Though she had made the unprecedented move of giving an open invite, her inhibitions kept her from screaming for him to quench the fire deep in her belly until she passed out from exertion.

It didn't matter because Justin took her cue and kissed her long and deep. His tongue explored her mouth drawing on her responding passion. He nibbled on her lip, moving to her neck. With one hand, he pulled her head back baring the graceful line of her neck. Shelly held on to him for support. Her legs had given out on her at the first kiss.

From the soft indentation at her throat, Justin licked a trail up to her jawline. Shelly couldn't keep the satisfying groan from escaping. "I think I'm about to faint," she gasped.

"Not until I'm finished." Softly in her ear, he teased, "And, I've only begun." He released her and pulled out a blanket that he spread on the bottom of the boat. Without saying a word, he kicked off his shoes, then pulled the shirt over his head, stomach muscles rippling with each movement. He left his shorts on and sat casually awaiting her.

Shelly walked over and straddled him. The break from his

searing lips gave her a moment to breathe, to think. There was no hesitation. There would be no regrets. Today, she would satisfy herself. It might be selfish, but she wanted Justin—here and now.

Catlike, she arched her back radiating under the sun's setting rays. He opened the small buttons of her blouse that provided a thin shield from his hands. With a slight movement, he brushed her breast. The reaction within made her shiver. "I don't think I'm going to survive this."

He laughed and kissed the valley between her breasts. "I'll just have to keep reviving you, then." In a quick movement, he pulled her offending blouse over her head and threw it to the side.

The removal of her clothes coupled with the feel of his chest crushing her sensitive nipples vaporized any further inhibitions. Shelly and Justin kissed with savage intent.

While he sucked and nibbled her shoulder, he removed her bra. Justin pulled away from her to admire. She bathed in his serious consideration.

His hand cupped her breast, his thumb playing with her nipple. His head lowered. The touch of his tongue stoked the flames tantalizing the peak. Each breast received equal attention, which responded to his erotic charms.

Shifting his position, he eased her back onto the deck. Shorts removed, it was her turn to openly admire him. Sleek, brown, and tight, he stood like an African king. His beautiful body, naked and free, reflected his desire, aroused.

Shelly followed his lead, and removed her shorts and panties, while he retrieved the little foil package. Later, she would think about her bold behavior, but at this time, it was hers to enjoy.

"Woman, your sophisticated beauty first caught my eye, your caring nature made me fall in love with you, but good 'googa mooga,' you've got a body that makes me wanna sing out loud."

She blushed, basking in his words. "Enough talk."

Without further delay, he covered her with his body. When he entered, her hips lifted slightly to meet his. Her legs wrapped around his hips and she gripped his back rubbing her hands over the taut muscles of his backside.

The boat's rocking increased as the frenzy of raw desire escalated. Sweat-covered limbs intertwined while their bodies pulsated to natural rhythms. Their unspoken language of love approached its pinnacle.

Slowly, pressure built within her, peaking and receding, teasing. Shelly craved satisfaction now. Her hold tightened with her legs squeezing tightly around Justin.

"Justin!"

Like an answer to her prayer, he took her to the summit where a dam had been erected a long time ago. With her full cooperation, the dam crumbled under Justin's artful strokes. When Shelly thought she would lose her mind, floodgates opened and she crested with him. Together, they brought each other to culmination, riding out the moment.

Clasped in each other's grasp, they rested comfortably. A lingering smile came to Shelly's lips. Justin's eyes were shut, but he also wore a smile. Each lost in thought over the very advanced stages of the relationship.

"I never thought I would find anyone so sensitive—so wonderful."

"Ditto." With a soft kiss on the tip of her nose, he stated, "It's time to get back to reality, though. Better yet, it's time to get dressed before we have the Coast Guard paying us a visit because they may think no one is driving the boat."

His last remark got Shelly moving. The tender moment over, she suddenly felt shy. Each dressed quickly taking a quick look around to make sure they didn't have unnoticed observers. The coast was clear, but not very far away.

They had drifted in the right direction in more than one way.

Twelve

Justin glared at the man sitting across from him in his office. Toby, dressed in a blue suit and a crisp white shirt, looked every part the banker. His visit, as it usually was, came as a surprise to Justin. He especially did not like the way Toby forced his way past his secretary.

With great effort, he invited Toby to sit. Mainly, his gesture was to stem the gossip that probably already had snaked its way to all floors. Besides, he wanted to know what Toby's next move would be.

Toby started the conversation. Arrogance oozed from him. "Happened to be in the neighborhood, and I thought about you and my last offer."

Justin kept his hands below his desk to keep his balled fists unseen. The gall of this idiot sitting before him as if he held the world in his power.

"I thought I made myself clear at our last meeting."

Toby adjusted his tie never taking his eyes off Justin. "Well, I figured with all the unrest that your depositors and shareholders must be experiencing from the latest news, you might have reconsidered."

In a shot, Justin stood, which sent the chair rolling back where it hit the wall with a short bang.

He leaned on the desk into Toby's face, but kept a few inches between them. "Be careful, Toby. Right now, you may think that you are above the law. But I know better.

You really don't want me for an enemy. Now that I see your intent hasn't changed, you can be on your way." He walked over to the door. Resting his hand on the knob, he said, "It seems that I'm always showing you the door, Toby. You would think that you'd take the hint. You and your money are not welcomed. All this attention on my bank is wearing. Take care of *your* turf."

The office remained quiet for a few seconds. Then, Toby clapped his hands, a cynical, dangerous smile in place. "It's only begun." With his cryptic message delivered, he left.

Out of frustration, Justin slammed the door. The whole week had left him exasperated. First, the boardmembers who were approached to sell their stock claimed that they were still considering the offer. They had been impressed by the big bank's show of its latest bells and whistles. Then, Connors couldn't unearth concrete evidence that the Gillis family had started the hellish rumors, although everything pointed their way. Now, the slick charmer had boldly reiterated his position.

There was no time to go off and sulk or storm about Toby's brazen act of war. Justin looked at the pile of manila folders in his in-basket, awaiting some action from him. With a sigh, he returned to his desk. He still had a bank to run.

"Mildred, do you like the change in our young friend here?" Phillip gestured toward Shelly.

Mildred considered her for a moment and replied, "To be honest, Mr. Thornton, I had my doubts when I first suspected the cause of the change. But, the whole thing has touched my soft side and it's just beautiful."

"Here, here."

"Both of you need to stop. There's no change in me."

Shelly's face felt hot. Their bantering directed at her was harmless, but she didn't want to be the focus of attention.

The old man sat in the wheelchair while Mildred and Shelly readied his bed. A look of concern shadowed his brow. "Please, don't let my comments upset you. I'm thrilled that you have changed. You seem more at peace. And I admit that I always hoped that you and Justin would—you know."

Shelly gasped. She dared not look at Mildred. "I don't want anyone depending or expecting anything." Flustered, she plumped the pillow continually, not noticing Mildred's outstretched hand for it. "There's no guarantee!"

She could hear Phillip maneuvering the wheelchair behind her. Her task almost completed, she just wanted to be left alone. It pained her that Phillip had such high expectations. She would love for the relationship to go on and on, but no one had nailed Justin down at this point. There was nothing special about her to change that.

"No, there are no guarantees. But, that's what life is all about, isn't it? But then, you don't need one, because you have the heart of the dearest person to me. That's why I know and can say without a doubt that Justin is yours," Phillip advised, concerned.

His words comforted, but then he didn't know the dark secret in her life. What kind of relationship could they have when she couldn't even tell Justin the whole truth? Every day, she lived with the fear that he might discover that his enemy was her demon. Then what?

"Want to join me for happy hour?" Mildred invited at the end of the day.

Shelly was slightly taken aback because Mildred didn't seem the type to go hang out at noisy bars, especially with her young family and recent husband.

Seeing Shelly's hesitation, Mildred offered, "I know it seems out of place, but the kids are at my parents' for the week in South Carolina. Bob is in New York for a sales conference. So, I'm free and plan to enjoy every minute. A girls' night out."

"Well, in that case, I would love to join you." She herself was free for the evening. Actually, since Annapolis, her time shared with Justin had not increased. She realized that the present bank situation required his attention. But it seemed that before, he had made time to be with her. With firm resolve, she buried the annoying doubts.

The bar was already packed with the crowd getting off from work in the downtown Baltimore area. Everyone seemed to be having a good time, sharing stories, jokes, and their office-from-hell stories. Shelly waved from the bar where she had saved a seat for Mildred, who had just entered.

"I feel out of place." Mildred looked around, self-consciously. "You know, it's been a while since I just did something for or by myself."

Shelly chuckled. She didn't exactly feel like she belonged, but no one seemed to care. Mildred ordered her drink.

"Oh, look, they have a pool table in the back. Wanna play?" Mildred slid off the stool with Shelly following reluctantly. She didn't mind playing, but there were too many eyes to view her amateurish attempts. She squeezed through the crowd, contemplating several excuses why she couldn't play.

The sound of a man's laughter caught her attention. She couldn't identify if it was how loud he laughed or the slight hiccup style that was hauntingly familiar. In any case, her feet stopped. She panned the room slowly looking for the source.

To her dismay, Mildred cavorted with the enemy.

Toby and Mildred were in deep conversation. Every

once in a while Toby laughed, and Mildred tittered. Toby was putting the moves on her. Just then, she saw Mildred turn to look for her.

Without thought of what a spectacle she might be making of herself, she ducked behind a tall stranger, who gave her an indulgent smile. The bar was not particularly big and could not provide her refuge. With Mildred looking for her, it would be only a matter of time before she led Toby over to her.

The door seemed far away, but she kept ducking and dodging until she was safely a few feet away from the exit. She had to turn around once more to make sure. The one drink she had consumed may have caused her vision to be fuzzy.

She chanced one more glance. There was no mistake. From across the room Toby's cold eyes penetrated her being, leaving it cold and numb. His stare devoid of feeling didn't reflect any recognition, but Shelly knew better.

She had to get out of the bar. She pushed past the few remaining patrons, getting rude stares and comments. No time to apologize. Her breathing became ragged.

Her drive home occurred on remote pilot. Just from his observance, she felt soiled. Her clothes lay in a heap outside the tub. The hot water poured overhead as she lathered repeatedly.

Skin scrubbed and slightly tender, Shelly sipped on piping-hot tea. A thick, terry cloth robe covered her, providing some warmth. She stared at the phone. How she wanted to call Justin—but couldn't without having to explain. She put the mug against her forehead. What about Mildred? She'd have to tell her something.

With a trembling hand, she picked up the phone and dialed.

"Hello." The sound of Leesa's voice calmed her somewhat. But it wasn't whom she wanted to hear. Gently, she replaced the receiver. Again, she dialed.

"Yes."

Her resolve not to cry disappeared. "Justin, I—I didn't know who to call." She sobbed freely, her words muffled. "Can you come over, please?"

"Shelly?" Justin's concerned voice rose. "Did something happen to you?" He didn't wait for her answer. "Lock the doors! I'll be right there."

Within fifteen minutes, Justin stood at her door, pounding. Now that some more time had gone by, she was a little more clearheaded. This also meant that she realized the present crisis. Justin would want an explanation from her.

Slowly, she opened the door. He rushed past her looking around for the bad guy. Shelly closed the door and pulled the robe closer.

"There's no one here."

Justin spun around appearing confused. His eyes searched for an answer. "What happened?"

Shelly walked past him to the kitchen. "Let me get you some coffee."

"Coffee! Damn it, Shelly, what's going on? You call me sounding hysterical. I rush over, running red lights in the process. And here you are, serving coffee."

"I had a scare tonight."

Her mind raced to find the right thing to say. She had been ready to tell him what gnawed at her soul. But the thought of rejection or contempt for her stupidity sealed the secret. Then, the thought of what it would do to his reputation made her stomach churn. She had to protect him.

"I—I went out tonight with—" Mildred could not be brought into her story because he would question her. "With friends. A man at the bar got a little unfriendly. I thought I saw him follow me out of the bar." She busied herself preparing the coffee. "I guess my nerves got the better of me."

Justin held her from behind. She allowed herself to relax against his firm body. "Hon, I didn't mean to go off the way I just did. It scared me to think that you were hurt or in danger." He turned her around and held her face between his hands. Softly, he continued, "I don't know what I would do if you were in danger."

She hugged him tightly. "Can you stay tonight?"

"Sure."

Sipping coffee with the lights dimmed, they watched a cop drama on television. Her head rested comfortably in his lap. She drifted into a light doze while he stroked her hair softly.

The phone rang by her head. It jarred. She debated, having a dreaded feeling that it was Toby. Her false composure would fall apart if she heard his voice.

"Do you want me to get it?"

She stiffened. No, that wouldn't do either. If Toby recognized Justin's voice or if Justin recognized Toby's, Justin would be bound to think that she was working with Toby. She shook her head. "Let the machine get it."

Too late. The machine played her greeting, which they both heard. Panic set in; the response would be heard too. "Hi, Shelly. It's Mildred. What happened to you? I was talking to To—" Shelly's hand grabbed the receiver.

"Hi, Mildred." She listened to Mildred while keeping a calm countenance.

"I forgot about an appointment I had. I figured I would make my apologies later." Mildred accepted her weak excuse and hung up. Shelly sighed. She would to make it up to her friend.

Later, snuggled in bed, Shelly said what was on her mind. "Haven't been seeing much of you lately." She waited for him to appease her insecurities.

A weary sigh escaped from Justin. "Work has been never-ending and then, I still have Toby Gillis breathing down my back. Somewhere in the midst of all that you got lost." He kissed the top of her head. "I can't promise when the pace will slacken, but in the meantime, I have to attend a reception at the end of the week for bankers' top management and their significant others. Would you go with me?"

She nodded and rolled over to her stomach. "How come you're not married yet?"

He didn't look at her, but instead at the ceiling. No matter where, no matter what he was doing, he looked handsome. He had all the qualities of a good man, so it was only natural that she wondered at his bachelorhood.

"I guess I just never found the right person or maybe the M word scared me."

In that case, she knew not to give the inclination that she had thought about a life together with the ultimate commitment of marriage.

He turned the tables on her and asked, "What about you? You seem the traditional type."

The question had never been asked of her before, although it was her mother's constant thought. "I couldn't tell you because I don't know the answer. So far, the prospects have been less than desirable. As a result, I'm careful."

"Well, it seems then all we have is each other."

They both yawned and shifted into comfortable sleeping positions. It had been a rough day for both of them.

Justin sat in the back of the limousine staring bleakly out the window. He would rather spend the night alone with Shelly. But his presence at this high-priced dinner was another price he had to pay because of the leadership position he had assumed. He wondered how his father did it and still managed to have an understanding wife at home.

His spirit lifted once Shelly got into the limo. He kissed her, expressing his appreciation. "You look good enough to—"

She stopped his devilish thoughts by putting her fingers on his lips. He promptly kissed her fingers, which produced a giggle from her.

Content, Justin watched her put the finishing touches to her makeup. In his estimation, she looked perfect. But it amused him to see her fuss at minute details of her eye shadow and now her hair.

"Oh, stop smirking, Justin. You guys don't have half the worries women have of looking good."

"But all that isn't necessary. I've seen you without the painted mask and with your hair spiked you're awake." She jabbed his shoulder at his comments. "And, I'm still hanging in there with you," he added.

"I appreciate the sacrifice, but a girl's got to do what a girl's got to do."

Justin walked proudly into the hotel with Shelly at his side. Heads turned, openly admiring her. In a silver-sequined dress, she could have been one of those movie stars going to the awards show. The form-fitting dress stopped a couple of inches above her knees highlighting the slender legs in silvery stockings.

The couple walked into the lobby area, joining the growing crowd of bankers. Justin gave obligatory greetings as he guided Shelly into the room where the reception was held. There had to be over a hundred persons in attendance. There was a head table and several round tables scattered around the room.

"Over here, this table seems to be just right."

It was placed toward the back and only had three seats accounted for.

Justin leaned over and whispered in Shelly's ear, "Relax, this is supposed to be fun."

She looked around uncomfortably. "I wish I could, but I feel out of place with all of these important people." She twisted the napkin in her lap looking utterly miserable.

"Don't let these folks intimidate you. They're just like you or me. I'll be your knight for the night." He chuckled at his own joke, while Shelly rolled her eyes at him. His spirits lifted when he saw her smile and visibly relax.

After dinner, the keynote speaker addressed the group. For Justin, the speech lasted too long and was too boring. If he didn't have Shelly to play footsies under the table with, he would have had to plunge his fork in the back of his hands to stay alert.

As the evening wound down, the hired band played big band music. Justin led Shelly out to the dance area ready to impress her by his choreography.

"Ah, Justin." Toby Gillis seemed to step out of nowhere.

Justin halted abruptly causing Shelly to bump into him. He stood protectively partly shielding her.

"Hi, Toby." Even to his ears, he sounded faintly robotic, but he wasn't in the mood to pretend that a friendship or business relationship existed. "I'm on my way to the dance floor, if you will excuse me." He reached out to brush Toby aside, but the man was like a granite statue and didn't budge.

With a sly smile, Toby peeped over Justin's shoulder. "You can't hurry past me without introducing me to the treasure you're doing a poor job of hiding."

Justin blew a frustrated sigh and pulled Shelly beside him.

"Toby Gillis, meet Shelly Bishop." He felt like the perfect heel when he saw how Shelly reacted. Her face, devoid of expression, froze. Because he knew her, he recognized a frantic look in her eyes. Toby could be intimidating. He placed his arms protectively around hers.

Toby offered his hand and after what seemed like minutes, Shelly responded. Justin was becoming irritated with Toby's dramatics as he let the handshake linger a little too long before bringing her hand to his lips. Shelly reacted as if a snake had bitten her, and recoiled. Justin was actually pleased at her response. At least, he wasn't the only one who held Toby Gillis in revulsion.

They managed to get onto the dance floor after the encounter, but Justin couldn't get back the mood. Shelly was barely talking and he wondered if she was ill.

"We can leave if you'd like." He gave up trying to have a conversation with her. Her attitude puzzled him. It had changed when she had met Toby. Her dislike was strong; maybe she was angry at what he had put his father through. She did seem protective of the old man.

"Yes, please," Shelly quickly answered. "I'm coming down with a headache and I know I'm not good company."

"Excuse me while I pay a visit to the rest room."

Life was just not fair. While he stood at the sink washing his hands, the devil himself walked into the area. He leaned casually against the marbled wall.

"You've added another one to the stable. Seems a bit different from the rest, though."

Justin shook the excess water off his hands. He kept his gaze averted, trying to maintain his composure.

"Where did you find that one? Hope you're not planning to settle down with the likes of her." Toby looked at his manicured hands. "My guess is that she's after something, maybe your money."

Justin paused briefly. The anger burned fiercely in his chest. He walked toward the door. As he passed, Toby added, "You ever heard of the saying 'lie down with a dog and you get up with fleas'?" He flashed a cosmetic-aided, white toothy smile.

Impulsiveness was later Justin's excuse.

His fist connected to Toby's fragile chin with such force

it flung back Toby's head and then his body. He crashed into the full-size mirror, cracking it as his body slid down in a lump. Justin balled up the paper towel and threw it in disgust on the unconscious form. He checked his reflection, adjusted his clothing, and left feeling slightly better.

Thirteen

It was the first time Shelly was glad to be out of Justin's company. The night of errors couldn't have ended sooner. Neither one pretended at conversation on the return ride to her house.

Justin sat on one end of the limo rubbing the back of his hand. She noticed that when he went to the men's room, Toby had followed. But, she had also noticed that only one man came out of there.

Somehow a wall of silent tension stood between them. Shelly was at a loss as to how surmount it. The invisible shield prevented them from looking at each other or even sharing in a conversation. The mood had dampened considerably. She could only attribute it to Toby. Like a strong deadly poison, a little went a long way.

They exchanged lukewarm kisses when she arrived at her apartment building. There was none of the usual bantering or romantic farewells this night. Shelly took her time entering the apartment, enjoying the cool night air. It helped calm the waves of nausea.

The sickening feeling, a direct result of her inability to make things better, frustrated her. She turned to take a last look at the limo leaving. Usually, Justin left the window half down while he stuck his head out blowing kisses to her. Tonight, the windows remained up with only a reflection of the streetlights looking back at her.

She kicked off her satin pumps, leaving the pair in the living room. Then she unzipped her dress and tossed it over a chair. Her stockings landed in a heap outside her door. She wished she could discard tonight's memories in similar fashion.

The phone rang and she picked it up with Justin in mind. "Justin?"

"Sorry. I guess you're out of sight, out of mind for him." The voice of her nightmares responded to her greeting.

"How did you get this number?"

"No 'how are you?' No 'good to hear from you'? Rudeness must be a permanent quality. I've had this number for some time now. Used it once or twice, just to hear that sweet, lilting voice of yours. Even had a photo from my detective of you going to work at the Thorntons'."

Shelly sat on the edge of the bed, holding her head, the receiver pressed to her ear.

"Yo, Shelly, still there? I guess so. I can hear your sexy breathing." He cleared his throat. "But let me get down to business. I want to see you."

The line went dead.

It was an extreme act, but she didn't ever want to hear from him again. She pulled the line out of the wall. Then immediately went to each phone and took it off the hook.

Determined not to make any hysterical calls to Justin or anyone else, she continued with her preparations for bed. Toby was trying to return to her life. Actually, it seemed he had already entered. He had been toying with her. She remembered the mysterious telephone calls. Now he made bolder moves. He wanted to see her. Knowing what he was, it could only bring disaster.

The next morning Mildred waited to do battle with her. Shelly didn't even bother to defend herself. Instead she focused on Mildred's encounter with Toby at the bar. Questions swirled impatiently needing to be answered.

"Before I left the bar, I saw you talking to a guy. Who was that? He seemed familiar, but I couldn't place him." She kept her glance averted just in case Mildred saw the underlying eagerness there.

Mildred answered, unaware of her friend's motive, "Come to think of it, he never told me his name. But he was a high spender, though. He paid for my drinks and even played pool." She frowned, remarking, "It really is strange that we spent all that time together and I never got his name."

If Mildred wasn't happily married, Shelly would break her illusion of Toby. She didn't have to worry that her friend would fall for him. Mildred and Bob, after fifteen years of courtship, had only recently tied the knot. They wrote each other love notes and placed them in each other's lunches. At least once a week, Mildred received a bouquet of flowers from her true love. Whatever game Toby was playing, he would have to count out Mildred. Maybe she was being paranoid.

"At least I was able to impress him," Mildred added, chuckling. "He thought it pretty nifty that I worked for the Thornton family. But I couldn't take all the credit. So even though he hadn't met you, I did share the spotlight with you."

"You did what!" Shelly almost shouted. She felt trapped as if her world was closing in by a careless comment. Toby knew that she not only worked for the Thorntons, but she was more than casually acquainted with Justin. She didn't want to think of what his devious mind could create with such information.

"I—I only mentioned that I worked with someone else; then I pointed to you." Thinking that Shelly was upset at not be introduced, she reassured, "I would have introduced you, but then you hurried out of the place."

Shelly's legs quivered for a moment, the sickening dread physically overwhelming her. She had to maintain control. It had taken every effort to prevent others from seeing how she had crumbled from within, a year ago. She had hid the scars from the world with success. But she had grown complacent, especially in the security and love of Justin. With danger lurking, taunting her, she didn't know if she had the stamina for another dose of life's upheavals.

Trying to keep Mildred from worrying, it was her turn to reassure. "I'm okay. Just a little shy about meeting anyone."

Continuing on with her duties, she greeted Phillip. He lay quietly too weak to respond. It hit her that Phillip's condition was deteriorating. But, there was something else nagging at her. His will, which was so strong and vital before, had disappeared.

There appeared an overall tiredness to his eyes that used to hold such mischief. Even his skin had lost its tone. He blended into the beige linens on his bed, offering a weak smile, which tore at her heart.

She had broken the rule. An emotional attachment had formed. Not only had she fallen under the boss's charm, but she had surrendered her heart to his son. There was no turning back. She would have to plead guilty.

"Phillip." She pulled a chair closer to his bed. "What's wrong? Are you giving up on me?"

He smiled weakly, patting her hand. "My dear, it seems that I'm not having a good day." His words were spoken low and she had to lean toward him to hear. Acting on impulse, she took his limp hand and held it sandwiched between hers. The gesture was symbolic of what she hoped, that her vitality could be transferred to him.

In a deep raspy voice, he shared, "If you don't mind my saying, you're not exactly a picture of laughs."

She tried to laugh off his accurate perception. "Just a matter of too much to do in too little time."

He turned toward her, interested. He did seem to perk up whenever she visited. Her company he craved, while she needed a sympathetic ear.

"How was the reception last night? I tried to get Justin to fill me in on the details, but he barely seemed to want to talk. Did you enjoy yourself?"

"It was great, in the beginning. Then, it turned ugly."

"Ugly?"

Her voice took on a faraway tone, as she remembered the hostile tension. "Toby Gillis turned up. After that, the night wasn't the same."

Phillip sighed and leaned back into the pillows. "I should have guessed. Justin's mood was so dark, but I couldn't think of what was on his mind. Did they get into a confrontation?"

"No. Both remained civil in front of prying eyes." She, on the other hand, would have loved the opportunity to rip Toby's heart out and stuff it down his throat.

"Since I haven't had the chance to talk to Justin, I would like to share this piece of advice with you. You—both of you—have to remain strong for each other. Trying times, such as these, can sabotage any relationship. But if you and he are focused on each other and keep the lines of communication open, obstacles won't be devastating."

She nodded, understanding his message. But, she doubted he would feel the same way if he knew what Toby Gillis's presence really meant. She didn't want to be responsible for worsening his condition. And it would.

"Don't worry, child," he urged softly. "Trust Justin, he will take care of everything."

She did believe in Justin, but this might be out of his

league. He didn't need her problems to weigh on top of the current problems. No, she had to maintain her own confidences.

Phillip struggled to sit up in the bed. She helped him adjust the bed and arranged his pillows. He kept his eyes closed for a few moments. The seconds felt like an eternity to Shelly. She sat on the edge of the seat waiting for him to speak.

"Whew," he exhaled. "Just got a bit dizzy, there." He waved away her concern. "Nothing you can do about it, dear. My body has a mind of its own, I'm just along for the ride."

"Don't say that. You do have the power to make everything all right."

He laughed. An unusual touch of bitterness edged the sound. "I have something to tell you that may change how you feel. I also hope that when I'm finished, you won't hate me." His fingers fidgeted with the sheet.

Regardless of what he had to tell her, she could never hate this man. "Never."

"I appreciate your loyalty, but you should wait until you hear what I have to tell you." He cleared his throat. "A few months back, when I felt better than I do now, I began to think of everything I had. It was a lot for the average person. And I am truly grateful. There was one thing that I didn't have. With time running short on me, I didn't know whether I would have it." He paused, looking directly at her. "I wanted to see my son settled and happy."

An unsettling feeling crept in and Shelly tried to remain calm. She understood everything Phillip said, but the underlying meaning still unspoken was what scared her. She held her questions and waited for him to continue.

"Then came the Volunteer of the Year awards. Since the bank is the sponsor, I got to see the nominees' photos and bios. Child, your beauty was so fresh and exotic, well, I was taken with you. I had Connors check into your background."

Shelly gasped. "You checked up on me?"

"Everything was fine. Your family. Your friends. The more I knew about you, the more I wanted to meet you, have you meet Justin."

Words were being spoken to her, but she had stopped listening. Her day had turned into a living nightmare. A background check had been conducted on her.

Her secret was no longer hers.

"You knew . . . about Toby?" Her voice cracked.

"Yes."

"Mr. Thornton, I need a few minutes. Excuse me."

"Wait."

She stopped, but didn't turn around to face him.

"I knew you would hate me. I couldn't let it go on without you knowing."

"I don't hate you."

Without another word, she left.

Shelly walked up to her door with shoulders slumped dejectedly. Her problems weighed heavily and the hardest part was pretending to the world that all was well. She fumbled for her house key as she thought about the joys of soaking in the bathtub.

"Shelly."

A voice that she would have liked to remain in the past called from behind. Her feet turned to stone, frozen. Keys dropped unnoticed to the ground. She remained motionless, waiting.

She saw his hand come into view, retrieving the fallen keys. Nothing had come to mind for her to say.

"Here, allow me."

Then his full figure stood in front of her. Up close, he still had the ability to frighten her to the point where she held her breath. The blood rushed through her head like a roller coaster and a wave of dizziness caught her.

"Oh, don't look so mortified, Shelly. Here, I will open your door. Come on in." He entered her apartment and stood at the door as if it were his place. "Well, come on," he invited, clearly amused by her reaction. He stepped toward her. "Or do you want me to come and get you?"

She recoiled instantly. His touch would be too revolting. She sidled past him not going farther than the living room. With the initial surprise gone, her thought process started working and she found her voice. "What happened to your face? It looks like you had a fight with a truck and lost."

Instantly, he scowled. He muttered words barely audible. She did manage to catch a few unsavory words and decided not to pursue the matter of his disfigurement.

"What do you want, Toby? It's late. You're not welcomed here. And, we have nothing else to talk about." She kept her arms folded to hide the betraying tremble. Her legs were another matter. She only hoped that her pants hid the telltale signs of her weak nerves.

"Don't get on your high horse with me. Actually, I have thought about you a few times, more than I would have liked. This visit is purely business." He kicked the door closed and sauntered over to the couch. Casually, he flopped down never taking his eyes off her.

Under different circumstances, he would make a comical figure. The dark purplish bruise to his chin and swollen lip made him look like a defeated boxer. She wished she could shake the hand of the person who laid it into him.

However, under these circumstances, she only had two words for him. "Get out." She stated the words clearly. With stronger emotion, she ordered, "I said get out."

"I see you have grown some *cajones* since our last meeting." He flicked his hand at her, dismissive. "Let me get down to why I'm here since you don't plan to be the gracious hostess. Clear up something for me, will you? Do I have it right that you are not only the latest notch on Justin Thornton's belt, but you also work for him?" He paused. "Ahh, I struck a nerve there. Be careful, you might end up like his wife, at the bottom of the river." He laughed. "Didn't think you had it in you to go after another rich dude."

"You are the most sickening creature I've ever met." She spat the words at him. He made her sound manipulative and dirty. She wouldn't let him do this to her. Determined, she walked over to the phone and dialed nine-one-one.

Toby shot out of the couch and pulled the receiver from her ear. After hanging up, he turned to her, leaning in to add emphasis to his threat. "Don't get too cocky. Remember everything you do, it's because I allow you to do it. But hear me out and then I'm gone." He held her arm to usher her back to the chair.

She pulled away from him and hissed, "Don't touch me. You may be stronger than me, but I swear that if you put your hands on me one more time, you'll go away from here defective."

The quiet delivery of her words must have affected him. Toby backed away and walked over to the couch. "Okay, let me begin with what brings me here. It's no secret that I want to own Hopetown Savings Bank. I have plans and investors who will turn it into a truly moneymaking entity. Of course, Justin Thornton stands in my way." He turned his cunning glare on her.

Electric currents, deeply rooted in her rage, zapped their way through her. She waited. Her heart thudded.

"The news break about the bank being sold hurt your friends, but not enough. But, my fairy godmother must be looking out for me because just when I was trying to come up with another plan, in you stepped."

"Me!" Shelly sat in one of her dining room chairs. She needed something firm under her, but didn't want to be too close to him. Despite his seeming indifference, she didn't trust him. His sudden mood swings could be deadly.

"Yes, you. I couldn't believe my luck when I saw you in the bar, then on the arm of the man I hate. And then, my luck just kept getting better when I followed you from their lair." He threw back his head and laughed.

She looked at him in disbelief. He had followed her. The thought left her feeling vulnerable and exposed. Despite all the security around the Thorntons' house, it couldn't protect her against Toby Gillis.

With sudden realization, it hit her. The deep-seated fear that her past wouldn't remain hidden was unfolding. She could do nothing to hold it back. As she watched Toby's grinning face, Kim's words from their counseling session came back to her. She could see how people went out and commissioned hired guns. If he only knew what she was thinking, he would wipe that sickening all-powerful smile from his disgusting face.

"If looks could kill," he teased. "Anyway, as I was saying, I want something from you."

She looked at him blankly, dreading whatever deal he'd cooked up to demand her cooperation.

"I want you to put Mr. Golden Boy in a compromising position. A situation that would leave the listening and viewing audiences of the different media wanting blood. His."

"Have you gone mad!" Shelly stood, hands on her waist. Her explosive retort caused the vein in her neck to stand to attention. "How dare you!" she screamed. "You, the lowest level of life, come to me with a ridiculous plan that will get not only you, but me, in trouble."

The fact that Toby remained calm was not a good sign. He tended to be the hot-tempered, impulsive kind of guy. His reptilian facade of cool contemplation chilled her even further. This wasn't one of his half-baked plans. He had thought out every angle. Her voice died down waiting for the bombshell.

"Everyone these days needs compensation. I'm up on the times, so I'll provide you with incentive. If you don't go through with this, if you decide midway to warn your man, if this is botched in any way, I will smear you and your family's name in this town." He put his finger to his head as if puzzling over an important thought. "Mmm. I wonder what that would do to Mr. Thornton. I wonder if you will be the apple in *his* eye." He held his hands up like a moving director viewing the scene. "Could you imagine the great Thornton family vying so hard for respectability having a floozy piece of trash associated with their good name?" His eyes narrowed dangerously. "I'm going to leave now. I don't need your answer because you would be a fool to think you could go up against me." He stood to leave. "I'll be calling you in a few days when I get back into town. Then, we can discuss the details."

Immobile, Shelly remained in the chair. Had he gone mad? As she stared at him, willing him to be just a figment of her overactive imagination, there was no sign of madness. Instead, a cunning streak malevolently displayed glittered from his eyes as he described his master plan.

The fact that it involved her, against her will, left razor-edged bitterness. The alternative for refusing to comply didn't leave her much choice.

On the one hand, she could follow her instincts and warn Justin. But, when he found out about her trouble, he would forget that she warned him and be disgusted with her. Then, there were her parents, whose reputation would be maligned.

Her other choice was to be an unwilling partner in the hateful scheme and bring down Justin's and Phillip's dream. Justin might never know that she had aided in his demise, but *she* would know. It would tear her heart to pieces to see the look of defeat in his face. All she wanted to do was to enjoy her time with him, loving his touch, his thoughts, his words.

Could she be so selfish as to think about herself? Toby would never leave her alone. To think otherwise would be naive. He would continue to seek her out to commit dirty acts that he couldn't do himself. With her self-respect already damaged at his expense, she would hardly be able to stand herself if she aligned herself with him.

Sleep was out of the question. She picked up her car keys and headed out the door. It was late, but sleep had long taken a detour. Besides, she was on a mission.

Fourteen

Justin's anger had gotten the better part of him at the reception. That one punch had a lot of pent-up anger that got unleashed onto Toby's face. No regrets, but it did put a damper on the mood. Plus he'd allowed the infuriating man to get under his skin. His attack on Shelly had pushed Justin over the edge of intolerance. Again, no regrets. Although his bruised knuckles ached as a result of his hot temper, he couldn't deny the sense of satisfaction of seeing Toby lying in a crumpled heap.

In the limo, he'd sensed her distress, but he was too wrapped up in reliving the scene with Toby and didn't pay her any attention. He acknowledged that she did seem to be deeply affected by her meeting with Toby. Ultimately, he had invited her to accompany him and he was responsible for her not having a good time. He had to apologize.

"Mr. Thornton, will you be needing me any further?"

Mrs. Beacham interrupted his guilt-laden musings. She stood in the hallway after checking on his father. Still looking fresh at the end of the day, she was the only symbol of stability in his life. With all the things that seemed to be occurring at the same time, he welcomed her constant attention.

He shook his head. "How is he doing?"

Her face immediately reflected her sadness with a sad

droop to her mouth. "Sleeping now. But he did have a rough day today."

A pain formed between his eyes. His stress increased, mainly because of his continued frustration at not spending enough time with his father. As time drew nearer, panic rose because the inevitable had to be faced. It was the one time that he felt powerless against his fate.

It had been a long day and the news about his father made him feel wearier. "That will be all, Mrs. Beacham. I'm going to take a shower and hopefully fall asleep."

"Good night. I'll brew you some coffee if you decide you need a cup."

The bed looked inviting and he couldn't wait to put his tired body down on the comfortable mattress. It would be even more comfortable with Shelly at his side, making wild and passionate love to him. He smiled at the thought, thinking about her beautiful brown body stretched next to his. Following the urge, he picked up the phone.

"Blast!"

The phone rang, but Shelly didn't answer. And worse, the machine wasn't on. He and Shelly had made it a policy about not bringing their relationship into this house, but he was ready to break the rules tonight. Well, it served him right. Because of tonight, she was probably mad at him. Still, he wanted to hear her sweet voice laying its charm on him.

Sighing, he thought about work. Out of habit, he checked his messages, cringing at the automated voice reporting that there were six. He bypassed most of them until he heard the header of one from Connors.

As the message instructed, he called. He checked his watch when the detective answered. His curiosity overshadowed his guilt at calling him so late.

"What do you have to tell me, Connors?"

"Got some info on the type of man you're dealing with.

Thought you would want to know that Toby Gillis has a network of folks working for him. Most of them against their will since he seems fond of blackmail. Word is that the leak to the newspapers and televisions is only the tip of the iceberg of what he has planned for you and the bank. Those who know him say that he won't stop at that and to expect much worse."

Great, Justin thought. The news wasn't surprising. Nevertheless, his stomach churned, sickened at having to deal with more dirty actions. He felt like a hunted man. It had gone beyond just acquiring the bank. Toby was trying to dominate him, crush him, annihilate him. The fight was far from being over.

"Okay, Connors. Anything else?"

"Well, sir." Connors hesitated. "I did find out that he plans to use someone close to you to help him."

"Who?"

Justin would have the head of any of his employees who thought they had the nerve to go up against him. Loyalty was an element he did not take lightly. The bank prided itself on its family atmosphere among the employees. It would have to be a new hire that hadn't learned the code. But wished he had.

"Who is it?" he asked again.

"Don't know. Toby has been bragging that the insider will have you begging him to take the bank."

"Find out who it is," he ordered. His temper shot up again and the familiar bitter taste of pure anger was back. "I want to know everyone he has paid money to or who is on his blackmail list. I want the information as soon as possible."

His headache increased and he swore he was seeing spots. The last time he had succumbed to his emotions with Toby, but this time he had to push back his fury. He had to be as cold and calculating as the enemy.

"Will do, sir." Connors stuttered, "Ah, there is the case of Miss Bishop and Toby."

"Shelly?"

"Yes, sir. I feel it's my duty to give you a heads-up, especially with the business about the bank and all."

The news held his interest, but also scared him. What connection did Shelly have with Toby? "You're holding something back from me. Spit it out now."

It was Connors's turn to be subdued. "Sir, I will give you the information you seek, but I need to talk to your father first."

"My father? Has everyone gone crazy? I hired you to do a job. Now you tell me that you have to talk to my father. I'm missing something here."

There was silence on the other end. Justin knew Connors long enough to know that he would not reveal anything further. What he had just disclosed was not a slip, but like he said, a heads-up.

Mechanically he went through the motion of disrobing and taking his shower. There was no satisfaction in the pulsating water beating away the day's stress, because in the final hours of the day his stress level had skyrocketed. A tight knot in the middle of his back between his shoulder blades accompanied his headache. It was if his body turned itself into a tight ball, bracing itself for the final blow.

Of course, sleep had taken the high road. He lay in bed staring up at the ceiling trying to overcome his shock and bewilderment. Despair knocked at his door and he struggled to keep it at bay.

In what way were Shelly and Toby connected? His active imagination left him sick at the scenario that played. But, it just couldn't be that they had been more than friends, or even that much. In his heart, he didn't want it to be that way. For if it was, he'd have to dismiss all the things she had said to him as pure lies.

He detested lies.

Looking for an explanation, he thought about how unhappy she appeared when Toby appeared. In fact, there was fear in her face and in her mannerisms. It was that look of terror that made him so protective of her. With Connors's revelation about blackmail, the matter took on an unpleasantness.

How far would she be willing to go to save herself?

With the devastating piece of news, she still laid claim to his heart. How could he deny what he felt with her? No woman had made him feel all the symptoms of love. It had been his hope that they would be together, forever.

The jaded side of him, which had been successfully stifled once he learned to let go of his fears, hadn't lost a beat. He felt cheated and betrayed. With male pride wounded, he wanted vengeance.

And then there was his father. What was his role? He had always felt that his father had manipulated Shelly into his life. But, with her secret connection to Toby, his father couldn't have gotten himself entangled with him.

He threw back the covers in frustration. It was no use fooling himself, he couldn't sleep. The whole matter left him feeling irritated, even a little angry, but mostly suspicious.

It didn't matter to Shelly that it was almost midnight. Focused, she steered her car through the almost deserted streets. Thunder rumbled ominously, the smell of rain in the air. The forecasters had reported a pending thunderstorm. Shelly thought the weather fitting, considering the developments to date. Thick drops fell slowly at first and then, as if someone threw a bucket of water on the windshield, the storm vented its fury.

Windshield wipers worked to clear her view. The rhythmic motion left to right mirrored the different opinions she battled with—to tell Justin everything about Toby and her or just to end it.

If she told Justin about what happened that night and then Toby's threat to use her, there was no guarantee that he would view the whole thing sympathetically. The fact that she didn't come forward and tell him that she knew Toby when Justin was going through his hell because of Toby would be in his mind. He wouldn't understand the deep-seated fear and insecurities that now took up permanent residence in her psyche.

But if she ended it, no one would be hurt, permanently. That was a lie. The thought of never seeing him, talking to him, or feeling his lips against hers ever again depressed her. But, despite her despair, her secret could remain; Toby would have to come up with another scheme; and Justin, dear sweet Justin, would go on with his life, meeting a truly respectable woman to settle down with, ultimately making his father happy.

Although all the ends seemed tied up neatly, she was left feeling despondent. She didn't want Justin settling down with anyone else. *She* wanted him.

She really didn't know where he would be tonight, since they didn't speak to each other after the reception. Considering Phillip's condition, she surmised that he was probably at his father's. She turned off the appropriate exit from the parkway.

The rain stopped and she perceived that as a sign that the decision she made was correct. If only her stomach wasn't so queasy.

With just a few miles to her destination, her doubts returned. First, how was she going to get into the house without waking all the occupants, especially Mrs. Beacham? Then, how was she going to tell Justin what was on her mind? Going back home was one way to deal with all of this. But she couldn't. She would be running away from her problems.

And so far, running away hadn't solved anything because her problems loomed in front of her. She turned into the residence and waved familiarly to the guard. His shift ended as she came to work. She was grateful that he had not questioned her, since she didn't have a smooth lie ready for him.

After parking the car, she walked up to the door. No lights were on in the front of the house, but Justin's room was situated in the rear. She entertained the thought of throwing pebbles at his window. With her lucky streak taking a hiatus, she would probably break the glass and set off the alarm.

Afraid to let the heavy brass knocker fall, she decided not to bring too much attention to her visit. She walked around to the side of the house, hoping that no silent alarms were being tripped. One of his windows overlooked the side of the house and Shelly was glad to see that a light was on.

Looking down on the ground for a pebble, she barely heard the scraping of a window opening.

"Shelly? What on God's earth are you doing here? Out there at this hour?" Mrs. Beacham hissed at her, clearly annoyed at her presence.

"I—I wanted to talk to Just . . . er, Mr. Thornton."

"At this hour, have you lost your mind? I think you had better get yourself home." Mrs. Beacham pulled the window down, clearly dismissing her.

It was now or never. Shelly ran over to the window. "Please, Mrs. Beacham, it is extremely important that I see him." Her voice broke toward the end. She had too much to lose and there was no turning back.

Maybe it was the desperation in her voice, the sight of her tear-filled eyes, or the fact that she was trampling the bed of wildflowers, but the formidable housekeeper hesitated. She pointed to the back door, motioning to Shelly to meet her there.

Shelly said a silent prayer of thanks. At the back door, Mrs. Beacham opened the door, but still glowered at her.

"What may I tell Mr. Thornton your visit is in reference to?" Her direct stare left Shelly feeling like an insect under a microscope.

"It's personal."

Mrs. Beacham didn't hide her impatience at Shelly's response. "You ran out on one today. Are you about to do the same to the other? Whatever your demons, you need to get rid of them or you'll never know peace."

Shelly was astonished at the length of time Mrs. Beacham addressed her; it had to be very important to the housekeeper to make such remarks. In her position, she got to see the drama of human life unfold. Shelly wanted to defend herself, but Mrs. Beacham, still dressed in her classic brown suit and dark hose, wasn't inviting confidences, just passing on words of wisdom.

"Well, come in and I'll go get him. There's coffee freshly brewed, you look like you need something."

Shelly gave a watery smile and decided to help herself to the coffee. In no time, Justin appeared behind Mrs. Beacham into the kitchen. He was clearly surprised at her unexpected and late visit.

"I need to talk to you . . . privately." She spoke up first before she changed her mind.

Confusion flickered across his face and he guided her to his office. Mrs. Beacham, the model of discretion, had a blank face as she retired to her quarters.

He closed the office door slowly and then turned to face her. "From the look on your face, I can tell this isn't going to be good news."

She nodded. If he only knew how much she hated to do this . . . but it was her only way out of the mess. She stared down into the coffee mug as she began. "There is no best way to say what I have to tell you. But, believe me, it is not a decision I made lightly."

He dug his hands into his pockets. The telltale tightening of his jaw showed he braced himself for the worst. He just stood tensely waiting for her to continue.

She took a sip of her coffee as if it would fortify her against the anger bound to be unleashed. "I think we should call it quits."

The room was quiet. He looked as if someone had punched him in his stomach and he was trying to catch his bearings. With her emotions on high and her senses tuned in to impending disaster, Shelly heard the soft ticking of the clock on his desk, felt a trickle of sweat drip down her back; and the coffee suddenly tasted bitter in her mouth. She restrained herself from running to Justin and hugging him close, apologizing for the moment of insanity.

"Say something," she pleaded.

"What would you like me to say?" he answered, softly as if talking to a child. "This isn't a discussion. You came and told me it's over. Does it matter what I think?"

"Yes, it does matter. Do you care that it's over or do you just say, 'oh, well' and move on?"

An angry glint flashed from his dark brown eyes. His mouth set in a thin hard line. "From what I hear, maybe that should be my attitude. What little game are you playing, Shelly? I am the pawn on your game board. You led me around like a fool and now, what?"

Each word struck a raw nerve, wounding deeply. He ob-

viously held her in contempt, thinking that she was a manipulative witch.

Defensively, she thought about who really played a
game. Phillip's confession came back to her. "Oh, but how
stupid of me," she spat. "This was all a game to you. You
and your father play with women's lives like a roulette
wheel, and this time I happened to be the prize."

"What the hell are you talking about?" He held his
hands up in surrender. "Okay, let's start at the beginning
because you are sounding a little crazy right about now."

"At the beginning? I think *you* should be the one to start
at the beginning. You brought out the charm and I fell for
it. It's time to end the ride and this is where I get off."

She slammed the coffee mug onto the desk, its contents
splashing over the side. She didn't care if it stained his expensive desk. Here she was feeling guilty about ending the
relationship and he acted as if she were a part of a devious
plot.

He grabbed her as she walked by him. "Now, just hold
up. Just like that, it's over?" He pulled her closer. "I
thought you felt something for me."

Her resolve was crumbling. His touch ignited her barely
dormant desires. She had to remain strong. Nothing was
what it seemed with Toby breathing down her neck with
secret threats and Phillip and Justin playing matchmaker
at her expense. No, she had to rid herself of everyone.

She pushed Justin away, as much as it pained her. "I
have to leave now. What we have was built on false pre-
tenses. It was forced. Outside of these walls, you wouldn't
have noticed me. You probably wouldn't have even acknowledged my presence otherwise."

Never mind that she would still have fallen head over
heels for him no matter where she had met him. Her love
was genuine and it broke her heart that it wasn't recipro-

cated. It was a good thing that she followed her instincts and brought closure.

Justin followed her to the door. He walked close on her heels. "You seem to be doing my thinking for me," he said, talking to her retreating back. "Is it some type of commitment you want? Was that the ultimate goal, but because you didn't get one fast enough, you're ready to cut loose? Is that the game you play with men—with Toby? I know about you and Toby."

She closed her eyes. *Please let this be a dream.*

Justin's words hit the mark. It wasn't just words, but the disgust in his voice when she turned to face him, his eyes narrowed at her reaction from his words. Grim-faced, he began to pace. Pantherlike, he walked back and forth in front of her, his steady gaze burning holes in her.

Maybe he waited to hear denial or at least an explanation. She could offer neither because the disaster she foresaw many times before was unfolding. With a sense of doom, she braced herself.

"Yes, I found out," he continued, despite her silent plea to stop. "And the whole thing makes me sick. I trusted you, but obviously that was wasted. I have dealt with women from different walks of life, but you deserve special mention." His eyebrows drawn into a scowl, he shook his head at her dismissively. "You're right, we should call it quits. Anything connected to Toby is unwelcomed. You can show yourself out or I can call security."

Her reaction was swift. The slap struck his face sounding like a loud clap. Her hand stung, but he deserved it. He had the nerve to look puzzled.

"Men!" She snorted in disgust and left, slamming the door behind her.

As if under direction of divine intervention, storm clouds that hovered over the house drenched Shelly as she emerged. Her heart-wrenching sobs mixed into the crashes of thunder, drowning her anguish. Tears streamed, but were lost in the deluge of rain beating on her head. Her fears had come true. Justin knew about Toby and rejected her.

She drove back to her house in a daze. Justin not only knew her secret, but they were also no longer together. Though everything was out in the open, she felt miserable and lonely. The elusive peace that Mrs. Beacham referred to remained as distant as the retreating storm.

All that remained was inner turmoil.

Fifteen

Shelly waited. Late into the afternoon with curtains still drawn, casting her bedroom into an artificial darkness. She wasn't sure what it was that made her experience a sense of anticipation. Maybe she hoped that her phone would ring and Justin would be calling to apologize. But as the hours went by, there was no phone call from anyone.

Desperately she wanted to talk to Leesa, although she didn't have any faith that her friend could untangle the latest complications. Never had she felt so alone. She remained curled into a ball in the middle of her bed, waiting.

Someone rang the doorbell.

The thing she feared most was at hand. The waiting was over, now it was time to face the devil. Toby.

Despite the continual ringing, though, she didn't budge. There was no need to rush toward the nasty scene bound to unfold. Extra seconds gave her time to perform some self-talk. She had nothing to lose and decided to say aloud words and phrases that once spoken empowered her to dispel her insecurities.

It also didn't hurt to beg. "Go away," she moaned.

The doorbell rang again, and this time the person kept up a constant ringing. Toby had the tenacity of a pit bull and he wouldn't leave until he got what he wanted. Uncurling, Shelly got of bed and checked herself in the mirror. Her fear could not be hid in the mirror's unbiased feedback.

Eyes swollen. Hair tousled. Heavy gloominess wrapped itself around her, enveloping her in a shroud. Regardless of how devastating she looked, one major contributor to her hell was about to be extinguished. A person could be pushed for only so long and so far.

The other cause—well, she sighed morosely. Her heart would ache for a long time.

With leaden feet, she walked to the door. An unusual calmness flowed through her as she opened it. She had no time to question the source of her calmness, but was thankful that it kept the jitters at bay.

Toby brushed past her angrily. "What the heck took you so long?" He was clearly agitated.

Shelly closed the door, giving the simple action undue deliberation. She didn't bother to answer him. It wouldn't have made a difference because he was so furious. Although her decision had her full commitment, riling Toby any further wasn't in her best interest.

In the living room, she sat deep in the chair, clutching a pillow. He sat next to her. Frown still firmly in place.

"I don't have time. I expected you to call me this morning. Now that most of the day is gone, let's get on with the plan." He leaned forward with a sick eagerness that Shelly found repulsive.

Though he chattered on with his elaborate plan of conquer and humiliation, Shelly mentally took a step back. Her body would have to endure Toby's dysfunctional behavior, but her spirit no longer cared or wanted to be involved in his caper. His lifelong ambition seemed to be ruining lives and crushing spirits. Shelly was quite sure she was not the first to have been threatened by his cruel nature. For the first time, she was pleased that Justin would not be dragged into the quagmire of her life.

Toby sized her up, frowning at what he saw. "Why are you looking disinterested? Do you think I've changed my mind?"

"Why am I so important to your plan?"

"Why? You owe me."

That pissed her off. "Owe!" she yelled, eyes blazing. Had he gone completely over the edge?

"If you hadn't acted like some shy schoolgirl, teasing me, I wouldn't have gotten mad and the lawyer wouldn't have been needed."

Shelly listened, not believing how illogical Toby sounded. He evidently blamed her, despite the fact that she had to go the doctor to treat her bruises. Her emotions were another matter. She had to tend to those herself.

"As usual you're hobnobbing around money with Thornton, like you did with me. This time, it's gonna bite you in the butt, because if you screw this up, it means your demise. Your precious boyfriend won't want to be with you, then. Can you handle that?" He grinned evilly into her face.

Shelly clutched the pillow tighter to her body. Physically, she felt exhausted with no reserve energy. To her surprise, her inner self was undaunted at Toby's menacing presence.

Shelly focused on this to face him. "It's my turn to ask whether you can handle the fact that I won't take part in your plan. The reason that I'm a part of your world of chaos is what you think you have over my head. Knowing you, you probably didn't even come up with a plan B because you were so sure that I would help you. I would suggest that you start thinking of alternatives."

He grabbed her up from the chair and shook her. Shelly felt as if her head would be shaken off her neck as it snapped back and forth. She struggled to get loose to no avail. His desire to control swept him up in the emotion.

"Are you playing games with me? Is it that you think I won't do as I say?"

He stopped shaking her and let go. Shelly fell to the floor, giving her head time to settle. Talking between gasps as she tried to shake the dizziness away. "Your threats are empty, Toby. You can't hurt me anymore."

Pulling up herself, she stood face-to-face. Her words reinforced the inner strength that may have been only the size of a kernel. The more she stared back at Toby and his dark soul, her strength grew because she was no longer afraid.

Determined and riled up, she brushed back her hair. "It's over, Toby. Whatever you had planned will have to go on without me. I've broken things off with Justin."

Toby's face resembled a mask of madness, eyebrows arched with a deep-furrowed brow. His mouth had an unnatural shape that expressed the depth of his anger and frustration. "Do you think that's it for you, then? After I crush the Thorntons, I will turn my attention on you." He pointed a finger at her. *"You* will be next."

With the new fortitude, Shelly surrendered to her new sense of self. With this attitude, she brought a close to the evening. "Toby, I think it's your turn to be on guard. Threats only work when the victim is afraid or has something to lose. For some time I have given you that power over me, making me think that I had lost something that couldn't be regained. Behind every bad thing is something good. I lived in darkness, in fear, ignorance, and self-loathing because of what you put me through. No more."

She walked over to the door and with a decisive gesture pointed to the opening. "It's time for you to leave. You can expect to hear from my lawyer. I would suggest you focus on yourself and forget about the Thorntons. Your troubles are only beginning."

He laughed cruelly. "Don't play with the giants, you'll get stomped on. Lest you forget, you signed a waiver."

"Yes, I signed the papers that you coerced me to sign. But don't you forget that I never took a penny from you."

For the first time since she knew him, he was left speechless. Disconcerted at her new independence, he shifted uneasily, unsure of what to do next.

"There's nothing for you to think about, Toby. It's over. Good-bye." When he was safely out of her home, she taunted, "Don't leave town." With that, she slammed the door shut.

Leaning against it, she smiled. In no way did she think that the actions she had just taken part in would receive positive reactions. With her sincere desire to seek justice in the pursuit of moral retribution, she would need help. With a dependability that she found comforting, she knew she could turn to her parents and Leesa.

She only wished that she could share her triumph with Justin, but it was too late. She couldn't very well call him up and explain it all. Besides, Justin already suspected the worst between Toby and her. She couldn't bear to hear his sarcasm if she was to bring him into her confidences.

Tomorrow was another day. Her battle would continue then.

After Toby's departure, she had to regroup. The only way to beat Toby was to outthink him and prepare for his counterattack. By giving him notice, Shelly knew Toby's reaction would be swift.

Finally, the phone rang for the first time that day. Shelly answered. It was Nancy from the agency.

"Hey, haven't talked to you in a while. Things must be going great for you." Nancy's upbeat voice lifted her spirits.

"Yeah, great," Shelly lied. "The reason I paged you earlier is that I need to take a few days off from the job to take care of personal stuff."

"Anything I can help with?"

"No, I just need you to clear it with the Thorntons. I am not due back for another day, but I'll be leaving tonight."

"I'll put a call through and get someone out there. How many days exactly?"

"Three." Again, she lied.

Her plan was never to return to the Thorntons' home. She did feel miserable that she would never see Phillip again, but she would write a note.

Then there was Mildred. Without planning to, she had gotten into something way over her head, giving truth to Mildred's warning. She shook away the intense guilt trip coming over her. She would have to make her apologies later.

After talking to Nancy, she went upstairs to pack. Her main desire was to conceal her movements as she prepared to fight Toby. Because of this, her parents' home wasn't an option. This left only Leesa as a person she felt close to and could get the support from that she needed.

She held the receiver between her shoulder and ear, waiting for Leesa to answer. Clothes and toiletries were tossed in randomly as she went from her drawers to the closet to the vanity.

Leesa's answering machine clicked on instructing the caller to have a message or to page her for an emergency. She left a message that she was on her way over for a couple of days.

She thought about how generous and thoughtful Leesa was. Anyone in distress could reach her twenty-four hours a day. The counselor had dedicated her life to rebuilding the lives of others. Leesa had offered her an open invitation to her house whenever she needed it, even providing her with a key. Their friendship had a special quality that

Shelly shared with no one else. It felt good to have a dear friend that expected nothing from her.

Packing completed, she had a small suitcase on wheels and a matching makeup case. Giving the room and then the entire apartment a once-over, she picked up her luggage to leave.

The doorbell rang, startling her. She expected no one, unless Toby had returned. She looked through the peephole on tiptoe. Exhaling noisily, she opened the door to deal with Austin Cooper, Toby's attorney. The devil's helper had visited her in the hospital emergency room for her signature. Her alarm grew at the sight of a thick-necked, wrestler type who accompanied him.

The brain and the muscle showed up at her door. Sarcastically she thought, now they were a complete person.

She didn't move aside for them to enter. Her home had already been contaminated with the likes of Toby. Anyway, she was on her way out and nothing they had to say could sway her.

"What do you two want?"

"Nice to see you, Miss Bishop."

Cooper's head was laced with perspiration despite the sun setting and slight breeze. His skin, the color of chalk, coupled with the continuous habit of licking his top lip, made her stomach churn. His outstretched hand offered in greeting was met by stony disregard.

He rubbed his hands together, she guessed, to give the chunky appendages something to do.

"May we talk?" His high-pitched whine irked her.

She frowned at him. "No. As a matter of fact, get off my property."

"Well, Ms. Bishop, if we don't talk now, Roc here will provide his personal escort service until you reach your destination. As memory serves, you've already had a taste of that." His smile made him look ghoulish with chipped, brown teeth.

Fear gripped her and she had to swallow the lump in her throat before continuing. However, she stood her ground. If she let them into her home, no one would be there to witness their heinous acts.

Although it was twilight, people were out jogging and walking their dogs before settling in for the night. The strange trio, a black woman and two white men, one resembling a blimp and the other looking like Hulk Hogan, drew stares. Shelly didn't know Morse code, but tried blinking, tapping her feet, even moving her lips to gain any passerby's attention.

"No one can help you."

Cooper had seen her weak attempts, and merely chuckled, before breaking into spasms of coughing. His huge girth bounced with each thunderous expulsion. Her thoughts turned dark at what she wished his fate to be.

He leaned against the railing outside the apartment. His sidekick remained where he stood, within arm reach of Shelly.

Cooper got down to business. "My client is very distressed at your threat. Realizing how emotional women tend to be, I tried to explain to him that it was probably that time of the month. Despite my best efforts, I could not ease his fears. And, here I am." He wiped his brow and flicked the sweat from his fingers. He continued, "I have to remind you that the contract you signed prohibited you from speaking about the events or you will be sued." He surveyed her apartment with contempt. "From what I can tell, you can't afford to be sued." Pulling up his pants unsuccessfully under his paunch, he laid down the ultimatum. "The decision you need to make today, right now, is whether you want to forget the whole thing, making your apologies to Toby, of course; or you can declare war and deal with the consequences."

The wrestler moved closer. Shelly thought she actually heard him growl. Instinctively, she cringed.

What was there to decide? Either she backed down and realized that she was out of her league, or be demolished. Crazy thoughts ran through her mind, which caused her to laugh with a touch of hysteria. Her guests didn't appreciate humor in the middle of their performance. Shelly wished she could stifle it, but it was a trademark of her nervousness.

She took a deep breath. Her nerves still shook and she concentrated on what she had to say. There was no turning back from what she had already set in motion. Her love for Justin had been sacrificed for what she had decided to do. It would all be for naught if she didn't go through with it.

"Mr. Cooper, you may think me a fool for not taking you up on your offer. But if I did, I couldn't live with myself and I would be no better than you." Her mother always said she had spunk. More than likely, she would probably add the words "too much."

"Justice is long overdue," she pressed, not allowing the attorney's shocked expression to affect her. "I'm not the one who started this. If Toby Gillis had stayed out of my life, I would probably have continued on, visiting therapists for the rest of my life. He's a menace and he has to persist until he has destroyed his victim. Here's where I put an end to it." She lied for self-protection, "The ball has started rolling. I've given a statement to the police and if I disappear or get hurt, your client will be the first person they'll come looking for. You're already in deep, Mr. Cooper. Abduction and murder will turn you into the monster you work for."

Silence was her reply. Only the crickets and other night

insects performed their symphony of night sounds. Tension thick as the humidity waited for the first person to give way. Determined and emboldened, Shelly stared down her opponents.

Finally, Cooper shoved himself off the railing. He glared at her, before addressing his assistant, "Roc, let's go. We tried. He'll have to do it himself." At the bottom of the stairs, he turned. "Your speech about my ethics and your high morals was cute. But, you're going to wish you weren't born."

Shelly watched them get into a small compact car. Both looked like giants in a toy car. She didn't move from the front door until their rear lights disappeared into the night.

As if she were awakening from a deep sleep, her movements were slow. She picked up the suitcases and walked away from the apartment. Her life was about to change.

Leesa lived about twenty minutes from her house. Frequently she looked into the rearview mirror for car lights that might be following. Traffic was fairly heavy because of the major league baseball audience leaving Baltimore after the game. The heavy flow prevented her from picking out any tails, but also provided her cover.

Driving out of the city limits, into Baltimore county, Shelly eventually pulled into Leesa's driveway and jumped out as if someone followed her. Leesa opened the door and ran out to meet her. The two women hugged tightly, drawing strength from each other.

Leesa held her friend at arm's length. "Are you okay? I called your house after I got your message. There was no answer and I expected you much earlier."

It was at this point, when Shelly felt safe, that her emotions gave way. She sank into her friend's arms that supported her. The two entered the house with Shelly leaning heavily on Leesa's arm.

Shelly sobbed into her hands. "I think I've lost my mind." She wiped tears away and leaned back, staring at the ceiling. Forcing back a fresh wave of tears, she brought her friend up to date from the ill-fated day that she saw Toby in the bar up to the show of intimidation she had experienced a few minutes ago.

Leesa listened without interruption. The only sign that she was agitated was the furious twisting of her locks. When Shelly's voice died at the story's end, her hands stilled. "You make me proud. Let's get you settled. Hungry?"

Shelly shook her head. Food would feel like lead in her stomach. The thought made her feel nauseated.

"Coffee, then?"

"That's fine."

Leesa led her through the ranch-style home to the bedrooms. The room she adopted for her brief stay was not overly furnished.

"Didn't move too much in here. That way, you could do whatever you needed to make it your home away from home."

Shelly hugged her friend tightly. "I don't know what I would do without you." Her voice caught. "Thank you."

Leesa tried to be nonchalant, but tears filled her eyes and she accepted her friend's show of appreciation.

"I'll leave you to unpack. Meet me in the kitchen when you're done. By the way, there is a phone in your room."

Again, Shelly was overcome with her friend's generosity. The room was uncarpeted with highly polished floors. The scatter rugs blended with the main colors of the room. Always attracted to natural lighting, she walked over to the windows. The neighbor's house was close enough for her to make out a child's bedroom directly across from hers.

A small face came into view. A little girl with pigtails

played peekaboo with the bedroom curtain. Shelly offered a friendly grin and waved. The little girl ran out of the room. She envied the child's innocence. Life's lessons were sometimes harsh, leaving one to wonder why. Sexual assault was one lesson that no one should have to learn.

Unpacking didn't take much time. Shelly followed the aroma of fresh coffee, which led into the kitchen. Leesa was seated in the eating nook sipping her coffee and reading the newspaper.

"Join me. I'm just catching up on today's news." She folded the newspaper, putting it aside.

Shelly pleaded, "Oh, no. Please, I don't want to take you out of your schedule. We don't have to talk now."

"You're right, we don't have to talk now." She clicked on the television.

Nightly news was already in full swing. The network featured community news and tonight's feature was the unknown fate of Hopetown Savings. The story's focus was its concern for the employees and the possibility of layoffs if a merger occurred between Hopetown and Stockton National Bank.

Shelly and Leesa watched with quiet intensity as the newscaster interviewed several individuals who worked for both banks. Her insides knotted at the anger expressed by a few scared about their future, based on her empathy for what Justin must have to deal with on a daily basis until he squashed the rumors once and for all.

After the news segment, Leesa turned to a sitcom. Neither woman watched it, each in deep thought. Shelly stifled a yawn. Suddenly, the events of the day and her tumultuous breakup had finally caught up with her. She really wanted rest.

"I'm going to turn in." Shelly yawned again. "I am truly tired. Tomorrow, we can discuss what I should do next."

"I can tell you now. Talk to Justin."

Surprised at Leesa's advice, she stopped. "Justin is out of the picture now."

"I know what you said, but it may be time to reconsider. Let's not go into it. Go to bed. See you tomorrow."

Shelly stared at her friend a little while longer, but Leesa was finished with the conversation and opened her newspaper again. The thing she was afraid of was that by Leesa suggesting she contact Justin, the weak side of her now had an excuse. He was in her every thought and she didn't need encouragement. She needed to be strong.

Before she gave in to a heavy sleep, Shelly called her parents. They were out of the loop, which was a direct act on her part. Eventually, she would need their help, but right now, she needed some time to herself to sort out the conflicting emotions raging within her. Looking at the lateness of the hour, she was sure her mother had already called her house.

"Hi, Mom."

"Honey, where have you been? I've been calling because there's a big sale at the mall and I thought you would be interested. Maybe buy matching outfits for you and Justin."

"Don't think so. I hate matching outfits." She rolled her eyes at the image. "Anyway, just wanted to let you know that I'm staying with Leesa for a couple days."

"Why?"

"Oh, uh, she's helping me with a project. I'm bushed and about to jump into bed. I'll definitely call you tomorrow because I'll probably need your help too."

"I know something is wrong. I can hear it in your voice. But I'll wait for you to tell me." Her mother's voice held uncertainty. The news of her staying with Leesa when she had an apartment that was all hers didn't make sense. As a result, her mother would worry. Shelly read out the phone number and then hung up the phone.

It wouldn't be easy. During her first crisis she had turned away from her friends and to some extent shut out her parents. This time, it would be different.

Sixteen

Many times Justin picked up the phone to call Shelly. Today was no exception. At the breakfast table, he set the receiver back on its base. This time he allowed the call to go through, but it rang with no answer.

It was six in the morning, where could she be? He sighed with exasperation. He didn't want to talk to her, but he didn't like not knowing where she was. Remembering how afraid she was a few nights ago, he hoped something bad hadn't occurred.

Mrs. Beacham entered quietly with a pot of coffee. She poured silently without interrupting his brooding.

"Is my father awake, Mrs. Beacham?"

"Yes, he is." She stood waiting respectfully, coffeepot in hand. "Why don't you go see him?"

Justin rubbed the tiredness away from his eyes. Dark circles outlined his eyes that were slightly puffy from sleeplessness. He nodded and took his coffee cup with him.

Knocking lightly, he entered the room. Curtains were already drawn back, allowing dawn's early light to enter. This highlighted the physical deterioration of his father's condition. Justin's hand shook. His grief numbed the sting of burning liquid that spilled. Tenderly he greeted his father. His forehead deeply furrowed as he restrained his emotions.

"Am I going to see a grown man cry?" His father's taunting was tempered by his weakened voice.

As Justin walked closer to the bed, his father squinted at him. He put his glasses on and inspected his son through the lower section of the bifocals. "You look like hell."

Trust his father to be blunt. He tried not to let his miserable circumstances consume him to the point that he wore them like an outer skin. Even the smile he showed his father didn't offer any of his usual warmth and exuberance.

"I didn't come in here to talk about me. I came to see you and spend quality time with you."

"Changing the subject, I see." His father raised his hand at his son's protest. "All right. All right. I'll leave you be." He looked toward the window. "It's been a while since I've been outdoors for reasons other than going to that infernal doctor."

"Maybe we can work something out. Roll the bed out to the patio for a half hour or so."

"That would be nice." His father gave him a grateful look. "I miss going out there with Shelly. She truly appreciated nature's beauty. Gosh, what a gal! But, you know that already."

Justin's hearing had tuned in at the mention of Shelly's name. Shelly was quite a gal with all the sneaking tricks of the trade. His wounded ego festered. He cursed the day he laid eyes on her. If he had only been thinking with his brain, he would have kept her at a distance like all the others.

Phillip sighed, absentmindedly picking at the comforter. "I guess I'll have to make do until she returns."

"Where did she go?" Her sudden absence disturbed Justin. "Was this planned?"

"All the agency said was Shelly had to take an unexpected leave of absence." He paused. "It's all my fault."

Justin shot his father a sharp look. "You know something."

"How do you figure?"

Justin leaned toward his father. He looked into eyes that mirrored the same shape and color. His father, who meant everything in the world to him, could never hide anything from him for long.

"Spill it, Dad."

Stomach muscles tightened instinctively for whatever news his father would impart. Since his father wasn't grinning and oozing self-confidence, he prepared himself for the worst.

Phillip patted his hand. The old man's face reflected his deep love for his son. "Okay, son. But, let me explain my position first."

The way his father spoke with quiet sadness added to his queasiness. His gut instinct told him that what he was about to hear would affect him, probably change his life. He nodded once he mentally prepared himself for the impending news.

"My time is drawing closer, and—"

"Don't. You can fight it."

"The spirit may be willing, but the body . . . You'll have to come to terms with it and be strong."

"Strong? For whom?" Justin's voice rose, the anguish evident in his tone. "I don't want to be strong and dignified. It's not fair and I won't accept it."

"You had no one else, until Shelly. That was my greatest wish come true. I wanted to see you happily settled down with someone you could spend your life with." His expression grew sad. "I hoped it would've been Shelly."

The news shocked Justin, but surprisingly not with a great impact. For the first time he admitted that he had never stopped suspecting that his father had manipulated the entire thing. Despite knowing this, he had looked forward to playing along in the game.

"I'd hoped that both of you would have recognized the wonderful strengths in each other and that any weaknesses you could overcome." He sighed. "It was an old man's wish."

"I did recognize her strengths. And because of them, I fell in love," Justin admitted to ease his father's doubts that all had not been a failure.

Though the words were said a little too late, he had to say them. Once they were said, his heart kept screaming, *I love Shelly.*

There was a dark side to the sensitive scene. Because of her weaknesses, he had learned to despise her. He couldn't let his father sense the strong, raging flow of emotions that crushed his being and threatened to drive him to distraction.

"So you don't hate me for playing matchmaker, for butting into your life?"

"No." It was his turn to pat his father's hand, reassuringly.

"Shelly does."

"What? She knows?"

"I only wanted to—"

"How long did she know?"

"—to make you happy and after I got to know her, make her happy too."

Justin barely listened. His thoughts raced. Her parting words came back to him. Stubbornly he resisted the urge to clear her of any wrongdoing. There was still the matter with her connection to Toby.

"Son, I know she loves you. I could see it. Anybody could see it." He glared at his son. "You would have too if you weren't so damn complicated. Now, she's gone. You're alone. And, I, well, I'm here."

"It's all very well to pretend that my life is some fairy tale, Dad. But, there was one thing that your little plan didn't account for."

"What's that?"

"Toby Gillis."

Justin expected shock, maybe even dismay. Instead, his father remained looking at him as if he had lost his common sense. Never mind his level of intelligence. His father was *not* surprised.

"You knew!"

"I know a lot of things. What exactly are you accusing me of?"

The tired look was gone from Phillip's face. His verbal sparring with his son gave him a spark of energy that added a devilish glint in his eyes. It was obvious that he needed constructive projects to keep his motivation on the upswing. Too bad it had to be at his expense, Justin reasoned.

"I haven't begun to accuse you of anything. I just want to know what the connection is between Toby and Shelly. I want to know why Connors suggested that I talk to you. I want—"

"Connors has a big mouth," Phillip interrupted. "I hired him to do a job, not run his mouth—"

Justin frowned. "Hired?" It was Justin's turn to interrupt.

"I hired Connors to look into Shelly's background." Phillip kept his eyes averted from his son's glare. "There was an unpleasantness in her past with Toby Gillis."

Before he delved into any more secrets that had once lain hidden in Shelly's life, Justin wanted clarification. "So, she's not connected with Toby on any underhanded scheme?"

"Hell no!" yelled Phillip. "What nonsense! Who said that she was?"

Justin tried to calm his father. It alarmed him how feisty the old man got over Shelly, and at the same time, it surprised him. Shelly had managed to work her way into the hearts of the Thornton men.

"I thought she was. I accused her of such." Defensively, he finished, "But you don't know for certain what happened between her and Toby. Like me, you were suckered into believing that title, 'Volunteer of the Year.'"

His father groaned. "If you weren't suffering from a broken heart right now, I would call you a big-headed idiot. You're right, I don't know much about her dealings with that ass, Toby. But, I believe that young girl is honest and kind and deserves the same in return." His father rubbed the salt deeper into the wound. "Are you man enough to handle that?"

"What happened with her and Toby?" Justin asked, a notch subdued. His father could always humble him.

Phillip leaned back exhausted. Despite the exciting conversation, his endurance fizzled. "Son, Shelly will have to be the one to tell you. If you truly love her, you'll go to her before it's too late. Think about what you want in the future and who you want to spend it with. My heart goes out to her. She's strong, beautiful, and has a generous spirit."

Touched by his father's words, Justin wished he had been more perceptive. The destructive nature of jealousy he experienced when he heard Toby's connection with Shelly made him react irrationally. Now that his male pride had fouled everything, he wouldn't waste any more time.

He kissed his father's brow. "Thanks, Dad. I love you."

"I love you, too."

The strong family bond was the foundation of the tender scene between father and son. For so many years, they had no one but each other. Justin had protected himself from the early loss of his mother and impending death of his father with a deliberate distancing of anything that required his emotional commitment.

For his troubles, his protection from the world had hardened his heart. Although many ladies, beautiful, rich, and holding celebrity status, had sashayed their way into his life, he had coldly kept them at bay. He enjoyed what they offered, but his heart wasn't for sale.

Then came Shelly.

Immediately she had found the chink in his armor. With all her charm, sensuality, and intelligence, she had burrowed into the inner region of his soul. Like a conqueror, she had laid claim and he had willingly offered no hindrance.

With mystical proportions, she possessed him. No matter how much he had wanted to hate her when he suspected her role with Toby, her spell over him forced him to reconsider his negative perceptions.

With his soul ready to be bared, he stood in front of her door. In his car on the way over, he had rehearsed all the right things to say. He had even pulled over to the side of the road at a curbside flower vendor. Like a remorseful suitor, he held a bouquet of red, white, and yellow roses. They represented the passion, friendship, and love he wanted to share with Shelly. In a heady scented cloud, he kept his finger on the buzzer.

He glanced over at the parking lot but didn't see her car. He leaned over the rail to see if he could make out whether there was a light on in the apartment window. He could only see into the living room. Everything sat neatly in its place.

"She's gone."

Justin jumped from the voice behind him. He turned to acknowledge the messenger of bad news.

"Gone?"

"Yep." A ten-year-old boy stood at the bottom of the stairs chewing gum with great gusto. He rocked from side to side staring at Justin.

Justin sighed. His apology wasn't going to be easy with

Shelly vanishing. From the looks of things, the little boy wanted to feel important and was not going to impart any news with urgency.

"Where to?"

"How much is it worth to you?" The boy grinned, clearly enjoying his important status.

"Boy." Justin used his authoritative tone, deepening it even more. "Don't play with me. I'll come down there and snatch you up off your fee—"

"Mama, Mama." The boy ran to the apartment building next to Shelly's. His high-pitched screams had many people sticking their heads out to see the cause. Justin felt like a heel.

A woman who resembled the little boy, probably his mother, came out to investigate. The boy wasn't too far behind her, sticking his tongue out at Justin.

Justin tried to keep focused on the woman, instead of showing the little boy his fist and then holding it up to each eye to demonstrate what he would like to do with him. No, it wouldn't be a good idea. His mother looked like she could beat the crap out of him and send him screaming for his dad.

"She's not there, mister." She scrutinized him from head to foot. "I've seen you around here before."

Justin nodded.

"She's been gone for a few weeks. I collect her mail for her."

"Does she pick it up from you?" he asked hopefully.

"Naw."

"So, you have her address?"

Shelly's neighbor was making the entire process tedious. Justin forced himself to remain calm. He had a feeling that, if he pushed her, she would clam up and go back into her house.

"Yeah, but she told me not to give it to anyone."

Justin wanted to scream. Calmness, tranquillity, serenity, he repeated the mantra to keep grounded. Then, a small lie began to form in his head. "I have news about her mother, Clara. It's important that I let Shelly know what happened to her."

The woman's eyes narrowed, suspicion firmly in place. "I don't believe you." She turned to go back into her apartment.

Justin had expected his charm to work, it usually did. Shelly's neighbor wasn't having any of it, though. Nothing left to do, but throw himself at her mercy. "Look, I'm a friend of hers." *Some friend,* his conscience chided. "She may be in trouble and I would like to help her."

"I've seen you here before." She smirked, "All lovey-dovey. Then, you stopped coming and the other guy started to visit." She leaned toward him and whispered conspiratorially, "He didn't know I was watching, but I saw him a couple of times sitting in his car staring at her building. Then, after a while, he'd drive off." She looked toward the parking lot.

Justin followed her gaze, imagining. The vision wasn't pleasant. Did Toby pick up where he left off?

"Can you describe the guy?" His tone was cold and flat.

Delighting in her topic, the woman launched into her story with hands gesticulating and eyes rolling for added flavor. "Everything about him was perfect. A little too perfect, if you ask me. He reminded me of a snake just a-slinking along with his good looks, clothes, and that fancy car. He's the kinda guy that just when you think he's okay, he jumps up and bites you." She turned her sharp glare onto Justin. "I don't know what happened between the two of you, but that creep wasn't the answer." She shook her head. "Talking here with you, I think you're all right. I can spot a jerk a mile away. I'll tell you what you need to know. I send the mail to her mother's."

Justin didn't waste a minute. After thanking her, he ran to his car and headed for Annapolis. The steady humming of the tires against the asphalt and the rhythmic flashing of the Parkway signs had him in a quasi-hypnotic state as he conjured Toby and Shelly together.

According to his father something unpleasant had occurred between the two. Yet her nosy neighbor said another guy, and her description matched Toby, had visited several times. If it had been so unpleasant for her, why did he make it past her front door?

He banged the steering wheel, causing the car to lurch into another lane. With concerted effort, he tried to focus on his driving—to no avail.

Of all the people she had to be seeing behind his back. Toby was the enemy. She knew this. It left Justin with only one explanation, that they had planned the entire thing. Their goals were to take the bank his father had helped build and at the same time make a fool out of him.

He looked at his reflection in the rearview mirror. "Well, she succeeded. You are a fool."

Earlier he had left his father's side ready to apologize and declare his undying love to a treacherous wretch.

Why did he let down his guard? His behavior was like a lovesick teenager's.

Now, there would be no show of remorse. He still wanted to see her, but the image of him embracing her left him with a sick feeling. She would be lucky if he managed to keep his temper in check.

He pulled up in front of her parents' house. It was nine o'clock, but lights were still on in the lower level. As he walked up the path, he pasted a smile on his face. It didn't have the effect he intended. Instead it heightened the tension in his face bringing more attention to the false emotions he showed.

The door opened almost immediately when he pushed

the doorbell. Clara smiled warmly, opening it wider for him to enter. "Hi, Justin." Then as she realized the lateness of the hour, her smile vanished and she held his arm. "Is Shelly okay?"

Justin felt rotten at having to pretend. "I'm here because I'm concerned about her. Frankly, Mrs. Bishop, I don't know how to reach her."

"Oh," Clara remarked thoughtfully. "Let's have a seat. Maybe we can help each other and my daughter."

It seemed a long time ago since Shelly's birthday. He could honestly say that he was in love, then. They were both happy, thinking life was truly great with all her friends and their parents there to share in her day. His heart swelled with pride that he had contributed to her joy in planning the entire affair. Her elation held him under her power.

He and Clara sat at the breakfast bar sipping coffee. Bill joined them. Justin felt nervous, especially since he harbored such negative feelings toward their daughter.

"Young man, you and I haven't chatted much. And there's a time and place for everything, but not today and not now. My daughter has disappeared. She calls her mother every day, and we know where she is, but we also know something is terribly wrong." He delivered his words eye-to-eye, man-to-man. With the same serious contemplation, he added, "I also feel that you are wrapped up in this somehow. That's my little girl out there. So before we tell you what you want to know, you need to tell us something. Shelly hasn't talked yet."

"We're supposed to be meeting tomorrow for lunch," Clara added. "She said she will tell me then."

Justin exhaled all the anger and frustration that had built up on the drive over to the Bishops' home. Understanding the love and concern for their daughter, he would be careful of how he expressed himself. "I don't know how much Shelly told you about us."

"She said she loves you," Clara offered.

"We had a bit of a misunderstanding."

"About what?" Bill asked bluntly.

Justin hesitated for a second. "Her involvement with Toby."

"Involvement?" Clara fairly shouted. "That was sexual assault, attempted rape. Choose whatever words you want to use, but there was no involvement."

A bombshell had been dropped. Justin was certain he could hear his heart beating in his ear. Words didn't come easily after such a revelation. He clutched the mug to remain focused.

Of all the things crossing his mind, attempted rape hadn't been a consideration. Her acceptance speech replayed in his mind. Not once did he think that Toby was the cause of her pain. He closed his eyes at his insensitivity toward Shelly. How callous he'd sounded, even to his own ears. He was ashamed. But, she never said, even after his accusation. How could she with his attack?

Shelly's dad reached out to touch his shoulder. "This is a shock to you, I can tell."

"I didn't mean to yell at you," Clara said apologetically. "I'm just a little tense. I take it she never told you. Why did you think they were involved?"

"With Toby Gillis breathing down my neck about the bank, I only found out recently that they knew each other and he had been visiting her home. I assumed—" Chastened, he apologized.

"Don't fret," Clara reassured. "I know Shelly loves you with all her heart. If both of you can forgive each other, you still have a marvelous life together to look forward to."

Satisfied with Justin's nod, she admitted, "Shelly's at Leesa's. Why don't you come with me tomorrow and you can talk to her? Maybe reason with her that running away isn't the answer."

"Thanks, Mrs. Bishop."

"Clara, please."

"Thanks, Clara."

It seemed like a decade ago that he had experienced happiness. But the thought of seeing Shelly tomorrow made him feel invincible and good old-fashioned happy at the same time. He hugged Clara, shook her father's hand, and left.

Shelly would have the surprise of her life. He just hoped she wouldn't refuse to see him. Since she felt manipulated, it was up to him to win her trust back. He swore he would win not only her trust, but also her love again.

can. As much as she could love, she needed someone to
love her in return.

The way she felt and looked at him, that flip-flop sight was
a comfort only she had that truly reflected her concern for him.
But she wasn't sure how she would act once he smiled or, Lord
forbid, if he had a fit of laughter.

Lord help her, she was reaching for straws. Not a single
smile passed over his face since he'd boarded and threatened
her with Quiet, lady, or I'll see to it you won't ever utter a_
sound.

Seventeen

Now that it was morning, Shelly could stop pretending
that she was asleep. Justin was the cause of her restless
night spent tossing and turning with her indecision to call
him. It wasn't going to be easy moving on with a life without him.

If she didn't call him, he could return to life as usual.
There would be no one to bring humiliation and disgrace
to his family or business concerns. And his father would
have to find another willing victim.

She punched the pillow under her head viciously. It
wasn't right to be mean-spirited about Phillip. Breaking
the rule, she had nurtured a personal relationship with
Phillip, even if it was all his handiwork. She didn't have to
go along with it, but immediately she felt a special connection to him. Out of all her mess, she treasured her
special friendship with him.

Because of her, his dream had been smashed to pieces.
When things died down a bit, she had to return to Phillip
to make amends for her rude behavior.

There would be no Shelly and Justin.

The problem with Phillip's dream was the assumption
that love would naturally occur and everything else would
fall into place.

Witnessing twenty-some years of happiness and stability within her parent's marriage, she wouldn't settle for

less. As much as she could love, she needed someone to love her in return.

The way Justin had looked at her that ill-fated night was a mirror into his soul that truly reflected his contempt for her and his anger. It was clear he would not be the candidate to love her as she needed to be loved.

Leesa popped her head into the room. "Wake up, sleepy-head." Her friend dressed in jogging attire walked in and plopped onto the bed. "I want us to go work out this fine morning."

Although Shelly wasn't sleepy, a jog first thing in the morning wasn't in her plan.

"How about you go jog and I'll stay and make us breakfast?" She hugged the pillow tightly as if it provided an anchor to the bed.

"No way. Breakfast for me is cottage cheese and a grapefruit." Leesa extended her arms. "Got to keep that flab off these arms." Then she stood and modeled her thighs, flexing her quads and hamstrings. "Also got to keep that cellulite away from these thighs."

"You make me sick!" Shelly didn't complain about her size, which was still in the single digits, but her endurance could stand some improvement. She threw off the covers and pushed Leesa out of the way. "Okay, let's go before I change my mind. So with all this exercising, is there someone else appreciating the effort?" teased Shelly.

Leesa skipped out of the room, and answered over her shoulder, "Maybe. See you outside, slowpoke. Gotta go warm up."

Sitting on the deck off the dining room, Leesa and Shelly enjoyed the coolness of their grapefruit after a thirty-minute jog through the neighborhood. If the morning was any indication of the day, it would be beautiful and sunny with low humidity. The heat wave appeared to be over and in a few weeks, fall would officially begin.

"Mmm. This is good," remarked Shelly with new wonder. "Can't promise to make this a daily habit, though. However, sitting out here soaking up the rays is ideal."

Leesa agreed. She fanned out her locks and leaned the chair into a semireclining position. "This is where I come to meditate. The woods back here make me feel separated from the hustle and bustle of city living. My immediate neighbors don't have young kids, so it's very peaceful." She threw a sidelong glance at her friend. "By the time I go back indoors, I've solved whatever problems are simmering." She added encouragingly, "Why don't we try to solve yours?"

Shelly knew where Leesa was headed before her last remark. She didn't see much reason to pursue a solution. Her mind had presented an answer, or perhaps it did and she refused to acknowledge its prompting. However, sitting outside and communing with nature seemed like a waste of time. She'd keep that opinion to herself.

"If I could grant you your wish, what would it be?" Leesa prompted when Shelly didn't reply.

Shelly thought about only one thing, one person. "Justin."

"Then, what's stopping you?"

"My past. He knows about me and what happened." She turned to Leesa, her face contorted with anguish. "He looked at me as if I were something a dog left behind and he stepped in it. I couldn't let him see how much he had hurt me, made me feel unworthy." She finished softly, "Because of that, I can't ever go back to him. It's over."

"Do you control the weather?"

Shelly looked at her friend to make sure she understood the question. What was she getting at? She looked around as if the answer lay among the trees or on the lawn.

"Do you control the weather?" Leesa repeated slowly.

"No."

"Okay. Do you like this weather?"

"Yes, now what has this got to do with anything?" Shelly muttered. She hated it when Leesa went all New Age on her.

"Calm down. My point is that there are some things in life you have no control of, but you can have a perception based on your experience. I bet you liked the weather because a sunny day means outdoors, beach weather, cookouts, and so on. Likewise, a wet day would be the opposite of all those."

"So?"

"It doesn't have to be, Shelly. Think about it. You have control over your destiny, but based on your experiences you're letting your perception of life drag you down. Did Justin ever say you were unworthy of him? Yeah, he's struggling with a few things himself, but no one should have the power to make you feel less than who you really are." She stood to leave. "I'm going to leave you now. I've got to get to the center. Look inside yourself, Shelly. Love who you are, and all those around you will also."

The tears started brimming and running over like a dam bursting. Her shoulders shook with the intensity of her sobs. Ever since Toby had made her feel like damaged goods, she admittedly indulged in self-hate. Looking at herself was a painful process, but she was also a survivor.

With a sudden ferocity, she wiped away her tears. Self-pity had its place, but it was time for her to take charge of her life. Along with getting rid of the bad that inhabited her life, she had to hold on to what was good. After all, she had decided to press charges against Toby. Somehow that seemed easier than meeting with Justin and fighting for the one thing that could bring ultimate happiness—his love.

Showered and dressed, she called her mother to arrange where they would meet. She missed her parents terribly, and looked forward to spending some time with her mother. She would have to call her father later. Thank goodness they were not the type of parents who would be holding a candlelight vigil until she returned, worrying her to death in the process. Her parents always gave her space. Her mini retreat had to be done without interference from anyone.

In her usual style she arrived about fifteen minutes late. Her mother knew her habits, so Shelly wasn't worried that she would leave her. Spotting her mother's sedan in the parking lot, she walked quickly to the entrance. She really did miss her.

The hostess took her back to where her mother was seated. They embraced, exchanging warm greetings.

"I feel like I haven't seen you in such a long time, although it's only been a few days. You have me worried, honey."

"I know, Mom. I just needed a few days to do some soul searching."

"And?"

"And, I have made some decisions that will require your support."

Her mother held her hand across the table. "Anything, baby. Your father is beside himself with worry. You know he doesn't say much, and now he's even quieter."

"I'll call him tonight. I'll come by in a day or two. I've got to put closure to some other matters."

Her mother looked at her speculatively. "Yes, you do." She stood, and added, "That's why Justin is here and I'm leaving so you two can talk."

The pounding began in her heart and spread throughout. Her hands turned cold and clammy. Butterflies fluttering in her stomach turned into raging moths. Words failed her and she stood openmouthed as her mother left.

From the shadows in the rear of the restaurant, he emerged. Shelly sucked in her breath. He was a vision of perfection that shouted strength, handsomeness, and virility. Dressed casually, he still looked like a million bucks. Her eyes took him all in and the experience made her feel drunk.

He had not spoken, but remained standing at the table. She gestured to the seat recently occupied by her mother. Her hands trembled slightly. From the time he appeared his eyes never left her face. His face was serene as she sat in front of him. The hostility that had been so visible was gone.

Taking a deep breath, she spoke a bit unsteadily. "H— hi, Justin."

"Hi, babe."

His words melted away the fears.

"Oh, Justin. What happened between us? What went wrong?"

He held her hands between his and put them to his lips. The soft kiss he placed on her fingers ignited the embers of her passion. She welcomed his touch. With an effort, she pulled away from his hand.

"I'm sorry," he offered.

"It's not that I don't want you to touch me." Her words erased the hurtful look. "I just think we need to talk. And honestly, I can't think when you're near me, much less touch me." She looked into his eyes like dark pools in which she felt she could happily drown.

He nodded. "Let's get out of here," he suggested. "Some place more private." He quickly added, "A neutral place."

His consideration for her feelings brought renewed hope that she was doing the right thing. "We can go back to my place."

"Are you sure?"

"Never more so."

Justin followed her back to her apartment. Shelly had to put on the air-conditioning in the car to cool down the sudden heat encompassing her body. Physical attraction was necessary to a healthy relationship, but she wondered if her addiction to Justin was a little overboard. Her heart, soul, and all of her body were his. Remembering how he could satisfy all three made her increase her speed toward home.

Maybe a neutral place was necessary.

Shelly closed the front door, watching Justin walk into the living room. From behind, he was all good. Leaning against the door, she licked her lips.

Seeing the suggestive gesture, Justin beckoned to her. Obedient, she approached him. The cologne he wore drove her senses wild. Hairs on his chest peeked through the un-buttoned shirt at his neck, driving her to distraction. She wanted to feel the wisps of hair curl around her fingers.

"Don't look at me like that, Shelly, 'cause I won't be able to say what I have to say."

She blinked several times, smoothing her clothes comically. "I'll behave, but hurry up," she said, standing with her hands clasped behind her. Then she grinned wickedly. It was amazing how the sight of him made all her inner turmoil seem ridiculous.

"Baby, I've behaved like such an ass. Sometimes people take each other for granted. You know they will always be there. You know what they like and dislike and you get comfortable. Then, when Toby entered the picture and Connors mentioned—"

"Who's Connors?"

"The detective I used to investigate you," he confessed sheepishly.

"Ah. We'll get back to that. Go on."

It was his turn to show his nervousness. "Okay. Well, when Connors mentioned that there might be a connection to Toby, I just reacted. I didn't think. All I could feel was betrayed and so angry."

"You didn't trust me enough to give me the benefit of the doubt."

"And you couldn't trust me enough, either."

"You got me."

"I was selfish," he said, humbly. "I thought only of me and what you were doing to me. Knowing Toby, I automatically thought that anyone connected to him was of the same caliber."

She flinched.

He touched her lightly under her chin. "Look at me, Shelly. I didn't know about your troubles with him. Even when I yelled at you that night, spitting out that poisonous dribble, I didn't know."

"Who told you?"

"Your parents."

Her eyes opened wider in surprise.

"I had to state my intentions before they told me," he defended hastily. "At first I couldn't understand how a sweet person like you could be with someone like Toby."

"It was a mistake. A costly one."

"I know. We will move on together and leave that behind because I love you."

She nodded. "I've carried the hurt around for too long. I'm tired. I need only you."

"Trust me, my love." He lowered his head. "Together we can overcome anything."

She ached for the touch of his lips. "I believe you," she whispered.

Her eyes closed and she leaned into him. His kiss was tender and lingering; then he trailed the tip of his tongue to her earlobe. He nibbled, drawing a moan from Shelly. She wrapped her arms around him, arching into his frame.

"I don't think I can stand to wait to take you to the bed."

Shelly unbuttoned his shirt and pulled it out of the waistband. "I don't want you to. Take me here. Now."

She knelt in front of him and unzipped his pants, planting soft kisses around his belly button. He gripped the back of her head and groaned.

Holding fast to the sides of his jeans, she pulled the legs

down, revealing Justin's aroused state. With her finger, she traced its entire length.

He gripped her wrist and growled, "Be careful, girl. I'm trying to restrain myself, but you're bringing tears to my eyes."

Her response was a kiss on the tip.

"You done gone and did it." He pulled his jeans off, hopping on each leg to get loose. Standing in his underwear and socks, he still could make her moist.

"Ready?" He grinned.

She tried to appear nonplussed leaning back propped on her elbows. "I think you ought to close the blinds."

She needed time to catch her breath. There was no telling what surprises Justin had in store, but she looked forward to them.

"Your nosy neighbors probably already had their fill." He closed the blinds and turned to address Shelly, "Think you're up for what I have to dish out?"

"We'll see who calls whose name first," she taunted.

"Mmm." With a secretive smile, he bent over to kiss her forehead. "We'll see," he challenged. "By the way, if you can't say my whole name, Jus will do."

To Shelly's amazement, he took his shirt and ripped it into two pieces. He certainly had her attention.

"My turn." He unbuttoned her shirt and then unfastened her bra.

Every brush of his fingers against her skin sent flickers of delight coursing through her. How she ached for him to stop toying with her. It was fun when she did it, but she was hot and ready for him.

Without telling her what he had in store, he pushed her gently onto the carpet. Shelly stretched sexily, extending her arms over her head. Before she knew what was happening, he tied each wrist to the legs of the coffee table.

"Justin."

She had to admit she was a little frightened, but that only made her more excited.

"That counts as one. Before the night's over, the neighbors will know my name."

With his tongue, he traced a path that traveled from the base of her throat through the valley between her breasts.

"Shh." He attempted to calm her fidgeting. "I'm going to teach you to trust me."

"I trust you," she moaned.

"We'll see after I'm done paying homage to you, my beautiful queen."

Shelly thought she would faint. Hands clenched, she writhed from the hungry passion that demanded satiating. Her body arched as he sucked on each taut nipple.

"I think I'm going to pull my arms out of the socket," she gasped. "I can't take this."

Justin kissed her lips, silencing her protests. Their tongues danced together. He covered her face with quick brushes on her cheeks, eyelids, and the tip of her nose, still teasing.

"Justin, please."

"That's two," he said, cruelly.

"I hate you," she sighed.

"That's okay, 'cause I've got enough love for the two of us."

When he undid her shorts, Shelly was sure the world was coming to an end. Eyes tightly shut, she surrendered to all the delicious surprises that Justin introduced her to. She heard the familiar tear of the foil package. Their intimacy reached new levels, as he acquainted her to the pleasures of his tongue.

"Are you ready for me now?"

"Yes." Her senses screamed their assent for him to take her to other mindless points of ecstasy.

He untied her wrists. Desire smoldering dangerously in his eyes. "I want you with me when we rock this building."

"Anything, baby."

She wrapped her legs around his well-toned body, welcoming him. The walls of her desire lay moist and willing and he plunged in with control. Raising her hips, she moved with deliberation, rocking to the beat of an inner natural rhythm. She could feel him going deeper inside and she clamped him with her thighs.

Soaring up to the heights of rapture, she dug her nails into his back. They reached climax together in a blazing glory with a flood of nature's juices flowing, intermingling. Like survivors in a storm, they clung to each other riding the waves of passion that built up, crested, and then released, until things returned to normal.

Exhausted, but beautifully satisfied, Shelly cradled Justin in the crook of her arm. She stared up at the ceiling while stroking his head. It was wrong to think about past relationships at a time like this, but with her limited experience no other man had made her feel and enjoy being a woman.

There was only one reason for that, Justin was the first man she had ever loved. He was the first man to love her. He was the first man she trusted with every fiber of her body.

Eighteen

Shelly filled the bathtub with scented oil and bath gel. The warm mist steamed the mirrors and rose up softening the light. It was their cozy den of wanton interludes. Stepping into the deep-sunken tub, she joined Justin already waist high in bubbles. His eyes hungry with naked desire drew her with a power that made her share his hunger.

They hugged each other in a sudsy embrace, kissing deeply.

The continuation of their wonderful lovemaking took place in the aromatic water. Shelly straddled her soul mate, holding his shoulders as he gripped her back. Wet hands slid across the tiled walls leaving a trail of suds as evidence of the frenzied shifts in body positions.

Justin groaned, the sound like a panther's growl. He buried his head against her breasts, nuzzling the soft mounds. His beard grazed her nipples, making her react with a tremor. Water splashed at each rocking motion, slowly at first, until they reached the point of no return. Exhausted, she fell against his hard chest.

"I have no shirt," announced Justin. He held up the two pieces of his shirt.

Shelly giggled. "I have an extra-large T-shirt in the bottom drawer." She pointed toward her chest of drawers.

Following her instructions, he held the T-shirt against

his broad chest. "Ah, I don't think big colorful flowers are appropriate."

"Do you have a choice?"

He said through gritted teeth, "This is all our fault. Why did you let me do this to my expensive shirt?"

"You were teaching me a lesson, remember?" she offered, getting dressed. Cocking her head to one side, she complimented, "I think you look kinda cute. The flowers bring out your rich skin tone and highlights the color of your eyes."

He reached out and grabbed her, silencing her laughter with a wet kiss. "That's for laughing at me."

"You can punish me any time."

"Gosh, I want you." He pushed her away. "But, I have to take a rain check." He grew serious. "Would you come with me to see my father?" He rushed on. "I know you're mad at him. But, he really misses you. Because of his condition, and all."

"Shh." She placed her fingertips gently against his lips. "You don't have to explain. I owe him an apology and a lot more. I would love to go see your father."

Now that they shared an intimacy that she could never have imagined a couple of hours ago, Shelly wanted Justin in every part of her life. The good times were always shared, but it was when the dreaded blues came and lingered threatening to send her into a depression that she would need him most. Although a big step had been made in her journey, there would be those dark hours. Her visits to the center had become a part of her life and would continue to be. Could they become a part of Justin's?

"I'm ready to talk about what happened with Toby." She sat on the edge of the bed and waited for him to do the same. "Are you ready to hear this?"

"Yes."

Courage. She needed it desperately. Drawing on her new

sense of self and confidence provided the necessary push to tell her story. She kept her focus on Justin's hands that had recently brought her pent-up passion to fruition and also conveyed his strength.

"I met Toby on the job. His aunt was ill and I was called in to care for her. The only reason he was there, he later told me, was that his aunt told him to come and meet her 'pretty little nurse.' I didn't immediately agree to go out with him because of the job and the entire situation." She laughed, harsh and bitter. "He isn't even my type. Too much the playboy. He loved to throw his money and influence in people's face. But I agreed to go out. First time, nothing happened. Second time, nothing happened and I started to think, maybe. But that third time . . ." She paused to compose herself.

"Take your time, sweetheart."

"I'm okay. I had him pick me up from home and we went to a restaurant bar. I had a few drinks. I was so gullible not realizing his motive. He kept ordering drinks, but he was barely touching his. By the time we left, I needed his help to get back to the car. I started to feel really dizzy in the car. He claimed he pulled over to help me, in case I got sick. I remember him opening the car door and holding my hands at first. Then before I knew it, he was pushing me down in the car. He hit my face a couple of times. I got scared." She shuddered, wrapping her arms defensively around herself.

The memories had carried her back to where it happened as if it were yesterday. "Something snapped when his hand moved between my thighs and he touched me. I don't remember his face. I don't even remember if I was screaming, but I brought my knee connecting to his crotch. He backed out of the car and then I kicked him in his face. Blood gushed. Everything was red. I closed the door and drove away."

She broke down weeping. Justin pulled her to his shoulder stroking her back, letting her feel his support. "I was at the hospital when his lawyer came with all these papers," she went on. "They were going to have me charged with drunk driving, car theft, assault, and anything else they could invent. I was scared and couldn't think clearly. My shoulders were bruised, my face throbbed, but he would claim that I fell while I was drunk." She drew a ragged breath. "So, I signed the papers." She looked up at Justin. His face was a tight mask concealing his emotions. "I didn't take any money. I just wanted to be left alone."

He held her close. Instinctively, she knew everything would be okay. He didn't hate her or push her away in disgust.

"I'm glad you shared that with me."

"Justin, I am part of a group that receives counseling at a rape crisis center. Although I didn't have to endure the horror of rape, sexual battery is also a major problem." She closed her eyes in an effort to concentrate and keep the tears at bay. "I would like you to attend a session with me. Not everyone in the session was raped or is a rapist, but someone close to them had endured the ordeal. It's a chance to see the different perspectives and how we all live with ourselves. Would you come?"

"Oh, darling, yes. I'll do whatever you want me to do. Your strength amazes me. I only hope that I can be strong enough for you."

"We will be for each other," she said firmly.

The phone rang and Shelly answered.

It was her father.

She gestured to Justin to remain quiet. After she explained that she was fine and Justin was back in her life, the call ended.

"Don't want Daddy to know I'm here?" he teased, planting kisses around her neck.

She squirmed away from him to fix her hair that resembled a mop on her head. "I'm Daddy's girl. I don't care how old I am, I'll always be that special girl to him. He knows what's up, but I don't have to flaunt it."

With her hair parted on the side, Shelly looked like a young college student. Her fine features, exposed without the usual framing of thick hair around her face, were breathtaking. Her eyes outlined by dark lashes had an exotic charm that glowed from her gentle nature inviting attention. As she applied her lip color, blotting her lips with tissue, her lips curled exhibiting an innocent sensuality.

"Anyone ever told you that you look like Dorothy Dandridge?"

She laughed at him. "Only your father."

Justin walked up behind her and held her against his frame.

"It's true. If you could only sing, we could make millions."

"You've heard me sing."

"Yeah, like I said. If you could only sing."

She punched his arm playfully.

Becoming serious, they looked at each other in the mirror. A striking couple obviously in love, with his height and toned physique, against her small stature. Each had gone on a personal journey rediscovering the other and sharing a quest to reach for the gift of love.

Resting his chin on top of her head, he said, "I'm the only child for my parents and you are the only girl, which automatically makes us special to them. But, I've heard about that special bond between a father and his daughter. I can only imagine how your father must feel about his little girl because I know how strongly and deeply I care for her." He moved his hands to her hips and stomach. "When we have our daughter, she won't be dating until she's in her thirties. And there certainly won't be any man in her house unless she's married."

Shelly chuckled. It felt safe and comfortable snuggled within Justin's arms talking about the future—theirs.

Then it hit her.

Her mouth opened in a perfect O. He had mentioned "our daughter." She looked at him questioningly. His eyes had never left her face reflected in the mirror.

"Yes, baby. You guessed it." He turned her around to face him. "Shelly Bishop, would you do me the honor of being my friend, my wife, my lover—my everything?" He looked ruefully at her. "Sorry, I haven't picked out a ring, as yet."

Her response was a high-pitched squeal and a loud "yes."

Momentarily stunned, she held her face while her thoughts collided in a jumble. "I have to call my parents. I have to call Leesa. Ooh, we have to tell your father." She put her hand on her chest, panting from emotional exertion. "When will we do this?"

"We can do it any time, but I'm not into any long engagements."

"I know how much this means to your father and to my parents, especially my mother when she hears. I would like to do it soon for Phillip's sake. Something small and private so he can be a part of it."

"Baby, you're so thoughtful. I don't want you to feel pressured. My father will understand if you want to plan a big wedding later on down the road."

"No, this is what I want. In a month?"

"It's a date."

Justin's eyes danced at his new fiancée's thoughtful repose. She was already in a state of planning. "I'm going to head on to my father's so I can get into something a little more my style. Go ahead and make all your calls. I'll see you in about an hour?"

He kissed her and left.

* * *

As he drove, Justin took deep breaths to calm his rapid heartbeats. His marriage proposal had taken even him by surprise. There were no second thoughts, only fears that he might not be able to make her happy for the rest of her life. The thought of spending a lifetime with her and having children with her thrilled him. He yearned for the deep sense of family and tradition his father espoused.

Sharing her ordeal with him was the best gift she could have given him. It did make him sick with thoughts of revenge. But what was important was that Shelly felt his support. Glad that she had also invited him to the center, he felt it marked the beginning of a new chapter in their lives. It made him angry at how many people were affected by one person's obsession with power. After the monster moved on without a care in the world, those people affected had to reassemble their broken lives.

News about similar monsters drew a sympathetic air whenever he heard a sensational story. The difference with this story was its personal nature. Since it was close to home, to his heart, his woman, he wanted the whole world to be outraged. However, reality dictated that only those concerned would be moved.

"Shelly, I promise to protect you, honor you, and serve you as I love you for the rest of your life."

Justin was dressed in no time and waited impatiently for Shelly to arrive. Nerves wracked him, causing him to pace and continuously look out of the window. Just as he picked up the phone, he heard the crunching of tires on the gravel. He ran to the door before a surprised Mrs. Beacham could do her job.

Openly taking Shelly by the hand when she entered, he

announced, "Mrs. Beacham, please welcome the future Mrs. Justin Thornton to the family."

He knew the news would shock the housekeeper and expected her to be coldly indifferent.

Instead, Mrs. Beacham beamed. "Congratulations to you both. I wondered how long it would take for both of you to come to your senses. Welcome, dear." She hugged them both, wishing them well.

Mrs. Beacham was part of his family and Justin had secretly wanted her blessing. He gave Shelly's hand a reassuring squeeze, after seeing her shocked expression. All would be well.

They approached his father's suite. "Could you give me a couple minutes to talk to Mildred?" Shelly whispered.

Mildred, seated at a table, deliberately kept herself immersed in a magazine. Understanding Shelly's motive, Justin excused himself and went into his father's room. He had no doubt that the two women with a budding friendship could overcome whatever misunderstandings stood between them.

Justin knocked and entered his father's room.

"Hi, son," greeted Phillip.

An oxygen tank had been brought into the room and two tubes led from it into his nose. Other heavy-duty medical equipment monitored his condition with electrodes taped to his chest. It was a blight on the wondrous occasion, but Justin resisted the urge to sink into despair.

"Dad." Justin called softly. He had good news and today they would not focus on the overpowering presence of terminal illness.

"Did you talk to Shelly? Iron out everything?"

"I did more than that, Dad."

Shelly entered, Mildred close behind, looking bewildered. With a radiance that could only be born of love, her presence brightened the room. Both men matched her beaming smile with smiles of their own.

"Shelly," cried his father. He struggled to sit up, sending the monitors bleeping noisily.

"I'll come to you." She rushed over and they exchanged warm hugs. "I've missed you."

With his father blinking back tears of joy, and Justin's heart bursting with pride, he determined that luck could not have orchestrated all of this. It was something akin to a fairy tale with its many versions of perfect love. He was certain that no matter where they were in life, they would have found each other. A unique tie connected them and bound them for all lifetimes.

His voice shaking a little, Justin announced for the second time that day, "Dad, Mildred. Shelly and I are engaged."

Phillip's immediate reaction was to hold his hands up in prayer. He repeated, "Thank you, thank you, thank you." Looking at his son and future daughter-in-law, he said, "I always had hope. I had hope that you would find someone and that when she came along in the form of you, Shelly, you would fall in love. Even when things didn't seem to be going according to my desires, I held on to that small nugget of hope. Shelly, I loved you as a daughter from the first day you walked in here. I feel honored to share my family with yours."

Justin held Shelly close as she sniffed, brushing away her tears. The tender scene was more than he could have hoped for to bring such happiness to his father. Always striving for his respect and wanting to please him above all else, he had fulfilled those goals with the only person who could. Shelly.

"Mildred." Shelly embraced her friend, who wept openly. "You know I'll be counting on you to give me all the advice on this marriage stuff."

"Keep the bad news to yourself, though," Justin joked.

They all laughed and Mildred excused herself from the room.

"I have to apologize again for playing matchmaker—" Phillip said.

Shelly interrupted, "I should be the one to apologize. What you did didn't harm anyone. I was afraid that Justin was involved in some elaborate scheme to use . . . use me."

"Never," said Phillip forcefully. "He didn't know. Suspected, yes. It's me, a lonely old man with an insane plan."

"This was meant to be, Shelly," Justin offered, placing an arm around her shoulders. "With all our imperfections, we have managed to come together because love can bridge all things. I finally opened my heart that had remained locked for so many years and now, can welcome you in without reservation."

"You have always treated me like a lady. Your love has given me the strength to get rid of my inner demons and for the first time in a very long time, I feel good. Because of this, I can love. And I love you." She looked at both men. "I have also decided to file charges against Toby Gillis. I realize that will bring you all kinds of unwanted publicity."

Justin tensed every time that name was mentioned. "Don't worry," he reassured. "I've handled whatever he dished out, and together we'll fight him off."

Shelly disengaged herself from Justin. "There's more." She focused on a point on the wall and spoke. "He has a plan to publicly humiliate you."

"I know," answered Justin.

"I was supposed to be part of that plan."

"That bastard," Phillip muttered. "Did he threaten you?"

"Did he?" Justin repeated the question. A dangerous gleam entered his eyes. His brows were drawn angrily together.

"I have to help him in his plans or he will expose your involvement with a woman of loose morals." She shuddered.

His banker life demanded that he use calm, rational decision-making. It was this talent that had helped place the bank in a better financial position, considering the number of banks that closed or were eaten by bigger entities.

Already a plan came into his head and he wondered if they were all up to taking down Toby Gillis once and for all.

Nineteen

Being a hero was never her goal in life. Shelly just wanted a good job, a nice house, and a loving husband. The responsibility of being a role model or standing out from the crowd frankly scared her.

Yet here she was, driving out to the state university library to meet Toby. She hoped that one day in the future she could look back on this as a gutsy move. So far, it rang of insanity.

If she made one wrong move to make Toby uncomfortable, the whole thing would be over. No raging storm matched his wrath with his new driven thirst for vengeance.

The library in the summer months did not have the heavy flow of students reading and researching. What she wouldn't give to be back in college studying for a simple final exam. Taking a seat in a corner, Shelly sat with her back to the window waiting for Toby.

Half an hour passed and there was no sign of him. He had not been easily swayed when she placed the call requesting to see him. She would give him another fifteen minutes and then leave.

Flipping through a technical magazine on computers to while away the time, Shelly did not notice when Toby approached. He pulled a chair out opposite her and sat.

"Oh, I didn't see you." He'd startled her, causing her pulse to shoot up and stay at hyperbeat.

He looked around the room and then faced her. "You

weren't meant to." Suddenly, he leaned over and grabbed her shirt under her chin and quickly patted her chest and shoulders. Shelly brushed his hands away. "Get off me. What's wrong with you?"

He threw another glance over his shoulder. "Can't be too careful. You may be trying to set me up. The other day you treated me like scum." He leaned in to about four inches from her. His hot breath bathed her face. "Few days later, you call me up to make a deal. What would you think?" He squinted at her, trying to read her expression.

That you are the biggest fool alive and your days are numbered. Because that would get a reaction, she merely smiled.

"Knowing how your devious mind works, I wouldn't put it past you to try something." He steepled his hands on the table and rested his head. His eyes never left hers.

Shelly gulped. She figured that she might be in over her head. "My agreeing to this scheme is for personal reasons, which by the way is still a bit screwy. I haven't changed my mind about what a low-life piece of sh—"

His hand shot out and covered hers in a painful grip. "Watch your mouth! I get the picture."

Shelly pulled her hand away rubbing it with the other under the table. Her knees started a tremor that worked its way up her legs. She held on to them, trying to keep calm. Screwing up now at this point wasn't an option. And Toby definitely scared her. If anything went wrong, there would be no lawyer coming to have her sign papers. Roc would be her surprise visitor.

"Okay. Let's both calm down." She glanced at her watch. "I'm going to have to be leaving soon, so let's get down to business."

Passersby stared as Toby laughed openly, some even gestured that he be quiet. One evil look from him sent them scuttling on their way. The grin dropped from his face, the frigid depth of his stare never left. "First, tell me why the change of heart."

She shifted uncomfortably. "I'd rather not."

"Then, it's over." He stood calmly staring down at her.

"No." She stood also. "Wait. I'll tell you."

A smug smile appeared. Toby liked being in control. He resumed his seat.

It killed her to make the admission, but she had no choice. "When you first came to me I couldn't see myself betraying Justin. I chose to break it off instead. But, I've realized that I'm giving up a lifestyle that suits my needs. As long as I can keep him happy and he doesn't suspect anything, I'd rather he lost the bank than lose him. With the money he'll get from you, he'll be sitting pretty anyway."

Toby measured her words. How could she even think to be involved with him? He had the looks, but they were all veneer. What a mistake.

"I knew you had it in you." He slapped the table forcefully. "Haven't found a woman yet who didn't go crazy over the dollar. With all that 'girl next door' look and attitude, underneath you're like all the others."

His words felt like a shower of dirt falling on her. For him to comment about her in such a manner made her furious, but she held back a retort. *Moron!*

Feeling proud of himself, Toby leaned back triumphantly folding his arms.

"What's your plan?"

"That's on a need-to-know basis. I just want you to have Thornton Junior at the chamber of commerce reception next Saturday. In fact, make sure he has a room at the hotel for the weekend. You have until Wednesday to get me the room number." He stared pointedly at her breasts. "You should tag along. Make him feel comfortable." He licked his bottom lip. "You know what I mean. That thing you do best."

"Then, what?" Shelly didn't bite at his comment, at least not outwardly.

"That's it. That's your job."

An uneasy feeling came over her. "You promised to keep me out of this."

"I promise," he sneered, raising his right hand. "Feel better?"

Here she was making a deal with the devil and wondering if she could trust him. If she followed her instincts, she would get as far away as possible from this man.

"See you around."

He walked away without looking back. His swagger drew appreciative glances from young college girls. Shelly wanted to shout out warnings to all of them.

Due to have lunch with Justin, she picked up her pocketbook to leave. A young man in the latest designer athletic wear pulled the headphones from his ears. He gave her a thumbs-up sign and then went back to the headphones, bopping to the beat.

"How was your morning?"

Because Justin was swamped, they were sharing a sandwich from the cafeteria. The change in plans didn't bother her, though. Being in his company was sufficient.

"Uneventful," she remarked, taking a bit of the chicken salad sandwich. Wiping the corner of her mouth she stated, "Except for my meeting with Toby."

"So, he actually came. What are my marching orders?"

She repeated Toby's instructions. Justin chewed, deep in thought. "What could he be planning? Something public, you think? There will be politicians and businesspeople attending." He pondered the possibilities, then leaned over and gave Shelly a quick kiss on her cheek. "Got to make

some calls and start the ball rolling. I'll see you tonight?"
He waved her out of his office.

Miffed, Shelly took the hint and left Justin's office. She
didn't want to be a part of any plan, Toby's or Justin's.
Since Justin had learned of her disposition with Toby, he
had gone to the extreme of proving that he could protect
her. His counterattack was by far the most extreme and
dangerous.

She punched the elevator button in anger. The male ego
testosterone levels of these two men were building to a
critical point. Somewhere in the middle she felt lost.

Toby didn't think her worthy enough to give her the full
details of the plan. Meanwhile Justin only talked in vague
terms about what his next move was. His excuse was that,
if anything went wrong, she would be truly innocent. She
only had to trust him.

What bothered her was how deep Justin's preoccupation
with Toby started to penetrate their relationship. She was
having her doubts that she was really the object of his plan
to crush Toby or whether it had become a battle of wills.

Calls made, Justin only had to wait. It was hard to believe that everything seemed to be falling into place. He
had to strive not to get overconfident, mistakes could be
made then. He had to ensure that Toby would make a mistake.

He would stoke the fires.

He clicked on the intercom. "Doris, I'm leaving for the
remainder of the day. I don't want to be paged unless it's
an emergency. Tell everyone that I'm tied up in meetings
all day. And I mean everyone."

"Understood, sir."

Doris had worked long enough with him to know what
he wanted before he asked for it. Without saying it, she

would provide the same message to Shelly. He only felt a momentary pang of guilt for not including her, but he would explain everything later.

Provided with Toby's schedule, Justin took the chance that Toby would be taking a long lunch at his health club. Although Justin wasn't a member, he would gladly pay the exorbitant daily fee in pursuit of his goal.

Gym bag in hand, he entered the posh club. Justin preferred outdoor sports to keep in shape. A glance around the facility showed that the club was equipped for health and fitness. It also provided a fringe benefit for its male patrons who lounged at a health food snack bar admiring the women dressed in two-piece, one-piece, and thong-styled leotards.

In the locker room his luck got better. Toby was about to change into his gym clothes. "Ah, I knew I'd catch you here."

"What are you doing here?" Toby was shocked.

Clearly, Toby hadn't ever considered a counterattack. Justin provided him with a toothy smile. "Actually, I came here to whup your butt in racquetball. The first time, I kicked your ass in private so only you would know that I'm the man. Today, I'm going to cream you in front of your peers out there so *they* know I'm the man." Justin prayed that his delivery wouldn't antagonize Toby to the point where he would just leave.

Toby continued to change his clothes, tensing his muscles with each movement. He threw the rest of his things in the locker and slammed it shut. Then, he walked close to Justin, brushing his shoulders. "See you on the court, punk."

Yes. Yes. Yes. Justin was more than a little pleased with how fast Toby took the bait. Now, all he had to do was live up to his boast and everything would be fine.

When he emerged, Toby had already spread the news of

the impending match. Many onlookers had positioned their seats in front of the glass-enclosed court. Toby had begun practicing, showing off stylish moves.

Justin opted to loosen up in the next court. He practiced his serve and rallying moves without flamboyance. Skill was needed to play at this level, but being a quick thinker could be the difference between winning and losing.

Toby tapped on the glass, motioning he was ready. Justin saluted him with the racquet. He walked through a gauntlet of Toby's supporters who shouted their encouragement. Maybe he shouldn't have given Toby home-court advantage. To decide who would start first, Justin tossed a coin in the air.

"Heads," Toby called.

The head side landed up allowing Toby to decide whether he wanted to serve or receive. He grinned wickedly and announced, "I want to serve."

Collectively, the crowd of onlookers had taken on roles as referees. "Zero serves zero," they shouted, signaling the start of the match.

Totally unprepared for Toby's style of play, Justin lost the first three points to him for his serving aces. It didn't help Justin's concentration when he noticed one spectator holding a photo of Toby receiving a cup for winning a racquetball championship.

"Sure you want to continue?" Toby panted.

"Why not? Just 'cause I let you win a couple of points, don't think the game is over."

"We'll see." Toby slammed the ball into the front wall keeping it low. Justin barely tipped it back without much power and Toby couldn't get to it in time. It was Justin's serve.

No one took time-outs. Neither wanted to provide the other with an advantage of resting, even if it was for only thirty seconds. Both men played with determination, diving and performing small acrobatic feats to finish rallies in their favor.

As much as Justin didn't want it this way, Toby won the first game. He would have loved to win the first two games, thereby winning the match. In this situation, the second game became crucial to him if he wanted any chance of walking away a victor.

Toby waved and bowed to the crowd. Grinning at him, he pointed to Justin with his racquet. "Don't be too hard on him. He's a dreamer at heart, but I'm the dream catcher," he announced to the crowd. He walked toward Justin and stopped with their foreheads almost touching. "I'm gonna send you crying back to your mama. Oops," he exclaimed, with apologetic exaggeration. "She's dead."

Justin stood still fighting the urge for violence. The way to beat Toby and crush him wasn't through brute force, but covert manipulation. He'd like to claim that ability. Today was the first step to that path. In his dealings with all types of people, various backgrounds, skills, and so on, Justin couldn't think of anyone who could compare to Toby Gillis. While Toby profiled and played to the crowd, Justin became quieter.

Rest period over, Justin began game two. Comfortable now with muscles loosened, Justin maneuvered around the court with expert skill, performing hard Z serves that frustrated his opponent. When it was Toby's turn, he rallied viciously sending the ball ricocheting off the walls. After forty-five minutes of slipping and diving, the score was fourteen even.

Sweat dripped in Justin's eyes, blurring his vision with a stinging sensation. He wiped off what he could with his arm. His heart pumped madly from the flow of adrenaline. It was Toby's serve. If Justin couldn't return the serve, it would be game for Toby.

"You know once I serve, game is over," Toby taunted.

Justin remained silent, focused.

The crowd's boisterous cheering earlier in the game had grown quieter over the duration. Many had switched sides choosing Justin.

Like a bullet, Toby whacked the ball into the front wall, but it rebounded to the back wall before touching the floor. Recognizing the force, Justin did not rush to hit the ball. "Out," he called.

Toby glared at him and prepared to serve again. This time his feet stepped over the service line.

"Out," the crowd immediately yelled.

"Out? Are you blind?" Toby stormed toward the glass door. "You stepped over the line. Give up the ball," one brave soul responded.

"This is bull—"

"Look, it's no use getting sore. You either give me the ball or they'll call you a cheat." It was Justin's turn to be smug.

After that argument, Justin aced the serve with no effort because the wind had been taken out of Toby.

With a five-minute break before the last game, Justin took some time to get a drink. Sizing up Toby, he felt sure that his game had fizzled mainly because of his emotional state.

He watched Toby approach to buy a sports drink. "Why me?" Justin asked, figuring he had nothing to lose.

"Why not?"

"Why couldn't you take no for an answer?"

"Are we talking about Shelly or you?"

"Both."

"In Shelly's case, she was uptight and I was just trying to loosen her up. Boys will be boys." He threw his head back and gulped down the drink.

Justin wanted to land a karate chop across his windpipe, but chose to finish his drink, too.

Toby wiped his mouth. "In your case, you just irritated me

with your high-handed manner as if you were too good to be associated with me. So, I made you my personal goal."

"Even if it means criminal activity."

"Prove it."

Justin stood. He had had enough. "If you don't mind, forget the time-out period and let's go to work."

"Fine by me, Hos."

Class was in session and Justin was the teacher. Anger in full boil, he marched onto the court. With the same attitude, he scored consistently, despite Toby's tactics of hard body contact and slamming the ball into his arm, back, and leg. Each area stung and he couldn't wait to go home to tend to his injuries. But he would do so after winning this game.

In twenty minutes, Justin won. His supporters clapped and cheered loudly. He saw bills being exchanged. At least he had contributed to some winnings.

He extended his hand as a gesture of friendliness. "Way to go, man."

Toby hesitated, but didn't want to call any more attention to himself. He shook it without saying anything.

Justin held on to it firmly. "Now, they know I'm the man." Then he released it as Toby pulled it away. Justin merely smiled and sauntered off, imitating Toby's bad-boy gait.

Justin eased into the hot water, groaning.

"Are you going to tell me what on earth you were doing?" Shelly had seen the deep purple bruises that were like knotted lumps dotted around his torso. He had not spoken a word, only groaned with each movement.

"Can you bring me two tablets for this pain?"

"Sure, but you'll tell me first what meeting you were in that caused these welts?" At least he had the decency to look embarrassed.

Standing over him with tablets and a glass of water, she

waited for him to confess. She didn't like the fact that he didn't tell her beforehand, but came crawling to her after the fact.

"Baby, I went to the gym."

"The gym!" she exclaimed.

"I had a racquetball game. A very important one."

There was more and she remained quiet for him to continue.

"It was against—"

"Toby." She closed her eyes and almost popped the pills herself. A headache was forming. "Why, Justin?"

"In order for everything to work, I had to make sure he would be so worked up that he would make mistakes."

Her voice rose. "But, was it really necessary or was this only for your male ego to be satisfied?"

"Why can't you understand? This is for you. I want to show you that I can protect you."

She slammed the glass down on the side of the tub. He barely caught the pills thrown at him. "Protect me from what? What happened to me happened before I met you. Nothing you do now will erase that. I need you in the present, not wasting time over Toby. Remember, we're getting married. How about focusing on that for a change?" She stormed out of the bathroom, slamming the door on his reply.

If she thought Justin would be apologetic when he came out of the bathroom, it was not to be. Shelly sat on the bed staring blankly at the television screen, her back to the bathroom door, pointedly ignoring Justin when he emerged.

He spoke to her back. "I think you're overreacting. My focus is on us and our future. And that includes the bank. Toby is threatening my family's bank's survival and I will not lie down and let him do as he pleases."

"I guess in my case, I lay down for him to do as he pleased," she replied, icily.

"That's not what I meant. You're twisting my words."

She turned to him. "Let's forget about this crazy idea of yours," she pleaded. "We have happier things to think about, you and me. I just don't have a good feeling about it."

Justin dressed and headed for the door. "I can't just forget about it. The bank is near and dear to me. I'll see you tonight."

The bank. The bank. That's all she heard from him. Maybe, subconsciously, what she had told Toby had a ring of truth. Would she have to compete with the bank for his attention? She couldn't shake her intuition that it was about to get worse.

After such a heated discussion, they headed to their engagement party at her parents'. She would have to put on a happy face, although she felt like her perfect world was crumbling.

Lying on the bed, she thought about how happy they had been when she hadn't revealed her acquaintance with Toby. She cursed the day that it all came tumbling out because regardless of what Justin said about his doing this for his bank, there was an element of revenge in his new obsession.

In the meantime, she was about to be officially engaged on a day marked by deceit, tempers flaring, and misunderstanding.

Twenty

Shelly felt like a hypocrite, playing the role of the happy fiancée. Thank goodness it was a small affair, nothing like her earlier birthday celebration. It didn't help matters that Justin hadn't arrived yet.

Until he did, she'd have to answer on his whereabouts, which highlighted the fact even more that he was not present for his engagement party. If he didn't show up in another hour, she was ready to answer, "What wedding?"

"Speak of the devil," she muttered, spying him squeezing through the door. Always the perfect gentleman, he kissed her on her cheek and apologized for his lateness. No one could have guessed at her mixed feelings.

The turmoil wasn't about whether to remain with Justin or not, but whether they were better off as long-standing friends. She studied him across the room, interacting with and charming everyone. The fact that he had proposed without a ring meant that it was spur of the moment. She smiled; it had been after they made love. It could have been the heightened emotions they both shared that made him impulsive. She watched him laugh at her mother's comment, while her father looked on, pleased with his soon-to-be son-in-law.

"Shelly, join us," Justin called, waving to her. "Your mother is regaling me with stories about her rebellious teen daughter."

"Oh, brother. Mom, stop embarrassing me."

"Frankly, I like hearing about the wild side of my beautiful bride-to-be." He put his arm around her, drawing her toward him.

"Count me out. No need to relive my exploits," Shelly remarked and twirled out of his arms. She felt prickly tonight.

When everyone was seated at the dinner table laden with home-cooked dishes, Justin rose to propose a toast. Shelly didn't know what to expect.

"Please, may I have your attention?" Everyone looked up at Justin with undivided attention. "I would like for you to join me as I pledge my friendship, love, and soul to the only one for me."

"Here, here," a voice boomed. Everyone raised a wineglass, saluting her and then Justin.

Shelly accepted the toasts and well-wishing, hoping that the night would be over soon. Right after that thought, Justin's new pager buzzed in the middle of dinner. It wasn't quite the distraction she looked for. She leaned sideways toward him, remembering to keep a pleasant face. "Who's paging today?"

He clicked on the display button and mouthed the word, "Good" to himself. "Project at work," he answered in a whisper.

"Clara, please excuse me. I have a sensitive project in full gear and I need to use your phone. Then, I'll probably have to leave."

Clara beamed. He could do no wrong, thought Shelly. The only project he was working on was Toby. She was a part of the plan. Lately with his actions, she felt more like a spectator.

Justin left the room to make the phone call. Shelly played with her food, preoccupied.

"What's up, honey?" Her mother had switched chairs and now sat in Justin's chair. "You're deep in thought."

"Little tiredness, that's all."

"Mmm. That's understandable with everything."

Justin returned to the table. "Well, ladies, I was right. I'll have to leave."

"Must you go? Can't someone else handle it?" Shelly asked, eyebrows arched over a piercing gaze.

"No."

"What project is this?"

"I wish I could stick around to explain, but I have to get going now. I'll call you tonight."

"Fine," she replied, between clenched teeth.

He kissed her on her cheek and left.

"Stop pouting," her mother scolded. "You're marrying an important man. You didn't think you would have him all to yourself, did you? You can't have it all."

Shelly merely nodded. Her mother didn't know about the plan in motion and Justin had sworn her to secrecy. Besides, just because doubts crept in, she didn't have to pass them on to her mother.

Later that night, Shelly lay in bed flipping through bridal magazines. Trying to pick out her wedding dress brought thoughts of how married life would turn out with Justin. It was late, but she had to talk to him. She dialed his private number. The machine started, but he picked up the receiver in the middle of his message.

She came straight to the point. "Justin, we need to talk."

"You sound upset." His voice turned worried.

"Are you having second thoughts about the wedding?" She hated asking the question because she might hate the answer.

"I think I should be the one asking you that question."

Silence.

"Are you having second thoughts, Shelly?"

She wanted to scream "yes." But some part of her held back. She had to be patient. An irrational act on her part could change her destiny forever. "No, I just got the feeling that you weren't thinking about it. You're so busy and preoccupied lately."

"The wedding is all I think about, it's what keeps me going. I know I'm being secretive, but what I'm working on is as much for you as it is for me." He sighed. "It'll be over, soon. I promise."

Her muscles instantly relaxed at the sound of his deep voice. It soothed her, taming the flames of jealousy ready to ignite into a full blaze.

After the call, she snuggled under the covers and plumped her pillows, waiting for sleep to overtake her. In the meantime, she acknowledged that her insecurities were making her second-guess and worry about inconsequential details. She had to learn to trust.

It was strange how the relationship between Phillip and Shelly had changed. He had employed her, but her falling in love with his son and planning a wedding altered the employee/boss alliance. She was glad he had the insight to bring Justin and her together. If any commitment between them was dependent on their stubborn personalities, there would be none.

"Why are you grinning? I hope it's not me."

"No, it's not you, Phillip. I guess I'm thankful for what you did."

"My handiwork."

"You have to forgive my rudeness. I had a lot weighing on me at that time."

"Please, child. I'll forgive you, if you forgive me."

"Agreed."

She read some of the get-well cards that came in the mail daily. The touching verses in the cards brought tears to her eyes many times. She knew the kind thoughts of friends and distant relatives were important to Phillip. In this time of pain and hopelessness, she was only too happy to bring him the tiniest nugget of joy.

Mildred entered with a huge bouquet of lilies. The massive floral display covered her from the chest upward to her head. She had to peek around the long stems to see her way.

As she got closer to where Shelly sat next to Phillip, the room filled with the sweet scent of the delicate flowers. Shelly cleared an area on the bedside table and positioned the vase to catch the light.

Phillip's eyes lit up at the surprise gift. "Who did this?"

All eyes turned to Mildred for the answer, but she remained silent with a mischievous twinkle in her eyes. Then, Mrs. Beacham entered with a cake, freshly baked. She carried it on a platter outstretched in her hands as if bearing gifts to a king.

Shelly looked to Mildred for an explanation, but the idiotic smile was still in place. Mrs. Beacham placed the cake on the tray and rolled it over to Phillip's bed. With sudden revelation, it hit her. Mildred already knew.

Mrs. Beacham was in love with Phillip.

The revelation automatically transformed the housekeeper in Shelly's eyes. The sweet nature of her feelings softened the forbidding exterior. Her eyes soft with emotion drank him in, as she fussed with him. His irritation at her close attention didn't deter her, but Shelly caught the slightest smile to Phillip's lips.

Witnessing this human side to the housekeeper touched her. She wondered how painful it must be for her to serve him for many years to have it end this way.

"So, what are we celebrating?" Phillip asked.

"Another season that you are enjoying."

"Yes, it is, isn't it? Thanks for thinking of me." Phillip turned to explain to Mildred and Shelly. "You see, as every season draws to a close and I'm still hanging in there, Mrs. Beacham celebrates. She always said the doctor's prediction was wrong." He sliced the cake with shaky fingers, but resisted any assistance. Mrs. Beacham place a slice of the angel food cake on napkins and passed it to each woman.

"None for me, thanks. Can't keep anything down. Eat up and each of you eat an extra slice for me. It's my favorite," he urged at their sad faces.

"So, Mrs. Beacham, you must bake a lot for the family?" Shelly asked, trying to dig a little deeper behind the housekeeper's mysteries.

She turned a sharp eye on Shelly. "I have no family, except the Thorntons. My husband died a long time ago, and I never remarried, nor do I have any children."

"Oh." What a lonely life, Shelly thought.

"Don't look so sad for me. I survived and now enjoy life at a leisurely pace."

"Mmm."

Shelly was still not convinced of the bright side. Especially since it was clear Mrs. Beacham loved Phillip, but wasn't in a position to do anything. She was much too proper to indulge in any questionable activity with the boss; unlike Shelly, who went after the boss's son.

Tossing her troubles aside, she scolded herself for being so selfish with Justin's time. When she thought her troubles were tremendous and weighed heavily upon her, she only had to look around and see. Here were two persons sharing a deep, special love that would never be fulfilled. Yet they were contented to accept fate and deal with what they could share and enjoy. When she was done for the day here, she would go visit Justin.

Glad that the federal agents didn't come with badges flashing, Justin visibly relaxed when they were shown into his office. Doris looked at him questioningly, but he pointedly ignored her. "I don't want to be interrupted under any circumstances."

"Yes, sir. Can I get anyone refreshments?"

Justin opened the door for Doris, indicating he wanted her to leave. "I'll take care of that."

The three agents shook their heads.

Justin walked over, loosening his tie. He pointed to chairs in his office and the couch. "Have a seat, please."

"Let me introduce myself, Mr. Thornton. I'm Heather Carr. And this is my partner, Tom Jeffries, and my boss, Captain Chuck Stokes."

Justin shook everyone's hands. Noting that the woman, Heather, had the right look to play the part. With her five-foot-nine-inch frame, with thick, shoulder-length hair, and a face and body that could compete with Tyra Banks, she would do.

"Have you learned much more than the conference date and location?" Captain Stokes questioned.

"No. Toby didn't tell Shelly anything further. And with what I heard on the street, I think he's going for the prostitute setup scenario."

"Yeah. That's why Heather was called in. Tom will be nearby, just in case."

"You expecting trouble?" Justin inquired, a bit worried.

Captain Stokes scratched his balding head and nodded. "Considering what you have planned for him, with his back against the wall, he may feel he has nothing to lose."

Heather smiled, flashing a brilliant smile of perfect

teeth. Her lips created a perfect Cupid's bow. "You do realize the extent of the damage that will be done if it goes
as planned."

Honestly, he didn't like noticing her physical attributes.
He felt as if he was cheating. But, if she was chip-toothed,
with bad breath, and had a face that could curdle milk, he
would be downright worried and more than a little hesitant
to go through with the plan.

"Has he contacted you since the game?" Tom asked.

Justin shook his head. He'd hoped that Toby would be so
furious that he'd be in his face. Instead, Toby had vacated
the scene. No one knew where he was or was admitting
where he was hiding.

"He's still out there. Waiting for the weekend to arrive
so he can fulfill his goal of humiliating you. It's amazing
that this man with a bank to run seems to spend so much
time away from it."

"It's because his focus is not the bank. His obsession is
with power and control. He lives to dominate. First, he
tried to dominate Shelly and now, I'm his target. I plan to
put a stop to his madness before anyone else is hurt by
him."

"Mr. Thornton, I am glad you came to us. We, at least,
know what direction Toby is heading toward. As long as
you don't disappoint his expectations, we will reach out
and grab him for the good of mankind."

"Sounds like a winner to me."

Everyone shook hands. Justin grabbed his briefcase and
jacket. He wanted to spend some time with Shelly. She
already felt neglected and he wanted to make it up to her
until he could tell her everything.

Outside, a blue official government car was parked. The
driver pulled alongside the curb when they emerged from
the building. Captain Stokes and Tom climbed in, while
Heather waited to talk to him.

Like a bad dream, he saw Shelly pull into the parking lot area. The bright smile she offered when she saw him froze. He waved, but her eyes narrowed suspiciously. It didn't help that Heather had leaned toward him to speak.

"Justin, you need to keep this on the down low from Shelly."

He shifted uncomfortably. "Why?"

"Since Toby didn't take her into his confidence, she wouldn't know what the plan was anyway. We need it to run smoothly and as naturally as possible."

"Well, it's too late for that. She's parked over there and shooting daggers with her eyes."

Heather appeared startled. "Then, I best be going. Remember. It's my butt on the line too. So, mum's the word." She climbed into the car quickly and closed the door.

Justin had to step back as the car raced out of the parking lot.

Justin adjusted his suit and pasted on a chipper smile. He would have a lot of explaining to do tonight.

Shelly waited until he was a few feet from the car. "Who was she?"

"Oh, a colleague."

"I want you to know for the record that I don't believe you. But until I have further proof, you can get into my car. And for the remainder of the night, convince me that your nameless colleague is just that."

"Yes, ma'am."

Twenty-one

An uneasy silence lay between them. Shelly would rather be anywhere else, but tonight was the night. Everyone had a command performance. Her stomach tightened in protest. Justin's grim face was tight with unease as he walked into the hotel.

"You're looking as if you're expecting something to happen." Shelly looked worriedly at him. "Just a reminder, you can't know anything. Only I am supposed to know what's going on."

He exhaled and grimaced. "I know. Just a bit nervous." He played nervously with her hair. "We'll make it through this."

She nodded, but wasn't completely convinced. Without having a clue as to what direction Toby would take his vendetta, she could only imagine the worst.

They moved quickly through the registration process. Because they arrived early, Shelly was able to study the other attendees. No one looked out of place: well-groomed, dark business suits, conservative types. Justin went to the hotel front desk for the room key and to signal his official check-in.

"Got the key. I'm going to take the bags up to the room."

She looked around, rubbing her hands together to dispel her fear. "I wish he would get this over with. I don't want to be here all weekend, waiting."

"Now it's your turn to look pleasant and adoring." He stared into her eyes until she visibly relaxed.

"Okay, I'll wait for you down here, just in case."

Shelly walked out to the lanai, ordered a drink, and sat in a wicker chair. From her vantage point, she could see clearly into the common area as she looked for any suspicious characters. She wasn't completely hidden so that, if Toby wanted to find her, he could.

Sipping on her juice, she noticed a young man heading her way. He kept eye contact with her. She wondered if he was the one. His direct, intense survey of her left her unnerved, naked. She squirmed in her seat, crossing her legs and closing her jacket as some form of self-defense.

"Hi there." The man stood unsmiling, hand extended. "Here for the conference?"

She shook his hand not wanting to appear rude.

"In a way, yes."

He pulled a vacant chair next to hers and flopped down, not taking his eyes off her.

"Was that your husband I saw you with?" He looked at her ring finger.

She leaned back away from him. "Who are you? What do you want?"

He held his hand up. "Take it easy. I just wanted to know how my chances were for us to get to know each other."

The man was trying to pick her up and meant no harm. Although flattered, she had no time to play games or be diplomatic. "Sorry, but that's not possible."

Then she spotted the elevator door opening and Justin emerged. "As a matter of fact, my fiancé is on his way."

Before she could excuse herself, she saw Justin smile at someone out of sight. Curious, she stood and looked in the direction that held his focus. Dumbfounded, she gripped the column for support—for something to dig her nails into.

"Looks like your fiancé may be tied up." The man, now

annoying, stood too close to her. Did he really think that this episode playing out like a nightmare made him more appealing to her?

Fat chance.

Her blood boiled and she was ready for a fight. She turned her attention back to Justin and the woman he was deeply engaged in conversation with. The same woman that was "a colleague." Tonight she wore a bloodred pantsuit with pumps to match. Among all the dull blue and black suits, she added a splash of color and a lot more. Appreciative glances turned her way. But she ignored them, as she sidled up next to Justin laughing at his comments and placing her hand, first on his hand, then his chest, and now, she had slipped her hand through the crook in his arm.

Shelly didn't remember making her way over to Justin. But suddenly she was there, standing next to him. "Justin, are you ready to look around before the reception?" she inquired, allowing the saccharin sweetness to drip from every word. She made no attempt to include or soften the glare toward the other woman who still had her hand on Justin's.

"Shelly." Justin grinned sheepishly. "Meet Anne Landis." He continued on, licking his lips, "She is the colleague I was—you saw—she's the one."

"Ms. Landis, would you excuse us?" It irritated her that the woman hadn't released him, but it didn't help that he hadn't disentangled himself from her, either.

"Honey," Justin pleaded, "I need to talk to Mrs. Landis about something extremely important, but why don't you wait here? I won't be long."

Shelly smiled at both of them, her eyes like points of glacier. "You'd better not be."

The night was turning into a disaster. She wanted to leave, but Toby's threats stopped her. Everything was going fine until this woman started popping up too conveniently.

Back on the lanai, she fumed, tapping her nails with frustration.

"It would appear my little flower isn't having a good evening," Toby drawled. "Your dear boy seems to have moved on to greener pastures."

He leaned against the rail where she stood. It took all her control not to slap the smugness off his face. The thought still made her smile, albeit evilly.

"Who is the she-devil placing the moves on your fellow?"

"A colleague."

"Hah."

Annoyed at being laughed at, annoyed at being made a fool, she felt her patience was dangerously thin. "Why are you here?"

"Where else would I be?"

"Well, you could take your offensive body to the other side of the room."

"Touchy broad," he retorted. "Sure, I'll go to my side of the room while I watch my creation play out." He laughed contemptuously at her. "There's not a damn thing you can do to stop it, but enjoy the ride." He moved off, giving her a quick salute.

Why did she ever agree to this scheme? The part in this nightmare that she didn't like was how insignificant she felt. Bits and pieces of the plan could be happening right under her nose and she wouldn't realize them. Or, something could be going dreadfully wrong, and she couldn't correct it. Her nerves would be shattered after this night. She needed Justin.

"Don't look so scared." Justin took Toby's spot next to her at the rail.

"It's a bit hard not to. Aren't you?"

"Actually, I'm terrified. But I keep thinking about you and what this will mean to us in the long term. We have to get this parasite out of our lives." He turned her toward him. "It will mean that you have to trust me. I have reasons for everything that I do or say. And I won't hurt you in any way."

She nodded. "But, I still don't like Anne Landis." When he didn't say anything, she held his face in her hands. "Is she part of the plan?"

"I—I can't."

"Is she Toby's person?"

"Yes and no," he replied evasively. He acquiesced to her piercing look. "Government."

"Oh." Shelly looked across the room for the woman. "Seems too pretty for that."

"Hadn't noticed."

"Good answer." She winked at him and he kissed her lightly.

"What would I do without you?"

"I'm afraid to consider."

They walked to the conference room where the seminar was about to begin. Shelly hoped that she appeared calm, because her stomach's queasiness had increased. The only good thing from this ordeal was that, in a few hours, it would be all over and she could move on with her life.

The meeting was about to start. Justin took a seat next to the aisle, while Shelly sat on the inside next to him. She dared not look around for Toby. He wasn't in the front, but she knew he was close by. As she wondered about his whereabouts, Anne Landis used the aisle as a catwalk, drawing glances as she made her way to the front row, aisle seat.

Once seated, Anne turned and looked over her shoulder. She made eye contact with Justin and smiled. Then, she turned back to the front. Shelly had to forcefully remind herself that the woman with thick, silky black hair was a government agent.

It would be a long night.

The speaker droned on with his presentation. Shelly

kept a constant observance of Toby for some kind of inclination that the plan was under way. After her initial
acknowledgement to Justin, Anne had not turned again.
Shelly glanced at her watch. The speaker was winding up
his remarks, and in a few minutes everyone would leave.

After the applause died, she followed Justin into the
crowd exiting the room. Although Anne was in front of the
room, she managed to have been in the first group that left.
As they walked toward the lobby, she was stationed casually against a large potted plant. At their approach, Shelly
stiffened. Feeling her reaction, Justin looked at her questioningly and then followed her stare.

Anne broke into a lazy, seductive smile for Justin's benefit. She pushed off from her sultry pose against the potted
palm and sauntered toward the elevators. Her swaying hips
sent nonverbal cues that were only to be heeded by one
man in the crowd, Justin.

Shelly whispered in his ear. "I'll be waiting for you."

"Here goes nothing, babe."

Shelly walked toward the bar. Waiting in their room
would absolutely kill her. She needed to be around people.
And in the bar, at least there was a television that featured
sports to hold her attention. Shelly took a seat in the corner, ordered a chardonnay, and waited.

When Shelly left him, Justin took a deep breath. He
leisurely strolled toward Heather. It was bad enough that
his peers saw him with her, especially given his near mar-
ital status with Shelly, who was still in the vicinity.

Heather slipped her hand around his arm and pressed
the elevator button with a red fingernail. She flicked her
hair back. "It's show time."

They stood shoulder-to-shoulder in the elevator. They

were its only occupants. Both stared at the lighted numbers signifying the floors as the elevator went past.

Justin asked, "Your people are in place?"

"Yes, don't worry."

The doors opened and the two walked out with Heather slightly in the lead. Justin looked around, mainly for Toby, but there was no sign of him.

Heather opened a room at the end of the hall and held the door for Justin to enter. He hesitated, looking down the hall one more time before following.

"Now what?"

Heather picked up the phone, placing her finger against her lips for him to be quiet. "Mr. Gillis, I'm afraid I have some bad news for you. I've decided that you need to add a few more hundreds to what we agreed upon." She gave Justin a thumbs-up sign. "Hey, watch your mouth. If it's such a problem, then you come up here and do it yourself." She slammed the phone on the receiver.

"You sure he's going to bite?"

She shrugged. "Let's hope so." Pointing to a chair, she offered, "Have a seat."

He complied. "Are you winging this?"

"Basically, yes." She sat on the edge of the bed. "How's Shelly doing?"

He shifted uncomfortably. "It's a strain on her. Sometimes I wonder why I even went this route. I should have just had him arrested when he tried to blackmail her." He leaned his head back wearily. "Blame it on ego, but I wanted to nail him, make him pay, and have an ironclad case against the bastard."

"Mind if I smoke?" She pulled out a cigarette.

"Go ahead."

She lit the slender stick and inhaled deeply. "You realize that the anger you feel won't necessary disappear even after he's caught."

He shook his head. "Yeah. I guess."

Their conversation was cut short. Toby was at the door banging furiously.

In an instant, Justin shot up and tiptoed toward the bathroom. Heather had also moved into action, giving the room a once-over to remove any signs of Justin before moving toward the door. He closed the door quietly and waited.

The mirror over the sink didn't hide the effects of the adrenaline rush surging through Justin's body. Perspiration beaded his brow, and his jaw clenched and unclenched. Toby's voice brought an immediate hate-filled reaction.

The door slammed against the bathroom wall. Justin jumped back, anticipating Toby to barge into the small room. From the gist of the conversation, Toby's focus was on Heather's betrayal.

"What games are you playing? You're out of your league and I will kick your pretty little butt around this room if you don't go through with what I hired you for."

"First, don't threaten me or you'll be sorry."

Justin had to give it to her for sounding so calm.

"This guy, Justin, is a little attached to his woman. So, I will have to do more blatant stuff, which means that more people will see who I am. For the extra risk, I want more money."

"Where is he? I saw him come up with you."

"Yeah, he came up, but then I got off and he said he was going up to his room. Said he was tired."

There was a long silence. "I don't have any more time to argue, so how much do you want?"

"How much I want for what?"

"Geez. This is what I get for hiring strictly on looks, because your brain is clearly missing."

"You like to talk a lot of trash."

"For the last time, and it better be for your sake, here is an easy five thousand dollars to scintillate Justin Thornton. I want you to bring him to his knees with your female wiles."

Heather chuckled, the sound of paper crackling as money exchanged hands. Justin kept his ear to the door, wondering what the signal would be to alert Heather's people.

"Justin Thornton, your ass is mine," Toby announced. "Hey, how about a sample before you get started on your job? Just a little action down south should get me back in a good mood."

"Sure." Heather walked back toward the bed. "But, I don't think you'll have time to enjoy."

"Why?"

"'Cause, my friend, you're busted."

Twenty-two

The sound of agents bursting through the door was all Justin needed to prompt him from his hiding place. The room filled with agents, including Captain Stokes and Tom Jeffries, busily carrying through their respective duties. The only person not in a frenzy, besides himself, was Heather. She sat on the air-conditioning unit, inhaling another cigarette, squinting through the thin smoke at a very distressed Toby.

No one paid Justin much attention, which afforded him the opportunity to witness every humiliating aspect of Toby's arrest, as his rights were read to him. Toby looked confused and every chance he got, he fought against his restraints.

Twisting to break free, Toby spied Justin motionless near the bathroom. "Is this your handiwork? You punk. You're gonna pay for this."

Justin thought Toby looked mentally unhinged. He couldn't have planned this better himself. Gone was the suave cockiness that had plagued his existence. Before him was a man who cursed with such vehemence in one stroke, then broke down into a stuttering state in another. Justin thought Toby might be headed for psychiatric evaluation, instead of a cell.

"Come over here so I can kick your ass and wipe that smile off your face."

"I think with that government jewelry around your wrist, the only ass you may kicking for a while is Bubba, your cellmate," Justin replied.

The whites of Toby's eyes seemed to enlarge. He breathed through gritted teeth, causing saliva to shoot out indiscriminately. "You've got nothing on me. Nothing, you hear!"

Captain Stokes left the room.

Heather walked over to the television set toward Toby. "Mr. Gillis, you have been recorded and videotaped from the time you met Miss Bishop in the library. And, as you have been told, these pieces of evidence will prove the government's case of blackmail, solicitation of a prostitute, and a whole host of other offenses." She crossed her arms and looked at Toby with contempt. "And, there is still the business of sexual assault and battery. But, just to ensure that your days as a thug are over . . ." With an added flair, like a television game show host, she stepped aside from the television. "Let me present Captain Stokes."

Justin moved closer.

Captain Stokes was live on TV in the hotel's lobby. He stood behind a podium with several microphones from different network stations aimed toward him. Flashes from photographers captured the moment for the next morning's edition of the newspapers.

Justin couldn't help smiling; the same news media that Toby had summoned to turn his life inside out when he would be caught red-handed with a prostitute had backfired. The sharks attracted to blood didn't care who was the bleeder. For their pleasure, it would be Toby.

Heather turned up the volume.

"Ladies and gentlemen of the press, we have just arrested Toby Gillis on the following charges." Captain Stokes stated the basic facts of Toby's illegal activities with subliminal innuendoes to his integrity and moral character. He answered the rapid-fire questions without providing substantive information. Each morsel fed to the group was just enough for them to add an edge of controversy.

Justin turned his attention to Toby. The man who had bullied so many now sat with slumped shoulders, head bowed to his chest.

A small commotion at the door revealed Shelly trying to enter, but the agent responsible for guarding the area restrained her.

"It's okay, Evans," Heather intervened. "Let her through."

Justin rushed over and embraced her. In that hectic moment, he thought about how wonderful her hair smelled, the way the edge of her eyes crinkled when she smiled, and how happy he felt when her arms held him.

"It's over, baby," he whispered in her ear.

She looked at him, a frown still in place. "Are you sure?"

"Yes," he replied firmly. He held her with a new sense of self.

He had needed to complete this mission as part of his personal development in opening his heart. For many in her plight, closure was sometimes missing. He didn't ever want to have her live with regrets.

"Miss Bishop, I'm sorry for all the cloak-and-dagger behavior Mr. Thornton had to put himself and you through. I felt it necessary for the success of the operation."

Shelly nodded. "I'm just glad it's over. Now, we can have no further distractions."

"Well, it's time to do the boring stuff, like paperwork. I'll see you tomorrow for your statement?" Heather left with Toby in tow, directing explicatives at Shelly, following.

Shelly didn't cringe from Toby's shouting crude language at her. Instead, she met his enraged behavior with a steady, fearless stance. "You'll pay for all the misery you've invoked. When I testify against you it will be with the greatest pleasure."

Later, as they left the scene, she wondered if it was

healthy to be happy that Toby's downfall was no longer a dream. Should she feel compassion? Should she forgive? Those were feelings she would have to deal with as she went through rebuilding herself. At the moment, she wanted to scream out loud with a new invigorated spirit.

It was finally over. Toby Gillis would be out of their lives for good. Even if high-priced lawyers negotiated with the prosecutors for their client, his reputation was severely damaged. The same thing he wanted for Justin had been turned on him. For the first time in his miserable life, he would experience what he had put so many others through.

Long after the media, onlookers, and federal agents had left, Justin and Shelly sat in the hotel lounge. It was their refuge until much of the hoopla died. Hotel staff was kind enough to allow them haven for a couple of hours.

"I think we make a good team." Justin smiled at her, brushing her cheek with the back of his hand.

Blushing under his attentive gaze, she nodded in agreement. "It's wonderful to hear those words from your lips."

He stretched, yawning widely. "I'm drained."

"Me too. Let's get out of here."

They walked hand in hand toward the elevator on their way to the underground parking lot. Despite the dishevelment from earlier activities, they made an attractive couple. Tuxedo jacket slung over his shoulder, he placed his arm casually around Shelly's bare shoulders. She looked up at him, love shining in her eyes.

"Gosh, I want you," he remarked in a regular tone. They were the only occupants in the elevator. "Got to stop at the house first, though."

She couldn't wait to have him all to herself. Although they both were tired and fatigued, there was some energy in reserve for special occasions. Feeling his naked muscled body touching hers would automatically chase away any sleepiness. It had been a while since they woke up in each other's arms and lay there talking quietly about their dreams.

"You know," Justin began, upon entering the car, "Dad will be waiting to hear how everything went." His face lit up with the sweet victory of success. "He'll want every detail."

"I want to hear every detail, too." She raised her eyebrows and gave him a sideways glance. "Especially when you and Miss Heather sauntered off to the suite. Exactly how soon did the agents come in?"

Patting her knee, he reassured, "Baby, you don't have to worry about a thing. Everything was taped and video-recorded, so we had no choice but to act morally."

Nonchalantly, she looked at her nails. "Seems to me there's a touch of sadness in your voice."

"Only that you weren't there with me."

"Liar." She chuckled. She was only teasing. There was no doubt after witnessing the extent and complexity to Justin's plan that she appreciated how deeply he wanted to make everything as right as it could be for her.

Watching hypnotically as the streetlights flashed by, she thought about how a simple action on Phillip's part had changed their lives forever. School and college crushes couldn't compare to the level and intensity of her love that was pure and sincere. In her heart, she could boldly admit that Justin was the only man for her and she was the only woman for him.

They would have to prepare themselves for the inevitable delays as court dates, proceedings, and settlements were negotiated or fought by a panic-stricken young man facing jail time. But they had known this going in and had decided to act.

"I feel exhausted." Shelly kicked off her shoes, flexing her toes. "I'm ready for a strong cup of coffee and a back rub—hint, hint."

"Give me those corn-chip-smelling toes. I'll start with those. Then depending on how you treat me, I'll rub more than your back." He massaged her feet resting in his lap while he drove in comfortable silence.

As they turned onto his street, a pulsating light penetrated the darkness. The constant, rotating red and blue lights sent an eerie message.

Something bad had happened. Justin and Shelly exchanged looks, bodies tensed, straining against the seat belts. All the houses they passed didn't contain the source of the emergency lights. Neither dared suggest what was on each other's mind.

Pulling up to the entrance of the property, they saw an ambulance parked in front of the house. The attendant had just closed the back doors and was poised to jump into the driver's seat. Coming into the scene at the tail end of the situation set them at a disadvantage.

Justin drove the car up to the ambulance's rear, tires squealing as he slammed on the brakes. Without turning the motor off, he jumped out and ran to the back door.

Shelly followed closely behind him and came up alongside where he stood. They both peered into the darkened window. But she didn't have to see. Her intuition told her it was Phillip. Without saying a word, she held Justin's hand for a moment.

The tortured look on his face tore her apart. He whirled away from her. She watched him frantically hit the side of the ambulance with his hand so they won't drive away. The driver leaned out and looked questioningly at the two running toward him.

"Hey, what's going on here? Is it my father?"

"Who're you?"

"Justin Thornton. Phillip Thornton's son."

"Oh. We got a call half an hour ago that he was having

difficulty breathing. By the time we got here he was in cardiac arrest, but we managed to pull him back. Gotta go."

"Which hospital?"

"University Hospital." The driver pulled off leaving a stunned Justin standing in the driveway staring after the ambulance. Shelly led him toward the house. "Come on. Let's change. We've got to hurry. It's time."

For a moment he stared vacantly at her. Then, as her words sank in, he looked around. "Where is Mrs. Beacham? Mildred?" he shouted frantically.

She understood he was in a state of shock and attempted to process everything rationally. But no matter how many families tried to prepare themselves, when the moment came, the blow was a mighty one. Pain and despair would be his company for a while, until he pulled himself beyond its reach. In the meantime, she had to urge him to act quickly. Time wasn't on their side.

"They may have already left."

"Shelly. Mr. Thornton." Mildred ran out of the house with Mrs. Beacham, visibly flustered, following.

Shelly ran toward her. "Are you all okay to drive?"

"Yeah, I'll take Mrs. Beacham. Do you have everything ready or will you need my help?"

"No. Don't wait for us. We'll be right behind you."

Shelly turned to see Justin hugging Mrs. Beacham before she sat in the car. Her cheeks shone from her tears. Gone was the efficient, well-groomed woman. Tonight, she seemed frail, emotional, and human. Shelly was glad Mildred's levelheadedness would get them safely to the hospital.

Justin had already walked into the house. She respected his need to be alone, to face the inevitable. They had talked about this moment. Despite all the planning and coming to terms with a part of life's cycle, the shock and hurt were no less apparent. She called her parents and then Leesa. They would meet them there.

It wasn't the way all brides pictured their wedding day. There would be no bridesmaids to attend to her, no limo to take her to the church, and no aisle down which to take that cherished bridal march. In fact, what they planned to do she wished on no one for their wedding day. But this was different. Since Phillip had brought them together, he should get to see it legally and spiritually sealed before it was too late.

In one of the empty bedrooms, she removed her wedding dress from the closet, a simple tea-length dress with a tight bodice and full skirt. Struggling with the tiny buttons up her back, she missed her mother at that moment. Not letting her emotions take over, she blinked back the ready tears.

Dress and hose on, she slipped her feet into satin ballet-style shoes, making her look ethereal. Then, she placed a pearl sequined tiara with its short veil on her head.

Her heart raced at all the thoughts flitting by about her present, past, and future. There was no sight of Justin and she waited at the bottom of the stairs for him to come down. To keep her hands busy, she donned lace gloves and waited for the man who would be her husband in a few minutes.

When she heard his first step on the stairs, she looked up with anticipation. Openmouthed, she admired him, falling in love with him all over again. He wore a black tux, with satin trimmings for a rich edge. Underneath the jacket, a crisp white shirt with ascot and waistcoat completed the ensemble.

A soft smile came on her lips when she noticed the gold cuff links. Phillip had shown them to her once. They were the same that he had worn on his wedding day. She blew Justin a kiss, which he caught and placed next to his heart. He was a work of art and a touch of class all rolled into one.

He offered his hand as they hurriedly walked out to the car. She hoped they weren't late. With Justin's high-speed driving, she also hoped they would arrive in one piece.

"Give me your hand," Justin demanded when they arrived. He fixed an iron grip on her hand and fast-walked his way maneuvering skillfully around patients and visitors.

"Careful," Shelly warned.

He lowered his shoulders and cleared a path, while she threw out apologies in his wake. They drew stares, mostly curious, with their hurried gait and out-of-place costumes. Justin and Shelly represented what many in the hospital had lost, youth and vitality. Their wedding outfits, in direct opposition to the ill patients, symbolized unfulfilled hopes and dreams.

Following the directions on the hospital wall, they found the ICU in the cardiac wing. Shelly saw her parents first in the waiting room and waved to them.

"He's hanging in there." Her mother spoke to Justin. "I think he's waiting for you."

The doors to the ICU were closed. Silent and still, he stood in front of the doors. Shelly sensed he was working his courage up to enter and see what lay on the other side. She would go in with him. "Honey, you look so beautiful. I'm sorry it couldn't be under different circumstances."

Shelly blinked away tears. "I know, but I wanted it this way."

Her father had his arm around her. The familiar, safe feeling enveloped her. Family was indeed important. She was thankful to be loved by the most important people in her life. "I'll need you to be there for Justin," she said, hugging her father.

"Certainly. It's only now hit me that my little girl has

grown up to be a beautiful, independent, strong young woman. And, it's my cue to fade into the background."

"No, Dad." Her mouth trembled as she replied. "I'll still need you. Still will need your praise and your advice."

"You've got Justin."

"Yes, I do. But, I still need to be Daddy's girl."

Her mother snorted. "Please. The man who bronzed your baby shoes will not fill them with anyone else."

"Your mother's just jealous because her feet are too big for them."

"Humph," she muttered.

The door swung open as medical personnel exited. Everyone strained to catch a glimpse. Phillip was in the first bed, curtains partially drawn around it. They could see his body, lying still. A large tube was in his mouth to help him breathe. Doctors and nurses examined him, making notes on their clipboards.

The tension lay thick as the huddled group anxiously awaited some news, any news. Finally, one of the doctors, grim faced, came toward them.

"He is going in and out of consciousness. It's my belief that it's close. So if you would, one at a time, like to go in to pay your respects . . ."

Justin stood behind the doctor, his expression unreadable. Her heart ached from imagining what hell he must be facing. She wanted him to know that he didn't have to face it alone.

"Doctor, we want to get married now at his bedside." He reached for Shelly. Together, they waited for his reply.

"I'm afraid that's not possible."

The doctor hadn't even given the request a second thought. Was he so detached that he couldn't empathize with them?

Shelly saw Justin's jaw tighten. Quickly, she intervened. "Doctor, this is what Phillip wanted. We knew this time would come, maybe sooner rather than later. He brought us together. Since this may be the only time we have left with him, what can it hurt?" She grabbed his doctor's gown. "P . . . please."

The doctor turned to look back at his patient. He scratched his head weighing both sides. "Okay, but it has to be quick. Do you have a priest or pastor?"

A man stepped out from behind the small group and waved. "I'm Reverend Jackson, the Bishops requested me."

Shelly smiled appreciatively at her parents. Her father winked back.

"Only you three can come in." The doctor pointed to Shelly, Justin, and the reverend.

Shelly shook head in dismay. The plan was to have everyone at the bedside. This doctor was ruining everything.

"It's okay," her father consoled her. "Go on. We can see everything from out here." Knowing his daughter's stubborn nature, he pushed her toward the door. "No time to argue. Hurry."

Everyone in the group hugged and kissed. Tears mixed with smiles in a situation that was both joyous and sad as friends and family showed how much they cared for each other.

With everyone urging them on, Justin and Shelly walked through the automatic doors, hand in hand. Entering the room was like stepping into a different world. A powerful world filled with the latest medical technology noisily whirring, dripping, and beeping. But, even perfect equipment couldn't obliterate nature's imperfection, ridding Phillip's body of cancer.

His face was peaceful; only the weak reading on the monitor showed that he was still with them. The crisp white sheets diminished his body even further, robbing him of vigor. Shelly expected, more like wished, that he would open his eyes and give her a sarcastic comment about how she looked at him.

"Dad." Justin spoke softly. "Shelly and I are here—to be married."

There was no indication that Phillip heard.

"I need you to witness it, Dad, like we planned." Justin pulled Shelly to his side. "Talk to him," he said softly.

She didn't know what to say. But, she knew Justin depended on her repartee with his dad. Relying on her nursing skills, she pulled deep from her knowledge and heart. "Phillip, it's Shelly." Her voice trembled. "I'm wearing that white dress. You remember. I showed it to you in the bridal magazine. I'm all dressed up for you. And now you want to take a nap." She sat on the edge of the bed and held his hand. "I want to marry the man you and I both know is the right one for me. I want to be with my love this minute, but I can't if you don't wake up . . . Dad."

His eyes fluttered, but didn't open. Shelly noticed his fingers moved, and stroked them tenderly. She slipped off the bed, motioning for Justin to replace her. Then, Phillip opened his eyes.

"Dad." Justin strained to see some sign of recognition.

When his lips moved and he looked at both of them, they hugged each other, overjoyed. The reverend, realizing the brittle hold Phillip had on life, started the marriage ceremony.

The traditional long sermon on the meaning of love, commitment, and marriage had to be omitted. He went straight to the heart of the matter where the two exchanged vows they had written beforehand.

"Shelly, before I met you, my heart was encased, protected from the world. But, that is, before you were brought into my life. Your warm spirit and loving nature dissolved those bonds to free my inner self. As a whole man, I promise to protect, honor, love, and serve you as your husband for the rest of your life."

"My love, my conqueror, my hero, I have been brought out of the depths of my hell with your love and support. Like a new woman, I experience what true love is—faith, trust, and respect. As we face our destiny together, I promise to cherish and love you with all of me."

The reverend blessed the rings, talking briefly on their meaning. He then declared them married and directed them to kiss.

Shelly felt as if she were floating. Looking up into Justin's face, she felt her heart swell with pride at the most handsome man she had ever met. As he lowered his head, she felt like the luckiest woman.

The moment their lips touched and they began kissing, the heart line on the monitor went flat. Alarms immediately sounded. Shelly opened her eyes to see Justin staring back at her; neither one wanted to look over at the bed.

Shelly chanced a look. Phillip had passed on, peacefully. Like her mother had said earlier, he had waited for them. Turning the poison of death and mourning to medicine, she was glad that the last thing he saw was their commitment to each other. He had been victorious to the end.

A few nurses couldn't hold back their tears. The wedded couple was ushered out so that they could get down to the business of saving him. Justin and Shelly left the hectic scene of someone gearing up to use the fibrillating machine.

The Bishops rushed forward when Shelly and Justin emerged past the doors. They hugged their new son-in-law whose stiff composure gave way. Everyone knew that Phillip was gone and it wouldn't be too long before the medical staff realized defeat.

Leesa gave Shelly a gift. "I'm so sorry for your loss.

Michelle Monkou

But, you are a great person and I know you and Justin will pull through this. I'll miss seeing you."

"Why in the world will you miss me?"

Leesa gave a short laugh. "You'll be the busy banker's wife, hosting parties and attending business functions. You won't have time for the little people."

"Come off it. I'll still need your kind of help occasionally. And, I'll still need a dear friend to keep me straight."

"Well, it's a deal. 'Cause I need a friend like you, too."

Shelly said good-bye, since Leesa had to leave. It was nice that she could be there not only to see the wedding, but to see how her protegé had developed with her help.

"Why are people treating us as if we are going on a long trip and won't see them again soon?" Justin stood behind her, holding her in his arms.

She loved the feel of his body behind her supporting her. In his arms, she felt invincible. "I think they are trying to give us as much space to grieve as possible."

"I've grieved prematurely when he was at home. I have to celebrate life and its many gifts, as he would want me to."

"You mean as he would yell at you to do."

They both chuckled. The pain would sink in later, but now they would enjoy the success of knowing that Phillip had been able to share in the most special part of their new beginning.

Just then, the doors swung open and the same grim-faced doctor approached them. "I'm afraid he's gone." Instinctively, he took a step back. Shelly wondered what he'd do if she launched herself at him and cried copiously into his medical jacket.

Justin answered, "Thank you, Doctor. For everything."

"Sorry." He turned and went back to his world behind the doors.

Shelly's father came over to Justin. "Come on, there's nothing much more we can do. Your father was a special man. He and I did a lot of talking at Shelly's birthday party. I genuinely liked and respected him. Because of my fondness for him and my love for you as my son-in-law, I extend my fatherly role whenever you need it."

The touching scene between the two most important men in her life brought tears to her eyes.

They all walked out of the hospital after completing the necessary paperwork. Phillip had taken care of all details and they were only a matter of a few phone calls.

Four days later, they attended the funeral. The overwhelming number of people who came to pay their respect included friends and colleagues from his past. Phillip was dearly loved and had made an impact on the lives of many. Shelly and Justin accepted the condolences with numbing dignity. There were no tears left.

Epilogue

Remnants of their first anniversary still littered the lawn. Balloons and streamers flapped in the morning breeze marking the festivity. The party had gone on into the early hours of the morning. The neighbors had their first experience of the new tenants.

Justin and Shelly ate breakfast on the patio, as they had done almost every morning. Shelly perused the dismal sight wondering when she would have the time to clean it all. She sighed, exhausted at the thought.

Shelly looked over at the recently dug area near Phillip's time capsule. They had created their own time capsule as the highlight of the evening. All their guests were invited to place something in the box to mark the times, their tastes, or the event. Justin's parents had started the tradition, and she wanted to honor their memories by continuing in the same vein.

"Daydreaming again?" Justin teased.

An answering smile played on her lips.

"Time sure flies. But, I'm glad we're on the same flight together."

Contentment.

It was the only thought that came to mind to describe her feelings. Her wonderful husband, leisurely enjoying breakfast before heading to work, had presented her last night with a sculpted glass crystal in her likeness. Gone were the doubts and fears that kept her from living to the fullest. Every time he looked her way and winked devilishly at her, her knees weakened like a schoolgirl with a crush.

"So what time will you be back so I can get some lovin' going on?"

Shelly peeked over the lip of her mug. Her husband was always a little hungry.

"You know what the doctor says, 'too much sugar can hurt your tummy.'"

"Well, you can give it to me on the low-fat plan."

She blushed. Then, hearing Mrs. Beacham approach, she cleared her throat for him to behave.

Justin wasn't complying. "Morning, Mrs. B., my dear wife here wants to put me on a diet."

Mrs. Beacham looked shocked. "Now, why do you think this healthy man should be on a diet?"

"I didn't," she answered defensively.

Justin poked his tongue out at her.

"He's not talking about food," Shelly explained.

Mrs. Beacham cleared the dishes away. "I know." She reiterated, "But, he *is* a healthy man."

Justin roared.

Shelly's face was hot. "It's time for me to go." She wondered, *this must be how a hot flash feels.* Despite her summer suit, her embarrassment raised her temperature a few degrees.

Justin came over with his best apologetic expression, but it seemed insincere when he snickered into her neck.

"You are incorrigible and it doesn't help when Mrs. Beacham is encouraging you." She pouted. "I'll never win any battles with you and Mrs. Beacham."

He kissed her forehead. "That's why we evened the odds."

She smiled. "Yes, we did."

Just then, the wail of an unhappy infant floated out to them. Their newborn daughter wanted to be where the action was. Shelly and Justin played paper, rock, scissors to decide whose turn it was.

"Best two out of three," Justin retorted.

"Oh, brother." Mrs. Beacham walked toward the house. "I'll go get my little Poopsie."

"Justin, Tahndi is going to grow up thinking her name is poopsie."

"Tahndi Poopsie Thornton, sounds fine to me."

Shelly shook her head and followed Mrs. Beacham. "I'll get her. I have to take her to my mother's before I go speak at Anne Arundel Community College."

Since the fall of Toby, Shelly had developed as part of her therapy a speaking circuit at the area colleges and even some high schools. She felt it her duty to share and enlighten both young men and women. It had been successful and she had been approached to teach a course under the sociology curriculum.

With Justin's focus back on developing the bank after his father's passing, he had reorganized it to fund revitalization programs for inner cities. A small group of investors helped to manage the programs, bringing them to fruition.

Her husband, her daughter, and Mrs. Beacham made up her new family. Picking up her screaming bundle of joy, Shelly was thankful for whatever lay ahead on the horizon. Her faith was restored that their love and strength could conquer anything.

Dear Readers:

Thank you for sharing in my celebration of Shelly and Justin's story. *Open Your Heart,* my debut novel, touches on the serious issue of date rape and its lasting aftereffects. Shelly undertook a journey to heal the emotional scars long after the physical wounds had disappeared. At times, it proved painful, but through her family's love, her self-esteem strengthened. Once she learned to love herself, she could open her heart for Justin's love.

I love writing about overcoming great odds with a wonderful romantic touch. In my upcoming book to be released in June 2003, there will be new lessons to learn, hearts to mend, and people to fall in love. There will be some history about the Underground Railroad in Maryland interwoven in the story. Stay tuned.

I would love to hear from you. If you would like to be on my readers list, please send an email to MichelleMonkou@aol.com or write to: Michelle Monkou, P.O. Box 2904, Laurel, MD 20709-2904. Also, please visit my website and sign my guest book at http://www.michellemonkou.com.

Peace,
Michelle Monkou

ABOUT THE AUTHOR

Michelle Monkou sold her first contemporary romance to BET in January 2002. She attributes her success to discipline and respect for the craft and supportive writer networks like Romance Writers of America and online listservs, such as the Black Writers Alliance.

Michelle earned a B.A. in English from the University of Maryland and an M.S. in International Business from the U of MD's University College. She works for a leading trade association for the life insurance industry and writes reviews for Crescent Blues e-magazine.

Born in England and raised in Guyana, Michelle attributes her creative source to the cultural diversity that she experienced. She currently resides with her family in the Washington, DC metropolitan area.